Diamond Promises

Also by Anna Jacobs

THE BACKSHAW MOSS
SAGA
A Valley Dream
A Valley Secret
A Valley Wedding

THE BIRCH END SAGA
A Daughter's Journey
A Widow's Courage
A Woman's Promise

THE ELLINDALE SAGA
One Quiet Woman
One Kind Man
One Special Village
One Perfect Family

THE RIVENSHAW SAGA
A Time to Remember
A Time for Renewal
A Time to Rejoice
Gifts For Our Time

THE TRADERS
The Trader's Wife
The Trader's Sister
The Trader's Dream
The Trader's Gift
The Trader's Reward

THE SWAN RIVER SAGA
Farewell to Lancashire
Beyond the Sunset
Destiny's Path

THE GIBSON FAMILY
Salem Street
High Street
Ridge Hill
Hallam Square
Spinners Lake

THE IRISH SISTERS
A Pennyworth of Sunshine
Twopenny Rainbows
Threepenny Dreams

THE STALEYS
Down Weavers Lane
Calico Road

THE KERSHAW SISTERS
Our Lizzie
Our Polly
Our Eva
Our Mary Ann

THE SETTLERS
Lancashire Lass
Lancashire Legacy

THE PRESTON FAMILY
Pride of Lancashire
Star of the North
Bright Day Dawning
Heart of the Town

LADY BINGRAM'S
AIDES
Tomorrow's Promises
Yesterday's Girl

STANDALONE NOVELS
Jessie
Like No Other
Freedom's Land

JUBILEE LAKE SAGA
Silver Wishes
Golden Dreams

ANNA JACOBS

Diamond Promises

Jubilee Lake Saga Book Three

HODDER &
STOUGHTON

First published in Great Britain in 2023 by Hodder & Stoughton
An Hachette UK company

1

Copyright © Anna Jacobs 2023

A CIP catalogue record for this title is available from the British Library

Hardback ISBN 978 1 529 35141 5
ebook ISBN 978 1 529 35142 2

Typeset in Plantin Light by Manipal Technologies Limited

Printed and bound in Great Britain by Clays Ltd, Elcograf S.p.A.

Hodder & Stoughton policy is to use papers that are natural, renewable
and recyclable products and made from wood grown in sustainable forests.
The logging and manufacturing processes are expected to conform to the
environmental regulations of the country of origin.

Hodder & Stoughton Ltd
Carmelite House
50 Victoria Embankment
London EC4Y 0DZ

www.hodder.co.uk

Diamond Promises

I

Abigail Dawson hurried round the house, making sure everything was tidy and in the places her father insisted were 'right'. She did this every day just before he came home from his office because she didn't want him in a bad mood all evening. He didn't seem to realise that it was mainly he who left things lying around.

When she heard the key turn in the front door she lit the gas under the kettle at a low flame and turned to greet him as he came into the kitchen.

To her relief, he was smiling and didn't even wait for her to greet him before speaking.

'Wonderful news, Abigail. We're moving house on Monday.'

She stared at him in shock, her hand still outstretched towards the teapot. 'Moving house? Where to?' And why had he not told her before now so that she could prepare for it?

'I'll tell you all about it after I've had a quick wash and changed out of my shop clothes.' He ran up the stairs to their tiny bathroom.

She had done the same too when she'd worked in the shop for a couple of years after she left school. She'd hated the place and its sleazy customers, not to mention the dusty and sometimes smelly items they had to deal with.

Her mother had trained her as a small child not to defy her father or even protest once he decided on something. The trouble was, he never hesitated to make important decisions like this without consulting either of them, and sometimes there would have been better alternatives.

As she waited for her father, Abigail's thoughts went back eight years to when he'd also made a similarly important decision without consulting her. She'd been courting, looking forward to getting married and having a home of her own. Oh, the dreams she'd had about her future!

Sadly, after a few weeks her father had decided he didn't want her to marry Harold after all. He said the fellow was more stupid than he'd seemed at first and though he might have provided good-looking grandchildren, he'd not have given them good brains, which was a far more important attribute.

She'd found out the hard way. She had gone out on to the landing when there was a knock at the front door, but her father always answered it if he was at home. She'd been shocked and horrified when she heard her father tell Harold that he couldn't marry her or even speak to her again, and had started to cry.

Her mother had dragged her back into her bedroom and told her to stop weeping this minute – unless she wanted her father to go into one of his rages. It had been one of the hardest things she'd ever had to do.

Three months later, Abigail had wept again in the privacy of her bedroom when she found out that Harold had married someone else.

Shortly after that her father acquired an old piano in payment of a debt and put it in the back room of the shop. She'd fiddled around with it a few times when he was out and quickly learned to pick out tunes.

She'd told her mother how much she loved playing the instrument, and sighed at the thought of him selling it.

An unexpected look of determination had crossed her mother's face. 'Leave it to me, love.'

Her mother had chosen her moment carefully and suggested to her husband that he let their daughter have the piano at home, and even pay for her to take music lessons for a while. Abigail clearly took after him and was showing musical promise.

He must have been in a good mood because he had the piano delivered to their home the next day and found a man who played in a pub to teach her what he knew, which didn't include reading music, just putting the chords and popular music hall tunes together.

Fortunately, Abigail found out that, like her teacher, with a bit of practice she could play any tune she knew, picking out the notes by ear and then figuring out which chords to add.

After that she was allowed time to practise and became proficient enough to entertain her parents occasionally in the evenings. Her father even favoured them with a song or two then and to her surprise he had a sonorous baritone voice.

She saw Harold and his wife in the street about eighteen months after his marriage and was shocked at how scruffy and down-at-heel he looked. And he didn't look at all happy, either. He was scowling as he walked along beside a pregnant, weary-looking woman pushing a pram containing a pinch-faced baby, which was wailing loudly. He'd made no attempt to help the poor woman with the pram at any time.

Abigail realised then that her father had been right about the sort of person Harold was. But oh, how she wished she'd been allowed to find another young man. A piano was no sub-stitute for having a family and home of her own, and escaping her father's control.

Then, during the following winter, her mother died sud-denly of pneumonia, gasping her way out of life in just three days. Abigail didn't need telling that there was no chance whatsoever of her ever being allowed to marry from then on.

As soon as her mother died, her father told her to take over running the house. That weekend he said they would stop wasting their time at church on Sundays now that her mother wasn't there to be upset about it. And that was that.

Not going to church meant she had little chance to meet or chat to people. Her main consolation was that she much preferred looking after the house to working in the shop, even though it was hard work physically and she was lonely.

Music gave her another consolation. Her father bought her a better piano and still asked her to play to him occasionally in the evenings. He even let her hire a part-time scrubbing woman so that her hands wouldn't be spoiled for playing.

She jerked suddenly out of her memories of the past when her father came back downstairs. She poured his cup of tea, put in the usual three teaspoonfuls of sugar and handed him the cup and saucer. He was still smiling, so clearly he was extremely pleased about this coming move.

He took a big mouthful of tea, then gestured with one hand. 'Sit down and I'll tell you all about it.'

She did that, trying to look pleased at the idea of a change to their lives.

'A few weeks ago I had a chance to buy that big house at the corner near the top of Railway Road at a bargain price, the house we've stopped to look at and admire sometimes on our Sunday walks. I always did love the look of it.'

Another pause to slurp down some more tea, then he continued. 'I bargained them down a bit so it took a while to come to an agreement, but we signed the final papers at the lawyer's office today. I've sold this house to pay for the improvements we'll need to make at the new place. The sale will be finalised the day after we move out.'

Her heart sank. The new house was huge, far grander than this one, but the outside was shabby and she guessed the interior would be sorely in need of updating and renovating.

Her father was the one who'd always stopped to admire it. She'd certainly never done so and didn't feel happy about the move. A house that size would be much harder for her to clean and look after. Would she even have time to play her piano from now on?

She'd definitely need to do something about getting more help with the housework, which meant persuading him it was necessary. She'd have to work out how best to do that.

Her father sat sipping a second cup of tea, continuing to issue information and instructions between slurps. 'I've arranged for some tea chests to be sent here this evening plus some old newspapers for packing our crockery. More chests will arrive tomorrow morning. You'll be able to start packing after tea and get on with it again immediately after breakfast. I'll pack my own things on Sunday when I don't have to go into the office.'

He always called it 'the office' and spoke as if it were an important business, but the place was actually avoided by respectable people. Many of his customers couldn't borrow money from banks and her father arranged loans for them at a higher rate of interest. He had a pawnshop, too, with a second-hand shop next door where unredeemed pledges were sold. He also bought and sold other items from members of 'the trade' as he called it.

The business must be bringing in a lot more money than she'd thought if he could afford to buy the house in Railway Road, because he never got into debt personally; he said borrowing and paying interest was a mug's game. That didn't stop him making money by arranging loans for the mugs he spoke about so scornfully.

'Could we go round to the new house this evening, Father, so that I can see what it's like inside? That way I'll have a better idea of how to pack our things efficiently. I've only ever seen the outside so have no idea what the interior is like.'

'I'm afraid not. The tenants are moving out tomorrow, so the place will be in chaos till they've gone. I've told them to make sure they leave it clean. I'll take you round there on Sunday, early in the morning, and we'll have our usual walk up to Jubilee Lake while we're out. Just a quick one to the lower end because we won't have time to go right round it.'

He loved that lake and the weather had to be very bad to stop him going up there on a Sunday. He even went round the top end when he wanted a longer walk. Most people avoided that area because the ground there was so rough and overgrown. The path had been planned to circle the lake completely but the top part had never been completed.

When he spoke in that firm tone of voice she didn't contradict him, let alone try to get his agreement to do what she really wanted. Well, few people ever dared confront Charles Dawson. He was a tall, powerful man with a fierce temper and he rarely changed his mind once he'd decided on doing something.

Abigail wasn't foolish enough to disobey him – not only was she totally dependent on him financially, but she was as afraid of him as everyone else who had to deal with him. His rages were legendary in the poorer part of town, and bad things happened to those who crossed him.

Like her mother before her, she'd gradually learned how to manage him, most of the time anyway, so life wasn't as difficult now as it had been when she'd first taken over looking after him and the house.

Abigail sometimes stared at her reflection in her dressing-table mirror and sighed. She wasn't bad looking, at least she didn't think so, but at thirty-two, she was still a spinster living with her widowed father. She might be comfortably housed and fed, but the price for that was waiting on him hand and foot – and as he was only in his late fifties, nothing was likely to change for years. She'd long given up hope of having a husband or children of her own.

She spent the whole of Saturday packing their possessions. There weren't a lot considering the size of the house they were moving into. Why had he bought such a large place? That baffled her. Just to show off his wealth, or did he have a more specific purpose? Who knew? She couldn't even guess what it might be, and perhaps she would never find out.

On the Sunday morning Abigail and her father walked along the few streets to the house on Railway Road, so named because it ran down a gentle slope to Ollerthwaite Station. It was a better part of town than where they had been living until now. Most of the houses even had gardens.

It might be large but their new home looked even more run-down in the bright spring sunlight, unlike its immediate neighbours. But of course she didn't comment on that.

'I'll gradually bring the outside up to scratch,' he said as he took two keys out of his pocket and opened the front door. He handed her one of them. 'Do not have a copy made or lend this to anyone else.'

'No, Father.'

Inside, her worst fears were realised. The house wasn't at all suitable for just the two of them. There were eight bedrooms but no bathroom and only one inside lavatory, as well as the outside one at the far side of the surprisingly large backyard.

At the end of the upper floor were stairs which presumably led up to the attics. Abigail went to climb them but her father said sharply, 'Nothing to see up there. And we don't need the space, so I'm going to lock it up. Apart from checking for weather damage every now and then, we'll leave it be.'

That surprised her, but when she thought about it later, she wondered whether he had something he wanted to hide up there. He could be very secretive at times, he wouldn't even let her clean the room he called his 'home office', but always did that himself. Not a word about it being 'women's work' then, like the rest of the house.

He went up to the attic door, locked it, took the key out and put it in his pocket. 'Let's go back downstairs and check what needs doing in the kitchen and the rooms we'll be using for everyday living.'

The kitchen and scullery were generously sized, but they were dreadfully old-fashioned. She pointed that out as tactfully as she could. The gas stove had probably been one of the earlier types installed just after she'd been born and was very out of date.

Their previous home had at least had a meagre indoor bathroom with a gas geyser that gave them just about enough hot water for a shallow bath, but this place had no bathroom at all. How did he think they were going to manage without one? He loved his weekly baths.

She tried to find a tactful way to begin making him aware of the practical problems. 'Do you wish me to make a list of what will be needed to give you the comfort you're accustomed to at our present house, Father? That way you'll be able to work out the order in which to have the necessary improvements made.'

He always seemed to forget about the practical ways in which she took care of their daily needs, though he never seemed to forget the tiniest detail of what was happening in his business. He had very firm wishes about what he ate, though, and was a hearty eater. He expected a hot meal to be waiting for him in the evenings and snacks to be available at all times. No wonder he was growing fatter each year.

He looked at her now in mild surprise. 'I suppose there will be quite a lot of things that need attention.'

'Oh yes. And some of them will need doing quickly, too. The neighbours will be surprised if we don't make our house comfortable. They'll probably think we can't afford to do it.'

'Hmm. You may be right. People do tend to think the worst. But I don't like you to gossip with neighbours. Remember that.'

She said, 'Yes, Father,' automatically but was still thinking about what she'd need to get done. There were several other rooms on the ground floor and she couldn't even begin to think what they would do with them all. They were sparsely furnished and dusty. But they could wait.

When they got back to the rooms near the front door, her father walked into the largest. 'This can be our living room.'

'It's so big it'll be hard to heat in winter.'

'We'll have a gas fire fitted. But we can do that later when the weather gets colder. You'd better tell me what you would consider the most pressing needs.'

'I'd say that a bathroom with a modern gas water heater is a matter of extreme urgency. You know how you love your baths. Our bathroom at the old house is tiny but you can have a big modern one installed here with a water heater which supplies enough for a deeper bath.'

'I suppose so. But that can wait a little, surely? We can buy a tin bath to use in the kitchen for the time being. Your mother used to fill one for me every Friday and wash my back for me, too. I always enjoyed that.'

She looked at him in astonishment. 'It wouldn't be modest for me to see you without your clothes on, Father. In fact, it'd be quite shocking.'

'Oh. No, I suppose not. I forget sometimes that your mother is no longer with us. Go on.'

'It'll be difficult to cook your evening meal on time if you have your bath in the kitchen. I wouldn't be able to cook a meal at the same time as filling buckets from the gas geyser, or waiting outside the kitchen for you to finish bathing.'

She let that sink in then added, 'What's more, some of your favourite dishes, like roast lamb, need stirring or basting at regular intervals. It'd be hard not to burn your food if I can't check it. I suppose I could give you ham sandwiches on bath nights and make them in advance.'

He scowled at that and she waited for what seemed ages for a reply. Surely he wasn't going to insist on the impossible?

When the silence continued, she added, 'And we'll need to hire a full-time cleaning woman. I won't be able to manage such a large home on my own. But I suppose you've taken that into account.'

She almost held her breath after daring to say that.

'Oh. Yes. I suppose you're right. You're of above average intelligence for a woman, that's for sure, so I do listen to what you say about our domestic arrangements. You're right about needing to make certain changes so I shall have to find suitable men to do the work quickly. Leave that to me. But it'd be better if *you* found a cleaning woman.'

'She'd need to live in.'

He looked at her in horror. 'Surely not?'

'I can't work miracles. And it'd be very little trouble. She could use that small room behind the scullery.'

'You're sure it'll be necessary?'

'Very sure, Father. It's a lovely big house, but what's the use of that if you're not comfortable in it? As for a maid, how about Mrs Blaney? You knew her as a child, didn't you? I'm sure we could trust her.'

He nodded slowly. 'Very well then. You tell her.' He sighed and began walking towards the front door. 'That's enough domestic stuff. We'll just take a short stroll up the road to the lake before we go back to our old house and get on with the packing.'

As they set off walking at the slow, measured pace he favoured since he'd started putting on weight, he asked suddenly, 'Is that everything urgent dealt with?'

'Not quite. If you want me to unpack quickly after the move and make you comfortable, we'll need to employ Mrs Blaney from the beginning. We can get her to find a friend who can clean the house we're leaving from top to bottom after it's been cleared. We wouldn't want to leave a mess behind for the people who've bought it, would we? That wouldn't reflect well on a man of your status.'

They'd reached the lake so she kept quiet and let him enjoy the vista before saying, 'I shall need Mrs Blaney to start work full-time on moving day if you don't want to come home from work to a mess.'

'The tenants who moved out have left our new house quite clean. Why will it need the expense of cleaning again?'

'It's unavoidable that dirt and dust will be tramped in from outside when the removal men carry in our possessions. No one can prevent that and it looks like the weather will be showery, so there will be muddy footprints to add to the problems.'

'I suppose you're right. I must say, I didn't expect so many extra expenses.'

'It'll be worth it. We're moving into a nice big house, Father. You've done so well to buy a place like that. People will be jealous of you.'

There was a moment's silence as he mulled this over, but his frown vanished and he began smiling again. 'They will, won't they? I'll leave you to arrange all the practical details and tell Mrs Blaney about her new job.'

It didn't occur to him they might need to ask her if she wanted the job, Abigail thought. But she knew Mrs Blaney would be very happy to come and live in, as she was a widow who often struggled to make ends meet and had to share a cheap room with another woman.

Abigail didn't know why her father had to do all this in such a hurry. She'd be hard put to make the move in time.

What would her life have been like if she'd lived with a kind and thoughtful person and had a few friends to spend time with? She couldn't even begin to picture it; she had given up hope of a more normal life years ago. Thank heavens for her music and books from the library to read.

Mrs Blaney arrived half an hour later, out of breath and looking apprehensive. 'I got a message to come and see you at once. Is something wrong? The lad who brought it didn't know why.'

'Nothing wrong at all. It's good news, I hope. I'll make us a cup of tea while we talk, shall I? The kettle has just boiled.'

'I'd love one.'

When Abigail explained about the job Mrs Blaney beamed at her. 'Oh, that'll be wonderful, just wonderful. It'll be a step up in the world for me to get a job as live-in maid.'

'And you'll be more comfortable, not to mention eating better.'

She was given another beaming smile. 'I certainly will, miss.'

'You're already quite good at not upsetting father. That's so important.'

'I've noticed that. Don't worry. I can be quiet as a mouse when needed. Eh, I'm that pleased about it.'

'I'm pleased too. You're a good worker.' She saw her companion pull out a crumpled handkerchief and mop her eyes. 'What's wrong?'

'Nothing. It's just, it'll be so comfortable not having to share a room with Alice. And I won't have to worry about getting enough work to pay my rent and buy enough food to eat as well as the breakfast provided for lodgers. I'll have to tell the other ladies I do odd jobs for that I can't come any more, but I'm sure Alice will take my place, so they won't be left in the lurch.'

'When you come here you'll have your own bedroom and I'll make sure it's comfortably furnished with an armchair and coal for your fire, because you'll have to sit in there during the evenings.'

'I shall enjoy the peace and quiet, miss. I'll be able to buy a newspaper now and then to keep me occupied.'

'You won't need to do that. You can have my father's old newspapers when I've finished with them, if you don't mind waiting a day or two for the latest news.'

'Even better. Thank you so much for this chance. I won't let you down.'

'Oh, and one other thing. Make sure you never, ever tattle about what my father does at home,' she warned.

'I know that, miss. I knew him when we were both children and he was just as secretive then. Who'd have thought some-one from Sampson Street would do so well in business as he has?'

'Who indeed?' Abigail sometimes wondered exactly how he'd made his money. He never talked about his family or early life, and Mrs Blaney rarely did that either.

'Are you looking forward to the move, miss?'

'Not really. It'll be hard work running such a big house.'

'You're a good daughter to him if you don't mind me saying so. He's not easy to deal with, is he?'

'We manage. Now, perhaps on your way home you can ask your friend to help out tomorrow and I'll finish my packing.'

She felt quite sure Mrs Blaney would be a good help. In fact, her presence was one of the best things about the new life. It'd be good to have someone to chat to occasionally.

2

The move was accomplished without any problems on the Monday, thanks to Abigail's hard work and quiet efficiency, for which she knew she would receive no special praise or thanks from her father.

He left for work even earlier than usual and she was glad to see the back of him because he kept poking into her neat piles of items that had already been sorted out to see exactly what was in them, leaving them in disarray.

Shortly after his departure, Mrs Blaney's friend Alice arrived, followed by the movers with their pantechnicon. The men started work, carrying furniture, bundles and boxes out to the big enclosed dray.

Abigail explained what was needed to Alice and set off just before the movers finished. She enjoyed the brisk walk to the new house, where Mrs Blaney was waiting for her, having arranged for her own possessions to be taken there before the move.

She took Mrs Blaney round the house and showed her the room which would be hers, leaving her things there. She set her to wiping down the kitchen shelves, which they both felt were not clean enough.

Then the movers arrived and all was chaos, with Abigail needed to direct them where to put things. She decided to take the bedroom over the kitchen and not until the man in charge of them asked her which bedroom the master's things were to go in did she realise that her father hadn't selected a bedroom.

She crossed her fingers for luck as she said, 'The big bedroom over the entrance for my father's things. Please don't forget to set up the bed for me.' Then she left them to it and went down to the kitchen to start putting crockery and foodstuffs away.

She made sure to offer the men a cup of tea and some biscuits later. Such details usually made for more willing service, she'd found. After that, the men set off back to the old house to pick up the rest of the things and she started sorting out her father's clothes.

It seemed a very long morning and it wasn't till the movers finally left in the early afternoon that she was able to give herself and Mrs Blaney a quick meal of bread and cheese. It was a relief to sit down for half an hour.

Then she sent Mrs Blaney back to check that their former house was clean and to pay her friend for the work. It was good to be able to delegate some of the work and absolutely wonderful to have the new house to herself for a while to get a feel for it.

Abigail's father came home at exactly his usual time of half-past six and walked round the downstairs with her, looking suspiciously into each room as if expecting to find something wrong, when in fact most of them were empty as they didn't have any extra furniture.

He then led the way upstairs. 'I don't know how we'll go on with a maid living in the house with us,' he grumbled.

'She's a good worker and is looking forward to the peace and quiet of having her own room. You don't do much in the kitchen, so you'll hardly know she's there. You were at school with her, weren't you?'

He nodded. 'She was one of ten children, always hungry. No wonder she's looking forward to us providing her with food and a room of her own.'

'I said she could read your old newspapers in the evenings so don't throw them away.'

'No. And that won't cost me anything.'

She nearly said something sharp because she was so tired of him talking as if he were struggling to make ends meet, but she managed to keep her thoughts to herself. 'You didn't say which bedroom you wanted so I gave you the big front one,' she said quietly and led the way to it.

He went inside and turned round on the spot, studying it, then nodded. 'Yes, this will do me nicely.'

'I made up your bed but I left your boxes for you to sort out because I know you don't like anyone else messing around with your possessions. And my bedroom is along here.'

'Good. And you said Margie Blaney will have the room behind the scullery, so she'll be out of my way.'

'Yes. I'll show it to you when we go down just so you know what it's like. It's only small but it'll be cosy with the warmth from the kitchen.'

'Good. She'll be out of hearing of what we say in the sitting room there as well. Now, what's for tea? I'm hungry.'

She was utterly exhausted, so had taken the rash step of planning to go out to a nearby fish and chip shop to buy their tea.

She sent Mrs Blaney to check the old house and pay her friend Alice for the work and told her she needn't hurry back. Hopefully she'd be able to get her father settled into the house before their maid returned.

He stared at her in shock when she told him. *'Buy fish and chips from a shop?* Surely you can cook us some ham and eggs?'

In the past she would never have dared argue back, but something gave her the courage to stand up to him today. 'I haven't so much as sat down all day and I'm absolutely exhausted.'

'Mrs Blaney can do it.'

'She's gone to pay Alice and check the old house for me.'

'Yes, but—'

'You're asking too much of me, Father! And before I fall asleep standing upright, I shall need some more money to buy fish and chips occasionally, and also to buy things for this house tomorrow.'

'How much more?'

'I don't know. I got through the other money you gave me, with only a few pennies left, so another five pounds at least. Things are different here and we need extra bits and pieces for a bigger house. I'll let you know when I've spent it if I need more. And I'll have to open an account at a new grocer's tomorrow. The place we used before is too far away from here.'

'*Five more pounds!*'

She ran completely out of patience. 'If you can afford to buy this house you must be able to afford the extra money it'll cost to run it. I'm too tired to do anything else tonight, far too tired.'

'Do we need to buy fish and chips for Mrs Blaney? Can't she make do with bread and jam?'

'No, she can't. I already gave her the money for that because I didn't think you'd want to eat with her.'

'But—'

'I can't go on like this.' She whirled round and ran up to her bedroom. She had never done this before and wasn't sure whether it'd shock or anger him. Well, she didn't care. She was totally exhausted.

She dashed away a tear. If only she had some way of earning a living, she'd have left home years ago, run away and hidden in some other part of the country. But though she'd saved some money from the housekeeping secretly, she didn't have enough to leave. In some ways he treated her well; in others she was a prisoner.

She heard doors opening and closing near her bedroom, then her father's voice calling, 'Abigail! Where the hell are you?'

He must have already forgotten which would be her bedroom. She let him call a few times before she answered, 'I'm here,' and opened her door.

He didn't apologise, of course not. 'You'll have to buy the fish and chips whenever we get them. It'd look bad for me to go for them.'

His expression was implacable, so she scraped together the energy to walk along the two streets to the nearest fish and chip shop. She went slowly and her spirits revived a little in the fresh air. It was good to be out of a house full of dust and chaos, good to be away from her father, too.

She was served immediately because someone in the queue recognised her as Mr Dawson's daughter and told the shop's owner. No one attempted to chat to her. They just stared at her warily. It was impossible to get out of his shadow whatever she did.

She walked back quickly, holding the package wrapped in newspaper close to her chest for its comforting warmth on a chilly evening.

When she'd given him his food, she saw that Mrs Blaney had returned so nipped into her room to have a word with her. 'You'd better stay out of his way tonight. He's in a bad mood, doesn't like change.'

'Thank you, miss.'

'You can make yourself a cup of cocoa once we've moved into the sitting room. We'll be spending the evenings there and leaving you in peace. And would you give the kitchen a quick clear-up before you go to bed tonight?'

'Yes, of course. Eh, you do look tired.'

'Yes. I can't remember ever feeling so exhausted.'

Mrs Blaney patted her arm in a motherly way. 'I'm here to help you in the house now, at least.'

She nodded and hurried back to eat her own meal at the table with her father before it grew any colder.

After they'd finished eating, he said grudgingly, 'That was surprisingly good. The fish was nice and fresh, and warmer than I'd expected when you got it home. We might buy the occasional meal like that from now onwards.'

She knew it was as near as he'd get to an apology for the way he'd treated her. 'Whenever you like, Father. I must say, it was delicious. It's lovely that I can leave Mrs Blaney to wash the dishes and clear up and come straight into the sitting room with you from now on.'

'Will she think to do them without you to tell her?'

'She's already offered without being asked. You'll find her a very good worker.'

'Yes, I expect so. Ah, this is a much grander room. I'm going to enjoy living here.' He shook out his newspaper and disappeared behind it, so she got out her library book.

The following morning Abigail was woken by someone knocking on her bedroom door.

'Miss. Your father's downstairs and he wants you to get him his breakfast.'

She blinked and sat up in bed. 'Just a minute.' She slipped into her shabby old dressing gown and opened the door.

She found her father waiting for her in what he said they were to call and use as the morning room.

He scowled at her. 'You're late.'

'I overslept because I was tired. Did you get yourself a cup of tea?'

'Mrs Blaney got it for me, but I'd rather have you making it.'

For once she told him the truth. 'I'm the daughter of a successful businessman who has just bought a big new house, and yet you're treating me like a skivvy. What's more, you pay me no wages and give me barely enough money to manage on for the housekeeping, so it's worse than a skivvy; it's nearer to being a slave.'

He gaped in shock at this then opened his mouth to say something, but she continued talking over him. 'At this rate I'll be dying young like my mother did, because of overwork. We've got a maid now. *She* can get your breakfast if I'm not available.'

He tensed and clenched his fists. Though he'd never hit her before, she half-expected him to lash out at her. But he didn't. He slowly unclenched his fists and studied her face then stepped backwards. 'You do still look tired. You'll have to teach her to look after me properly, mind. It's a good thing Margie was available as our maid, because I'd not feel comfortable letting a complete stranger into my private life.'

He fiddled with the salt and pepper pots. 'It's fortunate she did get up earlier than you. I couldn't even make myself a piece of toast because I didn't know how to get that damned cooker to light.'

'I don't know either yet. It's a very old one and won't be as easy to use as our previous one. We need a modern cooker with a grill and then you'll be able to make yourself a piece of toast whenever you fancy one.'

She waited a few moments but he merely nodded, so she said, 'I'll go and tell Mrs Blaney what to get for you.'

When she was dressed she came slowly down to join him, whispering to Mrs Blaney that they'd have a more peaceful breakfast if they waited till after her father had gone to work.

In the meantime she knew he preferred her company over breakfast so she took her cup of tea and sat down opposite him in the morning room.

He looked up, not putting his hovering forkful of egg into his mouth. 'Aren't you having anything to eat?'

'Not yet. I don't feel hungry. I think I must still be tired.'

He cleared his plate quickly then said, 'I have to go to work on time. I might have promoted Dennis Bibby to take charge of the shops but I'm not sure yet that he's going to work out, so I still need to keep an eye on him.'

She was in such a strange mood today, and spoke bluntly again, 'I don't like that man. The way he looks at me is an insult.'

'Men always stare at pretty women. You'll never stop them doing that. I'll come back here just after ten o'clock. Please have a list ready of what we need to buy or arrange for. After that we'll go out shopping for the most urgent things, and one of the first will be a proper gas cooker.'

'If you can get the name of someone capable who does odd jobs of various sorts it'd help, Father. There are a lot of small things which need fixing all over the house. Like this.' She opened a cupboard door to prove her point and it hung crookedly, one of its hinges hanging loosely.

He shook his head and made a tutting noise. 'You're right. Check every single cupboard and drawer first so that you can tell him what needs doing.'

After he'd gone, she and Mrs Blaney sat down together to eat breakfast. It was beautifully peaceful without him.

Mrs Blaney finished her boiled egg and sighed happily. 'I'm going to enjoy my meals here.'

So was Abigail, but for different reasons.

Later in the morning, when her father came back, their tour of the house took well over an hour and she took careful notes as they went. She didn't want him claiming later on that they hadn't agreed on something.

They went out and ordered a new gas cooker at the only shop selling them, plus hot water geysers.

When her father asked about a handyman to do several minor repairs in their house, the shopkeeper said he knew a man who would not only fit the cooker as soon as it arrived, but fit the other items and do any other sorts of jobs they needed too.

'I also need to have a bathroom created from scratch. And quickly.'

The shopkeeper beamed at him. 'I can arrange that for you as well, sir. Riley Callan is a very good plumber and Rufus Shorrocks will be able to help him get things done more quickly. What's more, I have a bathroom suite which might suit you in stock in my back room. Would you like to come and see it?'

Abigail had noticed before how careful most shopkeepers were in her father's presence. They didn't chat much to her when she was out shopping alone, either, as they did to other women, but just talked about the weather and the items she was buying.

Her father had little to do with shopping and she didn't understand why he made the shopkeepers feel so nervous on the rare occasions he came with her.

When they'd finished, he told the man, 'Tell this Shorrocks fellow to come to my house early tomorrow and I'll try him out. Seven o'clock. I want to meet him before I leave for work.'

Outside he turned to Abigail. 'I need to get back to work now. You'll be all right walking home alone, won't you?'

'Yes, of course I will. Is it all right if I open an account at a grocer's? The nearest shops are better in this part of town as well as closer to our new home.'

He gave one of his rare smiles. 'We're going up in the world in several ways, eh?'

'Wasn't that why you arranged to move?'

'Of course.' He raised one hand in farewell and strode off down the street.

She walked up and down a whole street of shops, finding a better class of grocer whose shop she liked the looks of. She explained to the man who seemed to be in charge of it that her family had just moved into the area and she wanted to open an account with them, to be paid weekly by her father.

When she told them her father's name and where she now lived, she again received a flattering amount of attention. But they too seemed a bit nervous of her now. Why were people so very afraid of upsetting him?

3

In another part of the valley, trouble was brewing.

Ever since his wife had thrown him out, Terry Catlow had been living in a cave just outside town on the edge of the moors. There were several caves in the outcrop of rock known as Beckshall Edge.

At this time of year it was warm enough in a cave, though he missed a proper bed and his wife's cooking. But living here meant that no one knew where he was or what he was doing from day to day, which suited his present plans. And now Edward Ollerton was in his sights again.

His prey was no countryman. It amused the watcher greatly that Ollerton didn't seem to notice the man who occasionally followed him around, let alone realise that it was the one who had attacked him before – and who fully intended to attack him again.

But this time Catlow was going to take more care about when and how he attacked and killed Edward Ollerton. He didn't intend the police to catch him, so would take care not to do it on impulse but to plan ahead. Most important was to make sure he did the deed when no one was around.

Cliff Nolan, the local policeman, was retiring soon and wasn't the sort to put a lot of effort into checking out such a crime. Well, he barely left the police station these days.

Catlow was ravenously hungry today but didn't dare go back and push his way into what had been his family home to demand some food. His damned wife had sworn she'd stab him with her kitchen knife if he ever went near her or the children again, and she never made idle threats.

The bitch had even poisoned his children's minds against him so they were on her side now and it'd be no use asking them to help.

He would go back home one day, though, and beat her black and blue if she protested. He'd make sure that she was too afraid to disobey him again. But at the moment, taking all things into account, it'd be easier to keep an eye on the situation if he stayed on his own and killed Ollerton without anyone realising what he was doing.

Catlow rather liked it that no one knew exactly where he was. And he'd always liked camping out in spring and summer on the moors.

He was having to do occasional odd jobs for people to keep himself fed. He pinched food when he could but sometimes he had to work in order to buy it. He hated working for other people, letting them order him about.

He'd grown a beard and some folk didn't seem to recognise him, especially if he tramped across the moors to villages outside the valley and stayed away for a day or two. They were glad to get cheap labour, weren't they?

There wasn't always work to be found, though, or he felt too weary for long walks, so he wasn't eating as well as he used to. But Catlow didn't intend to go back to his family until he'd killed that fellow and avenged his grandfather's death.

Fortunately, Ollerton hadn't had any children so if he could be killed before he planted one in his new wife's belly, the family would be wiped out. Catlow, on the other hand, would be survived by six children. That thought always made him feel happy.

So the job of getting rid of the Ollertons wasn't finished, but he was getting into position to finish it off. One day soon he would smile as he watched Edward Ollerton take his final breath.

And if the man's wife showed any sign of carrying a child, she'd have to be got rid of too. Terry didn't fancy killing a woman – but if it was necessary, he'd do anything to wipe out the Ollertons.

4

The handyman arrived at Railway Road early the following morning and introduced himself to Charles Dawson as Rufus Shorrocks.

'Can you tell me about your experience with this sort of work, Shorrocks?'

'Yes, of course. I'm a former miner but came home to look after my widowed mother and little sister. I've worked with a lot of different tradesmen and learned from them all.'

'Get a lot of work, do you? I'm surprised you haven't found yourself a permanent job.'

Abigail was watching but to her surprise this man wasn't cowed or subservient.

'I make more money working by the day because I'm good at all sorts of jobs, so I ask for slightly more in payment as a consequence.'

Her father nodded and actually gave him an approving look. Clearly the man had passed some kind of invisible test.

'I'll give you a try-out at the job then, Shorrocks, and as long as the work looks good tonight, I'll be able to employ you for a few more days.' He glanced towards the kitchen clock and made an irritated sound. 'I have to go to my office now so my daughter will show you exactly what's needed.'

After her father had left, Abigail took Mr Shorrocks into the kitchen and offered him a cup of tea, which he accepted with alacrity. His table manners were excellent, and his voice was deep and gentle. She liked the sound of it. His gaze seemed kind, too.

'A lot of things are in need of repair. I know some of them but I think you may discover more when you look round and I'll take your word for that.'

'I won't try to cheat you, I promise.'

'You don't have the face of a man who cheats,' she said before she could stop herself, then blushed at speaking so frankly to him.

Luckily Mrs Blaney came in just then, carrying the ashes from the fire in the living room, so Abigail introduced her.

'We've met already,' Mrs Blaney said. 'I know Rufus's mother. Is she any better?'

'No. I'm afraid not.' He turned back to Abigail. 'I'll start work in the living room, then. Call me when you've finished in the kitchen and we'll examine it carefully.'

Mr Shorrocks proved to be very efficient once he started work. During their inspection of the house he pointed out some things Abigail had missed and which clearly needed fixing.

'There will be a full week's work if they're dealt with properly. I shall enjoy doing that because it's a lovely house and it'd be a shame to half-do a job. I'll begin by repairing the windows if you agree. That way we'll keep a lot more of the draughts out.'

He also made one or two other useful suggestions about future jobs. He showed Abigail where the water supply came into the house at the rear and therefore which room would be the most efficient place to install a bathroom in, an aspect she hadn't thought of before.

It was inevitable that Mr Shorrocks would need to ask her about various details as the day progressed and their encounters sometimes led to other topics of conversation. Like her, he read newspapers regularly to keep up with the wider world and he seemed genuinely interested in a woman's view of certain aspects of modern life, unlike her father.

She wished she could have someone to chat to like this in the evenings! Her father always talked *at* her rather than chatting with her as Mr Shorrocks did.

When her father came home from work that first day at his usual time, he took a quick look at the work done and glanced at her enquiringly. When she nodded to tell him all had been done properly, he paid Mr Shorrocks and told him to keep coming till the work was finished.

She had the evening meal almost ready, so as soon as Mr Shorrocks left she could finish it off because, as always, her father preferred to change out of his working clothes before eating.

Thanks to Mrs Blaney's labours the areas of the house they'd be using this evening were both looking and feeling cleaner, windows sparkling, woodwork gleaming.

However, she hadn't had time to wash and change her own clothes because he insisted that his meal be ready on time. She wasn't surprised when he stared at her untidy appearance with obvious disapproval.

'Why haven't you had a wash and changed your clothes, Abigail? You know I like you to look neatly dressed in the evenings.'

'Yes, Father, I do know that. I did my best today but I had to keep an eye on Mr Shorrocks and answer his questions, as well as Mrs Blaney, and I've only just finished the essential unpacking. There was also the small matter of cooking your tea.'

'Ah.'

'A larger house creates more work of all sorts, I'm afraid, and I haven't even started on the backyard, except for sending Mrs Blaney to clean the outside lavatory properly.' Which was a job she didn't miss doing at all.

'Well, I hope you'll manage to tidy yourself up from now on. You're sure Shorrocks did all the work properly? It looked all right to me. I had meant to come home early and do a thorough check, but I had to deal with an unexpected piece of business late in the day.'

'He's an excellent worker and got more done than I'd expected, you'll be pleased to hear. He did far more than other men who've done jobs for us would have achieved. He says it'll probably take the best part of a week to sort everything out, depending on whether you want all the rooms checking and their problems fixing or just those we'll be using. The former owners didn't keep up with maintenance very well, I'm afraid.'

'I shall want all of them putting right, of course.'

She didn't tell him that she'd asked Mr Shorrocks to clean out the fire and chimney in Mrs Blaney's room the following day so that their maid could have a little fire in the evenings without it getting smoky. It would be very necessary in the winter but fortunately this house had been well built and all the bedrooms had proper fireplaces.

A week later, her father said abruptly, 'The bathroom suite we ordered has arrived. There's only one plumber in town who has the skill to put in new modern bathrooms properly. Riley Callan and his assistant will be starting work tomorrow and Shorrocks can help them if necessary. I want it done very quickly.'

'Yes, Father.'

It was a chaotic few days because new gas geysers had to be fitted too. Then suddenly the bathroom and other jobs were finished and the house was quiet again. She missed having the workmen around to chat to or even just to smile at in passing, especially Rufus Shorrocks.

Life settled down and they lived as quietly in the new house as they had in the old one, neither offering hospitality nor being offered any. But at least she had Mrs Blaney to chat to during the daytime now. That made a big difference to her.

Abigail still played the piano and sang sometimes when she was alone, but her father seemed to be going through a bad patch at work and wasn't often in the mood for having a sing-song with her, or even letting her play. As always, when thinking about some new project, he wanted silence in the evenings. She didn't know what this project would be as he never told her in advance.

In fact, her new life was almost as unsatisfactory and lonely as her old one had been. After the interesting discussions she'd had with Mr Shorrocks about the wider world, she found her conversations with Mrs Blaney rather limited.

The only real outing of the week remained the walk she and her father took round Jubilee Lake when the weather was fine, and she watched the sky as the weekend approached rather anxiously, hating it when the rain kept them indoors.

She sometimes felt sad that she was as much a prisoner of her father's needs and whims here as she had been at the old house.

When Walter Crossley got up he unlocked the back door and strolled outside for a few moments to enjoy the beautiful sunrise. He was so lucky to live here at the farm. There were pleasing views whether you looked up towards the moors as he was doing now, or down into the valley from the other side of the house. It promised to be a fine day but there was a hint of an autumn chill in the air in the early mornings now.

He was the first to get up today, which was unusual, so when he went back inside he got the damped down fire in the kitchen range burning up again then filled the kettle with fresh water from his own spring. This tasted far nicer than the water pumped to all the houses from the reservoir by the local council, he always thought, though it was convenient to use that for other household purposes by merely turning on a tap.

He set the kettle on the stove to heat up the water for the day's first of many pots of tea and smiled. On second thoughts it wouldn't be unusual from now on for him to be the first up. His household had changed yesterday with the marriages of two of its occupants. And what a lovely day it had been.

He didn't mind if things continued to change in the same way if that meant new people moving to the valley and children being born to local families. The more outsiders he could persuade to settle here permanently the better. He wanted his valley to thrive, not fade away quietly with all the young folk leaving to get jobs elsewhere.

Decades ago when large, efficient modern machinery was created, manufacturers had needed to build huge new mills to put it in, which meant moving the spinning of cotton from small places like Ollindale to the bigger valleys and towns. It had seemed for a time as if Ollindale would die inch by slow inch, but first his father then himself and some other like-minded folk from hereabouts had found ways to tempt new people to come here, thank goodness.

His distant relative Maude was one of the ones who'd settled here with his help. She'd married another newcomer, Riley Callan, yesterday and they'd gone off to spend their wedding night in a friend's house. It was wonderful to see the pair of them shining with happiness whenever they were together.

They would be coming back to live at the farm for a while from tomorrow onwards, after spending another leisurely day together.

Such a nice lass, Maude, and a good cook too. She would continue to organise the daily running of the house for the family and take care of the chickens in return for the egg money earned by selling them at market. Riley would be busy establishing his new plumbing business.

But they'd no doubt find a suitable home of their very own and move out of the farm after a while, especially if they managed to start a family. They were both approaching forty but were in good health and still hoping for a child or two before they grew too old. He prayed they would manage that. Maude would make a wonderful mother, he was sure.

It had been a double wedding with Lillian, who had also come to live here recently, marrying another incomer. Edward Ollerton had bought the large estate that bordered Walter's farm. His family had once owned it, but one of them had gambled it away to the Kenyons. It was good that he'd now got it back.

The two of them would have to live in the former agent's house for a year or two until a new manor house was built to replace the old one, which had been destroyed by the incomers in a deliberately set fire.

It hadn't only been the house that had been destroyed in the fire but the livelihoods of the people who had previously worked there. The Kenyons hadn't settled happily in the valley and seemed to have very old-fashioned views, expecting the local people to kowtow to them.

Walter let out a snort of laughter at the mere thought of that. Lancashire people didn't kowtow to anyone, and why should they?

Edward said he wasn't building a house as big as the old one, but it'd still be big enough to need servants and gardeners, wouldn't it? And they'd be buying supplies for their household from the local shops.

5

As the months passed, the valley was buzzing with the news that the rebuilding of the old Ollerton family home was to speed up, which delighted most folk in Ollindale. When the original house had been burnt down, it had meant a loss of jobs and a reduction in custom for shops in the valley.

One result was that Rufus's life took a turn for the better. After doing various jobs for the newcomer and his architect, he was offered a permanent job as a kind of foreman at a much higher rate of pay than he'd ever earned before. He accepted it with alacrity.

Edward Ollerton was a pleasure to work for and Rufus thoroughly enjoyed his new job with such a courteous and friendly employer.

The only thing Rufus was sorry about workwise was when he got a message from Miss Dawson asking him if he could do some more work on the house and sadly had to turn her offer down.

He sent his regrets and they were genuine because he'd enjoyed her company earlier in the year. She was quiet and a bit shy, but had soon relaxed with him. She had an interest in the wider world that equalled his own. He'd read the name 'new woman' in a newspaper and thought it would suit her independent mind, even though she seemed physically trapped at home by her father. In fact, the man had her caring for him like a slave.

Presumably he held the purse strings and as Rufus knew only too well from his own life, you needed enough money to live on to be truly free. He was tied to supporting his mother and sister.

Sadly, Miss Dawson's father kept a firm hold on her and didn't even allow her to attend any social events with other ladies in their small town. Or perhaps they didn't invite her, given who her father was, because he wasn't exactly respectable.

If she hadn't been Charles Dawson's daughter, Rufus might have tried to get to know her better, but like other people he didn't want to be connected to that man. Anyway, everyone knew that Dawson didn't allow anyone to court his daughter. Pity.

Rufus was enjoying the work he was currently involved in but didn't enjoy the time he spent at home, because his feckless mother was getting more and more careless about the housekeeping money. She was still absolutely furious at him for letting his young sister stay on at school past the leaving age, because Nina could have worked half-time and attended school half-time as soon as she turned eleven.

She should have got a job and brought in a few more pennies, his mother insisted, but he didn't agree. It would have been a great shame for an intelligent girl like Nina to have been set to do a menial job such as rolling cigars, then leaving school fully at twelve.

'She should be paying us back now,' Rhona raged to her son regularly.

'She'll earn more in the long run by staying on at school as a monitor and becoming a teacher.'

'That'll all be wasted when she marries.'

'Having a well-trained mind is never wasted and besides, we can manage without the tiny amount of money she'd earn.'

'I would welcome it, you're so mean with me.'

He didn't enter into another argument about that. His mother would only waste any extra money, he knew. At first when he came back to live in the valley, she'd spent all the housekeeping money he gave for the week in a day or two, then come to him for more. He changed that to giving her money every two days and refused to give her more, buying food for himself and Nina secretly if it was necessary to tide them over.

Things had got a bit better at home this year during the long summer holidays when the schools were closed. Nina took over a lot of the housework and cooking and made the money last longer. But that caused worse rows than ever when he insisted she would be going back to school in two weeks' time.

Then one day he came home from work to find that his mother had fainted and Nina had had to call in their neighbour to help get her to bed.

'Mum, you must go and see a doctor,' he said. 'You need help.'

'There isn't one now that Dr Twilling's dead.'

'Of course there is. There's a very capable woman doctor who has taken his place. I've heard nothing but good of her.'

'A woman can't be a real doctor.'

'Why not? She's passed all the same university exams as a man would.'

'Women's brains aren't clever enough for them to be proper doctors, whatever bits of paper they show you,' she insisted.

'Well, Nina will be going back to school soon so you will have to do something.'

'She can't go back to school. I need her here. Do you want to kill me, making a sick woman do the housework?'

He tried every way he could think of to talk sense into his mother but she stubbornly refused to seek medical help. All he could do was insist on Nina going back to school and arrange to pay a neighbour to do some of the housework and keep an eye on his mother on her bad days.

He was at his wits' end trying to find a permanent solution to the situation. Nina had had to stay home from school a couple of times in the first fortnight of school because their mother couldn't get out of bed, and no neighbour was available to look after her.

He went to the school and explained the situation to Nina's headmistress in person because he didn't want Miss Wadley to think his sister was malingering, or being encouraged by her family to take days off.

'It's all right, Mr Shorrocks,' the headmistress said gently. 'I'm well aware that Nina would never willingly take a day off. She enjoys learning too much and each time she's been absent to look after her mother, she's made up what she missed very quickly.' She hesitated then added, 'I saw your mother in the street last week and if you'll pardon me saying so, she was looking extremely ill.'

'I know. But she refuses point-blank to see the doctor.'

The headmistress sighed. 'Some people become very difficult as they near the end of their lives.'

He felt upset all the way home from that meeting because he too had been wondering if his mother was getting closer to losing the battle against whatever ailed her. He felt sorry for her because she was such an inadequate person in many ways and always had been. Which is probably why his father had left them and never been seen again.

Only, if his mother did die, how would he and Nina cope? She'd only just started the new school year and was enjoying her studies as much as ever. Did he have enough money to hire a full-time housekeeper? If so, he would never save enough to start his own business.

Most men wouldn't have hesitated to find a wife to take over running the house, often someone who'd lost a spouse recently, but he wasn't most men. He couldn't have borne to be married to a dull woman he didn't care about for the rest of his life – and if that meant he was selfish, well, he couldn't change that. No, he'd have to wait till Nina was able to train and work as a teacher.

Then one day a lad brought a message to him at work from the neighbour who helped out to say that he was needed urgently at home. He'd been working with Edward Ollerton, marking out the ground in detail for the foundations of the new house, now that the ruins had been properly cleared.

They'd decided to build the house over the old cellars, which would save weeks of work on creating new cellars, so these were now being cleared and stabilised.

'Why am I needed so urgently?' he asked the lad, not wanting to go if it was just his mother playing up again.

The messenger glanced sideways at Mr Ollerton and said in a low voice, 'Your mother's been found lying dead on the kitchen floor.'

'Oh, hell!'

Edward, who'd inevitably overheard this, moved forward and put one hand on Rufus's shoulder. 'My commiserations. You'd better go home straight away and don't hesitate to take as many days off as you need to sort things out.'

'Thank you, Edward.' It was typical of this boss that he and his senior workers were all on first-name terms and that friendly hand on his shoulder just now had meant a lot.

The lad ran off again and Rufus gathered his things together and rode his new bicycle home as quickly as he could, over-taking the lad on the way.

He didn't know what he would do now, how he would cope with domestic matters, but he still didn't want his sister to lose her chance of a better life.

Mrs Lucas was waiting for him in the kitchen. His mother's body was lying on the floor, covered by one of their ragged sheets.

She greeted him with, 'Someone told that new police sergeant there'd been a sudden death and he turned up here. He told me not to touch or move her. He's poking his nose into everything, that one is, and he's a real stickler for doing things by the letter of the law. Because your mother hasn't seen a doctor for years, he's sent for the new one to certify death by natural causes. Did you ever hear the like?'

'Our former policeman would never have bothered. Where is this one now?'

'He got called out and said he wouldn't be long.'

Sergeant Hector McGill turned up again ten minutes later. Rufus found him pleasant and courteous, with a slight Scottish accent rather than a northern one. But he remained firm about a doctor needing to see the dead woman.

Dr Coxton arrived shortly afterwards. She examined the body then looked disapprovingly at Rufus. 'Could you not have brought her to see a doctor?'

'I tried to get her to see Dr Twilling, but she didn't like him. Then when he died, I told her she should see you. Only she wouldn't hear of it because she didn't trust women doctors. Ask the neighbour. She too tried to persuade my mother to get help. I think the truth is that Dr Twilling had put my mother off doctors for good.'

Dr Coxton rolled her eyes and muttered, 'That man!' She looked at the sergeant. 'I'm satisfied that there is nothing untoward here so I'll issue a death certificate.'

'My commiserations on your mother's death, Mr Shorrocks,' the new policeman said. 'I'll leave you in peace now.'

'Thank you. Look, if you pass any lads who look ready to act as messengers on your way back, could you please send one here? I need to call in the undertaker.'

'I pass the funeral parlour on my way back. I can easily go in and ask them to send someone to help you.'

'Thank you. That's very kind.'

'I consider it my job to help people in this valley in any way I can, not just to lock up the bad ones.' He nodded farewell and strode off down the street, following Dr Coxton.

'I'll get back to my housework,' Mrs Lucas said. 'If you need anything else, my son will be home from school soon and can take messages or run errands.'

His sister would be back soon, too, Rufus thought, as he was left on his own staring down at his mother's body. 'I'm sorry it ended like this for you,' he said aloud, knowing it was too late to make any difference but still needing to say it to her.

Then he went upstairs to check that her bed was tidy before he carried her body up. Only it wasn't tidy and the room smelled sour, mainly because she'd rarely washed herself or her clothing. So he left her on the kitchen floor, covered by the sheet, and waited for the undertaker to arrive and his sister to get home from school.

The undertaker turned up first, thank goodness, and Rufus asked for the cheapest funeral and the cheapest marked grave, and all to be done as quickly as possible. He'd have liked better for his mother, but Nina was his priority now and they were going to need every penny. He was glad that they took the body away before his sister got back.

Then he cleared up the kitchen as he waited for Nina, worrying about how to cope from now on. They'd have to ask the neighbour to help them until after the funeral then he'd look for a permanent way to manage their life. Only it'd probably take most of his wages to pay for help and food.

Nina came running in a short time later and when he told her about their mother, she flung herself into his arms, weeping.

Once she'd calmed down, he said, 'I've started to clear out her bedroom and we'll need to clean it thoroughly, then you can move into it. No wonder you slept in the attic. The room is filthy.'

'I'll help clean it and keep it clean afterwards.' She hesitated. 'Will I have to leave school and look after the house now?'

'Not if I can help it.'

'I love studying and I'm good at it. I so want to be a teacher one day, Rufus, but I'll help round the house as much as I can after school, I promise.'

'It won't be my fault if you don't get your chance to become a teacher. For the moment, I need to sort out some of our mother's clothes for them to bury her in. Is there anything that isn't too dirty or ragged? I'll take them to the undertaker's.'

She nodded. 'She hardly ever wore her best clothes. I'll get them. Can I come with you? I'd like to see Mum and – you know, say a proper goodbye.'

'Are you sure?'

'Yes. I won't feel she's dead till I've seen her. It feels as if she's just nipped out to the shops.'

So they sorted out some clothes and walked through the quiet streets of early evening, not saying much. It was enough that they were doing this together. They'd always got on well.

Eh, but how was he going to protect Nina and see she got her chance of a better life, as he'd promised? It was going to be hard to do that.

6

A few days later Abigail's father was late home from work. That was so unusual that after an hour had passed with no sign of him and no message to say he'd be late, she began to feel seriously worried that something had happened to him.

When someone knocked on the front door, she opened it to see the new police sergeant standing there. Hector McGill had only started work in the valley about ten days ago so she hadn't actually spoken to him yet, though he'd been pointed out to her by a shopkeeper as he strolled along the street. He'd been out and about a lot, apparently, getting to know his new place of work.

Standing next to him today was the new lady typewriter Miss Keane, whom her father had hired recently but whom Abigail hadn't taken to.

'May we come in, Miss Dawson?' he asked.

She looked behind him, half expecting to see her father, but there was no sign of him so she held the door open and led the way into the front parlour, her stomach churning with dread. What on earth could have happened?

She gestured to the sofa. 'Please take a seat.'

He waited till she'd sat down in her usual armchair and Miss Keane on the sofa, but he remained standing in front of the fireplace. 'I'm sorry, Miss Dawson, but I have some bad news for you.'

She waited, keeping her face calm, something she had learned to do to hide her emotions from her father. 'Yes?'

'It's your father – I'm afraid he's dead.'

The words seemed to echo round the room, they were so unexpected. She could hardly believe it was possible but the sergeant's expression was so solemn it could only be the truth.

She realised suddenly that Miss Keane was staring at her with what could only be described as a calculating look. She wished he hadn't brought her with him.

He hesitated then added, 'Sadly there's worse to tell you.'

What could be worse? she wondered. 'Go on.'

'I'm afraid your father was murdered.'

She couldn't hold back a gasp this time. How could that be possible? Her father was such a big, strong man. 'How?'

'He'd been stabbed in the back. We think it must have happened this afternoon when he went out to deposit money in the bank. The money bag wasn't there and the bank said he hadn't been in today, so we have to assume the money was the reason for the attack and had been stolen.'

Miss Keane joined in, looking excited. 'I was surprised when he didn't return at the usual time, because he's always so punctual, but I just thought he'd been delayed, and Mr Bibby did too.'

The sergeant frowned at her and took over again. 'The shopkeeper next door saw his body concealed in the alley between the shops, the one that leads to the back gate of your father's store. That was just over an hour ago.'

'I heard someone shouting for help outside at the back and went to see if it was Mr Dawson coming back, and there he was, lying on the ground, covered in blood.' Miss Keane sounded as if she was enjoying the excitement.

Abigail couldn't bear to look at her, and this time she had to bury her face in her hands for a few moments to hold herself together. She wasn't going to burst into tears in front of a woman she despised. She was relieved when she heard the sergeant ask Miss Keane to go and make her a cup of strong, sweet tea, then he suggested in a gentle voice that she give herself a few minutes to recover from the shock.

By the time Miss Keane came back into the room a few minutes later, Abigail was in full control of herself again.

The other woman was carrying a cup of tea so carelessly it had slopped into the saucer. Abigail said thank you for the tea, but didn't take more than a sip before putting the cup down because it was far too strong and horribly sweet.

'I can stay with you if you like,' Miss Keane offered.

'Thank you, but no.'

The sergeant seemed to realise she didn't want the woman hanging around and said quietly, 'Would you wait in the kitchen for a moment or two, please, Miss Keane?'

When the door to the sitting room closed, Abigail looked up, relieved that the two of them were alone, though he was still looking at her as if half expecting her to collapse.

'I won't faint on you, Sergeant. But I can't stand that woman so I'd be grateful if you'd send her away.'

He nodded but still looked at her warily.

'Have you any idea who did this, Sergeant?'

'No. Not yet, anyway. I shall do my best to find out, I promise you.'

'Where is my father now?'

'They took his body to the undertaker's.'

'I'd like to bring him home.'

The sergeant shook his head. 'I'm afraid I can't allow that yet. The doctor needs to examine him because it's a murder. Are you sure you don't want Miss Keane to stay with you?'

'No, thank you. I'd prefer her to go back to my father's office and keep an eye on things till I can get there.'

The woman must have been eavesdropping because she suddenly appeared in the doorway. 'Did I hear my name? Is there something else you want?'

The sergeant frowned at her. 'No, thank you, Miss Keane. Please wait in the kitchen, as I asked.'

The footsteps stopped almost as soon as she'd left the room and the door had been left slightly open. He put one finger to his lips and went out quietly, finding the woman standing close to the door to the living room. He pointed towards the back door. 'I think you'd better return to the office now. I'll see you out.'

She scowled, shrugged one shoulder at him and flounced out at a ridiculously slow pace. He made a mental note about her lack of respect for the law.

When he returned to the living room, he said quietly, 'She's gone now, and I locked the back door. I don't like to leave you alone here, though, in case the murderer comes after you next, Miss Dawson.'

She gaped at that. 'Why would anyone want to murder me?'

'Possibly because they might think you have other valuables or money here?'

'Any valuables are safely locked away.' She knew her father kept some money and who knew what else hidden in the room he used as a home office, and there might be something of value up in the attic here as well, but she didn't want to mention that possibility until she'd had time to think and check things out.

'After I've spoken to the doctor examining your father's body, I'll call in at his office and check that everything is all right there. You are your father's heir, I presume? There isn't anyone else we should contact?'

'Father never spoke of making a will, but I suppose I must inherit everything.'

'Who is his lawyer?'

'Mr Osgood. He has rooms opposite the town hall and lives in the house next door to it if you need to see him after hours.'

She didn't like Mr Osgood, because he was always so obsequious towards her father yet hardly acknowledged her presence. She thought him the sort who would do anything for money, but her father had been dealing with him for as long as she could remember and he'd seemed satisfied with his services, so what did she know?

'I'll call on Mr Osgood on my way back. You'd be wise to have someone staying with you till we find out more.'

'Our maid will be back from her afternoon off in about ten minutes. She lives here too. I don't have any close relatives. My father always said we were the last of the Dawsons.'

'Very well. I'll wait with you till she returns.'

'There really is no need. I'll see you out.' She led the way to the front door, then went back to sit down and try to work out what to do.

There really wasn't anyone she could ask for help, so she'd have to manage on her own. But at least she had Mrs Blaney living here now.

Rufus and his sister were sitting in the reception area at the undertaker's, waiting for the man who worked there to dress their mother's body in her best clothes and lay her in the simple coffin. He'd suggested Nina should wait to see her until that had been done, wanting to spare her any unpleasant sights he could.

Suddenly the outer door opened and two men began to struggle in with a shabby-looking coffin.

Rufus went across to them. 'That looks heavy. Shall I lend a hand?'

'I'd be much obliged, sir,' the older one said. 'The gentleman is rather heavily built.'

He didn't ask who this was but the man whispered a name anyway. 'It's Mr Dawson. Someone's gone and murdered him.'

His assistant nodded vigorously from the other end of the temporary coffin.

'Murdered?' Rufus gaped at them, shocked rigid.

'And what that poor lady will do without her father to look after her, I don't know,' the older man said as the three of them set the coffin down in the back room. 'Thank you for your assistance, sir.'

'What if someone comes after her as well?' the younger man asked.

Rufus shot a quick glance across to where his sister was sitting. Nina seemed very certain that she needed to see their mother one final time, but he could have done without this.

'I'll go back to my sister till you're ready for us to view our mother.'

The man whose job it had been to dress her said, 'I wonder if you'd mind bringing your sister in for a quick farewell straight away, sir. She's quite tidy now. We have to see to this gentleman as a matter of urgency and get him ready for the doctor to check exactly what happened.'

When he took Nina into the back room, she stared down at their mother for a moment or two, then stepped away and said, 'Thank you, Rufus. I had to see her to feel that she really was dead.'

'We'll walk home now, shall we? Some fresh air will be very welcome. Is there something to eat for tea?'

'If you don't mind bread and jam. That's all she ever bought recently.'

'I noticed. We'll buy something more filling on our way back, then.'

So they set off along the streets. As they were about to turn on to Railway Road and head towards the shops, Rufus saw a man walk through the gate of the house where the Dawsons lived, look round carefully then turn a key in the lock of the back door. Rufus didn't recognise the man. Why was a stranger letting himself in like that?

The way he had looked round before unlocking the door had been distinctly furtive. If the father had been murdered, would the daughter be safe now? He didn't like to think of Miss Dawson getting hurt, so he pulled his sister to a halt and said in a low voice, 'I think someone has just broken into the Dawsons' house. Run to the police station as fast as you can and ask them to come quickly. I'll check that Miss Dawson is all right. Go on! Fast as you can.'

Nina was off like lightning and Rufus ran across the road towards the house where he'd done quite a bit of work a few months previously. When he tried the back door, he found it still unlocked and no sign of the man in the kitchen, so went quietly through it towards the living room.

From inside the room he heard Miss Dawson exclaim, 'What are you doing here, Bibby? And how did you get in?' The name was faintly familiar, and he realised that this was the new manager of Charles Dawson's shop.

Miss Dawson didn't sound pleased to see him, so Rufus waited out of sight to see what would happen next.

7

Abigail was astonished to see Mr Bibby come into the room, and even more bewildered when he ignored her question and addressed her in a very earnest voice.

'I've come to help you, Miss Dawson. You won't be able to manage on your own in this dreadful time.'

'Thank you but I don't need your help. Please leave and go back to the office at once.'

'I can't do that. Your father would have wanted me to stay, I'm sure.'

'Why do you say that?'

Bibby took a step towards her. 'This isn't a good time to raise such a delicate matter, but he's been hinting for a while that he wants to find a husband for you and he asked me to come to tea one day soon and meet you with that in mind.'

Abigail stared at him in amazement. 'I don't believe you.' Her father would never have chosen such a person as her husband, even if he'd wanted her to marry, which she doubted. Even if he'd changed his mind about that, he'd have looked for someone of a better social status than this rather shabby fellow; someone with good social connections which would be useful in the business.

'I assure you that he and I have been discussing it.'

'Well, I don't want your help nor do I want to marry you, so you can just leave my house at once.'

'I can't do that. It isn't safe to leave you here alone. You need a man to keep you safe.'

Listening outside the room, Rufus heard a faint sound from outside the kitchen door. When the new police sergeant stepped inside, Rufus put one finger to his lips, gesturing towards the sitting room.

As the sergeant moved forward, he whispered, 'I noticed a man letting himself into the house. It's the manager from Dawson's shop and he's trying to persuade Miss Dawson to marry him.'

'He's proposing to her at a time like this? Is he mad?'

They fell silent and heard Bibby repeating once again that he'd been chosen by Abigail's father as a suitor. Through the crack in the door Rufus saw him move suddenly to grab Miss Dawson's arm and drag her towards him.

As he was almost as big as her father, she couldn't shake him off. 'Let go of me at once!'

'Don't be stupid. You're going to *need* a husband now and I can—'

The sergeant rushed into the living room and before Bibby saw him, he yanked the fellow away from her.

Bibby was about to fight off his assailant until he realised who it was. He scowled and let his clenched fist drop.

'Miss Dawson has just asked you to leave her house and if you don't, I'll arrest you for trespass and possibly assault if she presses charges against you,' McGill said sharply.

'Her father wanted me to marry her, Sergeant. I'm only carrying out his wishes.'

'I don't believe him,' Abigail said. 'My father would never have asked me to marry a man like him. And I don't appreciate how you behaved towards me just now, either, Bibby, grabbing me like that. I couldn't work with you in any way after what's just happened so you're fired.'

'You can't do that! I've helped build up that business.'

'She has every right to sack you. Please leave at once!' the sergeant repeated. 'And I suggest you take your personal possessions away from the office at once and stay completely away from there from now on. I'll be coming to check that.'

The look Bibby threw at Abigail was threatening, needing no words to say that he didn't intend to give up so easily, but he left the room.

Sergeant McGill escorted him to the back door, watched him walk off down the street then came back. 'It's Mr Shorrocks, isn't it? We met a couple of days ago. You work for Mr Ollerton.'

'Yes.'

'Look, I can't leave Miss Dawson here on her own, but I didn't like the look of that man, so I want to go and check what he's doing. Was he really your father's assistant, Miss Dawson?'

'Yes. Father gave him the job a few months ago. I've never trusted him, but I gather he frightened the customers, which was what my father needed sometimes.'

The sergeant turned back to Rufus. 'I wonder, could you stay with Miss Dawson for a while? Would that be all right, Miss Dawson?'

'Yes.'

He looked back at Rufus. 'I don't want to leave her alone till I find out what's going on and Mr Ollerton spoke well of you, so I trust you.'

Rufus turned to the woman now standing as if frozen, her face pale and her arms crossed in front of her in a protective gesture. 'If *you* wish, I can stay with you for a while, Miss Dawson? Though I'll have to bring my little sister here as well. Our mother has just died, you see, and Nina is only eleven, so I don't like to leave her on her own.'

'I'm sorry!' the sergeant said. 'I didn't know that. I'll find someone else.'

Abigail let out a long breath and studied Rufus. 'Then this is a bad time for you as well, so I can't ask you to do that.'

'I'm happy to do it. Nina and I have already dealt with the formalities and arranged a very simple funeral, so we're free to help you. And happy to do so.'

'You're sure?'

'Yes.'

'Then I would be extremely grateful if you'd stay for a while. I don't trust Mr Bibby, never have done. But I've only just heard that my father has been murdered so I've not had time to... to work out what to do. It was... unexpected to say the least.'

'I'll fetch Nina, then. It won't take a minute. She's waiting outside further down the street.' Actually, he and Nina would be more comfortable here than in their own home. He stole another glance at Miss Dawson, who was staring blindly down at her clenched hands. How dreadful it must feel to know your father had been murdered.

He definitely agreed with the sergeant that Miss Dawson shouldn't be left on her own. And he had his sister to act as chaperone.

Rufus went outside and beckoned to his sister, who came running towards him. He stopped for a moment outside by the back door to explain rapidly what had happened.

She stared at him in that wide-eyed way she had. 'So you saved her from an intruder?'

'Well, we both did. You got the sergeant to come here quickly. I was there in case of trouble, which I suppose helped. You must have run there fast.'

'I'm a good runner.'

'When we go into the sitting room now, be careful what you say. Miss Dawson is very upset and who wouldn't be if their father had just been murdered?'

'You already knew her, didn't you? I remember you pointing this house out to me when you were doing some work here a few months ago.'

'Do you ever forget anything, Nina?'

'Not often. You said you were enjoying working here and that she was a nice lady. You don't often say that sort of thing.'

'I enjoyed it very much. She's an intelligent woman and it could be a lovely house if it were brought up to scratch again.' He led the way inside, intending to go back into the sitting room, only Miss Dawson was in the kitchen pouring hot water from a kettle into a teapot. She was still pale and looking rather tense, but she seemed to have pulled herself together.

'The sergeant is checking the rest of the house in case someone else has sneaked in,' she told them.

It was a minute or two before he came back. 'There's no one else there, Miss Dawson.'

She turned towards the teapot. 'I thought we'd all be better for a cup of tea. The woman who was here earlier made some and it was so strong and sickly sweet it tasted horrible. I poured it down the sink. Would you like a quick cup, Sergeant?'

He hesitated.

'I can put some cold water into yours so that you can drink it at once.'

'Then I'd welcome a cup.'

She did that and as she turned to attend to the others' cups, he drank his quickly and set the cup down.

'Thank you very much. Could you please lock the back door after me, Mr Shorrocks? I don't want anyone else taking you people by surprise.'

'We'd better listen for my maid arriving, but she's not due back from her half day off yet.'

Rufus locked the door then gestured to his sister. 'This is Nina.' The girl responded with her usual politeness. He was proud of her manners as well as her intelligence.

'I'm pleased to meet you, Miss Dawson, and I'm sorry about your father.'

'Yes. It was a big shock. I'm sorry about your mother, too, Nina.'

Rufus's sister looked at him and he guessed she wasn't sure how to answer that. For some reason he didn't want to tell Miss Dawson lies so he stepped in.

'Our mother had been ill for a while, so it wasn't a shock like your father's death must have been.'

Miss Dawson nodded but didn't answer so he filled the silence to give her more time to pull herself together.

'We've just arranged the funeral but we still have to work out how to cope without someone to run the house. Nina is doing really well at school and has just been made a monitor, so I'm determined to find a way for her to stay on and become a teacher when she's old enough.'

Miss Dawson gave Nina one of the quiet smiles he remembered so clearly. 'Well done with your studies. Goodness, don't you look like your brother? Such a lovely colour of hair you both have, that dark red.'

'Your hair's reddish too. Did the other pupils at school call you names because of it?'

'Oh, yes. Children often call each other names. If it's not because of one thing, it's because of another. They used to call me beanpole because I was tall and scrawny.'

She wasn't scrawny now, Rufus thought. In fact she had a very shapely figure. And her hair was an unusual shade of reddish chestnut, the red predominating when the light caught it. At other times it looked brown. Then he got annoyed with himself for thinking about her appearance at such a sad time, as well as feeling guilty about standing around and letting her wait on them. 'Do you need any help?'

'No, thank you. I'd prefer to keep occupied, if you don't mind. I think best when my hands are busy with some simple task.'

He could understand that. He was the same, so when she again gestured to the chairs set around a big kitchen table he took the nearest one and Nina sat across from him on the other side, staring round the large room with her usual intense interest in anything and everything new.

He tried to keep an eye on Miss Dawson without making it too obvious and soon realised that she was studying them closely as well. She moved to and fro, setting out matching china cups and saucers, after which she put out a plate of biscuits and stirred the tea in the pot before setting it on a mat on the table. Finally she set out a jug of milk and bowl of sugar as well.

It all looked very attractive, served like that, but by the time she'd finished her hands were trembling slightly, as if reaction was setting in, so when she sat down abruptly Rufus picked up the teapot. 'I'll pour, shall I?'

'Thank you. It's beginning to sink in what I'm facing, I think, and I'm a bit too upset to pour steadily. Please help yourselves to sugar and milk.'

Nina poured some milk into her tea but shook her head at the sugar and took a sip, then a big mouthful. 'Ooh, what lovely tea!'

Miss Dawson relaxed enough to smile at the child. 'Only the best for my father. Have a biscuit. They're rather special too.'

The last thing Rufus had expected to be doing when he came here was to be chatting over a pot of tea drunk from elegant china cups, which were carefully refilled as needed from the big teapot. This seemed like an oasis of calm after the horrors of the day.

Miss Dawson had stopped trying to chat and was looking thoughtful, so he didn't say anything either.

When Nina finished one biscuit and looked at the others on the plate longingly, their kind hostess pushed it towards her and he nodded at his sister to take another, taking a second one himself.

Once they'd finished, they all carried their cups and the other items across to the draining board, then Miss Dawson took a deep breath. 'Nina, would you like to look at a book in the other room while I speak to your brother on my own?'

The child beamed. 'Yes, please. I love books.'

'Good.' Abigail turned to Rufus. 'I wonder if you and I could have a private chat, Mr Shorrocks? I have a suggestion to make.'

8

Rufus waited in the doorway as Abigail showed Nina into another large room, this one set out with the comfortable armchairs and sofa he remembered from his previous visits.

Abigail gestured to the bookcase. 'You can look at any of the books, Nina. Just remember to put them back in the same places.'

'Thank you.' Nina beamed and plumped down on her knees in front of the low bookcase.

'You'll never get rid of her if you show her rows of books,' he said as they went back into the kitchen and he pulled out a chair for her. 'Now, how can I help you, Miss Dawson?'

'I'm thinking we might be able to help one another.'

'Oh? Do go on.' If he could do anything to make this sad time easier for her he would, but he couldn't imagine how she'd be able to help him.

'First, let me get a few things straight. You're not married, are you?'

'No. And I never have been.'

'Are you courting?'

'No. And again, I've never done that either. I've always planned to set myself up financially before marrying and settling down. Anyway, it'd have been impossible to create a happy marriage with my mother around.'

She gave him a quick, sharp look.

'I'm not going to lie to you about her. To be frank, the older she got the more foolish she became, spending any money that she got hold of immediately, not necessarily on buying food, but on whatever caught her eye.'

Abigail was looking so sympathetic he told her more than he'd intended. 'Mum didn't even look after the house or Nina properly in the last few months. After her second husband died, I was the only support of her and my sister, which meant doling out money daily so that she couldn't waste it and taking any job I could. It's hard to keep a job when you may be called away at any moment because your mother is causing trouble. I'm lucky that I've been working for Mr Ollerton lately. He's very considerate.'

He looked sad, she thought, and what he was saying made her more certain that she should try her idea on him.

'It was difficult to make sure Nina ate regularly and was able to finish her schooling. She's such a clever lass, I won't let her leave school early if I can help it.'

He frowned and looked across at her, not sure where this was leading. 'Sorry to go on about it. Why did you ask?'

She took a deep breath and said slowly, 'I think you and I would be able to help one another in several ways if we got married.'

He could only gape at her because this was the last thing he'd expected to hear. Let alone women didn't usually propose to men, the two of them were near strangers and from different social backgrounds.

'Why?' he managed at last. 'We hardly know one another.'

'Because we're both facing difficult situations and have no family to help solve our problems.'

He could see some sense in what she was saying. People did marry for the convenience of having someone to help out in their daily lives. But he was puzzled as to why she'd choose him. Besides, she could afford to pay for help; she didn't have to marry it. 'Go on.'

'If you and Nina moved here, you'd have a proper home and she could continue at school. And it'd give me protection to be married.'

'Protection?' That was something he could understand after what had happened.

'Yes. Someone has killed my father and I shall need to sort out his business affairs, which will upset certain people, like that horrible Bibby fellow. I think you'd be able to help me do that as well.'

'You're serious about this, aren't you?'

'Yes, of course I am. I'd not have thought of it, though, if we hadn't got to know one another earlier in the year.' She went a little pink as she added, 'You did a really good job on the repairs to this house and – and I enjoyed your company greatly. I missed chatting to you after you'd finished the work and stopped coming here.'

'I enjoyed our chats too. You're an intelligent woman. And I could tell that you were lonely.'

Her voice was a near whisper. 'Yes. Very. I have been for years.'

Silence hung over them for a few moments, then she said, 'If you're going to turn me down, please do it quickly and never mind being tactful. I'm not going to beg. I've embarrassed myself enough.'

And he suddenly realised that he wasn't going to turn her down. She was right: they really could help one another and they had got on well before. So he said it aloud. 'I'm not going to turn you down.'

'Oh!' She blushed an even deeper pink, looking suddenly prettier and younger.

'Are you absolutely certain that's what you want?'

'Very much so.'

'Then I'd better call you Abigail, hadn't I?'

'Of course. And you're Rufus.'

They smiled at one another, then his smile faded. 'I am concerned that I'd be taking advantage of your current difficulties, though, and that you might live to regret it bitterly if we did get married.'

She sagged against her chair back, closing her eyes for a moment and covering them with one hand.

'Are you all right?'

'Yes. Just pulling myself together because I need to say something else that's embarrassing. I wouldn't regret it if you were kind to me and—' She sucked in a huge breath before adding in a rush, 'If you gave me a child or two. My father took that possibility away from me by keeping me a prisoner here and it made me very unhappy.'

'Is that how you felt? Like a prisoner?'

'Yes. But I didn't just feel it: I *was* a prisoner. Well treated but still "*cribbed, cabined and confined*" as Shakespeare's Macbeth said. I've never forgotten that phrase because it's exactly how I've felt for most of my adult life.'

He stretched out one hand and she hesitated for a moment then laid hers in it, still staring at him a little anxiously. He closed his fingers gently round that soft, warm hand. 'I can understand that because I've felt trapped for years, too. When I was younger I was trapped by my family's poverty, which is why I left Ollerthwaite to work in the mines, even though I hated being underground. I earned more money there, you see. And lately I've been a prisoner of my mother's foolishness and her illness. So I really do understand how you can be trapped by circumstances.'

She didn't pull her hand away and he didn't let go; he loved the soft warm feel of her skin.

'I enjoyed the way we chatted about our lives, and we're sharing our thoughts honestly now, Rufus, at least I think we are.'

'You're right. We are. So I'd be honoured to marry you, Abigail, and I promise that I'd always be kind to you. I have a condition to ask of you, too. I love my younger sister dearly. Nina would have to be part of any family we created and I'd want you to be kind to her in your turn. Very kind, if you could manage it. She's had so little chance of happiness with a mother like ours.'

'I think she's a delightful child and I'd welcome her into my life. I've known too few people, thanks to my father, and have always wanted children of my own. You'll have to tell me at first if I'm doing or saying anything wrong when I'm with her.'

He smiled. 'She's not hard to deal with. Treat her like another adult. She's very intelligent and has a questing mind. I really enjoy chatting to her.'

Abigail was still clutching his hand and he suddenly realised what she needed now, so stood up, pulled her to her feet and hugged her close, pressing a gentle kiss on her forehead. 'This is to seal our bargain.'

When she burst into tears, he rocked her to and fro, making soothing sounds till the sobs abated. 'Are you all right again now? You were crying so hard I was worried that you'd changed your mind.'

'No, I haven't done that, Rufus. It's been so many years since anyone has hugged me. And it's such a relief not to have to face life alone – and to have a chance of making a family.'

'I've longed for a proper family too.' He wiped her tears, thinking what pretty eyes she had and sneaked a quick swipe at his own, because he'd been upset by her pain.

He took hold of her hand again. 'You were very brave, proposing to me.'

'Maybe you're the brave one to accept me because I don't think it'll be easy for us to sort our lives out.'

'Oh, and just one more thing,' she went on. 'Mrs Blaney is our maid and a good one too. She has nowhere else to go. I hope you won't mind her staying on. My father's money will easily stretch to paying for her.'

'I'm happy to let her stay. This is a big house to look after.'

It was out before she could stop herself. 'I feel so better about the future now.'

'Only time will tell, but I think we'll stand a better chance together. I'll always do my best for our little family. No one can do more than that.'

'I shall try my hardest to make a good life for us all, too.'

'Good. Let's go and tell my sister. I think it will please Nina, too.'

Neither of them attempted to keep hold of the other's hand as they walked into the other room. They weren't at the stage of such public displays yet. But the warmth of her clasp seemed to linger in the palm of his hand, and Rufus welcomed the feeling.

9

They found Nina curled up in an armchair, so lost in the book she was reading that she didn't at first notice them come in. When her brother went across to stand in front of her she suddenly became aware of their presence and jumped to her feet.

'Sorry. This is such an exciting story I forgot everything else.'

Abigail joined them. 'What are you reading?'

'It's called *The Jungle Book*. I've never heard of it before but it's lovely.'

'It's a book for children but I like Rudyard Kipling's writing so I asked my father to buy it for me when it was published recently. He never used to read books himself, only newspapers, so wouldn't have known whether it was for children or grown-ups. He was generous about buying books for me.'

She blinked her eyes furiously, not wanting to spoil this moment by weeping again in front of the child. Her emotions seemed to be warring with one another about her father. She felt upset and grieving that he'd been murdered, yet relieved to be out of the prison he'd kept her in for so long.

Rufus looked questioningly at her, as if asking whether she wanted to speak, but she gestured to him to tell his sister their news.

'Let's all sit down, shall we? There's something very important we need to tell you, Nina love.'

The child smiled at her brother with such utter love and trust that Abigail felt it was another sign that he really was a kind person.

'Abigail and I have decided to get married.'

She looked at them, nodding as if this wasn't unexpected.

'You don't seem surprised.'

'My friend at school's mother died and someone told me her father would soon marry again, because men need wives to look after their houses and families. And he did. It's nearly the same with you, even though it's our mother who's died, not a wife.'

'You don't sound as if you mind?'

'No, of course not. I'm happy for you both.' She gave Abigail a quick shy smile.

'It'll mean us coming to live here.'

'Really? Ooh, living here will be wonderful. It's a lovely big house. Can I have a proper bedroom of my own?'

Abigail looked a little surprised but didn't hesitate. 'Of course you can. You can even choose which one.'

'Thank you. And look at all the books. Will it be all right to go on reading them, Miss Dawson? I'll be very careful not to damage them, I promise.'

'Of course it'll be all right and you should call me Abigail from now on.'

'Abigail! Abigail!' Nina twirled round several times.

Rufus grinned. 'She always twirls round when she's happy. And I knew there was a particularly good reason for us to get married – she'll be able to read all your books if you're her sister-in-law.'

They exchanged genuine smiles at his little joke.

There were sounds from the kitchen, three loud knocks on the back door followed by a key turning in the lock.

He stood up. 'Who else had a key to the house?'

Abigail put out one hand to stop him rushing out. 'Only Mrs Blaney, my – I mean our live-in maid.'

'We'd better tell her our news too.'

In the kitchen Mrs Blaney was putting a shopping bag on the table and looked surprised to see Rufus and Nina come in to join her.

Abigail said quickly, 'My father's dead. He's been murdered.'

Mrs Blaney gaped at her. 'Surely not!'

'I'm afraid so.'

'And Rufus's mother has just died too, so . . . he and I are going to get married.'

She looked at them in surprise then a smile slowly spread across her face. 'I'm that glad for you, miss. And you make sure you treat her nicely, Mr Shorrocks, or you'll answer to me.'

As she was a small, wiry woman and he was tall and strong that made him smile again, but he liked the way she was protective towards her mistress.

She turned to Nina next. 'You'll like living here. It's got the makings of a nice family home . . . now.'

Rufus didn't need to ask her what she meant by that. And to his surprise he agreed. He still felt amazed at the whole situation, as if this was happening in a dream – a good dream, though, not a nightmare.

Then he realised there were practicalities to be attended to. 'I shall need to collect our possessions and bring them here. I'd better do it quickly or they might get stolen, but I'm worried about leaving you three here.' He didn't say it aloud, but there was still a murderer at loose and he could see Abigail suddenly realise why he was thinking like that and lose her half-smile.

He snapped his fingers as the solution came to him. 'I know! There's a man I work with sometimes who lives nearby. I'm sure Steve will be happy to earn some extra money by joining you here till I've finished moving our possessions and arranging for our former home to be cleaned. I'm pretty sure our neighbour will do that for us if I slip her a few shillings.'

Abigail frowned at him. 'Do you think we're in that much danger that we need a bodyguard?'

'I'm not sure of anything except that it's a good idea for us to marry, and until I am sure of the situation, I'd rather be safe than sorry. Humour me on this.'

She nodded reluctantly.

'If my friend isn't at home, I know other chaps who live nearby and one of them is bound to be free to stay with you till I get back. And there's a fellow with a pony and cart who'll help me clear our things out of our old home and bring them here.'

'You seem to know a lot of people.'

'I do. And that's going to come in useful for both of us.'

'How many trips is it going to take to bring everything, or has your friend got a large cart?'

He'd only bring those things that were worth keeping, he added mentally, trying to hide his embarrassment as he explained, 'We don't have a lot of possessions, so it'll only take one trip to bring them. And I shan't keep much of it but even though our furniture isn't suitable for a house like this, there are people who would be delighted to have it. I don't like to waste anything.'

'Then that's what we'll do.' Abigail turned to the child. 'Nina, are you hungry?'

'I am, rather. But I can manage if you haven't got any food.'

'There is plenty so you can help me and Mrs Blaney put together a meal. We won't wait for your brother to eat ours, though we'll make something for him as well.' She added in surprise, 'I'm suddenly feeling hungry too, now.'

'It's about time you started eating properly,' Mrs Blaney said. 'And then we can sort out bedrooms for them both.'

When Rufus returned ten minutes later he was accompanied by an older man. Steve looked strong and was very polite to the women when introduced as their guard.

Rufus showed him quickly round the ground floor then left on a cart whose driver had been waiting patiently for him outside the house.

Used to preparing hearty meals for her father, Abigail got on with the cooking and told Nina she could continue reading her story.

'She can come up with me and have a look at the bedrooms while you're making a meal,' Mrs Blaney said. 'It's a good thing several of them have got beds in them and there's spare bedding in the linen cupboard.'

So Nina went with her and Abigail continued cooking, glad to have a little time on her own. Steve kept walking slowly round the house, keeping an eye on things.

When the meal was ready, Abigail called out to Nina and Mrs Blaney to come and eat and offered Steve some food as well.

He hesitated. 'Are you sure you've got enough, miss? You weren't expecting me, after all.'

'Yes, we have plenty.'

'Then I'd be very happy to join you. It smells delicious.'

It seemed strange to be eating with anyone but her father. She dished out the food, not even trying to chat to them.

Steve ate his meal quickly, then took another walk round while she served dessert, pieces of her father's favourite fruit cake. She stared at it for a minute or two, feeling a wave of sadness, then shook her head and told herself to get on with things.

Steve ate his cake just as rapidly, thanked her profusely and began walking round the house again, upstairs and down.

It seemed a long time before someone knocked at the back door.

'I'll answer that.' Steve hurried across to peep out of the kitchen window and turned to smile at her before unlocking the door. 'It's Rufus and Colin. They've been quick, haven't they?'

She realised then that she hadn't thought which room to put Rufus in but to her relief it turned out that Mrs Blaney had worked it all out.

'It'd be better if Nina sleeps in your bedroom till you're married, miss, if you don't mind me saying so. We don't want any gossip about you two.'

'Can I see the room you'll be using?' Rufus asked.

He nodded as he was shown it. 'Yes, I did remember correctly from when I did the repairs, it's quite a large room so we can fit Nina's mattress into it quite easily. I'll go and buy her a proper bed frame tomorrow.'

'There's no need. There are spare beds in the other rooms. She can use one of those if you'll help move it in for us. And they have comfortable new mattresses because we never had any visitors. I don't know why Father insisted on furnishing those rooms, but he did.'

'Perhaps it gave him satisfaction?'

She shrugged. 'Perhaps. I didn't always understand why he did things. Anyway, there are beds in most of the other bedrooms. You can choose whichever room suits you, Rufus. Mrs Blaney is sleeping at the far end. If you need more bedroom furniture – like another chest of drawers – just take it from one of the other rooms.'

'Thank you. But I doubt I shall. Nina and I don't have many possessions, I'm afraid, Abigail.'

She risked reaching out to pat his hand. 'That's all right. If either of you needs anything else, we can get it for you. She looks as if she's grown out of those clothes, so she'll need more straight away. Children do grow quickly at times, I gather from my reading.'

Especially children who were never bought new clothes until they desperately needed them, he thought. And how sad that Abigail only knew about that from reading.

It took less than an hour to unload the cart and when he'd paid Col and seen him out, Rufus came to find her. 'I've hired Steve to keep watch during the night because it's been a wearing sort of day and I'm so exhausted I couldn't guarantee to wake up quickly if there were strange noises.'

'As long as you haven't changed your mind about our arrangements?' she said in a low voice. She kept worrying that he might.

'No. I shan't do that, I promise you. You're still all right about it, aren't you?'

'Very much all right.'

'Good. I'm glad of that. I shall enjoy your company and enjoy living here too. And you'll be very good for Nina. I can see how she admires you already.'

'Not as much as she admires the books.'

That lightened the mood a little and they both chuckled.

Surely, Abigail thought, it was a good sign that they could laugh together, even at a difficult time like this.

Later, she lay in bed listening to the girl's soft even breaths from the other side of the bedroom, hearing the hall clock striking the hour until it was past midnight. So much had happened today that her mind wouldn't calm down for a long time. Well, no wonder. Her whole life had been turned upside down.

She shed a few more tears about losing her father, but she had no qualms about marrying Rufus Shorrocks: it felt absolutely right. He was a fine figure of a man, but more importantly to her, he was kind and intelligent.

And she'd have Nina living here as well as Mrs Blaney. What a delightful child his sister was!

She would be very relieved to have Rufus to help her deal with her father's old business. She knew so little about what he'd been doing in recent years. He'd always been very secretive.

She so longed for a normal family and friends and was sure she and Rufus could make a decent new life. She didn't need anything grand, just a more normal way of living.

10

When he left Abigail Dawson's house, Sergeant McGill decided to go to the undertaker's first and then to Dawson's office, on the principle that people were more important than inanimate objects. But with only him and a constable, who wasn't due to start work in the valley for a few more days, he couldn't do everything in as timely a fashion as he'd have wished.

He reached his first port of call just as the doctor was finishing examining the body and was shocked to find the town's female doctor doing such a task.

Dr Coxton looked across the long, narrow table at him, then gestured to the naked corpse lying between them. 'He was stabbed four times in the back. It looks as though it was done with a dagger, not a kitchen knife, and the person who stabbed him was probably right-handed and angry.'

He looked at her in surprise. He hadn't expected such a skilful analysis from a woman, together with her obvious lack of embarrassment about dealing with a man's naked body. 'Thank you. That's, um, very efficient. Can I see the wounds?'

'Yes. Give me a hand. He's a heavy chap.'

When he'd taken a good look, Hector helped her roll the man back and she gave him a wry smile that reminded him of his mother. That smile said she knew he'd been underestimating her skills merely because she was a woman. It probably happened to her a lot and he mentally vowed not to do that again. After all, if she'd trained as a doctor, she must be used to bodies, probably more used to them than he was, come to think of it.

She went on with her analysis. 'I'm not sure it's relevant but if this man had come into my surgery while he was still alive, I'd have told him he was eating his way into an early grave and he needed to eat less. He was overweight in a very unhealthy way with that big belly. I'd guess from his florid complexion that he also indulged in the sort of heavy, regular drinking that doesn't usually lead to a long life.'

'Goodness, you are thorough. Thank you so much for that information. You never know what will come in useful when you start investigating a crime, so if you think of anything else, do get back to me.'

'It's all part of my job. I am a fully qualified and experienced doctor, you know, and have been practising my profession for many years.'

'Yes. I can tell from what you say and do. I apologise for doubting your skills at first. I'll not do that again.'

'You shouldn't do it to any woman doctor,' she said.

He could feel himself flushing in embarrassment. 'No. I won't in future.'

She inclined her head in a gesture of thanks, then looked back at the body. 'Who did this to him, have you any idea? Does this attack mean we're going to be facing an outbreak of violence in our valley or was it aimed only at him?'

'I don't know yet but I hope it won't lead to more general problems, Dr Coxton. Stabbing him four times makes me think this was a personal attack, possibly by someone who hated him or envied his wealth.'

'Did they steal from him as well?'

'Yes. His wallet was missing and also the bag of money he was taking to the bank and his keys.'

'I suppose they went on to burgle his business premises?'

'I'm about to find out. His office is my next port of call. Unfortunately, there's only me to deal with everything in the valley at the moment and I felt I had to inform the man's daughter that her father was dead before I did anything else. The authorities in charge of this part of the county have appointed a constable to help me but he hasn't arrived yet.'

'He'll be a big help, I'm sure.'

'To add to the difficulties of this investigation, it was probably a couple of hours before anyone found the body, so the murderer will have had time to get away, I should think. That's partly why I haven't rushed to the scene of the stabbing.'

'Is his daughter all right, Sergeant?'

'She seems to be taking it very stoically. How do you find her generally?'

'I don't know her except by sight because she hasn't needed to see me about her health. Actually, no one knows much about her because she stayed quietly at home most of the time, and apparently Dawson didn't encourage visitors or allow her to have any friends. I've seen the two of them walk up to the lake at weekends several times, though rather slowly because of his size.'

Hector looked at her thoughtfully then told her the rest. 'I left Rufus Shorrocks keeping an eye on her in case anyone tried to break into the house and attack her as well. He saw someone sneaking into her house through the back door earlier and followed him in to make sure she was all right. Shorrocks has impressed me as a man of sense.'

She nodded. 'Yes. People say he's a clever chap and there are few household repair jobs he can't turn his hands to, which is probably why Mr Ollerton has recently hired him as foreman. He was very kind to his mother, too, considering the poor woman's problems.'

'Was she one of your patients, Dr Coxton?'

'No. But I was treating her neighbour who mentioned her once or twice, worrying lately that she seemed to be getting rather forgetful. That sometimes happens as people grow older, as you'll appreciate, but unfortunately we doctors can't help at all with the condition. Even rich people can't buy cures for all the ills brought on by old age.'

He knew he should be going but she was sharing information with him that might be useful in this new job and he couldn't resist lingering. 'I gather there aren't many rich families in the valley.'

'There are one or two who are very comfortably off, like Walter Crossley. You'll find him a very helpful chap. Mr Ollerton is probably the richest person but he doesn't make a display of his wealth like some arrogant folk I encountered in London. He's rebuilding his family home, which burned down, but spending the money carefully by the sounds of it.'

'Your observations are very helpful.'

'I'm not a gossip but we doctors can't help hearing what's going on, Sergeant, and I know you're not asking questions out of mere nosiness. I'd guess you're trying to find out about your new place of work as quickly as you can in order to do your job properly. Am I right?'

'Yes. Anything you can tell me now or in the future will be much appreciated and kept confidential. I see my job as to prevent crimes wherever possible, rather than merely dealing with the results of the worst ones.'

'In that case I'll let you know if I hear anything that worries me.' She looked down at the body again and opened her medical bag. 'I'm used to seeing people dying but this is the first murder I've encountered. Will a normal death certificate do or shall you need me to fill in some special form?'

'A normal death certificate will be fine. I'll have to inform a magistrate about the incident as well. Who should I speak to?'

She gave him the details, adding, 'I've always found him a decent sort of chap to deal with.'

'Thanks. I'll continue to hunt for the murderer, though he'll probably be long gone and it'll not be easy to find him. I might start by questioning the manager of Dawson's shop who'll be keeping an eye on things there at the moment, I assume. I didn't much like the looks of Bibby. He'd sneaked into the house and was actually pestering Miss Dawson to marry him and let him run the business for her – at a time like that!'

'Good heavens! I'd not want him running anything for me because I don't trust him, though I can't say why. I do wonder how she'll cope with her father's business, though. It won't be easy.'

'Who knows? People do mainly cope with what life dishes out, I find.'

She filled out the form and handed it to him. 'Oh! One other thing. I was speaking to Walter Crossley the other day and I give you fair warning that he wants to get people interested in volunteering to help finish work on the upper end of Jubilee Lake, and when he wants something as much as that, he usually gets done in the end. He'll no doubt try to get you involved in that.'

Hector chuckled. 'You're too late with your warning, Dr Coxton. He's already mentioned it and I've agreed to help. It sounds like a worthwhile project, a good way of marking the Queen's coming Diamond Jubilee. 'Ninety-seven will be a very special year for her and the country if she's still alive then, won't it? She's already lived longer than anyone expected.'

'Yes, but she's another who's eating too much, judging by recent photographs in the newspapers. Now, I really must get on with my day.'

11

Hector left the undertaker to deal with the body then walked briskly across town to Dawson's office and shop, which were at one end of a row of small shops. He was getting to know the central area of Ollerthwaite now and some of the people who lived or worked there.

There was no one hanging around outside it today as he'd seen when he walked past yesterday. Perhaps they'd heard about Dawson being murdered in the alley, which led to the rear entrance, and didn't want to risk getting attacked.

He went up to the front door first and read the roughly scrawled notice saying *Closed due to death of proprietor.* It was attached to the inside of the glass window which formed the upper part of the door and had iron bars across it. He tried to open the door but it was locked, so he banged on it for attention.

There was no answer, so he thumped it again, but with a similar lack of response. Where was Bibby? And that female clerk was supposed to be here too.

Hector tried to get round to the rear of the shop but found a high fence and side gate opening on to the alley. The gate was also locked. He hammered on that and yelled loudly for someone to let him in but still got no answer.

In the end he climbed over the gate, not without some difficulty, because there were spikes on top. He used a dirty old sack that was lying in a corner with some other rubbish to cover the spikes, got up carefully then jumped down into the backyard and stared round.

This area was surrounded on all sides by high fences. He'd never seen a shop made so secure. The yard was bigger than he'd expected, because it went further back than those of the nearby buildings. He unlocked the bolts on the gate so that he could gain access in future and started to pull the sack off the spikes at the top.

'Hoy!' a man's voice called from behind him.

Hector swung round.

'What the hell do you think you're doing?'

He saw a man peering over the nearby part of the fence and flung the sack to one side, ready to defend himself.

The man looked surprised. 'Sorry. I didn't realise you were a policeman. That sack hid your uniform.'

'May I ask who are you, sir?'

'Brad Peters. My family and I run the tripe and pie shop next door.' He jerked his head towards the building, which was not only smaller than Dawson's establishment but distinctly shabby. 'What's going on?'

'You know that Mr Dawson has been murdered?'

Peters nodded. 'Aye. I doubt there's anyone in this part of town as doesn't know that by now.'

'I'm trying to get into the shop to find out whether anything's been touched there. I'd expected to find the manager here.'

'You've just missed Bibby. He came rushing along the road a couple of hours or so ago and went inside.' He frowned. 'Maybe it was a bit longer ago than that. I wasn't paying attention to the clock because I had a shop full of customers.'

When he paused, Hector said, 'Go on.'

'I could hear Bibby yelling when I went into the back room for some more pies. He told everyone to leave quickly, the customers waiting and the two shop assistants. He said the police had ordered him to lock the place up.'

'How do you know that?'

'One of them came in for a pie and told me. He said Bibby looked really agitated and had locked the door and gate on them the minute they left. Bibby's the only one I've seen who has a door key, apart from Mr Dawson.'

Hector frowned. 'Well, I only saw the man briefly at Dawson's house. I told him to get back here quickly and keep an eye on the place till the new owner could sort out what's going to happen to it.'

'Well, he didn't do that. He's not into cooperating with others, that one isn't, doesn't even try to get on with the rest of us shopkeepers in the street. I'd never have hired a man like that. He's out boozing most evenings, an' not in places patronised by decent folk, no, not him.'

'I'd expected to find him inside the shop waiting for me, but it's all locked up,' Hector said.

'Well, you've missed him by half an hour or so. He and that flighty female as calls herself a "lady typewriter" an' fiddles about half the day with that silly machine, came out again about an hour after the others left an' locked the place up. They were carrying some heavy bags and rushed off down the street.'

Hector gaped at him. 'I need them here to help me find out what's been taken.'

'Looked to me as if they were doing some of the taking as well as the thieves.'

'I'll look for them shortly but I'd like to take a quick look round the shop as well to see if everything is all right. There might even be someone else who's been attacked. Um, I wonder if you'd come in with me so that you can bear witness to what we find, if necessary?'

Peters nodded without hesitation. 'Yes, I can do that. My son can look after our shop on his own because we're nearly ready to close for the day. Someone told me Dawson kept everything of value in a ruddy great safe in the back room, so it'll probably be there still. You'd think he kept the Crown Jewels in it. He wouldn't open it if anyone was in the room with him.'

Dawson seemed to have been strangely secretive, Hector thought, and wondered why. What had he been hiding? 'Come round to this gate, Mr Peters, and we'll go into the shop the back way. We'll probably have to break a window to get inside because his daughter didn't have a key to the shop.'

'Pity if you have to do that. We don't want to leave the place standing open for any passing light-fingers to get in afterwards. It might make them think about burgling the other shops as well. Not that they'd find much in mine. I don't keep any money in the shop itself overnight, just the food, and anyway we live above it, so I'd hear intruders.'

'Yes, well, come on round quickly. We'll find a way to secure the place again afterwards.'

Peters arrived shortly afterwards carrying a walking stick with a big nobbly handle. He waved it to and fro in a threatening way. 'I'm not going in without a way of defending myself. Who knows what we'll find there? Have you got your truncheon handy?'

'Yes, of course.' Hector doubted there'd be anyone inside now but patted the side of his belt to reassure his companion. He knocked on the back door again and shouted, so that Peters could bear witness to him checking that no one was inside before he broke in, but of course there was no response.

He turned to his companion. 'You'd better stand back, Mr Peters. There are bars on the windows but if I break the glass, I'll be able to reach inside to the lock. The key will probably have been left in it. Most people do that, I find, which is making things easier for burglars. If it's not there we'll have to find an axe and chop our way in.'

'Let me break the glass for you, Sergeant. I can do it with the top of my stick.' He brandished it. 'I've allus fancied smashing a window, right from when I was a lad.'

Hector didn't allow himself to smile. 'Very well, but make sure you clear the bits of broken glass from the bottom edges afterwards so that I can reach inside safely.'

He stepped back, watching in amusement the older man's childish glee as he smashed the window. Allowing actions like this helped you to win long-term support in the community but it was hard to keep a straight face.

Once the bottom part of the window frame was clear of the visible glass shards, he covered it with the sack just to be sure he didn't get cut then felt round the metal lock cover. To his relief, he found that a key had indeed been left in it. Moving carefully he wriggled it out and used it to open the door from the outside, exclaiming, 'Got you!' when it turned easily.

As he led the way into a small lobby, he warned, 'Mind the broken glass on the floor and don't touch anything unless I tell you it's all right to do so.'

'Righty-ho.' Peters was all serious attention again after his moment of boyish pleasure.

Hector peered through the door that led into the shop at the front and saw all sorts of items strewn around on the floor and counter. 'Looks like someone searched the shop in a hurry. You say there's a big safe in the back room? Let's check in there, then.'

He opened the door at the rear and both of them stopped to stare in shock. The door of the safe was gaping open, with goods tumbled out of it on to the floor and some others piled on a big desk.

For a moment the two men were speechless, then Peters said, 'It looks as if he took the stuff he wanted out of that safe in a big hurry, don't you think, Sergeant? He was only in the shop for an hour or so. I saw him and that woman come out in a tearing hurry, both carrying heavy bags.'

'He left a lot of good things behind but I suppose they could only carry a certain amount of loot if they were on foot.'

'How did they get into the safe, though? Dawson might have given that chap a key to the shop door but he'd never have given him a key to the safe.'

'Bibby must have found a key in the dead man's pocket, which makes it even more likely that he's the one who killed Dawson. Where did Bibby and that woman go, do you think, Mr Peters? You know the town better than I do.'

'Yes. Born and bred here, I was. They probably went down to the station and caught the teatime train out of the valley but who knows where they got off it, eh? If they went to the very end of the line, they'd be able to catch another train to one of the bigger towns like Blackburn, then who knows where they went?'

'I suppose that's a good guess.'

'It happened once before. There was a chap escaped by train a few years ago after robbing his own uncle an' leaving him tied up. The nephew timed it well and it was a while before anyone found his uncle. That sod was never caught an' I bet Bibby won't be, either.'

Hector thought about this then nodded, telling himself he was only one man, as he often did when he failed to prevent a crime or deal with it properly afterwards. 'You could be right. Leaving by train sounds to be the most likely thing they did. I'm extremely grateful to you for your help, Mr Peters and can't thank you enough. Just one other thing. We need to get keys to this place. Is there a locksmith in town?'

'No. You'll have to bring one in from Halifax. There's a glazier, though, so you can get the window repaired, but he only does it part-time because he has a smallholding just outside Ollerthwaite. You can leave a message for him at the furniture shop.'

'Thank you. I shall have to find some way of locking this place up again and keeping it from being invaded by someone else looking to pinch stuff.'

Peters looked at him, opened his mouth, shut it briefly, then said, 'You ought to know one other thing about Dawson: I can't prove this, but it was probably the other way round half the time when it comes to stolen stuff.'

'What do you mean?'

'I've thought for a while that stuff which had been pinched was brought to the shop every now and then and Bibby bought it off the thieves for Dawson. I reckon that's why a chap like him got the manager's job in the first place. I used to see people slip in through this gate carrying bundles after dark. And sometimes Bibby came back after midnight and went in the back way. Did he think that wouldn't wake me up? He didn't even bother to oil the gate an' it had a sort of double squeak.'

'Did you report this?'

'I told Cliff Nolan what I thought was happening but he was old an' weary. He said he didn't believe me and insisted Mr Dawson was a respected member of the community. Which he wasn't. None of the other better-off folk did more than nod to him in passing.'

'And now Nolan's retired to live with his daughter somewhere in Yorkshire, I gather, so we can't ask him about it.'

'He'd not have tried to catch anyone with stolen goods. Towards the end, he couldn't have chased a ball down the street, let alone caught a burglar. I'm glad we've got a younger bloke like you as our policeman now.'

'I'm only one man.'

'Yes. But word is that you'll have a constable working with you soon. Is that true?'

'Yes, it is.'

'So the two of you will be able to maintain law and order here better than Cliff ever did, poor old sod.'

'I'll be giving keeping the peace here my very best go, I assure you, and I'll make sure my constable does the same.'

'Strong young fellow, is he?'

'I haven't met him yet.'

Peters studied Hector for a moment or two, head on one side, then nodded. 'Well, you're a big chap, so you're bound to get more done than Cliff. As for keeping an eye on this shop tonight, my son will do that if you like. He's a strong young fellow, my Jem is, an' he's like me, hates cheats and thieves with a passion.' He swished his walking stick about as if to emphasise this.

'I'll pay him five bob for his night's work.' Hector had a small fund for such extras. The new inspector in charge of policing this area was a big believer in using members of the community to help out, and had introduced this new tactic with a warning not to use the money too lavishly.

Peters looked surprised then smiled. 'That's good to hear. Jem's saving up to get wed and every shilling counts, doesn't it? The wife and I are looking forward to him moving out, not in a nasty way but he's a stomach on wheels that one is, eats you out of house an' home. He's a good lad at heart, though. I wish we had a few more sons like him, but it weren't to be.'

He looked sad for a moment, so he and his wife mustn't have been able to have other children.

Hector was slightly amused at how garrulous the man was. Still he was getting on good terms with him and finding out more about the town, which was what counted.

He gave his companion a minute to pull himself together again then said, 'You're being very helpful and I'm grateful. Even if we can't lock the back door, your son can bolt it from inside to stop anyone getting in. And tell him to leave lights on all night and never mind the cost of the gas. But he's to change the rooms that are lit a couple of times to show anyone considering breaking in that someone's there.'

'Jem's keeping an eye on our shop and he'll come round as soon as I tell him about the job. We always have a few late customers who nip in for cheap leftovers and broken goods. If I let them know he's keeping watch next door, they'll spread the word.'

'Good thinking. I'll let Miss Dawson know what I've found here but there's not much else I can do tonight. I'll ask her to meet me down here tomorrow morning so that she can give me some idea of what's missing.'

'Eh, she won't be able to do that, Sergeant.'

'Why not?'

'Dawson didn't let her come to the shop once she'd stopped working there. After his wife died, he kept that poor young woman under his thumb looking after him and the house. Some people do that, keep the youngest daughter at home an' don't let her get wed, so that she can look after them in their old age.'

Hector nodded. 'I've seen that happen a few times and felt sorry for such women. Again, thank you for your help.' He held out his hand and they shook, cementing what would become a useful alliance, he felt sure.

He was hoping to make a few connections like this with people in the valley. They could be invaluable.

He waited for young Jem Peters to come round to the shop and left him there to keep watch. Then he called in briefly on Miss Dawson to let her know what he'd found.

'The shop had been broken into but I don't think we can do anything else tonight,' he ended. 'I've put someone there to keep watch and I'll call on you tomorrow morning and go through the details, then perhaps we'll go and look round. Will that be all right?'

'Yes.'

He made his way home, tired now. He slowed down as he passed the end of a narrow street called Jubilee Lane with a sign pointing to the presence of a lake. He hadn't had time to walk round the lake yet but it was on his list of things to do. Perhaps this weekend he could take an hour or two off from his investigations if the weather was fine. His wife would enjoy a walk too, and they'd bought a sturdy little pram when he got promoted that both children could fit into.

He liked Mr Crossley's idea of finishing off the path round the lake. It would be good to have somewhere pleasant to go for walks, especially in the summer, but you needed a path when you were pushing a pram, as he hoped he and his wife would be doing for a year or two yet.

He also liked the thought that if he helped to work on the lakeside path he'd come into contact with more of the decent people in the valley.

When he'd been learning the job, the very experienced sergeant from his first police station, who'd taught him some really useful lessons, had stressed how much you needed the support of the people you were doing the policing for. You didn't get very far on your own and anyway, who wanted to be on his own against the villains of a town? He didn't, that was certain.

He liked the valley already and so did his wife. They would be happy to settle here for the next few years.

12

As he got out some food for breakfast Walter's thoughts were on his new project. He was determined to set up a proper modern nursing service for the poorer people of the valley, especially the mothers and children, so that they could receive free medical attention when they needed it.

Without such a service, many of the poorer women simply went without medical help if their husbands couldn't afford it. And if the husbands had something wrong, the men took priority when it came to paying the doctor.

It was crucial to poorer families that the main breadwinner kept on working, but Walter still thought it unfair that women so often went without the care they needed because of that. And he wasn't the only person in England to think that. There were some big changes happening in the country.

He hoped to see changes being made here from now on with the help of Flora Vardy, who had arrived in the valley recently, sent by one of the national organisers of the Queen's Nursing Service. She was a redoubtable woman, who had been highly recommended to him to help set up clinics and whatever else was needed.

And since she was lodging at the farm, he couldn't help noticing that she was still a fine figure of a woman even at sixty. Perhaps she was too mature to be called pretty but if you asked him to describe her, he'd say she was handsome, with a trim figure, still rosy and healthy looking.

Queen Victoria herself had donated money towards training this new type of nurse and from what he'd read in the newspapers, he reckoned it had been one of the best things their queen had ever done for her poorer subjects.

Flora said that after decades of hard work as a nurse she wanted a quieter life to end her days. That amused him every time he remembered it, because her idea of a quiet life was more akin to most other people's idea of being extremely busy.

He felt the same as she did about keeping active. He might be a decade older than Flora but he'd not stop trying to help the people of his valley until they carried him out of his beloved home feet first.

The new doctor who'd moved here recently was also a woman, not young but younger than Flora. It had shocked some people to have a female doctor, especially the older and more hidebound men. He reckoned they needed a second doctor in the valley but the other one had better be a man, because some of the local chaps were too pig stubborn in their attitudes to let a woman doctor attend to their needs unless they were at death's door.

He turned as he heard someone coming down the stairs and into the kitchen.

'Good morning, Flora. You've timed it well. The kettle will be boiling in a minute or two. If you sit down I'll make you a cup of tea.'

'That'd be lovely, thank you.'

But she didn't sit down straight away. Instead, she went across to stare out of the front window at the valley below. You could even catch a glimpse of the lake if you stood close to the glass and looked to the left.

After a few minutes Flora sat down and let him pour her a cup of tea. 'How lovely this view is, Walter.'

'Yes. I usually start my days by looking at it.' He looked at the ceiling. 'Was anyone else stirring when you got up?'

'No. Elinor's very nauseous in the mornings, poor thing. Some women are like that when they're expecting, but from what she tells me, she's started very early. There isn't much you can do about it except try to help them take things more easily. I really like the way your grandson looks after his wife. He's a kind chap – a lot like you, in fact.'

It wasn't often he felt flustered, but he didn't know how to respond to a compliment from a woman like her. 'Oh. Well, er, thank you for those kind words.'

'I may upset people by being blunt when I see something wrong, but I'm not backward about giving compliments where they're due, either.' She smiled. 'You'll have to get used to that.'

'Then I'll give you a compliment in return by saying how lucky we are to have you here now, Flora, to help us sort out a way of getting proper nursing care for the poorer folk. And while I think about it, you really don't need to move out into lodgings. I'd be very happy for you to continue staying here at the farm as part of my contribution to setting up such a service. There are plenty of bedrooms here and we always have food to spare since we produce much of our own.'

'Are you sure, Walter? I don't want to impose.'

'I'm very sure. Apart from anything else, I enjoy the company of someone of my own generation. If you don't mind being told that by a seventy year old?'

'I don't mind at all. I don't pretend to be young and actually it's useful having a head full of medical experience to draw on when sick people need help.'

'There you are, then. Stay here, Flora, and be as frank as you like. I'll help you with organising the nursing in any other way I can, as well.'

'You seem to make a practice of helping all sorts of folk in Ollindale, Walter. I admire that.'

He shrugged. 'The valley is my home and I love it here.'

'I'm starting to love it too. I haven't breathed such clean, bracing air for a long time.'

They smiled at one another and finished their mugs of tea in a silence that was as warm and friendly as any conversation.

After a while he asked, 'What about breakfast? Shall I make you something, Flora?'

'We can make it together.'

He was sorry when Elinor and Cameron came downstairs to join them, fond as he was of his grandson and wife. Chatting to Flora was a pleasant way to start the day. There was no denying things had been extremely busy in the past year or two, and at his age it would be good to slow down for a while.

Growing old wasn't for the faint-hearted, as the saying went, and he definitely didn't have the same vigorous energy he'd had in his younger days. But he'd been lucky so far and had enjoyed good health. He hoped to live for a few years longer, as people in his family usually did. Quite a few of his ancestors had made it into their nineties even, barring accidents like the one that had killed his son and grandson last year.

He sighed. Every now and then the memory of that dreadful time stabbed him hard. It had left a huge hole in his family and his heart.

He felt a hand on his arm and turned his head sideways to see Flora looking at him as if she understood what he was thinking about.

She gave his arm a quick squeeze. 'Come and take a stroll up to the edge of the moors with me, Walter, and leave your demons in the past. You can't change what's happened, only continue to move into the future and do the best you can with what's left of your own life.'

He clasped the hand that was lying warmly on his arm. 'I don't often brood on the past. And I'd very much enjoy a walk in the fresh air with you, my lass.'

She chuckled. 'I haven't been called a lass for I don't know how many years.'

'Well, I'm older than you so I claim the right to do it. What's more, you are a *bonny* lass.' A tidy armful, his father would have called her, with a face that was still youthful in spite of her silver hair.

As they walked along, he realised suddenly that he'd been flirting with her and she had seemed to enjoy it.

Was he imagining that?

No, he wasn't. And when he looked sideways, she winked at him. She often seemed to know what he was thinking.

He had felt so comfortable with her right from the first time they'd met.

13

Sergeant McGill got up extra early the next morning and wrote a letter to the area commander in which he summarised what had happened. After wolfing down breakfast with his wife and children, he set off for the railway station to speak to the elderly porter who was the only member of staff at the terminus of the minor railway line that Ollerthwaite was lucky to have.

On the way he posted the letter, pleased that the little sign on the mailbox in the wall of the local post office showed that he was in time for the earliest collection. The letter would arrive at its destination in Preston by last post today. He'd feel better when the weight of this investigation was not resting solely on his shoulders and Inspector Helton, who was based there, was always quick to respond if he felt he could help with a major problem or you were doing something wrong, though Hector didn't think he was with this murder.

Working so far away from other colleagues was an aspect of being in such a remote area that could make his job more difficult at times.

The porter remembered Bibby and his female companion clearly because they'd almost missed the train and had yelled for him to hold it so they could scramble on board.

'Is there any way of finding out where they got off it?'

'Unfortunately not, Sergeant.'

'Well, at least I now know that those two left the valley yesterday. I'll have to send another message to my inspector to tell him that.' He thought for a minute then added slowly, 'I shall also write to the police officer in the village at the other end of this railway. That's where you change to a major railway line that connects to the bigger towns, isn't it?'

'Yes, Sergeant, it is.'

'The porters there may or may not have seen those two but even if they haven't, they can ask around and maybe find someone else who did see them. They were carrying heavy, lumpy bundles from all accounts, so they might have been noticed, if we're lucky. I'm not counting on it, though.'

He then noticed the time on the big station clock and said a hasty farewell before hurrying up Railway Road to call on Miss Dawson. He felt as though he'd already done a full morning's work and it wasn't yet eight o'clock. He was hoping she'd be up by now.

To his relief the maid answered the door and said her mistress was just finishing breakfast.

'It's rather urgent that I see her.'

'I'll take you straight through, then, Sergeant. I'm sure she won't mind, given what happened and you being a policeman.'

She showed him into the kitchen where Miss Dawson was sitting with Rufus and his sister over the remains of their breakfast.

She was speaking to the child but broke off and looked anxious when she saw him standing in the doorway.

'I'm so sorry to come here this early in the morning, but there's only me to sort everything out. Could I speak to you privately about your father and the shop, Miss Dawson?'

She hesitated then looked at Rufus, who nodded.

'I'd prefer Rufus to stay with us, Sergeant. You see, yesterday he and I decided to get married because we've . . . um . . .'

'Known each other for a while and both have personal situations that we can help the other with by marrying now,' Rufus finished for her.

The sergeant tried to hide his surprise. 'Oh, er, congratulations.'

'We get on so well.' Rufus smiled at his new fiancée warmly. 'We met earlier in the year when I did some work here but her father didn't want her to marry at all, so I couldn't get to know her better then.'

It made her feel good when he said that so firmly, making their engagement sound less strange. She couldn't help giving him a quick smile.

'Well, in that case, I'm happy for Mr Shorrocks to stay with us while we talk.' Hector noticed Nina sitting at the table and added, 'But perhaps this isn't something that concerns your sister, Mr Shorrocks?'

'You're right.' He turned to the child. 'Would you like to go into the other room and read your book while we have our chat, Nina love? I think you should keep a book handy at all times from now on, because Abigail and I will have a lot of business to sort out in the next few days and we might not always be good company for you.'

'I like to read and there are lots of lovely books here but what about school?'

'We'll keep you at home for a day or two. It'll be safer.'

She stared at him solemnly then nodded as if she understood why and stood up.

'You might enjoy sitting in the big comfortable armchair next to the window in the living room,' Abigail said. 'It's where I like to read in the daytime. The sun shines into it for part of the day.'

'That'll be lovely.' Nina left the kitchen.

'Shall we sit down again?' Rufus gestured to Hector to take a seat then he sat down too, next to his fiancée this time, not opposite her.

The sergeant kept an eye on Miss Dawson's reactions as he went through in greater detail what he'd found at the shop.

'As I told you yesterday, I had to break into your father's business premises so I left someone there to keep an eye on things overnight until we can find a key to replace the one Bibby must have taken.'

'What exactly had Bibby done at the shop?'

'He'd gone through its contents and left a right old mess. And there are gaps on the shelves, so presumably he's stolen some items from the displays. He'd also opened the safe and it looked as if more things had been removed from that. The neighbour saw Bibby go in and later he and a woman came out carrying heavy bags. They ran down the street towards the station and were seen getting on the train.'

'Oh dear, only my father had a key to the safe and it was always kept on his watch chain. I don't know of any copies of it and he'd never have given one to Bibby, manager or not.'

'That reinforces what I'd been thinking, that Bibby must have been the one who killed him. The porter told me he and Miss Keane only just managed to get on the train before it left and they were carrying a lot of luggage.'

She nodded but didn't comment, so he continued, 'I was wondering if you know anything about the contents of the safe and shop. I can see gaps from which things must have been taken but I have no way of knowing exactly what's missing or whether everything was taken yesterday.'

'I'm afraid I can't help you with that. I haven't even been back inside the shop since I stopped working there after my mother's death, and that's nearly ten years ago now. I never had anything to do with Father's safe even when I worked there. No one was allowed into his office when he opened the safe, so I'm sorry, but I don't know any way for you to find out exactly what's missing.'

He looked at her in dismay. 'Oh dear. That's going to make it very difficult to investigate this case properly or to prove theft if we do catch him.'

'I wonder whether... ' Her voice trailed away and she frowned.

'Even a guess would be better than nothing,' Hector said quietly.

'Well, it is only a guess, but Father keeps some business papers here. He always locked them in his room, so I don't know what they are, but they may give you some ideas about what's missing. There may even be another set of keys there.'

'I didn't realise he had an office at home as well as the shop.'

'He didn't call it his office, just "my room", and I have no idea what's in there. I wasn't even allowed to clean it, so only caught brief glimpses of it when he opened the door. He did the cleaning himself, though not very often. I can't even let you in because I don't have a key to the door, let alone to the cupboards and drawers in there.'

'Good heavens!'

Both the sergeant and Rufus stared at her in astonishment.

'My father was always extremely secretive about his financial affairs,' she said apologetically.

'Yes, I'm beginning to realise just how secretive,' the sergeant said. 'That makes me even more sure that Bibby must have been the murderer.'

'Why would he do it, though? Father had made him manager of the shop. He was doing well by most people's standards.'

'Who knows why? Greed or he could have been upset about something. Perhaps your father had just fired him. Did he ever mention having trouble with the man's work?'

'He rarely mentioned anything that was going on at the shop.'

Rufus put his arm round her. 'Let's take the sergeant to look in your father's room here, shall we?'

'But I told you: I don't have a key to the door.'

'Then we'll have to break it down. He and I can probably manage that.'

Hector gave them a wry smile. 'Actually, we may not need to do that, Mr Shorrocks. I've learned a few tricks from the villains I've dealt with over the years, and one of them is picking locks. I could give this one a try, with your permission of course.'

'Oh, yes. Please do. I'll need to get in there myself now. Come with me and I'll show you which room it is.'

Hector followed them to the far end of the ground floor, along a broad and rather dark corridor with a couple of small, narrow tables at the side. They weren't dusty but there were no ornaments on them or mirrors on the walls above them, as might normally be set out to make a house look more attractive, only very plain everyday candlesticks with new candles in them and boxes of matches beside them.

Halfway along the corridor there was a window looking out on the street. It had a stained-glass pattern round the edges and the middle part was heavily frosted glass, which let in some light but would reveal little of what was inside to anyone trying to peep in from outside. What a secretive house this was!

Abigail gestured to the final door, which was set across the end of the corridor. 'This was father's room. It's bigger than the others.'

Hector tried the door but wasn't surprised to find it locked.

He took out his 'lock picks' and fiddled about for a few moments. He was just thinking this lock was going to resist his limited skills when suddenly there was a click. 'Aha! Here we go.'

He opened the door then gestured to Abigail. 'I think you should go in first, Miss Dawson.'

As he pushed the door further open she moved forward. 'I'd better draw back the curtains first so that we can see what we're doing.'

Even with the curtains fully drawn back the room seemed gloomy. It stretched across the whole width of the house, but the rear window looked out at a brick wall. The front one looked out on to the street but had heavy net curtains across it.

The whole room felt dusty and the windowsills and skirting boards were thick with it as if never cleaned. There were two huge desks with nothing on them except big blotters and pen stands. Hector tried the drawers and every single one was locked, as was the tall mahogany filing cabinet in the corner.

'What exactly did your father do here? Do you have any idea at all?'

'I'm afraid not. He always said he had "a few things to see to". He didn't come in here every day but when he did, it'd be towards the end of the evening and he'd tell me not to wait up for him, so I'd go to bed with a book. I knew better than to disturb him when he was working on his business affairs so I'd not see him again until morning. I sometimes heard him come up to bed in the early hours of the morning.'

She looked round and shivered. 'I've never liked the feel of this room. If you want to look for keys, Sergeant, you're welcome to pick the locks on the drawers and continue poking around. If you can't find any keys, don't hesitate to break into the drawers because I shall have to get into them somehow to deal with whatever they contain.'

'We'll see if we can find the keys first. But I'd be grateful if you'd stay while I hunt for them.'

Rufus put his arm round her shoulders. 'Come and sit down, Abigail. At least there's a comfortable armchair.'

But she suddenly stopped and looked at the low bookcase pushed back against the wall between the two desks. 'Try looking inside the books, Sergeant. I've got a vague memory of seeing Father hiding something in a hollowed-out book when I was a child. Even then I knew not to mention that I'd seen it. He's been very careful in recent years not to do anything connected with his business while I was nearby, but perhaps he still used books as hiding places.'

'Worth a try.' The sergeant began pulling out books and opening them to flick through the pages and make sure they really were books, then piling them on one of the desks. After a few minutes he suddenly exclaimed as he tried to open what looked like a book with gold-patterned binding on the spine and the words 'Charles Dickens' at the top of it. But he couldn't flick any pages because it proved to be a box covered in leather with the end made to look like the spine of a book. It wasn't locked and opened easily, proving to contain various keys in little felt pockets. These didn't clink if you picked the whole thing up or opened it.

'Your father seems to have been absolutely paranoid about keeping things secret,' Hector commented. 'I've never seen such careful hiding places.'

He'd been studying Abigail as he spoke. 'You didn't know about these hidden keys, did you?'

'No. I learned when I was a child not to try to find out what my father was doing. As long as I lived by his rules, he was quite kind to me in his own way, but I always felt like a prisoner. I'm sorry he's dead, of course I am, but I'm hoping to lead a more interesting life from now on.'

She glanced at Rufus as she said that and he moved closer to give her another of his quick, one-armed hugs.

'*We* are all going to lead a fuller life, Abigail, I promise you,' he said. 'I've been limited too, by my mother's health and foolishness, and so has Nina.'

He made her feel safer and more optimistic, and he was so tall and strong that his mere presence made her feel better.

'The more we find out about your father, the more mysterious he seems, Miss Dawson,' Hector said quietly. 'Could you bear to stay and go through the drawers with me? You may recognise some of their contents.'

'I suppose so.'

But she didn't look happy about it.

She saw Rufus glance at the clock ticking quietly on the mantelpiece. 'Can you spare the time to stay with me as I do this or do you have something you need to attend to? I don't know your daily work routines yet but I don't want you to get into trouble with your employer.'

'I think we need to sort out this whole situation before I start work again, don't you? I'll always try to be here when you need me from now on. Edward – Mr Ollerton, that is – said yesterday that I should take as much time off work as necessary. He's very considerate and I already consider him as much a friend as employer.'

He grinned as he added, 'I was looking at the clock because I was feeling thirsty.'

'I could do with a cup of tea too. I feel parched with all the dust in here.' She turned to include the sergeant. 'Would you like a cup as well before we continue our search?'

'I'd love one but would you mind bringing mine to me here?' Hector asked. 'I'll continue looking through the drawers while you're making it.'

'I'll come and help you, Abigail,' Rufus said. 'I don't want to let you go on your own in case Mrs Blaney has been leaving the outer doors open as she cleans the house.'

The sergeant gave him a quick half-smile when he said that and nodded slightly as if approving.

As they walked back along the corridor together, she said in a low voice, 'It feels as though I'm living in a nightmare, Rufus. Will I always have to worry about someone attacking me, even when I'm only going to make a cup of tea in my own home?'

Her voice broke on the last words and he put his arms round her, stopping her moving on for a moment or two. 'The danger will end and we'll build a happier life together.'

She leaned against him for a few moments and he kept his arms round her. 'I'll make sure you're safe even if they don't catch Bibby,' he added.

'I hope they do catch him, not just for my own sake but because I'd not like to put your sister in danger.'

That brought a fond smile to his face. 'You and Nina seem to be getting on well.'

'She's easy to get on with.'

'Good. She clearly likes you. And while we're at it, let me repeat that I shan't change my mind about us getting married. I don't make promises on idle whims and I always keep my word. Actually, I think us being together will work out very well. I really like you, Abigail.'

'I really like you too, Rufus. I've never felt as comfortable with anyone else in my whole life.'

He planted a quick kiss on her cheek. 'Good. I'm glad to hear that. And you'll not only be good for me but good for Nina in so many ways. She's at the age where she needs a woman to look after her and teach her things about grow-ing up. And talking of Nina, let's see whether she's still sitting reading and offer her some refreshments as well.'

But Nina was already in the kitchen, chatting to Mrs Blaney, who was making some scones and demonstrating how to get them light and fluffy.

'I hope you don't mind me doing some baking without asking what you want, miss?'

'It's an excellent idea.'

'And also – do you think you could call me Margie from now on? I don't really like being called Mrs Blaney because it's my husband's name. He was a violent brute and it was a relief when he died. Only it was more respectable to be a widow when I was looking for work.'

Abigail smiled. 'Of course we can call you Margie. It's a pretty name.'

Rufus joined the conversation. 'And thank you for showing Nina how to cook. Our mother didn't do any baking, so my sister has never had the chance to learn.'

Nina beamed at him and so did Margie.

'She's good company, that lass is. It's nice to have young 'uns in a house.' She turned back to Abigail. 'There's another thing I need to mention, miss: we're running low on some pantry goods and there are more people to feed now. Do you want me to go to the shops for you?'

'I'd rather go myself,' Abigail said. 'But it'll have to be later, because the sergeant still needs me. Could you make a list, please? There are some scraps of paper in the top drawer and there should be a pencil there too.'

'Yes, I can do that, miss. Happy to.'

'Don't skimp. And if there's something you particularly like to eat, please buy it for yourself.'

Margie looked surprised. 'Thank you, miss. Where do you shop?'

'We've opened an account at Prebble's. I'll go there later and ask them to transfer it from my father to me and to allow you to buy goods on that account.'

'We'll go together later,' Rufus said firmly. 'Don't go anywhere on your own yet, Abigail, even if it's only a quick trip to a nearby shop. The situation is still unclear and we don't want you running into danger. Bibby may not have been the only threat to your safety and others might have wished your father ill and turn on you now. We're not risking anything.'

'Very well.'

He turned to Nina and Margie. 'Same for you two. Go nowhere alone till I tell you it's safe to do so.'

Margie's nod and glance towards his sister reassured him. Like Abigail, the maid seemed to be coming out of her careful shell.

14

As they took the cups of tea back to the far end of the house, it felt to Abigail as if she was going from a sunlit day into dusk. She shivered involuntarily as they went into her father's private room.

Rufus saw that but didn't comment as he handed a cup of tea to Hector then concentrated on his own. As he swallowed a mouthful, he stared at the desks. Their surfaces were now covered in papers and envelopes. 'You have worked quickly!'

'The top drawers had keys to the other drawers in them. But most of these are simply household accounts from the shopping, as well as the bills and receipts for the legitimate expenses of running his own shop. Did you know he owned the building it's in, Miss Dawson?'

'I never really thought about it.' She frowned. 'I did guess he owned the house where we used to live before this one, because there was never any talk about a landlord or paying rent. He sold it when we moved, presumably to help pay for our present home. But I knew better than to ask about the details.'

'I still have a few drawers to go through, but I also found this.'

He handed her a large envelope and she saw that it was labelled *Last Will and Testament of Charles Martin Dawson*. On the back it bore the name and address of a lawyer in town: Granville Osgood. She'd met the man briefly after her mother died but not since.

She didn't even feel comfortable holding the big envelope.

'Perhaps you'd open it and check that you're your father's heir? I don't need to know the details of what you've inherited but it'll be easier if I know who to deal with as I continue to investigate.'

She hesitated then took a deep breath and used her fore-finger to pry open the envelope. It contained just one sheet of paper, leaving everything her father owned to 'my daughter Abigail Mary Dawson'. There was no message to her, only that bare statement, his signature and those of two witnesses, then the rubber stamp and signature of the lawyer.

She showed it to the two men and the sergeant nodded. 'That will make everything easier for me.'

She swallowed hard as she took back the sheet of paper and her hand shook. She was relieved when Rufus said, 'Let me.' He folded the will and slipped it back inside the envelope then held it out to her.

'I don't know where to put it,' she confessed.

'We could lock it in one of the drawers,' Hector suggested. 'Then you could keep the key.'

'Or Rufus could keep it in case we need to show it to any-one. And he should keep the keys to the house as well. Men have so many more pockets and can easily carry something with them, while women have to either put keys on a chain round their neck or put them into a purse, which someone can snatch quite easily. Would you mind, Rufus?' she asked.

'Not at all.'

He took the key and the envelope from her and slipped them into his pockets.

'You'll need to go and see that lawyer chap about the will,' Hector said. 'Perhaps you should do that this afternoon as well as the grocery shopping?'

'Most important of all is that we go to the town hall today and book our wedding,' Rufus said. 'Would that be all right, Abigail?'

'It would.' She didn't say it but everything felt so unreal that she was glad to have Rufus to help her deal with these matters. She'd welcome some fresh air too, and longed to be surrounded by normal people going about their normal daily lives.

'Is there nowhere else in the house where your father may have kept things?' Hector asked. 'What about the attic? We haven't been up there yet.'

'I've never been up there.'

Both men stared at her in utter astonishment.

'Father locked the door the day we moved in and kept the key, so I've never even seen inside it, though I've heard him go up there, usually on the nights he worked in his room.'

'Could we go and see it now?' Hector asked.

'Yes, of course. Actually, I'd like to do that. I always wondered what was up there. As long as you can get the door open for us again, Sergeant.'

'Perhaps we should take a lamp with us in case it's dark up there, Miss Dawson? Attics don't usually have big windows.'

'There are some lamps in the scullery. We can take more than one.'

She led the way to the kitchen. It was lovely to hear Nina and Mrs Blaney – no, *Margie* – chatting away happily. They sounded so normal. When her father had been out Margie had talked to her more openly as well.

He had controlled everyone who came near him and made them afraid to open their mouths when he was around. That was no way for human beings to live. She would definitely try to make sure Nina had a happier life and would encourage Margie to offer suggestions and chat to her.

For some reason she felt quite certain that Rufus wouldn't try to control her in that way. Surely she wasn't making a mistake about him?

She glanced sideways and he smiled at her. He smiled at his sister in exactly the same way. No, she decided, he really was kind. You couldn't fake a smile like that. Or fake the love he clearly felt for his little sister.

Maybe one day he'd grow fond of her too and she'd be more than just a convenient wife. She did hope so.

She told herself to stop letting her thoughts wander and opened a cupboard in the scullery, gesturing towards the top two shelves.

Hector said, 'Aha! Let's take a couple of these outdoor lanterns in case it isn't light enough up there.'

Rufus studied the one he'd picked up. 'These are good modern lamps.'

'My father liked plenty of light wherever he was.'

Without being asked Margie brought them a box of matches and the two men checked that there was enough oil in the lamps, then each lit one.

'I think two will be enough,' Rufus said. 'You can see from the road that there are skylights in the attic and it won't be fully dark for a few hours yet.'

Hector led the way, striding up the stairs two at a time, holding the oil lamp up so that it cast light ahead of them.

Abigail and Rufus followed and when she took hold of his hand as they walked slowly up into the dimness of the attic stairwell, he gave her hand a couple of little squeezes. It felt good to be sharing a pool of light with him.

Who knew what they'd find up here? she wondered as they came to a halt.

Rufus stole a glance at Abigail as they walked up the stairs, wondering why that father of hers had kept her so ignorant about his business affairs. She was an intelligent woman, though still rather cowed, but she seemed to be getting over that little by little.

When she slipped her hand in his that pleased him. He was growing to like the feel of its soft warmth.

He might be gaining money from marrying her, but that wasn't the main reason for doing it. He wanted a more normal life for himself and Nina. And in return he was determined to give Abigail a life that was far more interesting and enjoyable than living with her father had been.

He hadn't taken to Dawson when he did those jobs for him earlier in the year and hadn't been able to work out why, because the man had treated him perfectly civilly, had complimented him on doing good work and paid him generously. There had been a coldness in him, though, noticeable even when Dawson spoke to his daughter.

On the few occasions she'd relaxed with him back then, Rufus had found Abigail very good company. And now, well, she was pleasant to chat to. And she'd said straight out that she wanted children, so if he took care how he treated her, his own needs might for once be fulfilled as well, both for the human warmth of a woman's touch and for the family he too longed for.

He'd watched other men play with their children and smile at their wives without even realising they were doing that, and he'd envied them. If only the sergeant could sort out this murder and Rufus could help Abigail sort out the chaos that it had caused, he rather thought the two of them would stand a good chance of making a happy life together.

They would have what seemed to him a lavish amount of money behind them, and that would give all three of them security, which he valued highly. He had scraped some savings together pound by painful pound, but the big house and shop must be worth ten times more than he'd ever have managed to save during his years of hard work. Perhaps more, even. Would she mind that? He didn't think so. What she wanted, and indeed what she needed, wasn't money but affection.

He brought his attention back to the present as he waited for the sergeant to finish examining the lock and turn to smile at them.

'This one ought to be easier to open.' Once again he pulled out his picks and fiddled about. It didn't take nearly as long to open but the room it opened into was rather dimly lit. 'It's a good thing we brought the lanterns.'

'I think you'd better go in first, Sergeant,' Rufus said quietly.

They followed him and the three of them stood just inside the door with the two men holding up the lanterns.

'Look! Even the skylights up here have blinds pulled across them!' Hector exclaimed. 'No wonder it's so dim.'

'Your father took care to cover every door and window, didn't he?' Rufus said thoughtfully. 'What was he hiding?'

'Yes, he did. I don't know why. I even had to draw all the curtains *before* it got dark, upstairs and downstairs.'

'I'll pull back the nearest blind,' Hector said. 'I think I can reach it if I stand on that box.'

He did that and the darkness lightened a little in that part of the large attic, showing a space divided into several separate areas, with mounds of lumpy objects covered in tarpaulins in each one.

Abigail pointed to one side. 'That area looks less dusty than the others as if it's been used more.'

They walked across and when Hector pulled back the tarpaulin he revealed a chest of drawers.

'Oh! That belonged to my mother. I wondered what had happened to it. Why did my father bring it up here?' She opened the top drawer and found several small packages.

'Open one,' Rufus said.

She did and found a piece of jewellery. It was silver and very pretty but she didn't recognise it. She opened several of the packages and they were all similar except for the last one, which was in the form of a butterfly and made of gold and coloured enamels.

'I think I recognise that one,' Hector said. 'It was stolen from a Mr Sidford-Hayes a few years ago. It belonged to his wife and she'd apparently been very fond of it. He made a huge fuss about the police not catching the thieves who'd broken into their house in the country while they were away in London.'

He looked at Abigail, who was now looking at the piece in horror.

He hesitated then said, 'I'm afraid it looks as if your father was handling stolen property, Miss Dawson. I'll need to report the matter to my area inspector. Could you please not touch anything up here till Inspector Helton gives me instructions?'

She was clutching Rufus's arm with both hands. 'I don't want to touch it if it's stolen property. I didn't know anything about it, I promise you.'

Rufus gave her hand a quick squeeze. 'I believe you.'

'So do I.' The sergeant smiled. 'You have a very open face unless you're trying to guard your expression. Now, let me just check the other drawers.'

There were a couple of necklaces in the second drawer and some small dishes and bowls, again made of silver, in the third drawer.

'Why were these things left here?' the sergeant wondered aloud.

She could only shake her head. She had no idea.

'Will you give me your word not to come up here again until this whole business is sorted out?' he asked.

She nodded. 'Of course.'

'I'll need to send a telegram to my inspector before I do anything else.'

'Will it be all right if we go out to do our shopping and book our wedding in the meantime?' Rufus asked. 'I'm sure I speak for Abigail when I say we neither of us want anything to do with stolen property.'

'I agree,' she said fervently.

'Has your father always had secret storage places, Miss Dawson?' Hector asked, his expression grim now.

'I don't know what he had at the shop, but he didn't have anywhere to store things at home till we moved into this big house. Maybe that was partly why we moved here.'

She took a deep breath and went on, 'He was so gleeful about buying this house. A couple of days after we moved in, some men delivered the desks and office equipment for him to use in his room when he wanted to work at home and he told me to wait in the kitchen, so that I'd not be in their way. They probably took my mother's desk upstairs when I was in there.'

She sounded so agitated, the sergeant said quietly, 'I believe you, Miss Dawson.'

'He said furniture had been left up here by the previous owners.' After a pause for thought, she added, 'I didn't see him move any other large items up to the attics after our first week here, so if those bigger lumps are furniture, they must have been here when he bought the house.'

'He could have taken smaller objects in and out of the house without you seeing them, though,' the sergeant said. 'This doesn't look like a large-scale operation. If he sold smaller items regularly it'd probably have been enough for him to add a nice amount of money to his bank account without drawing attention to himself.'

It made Abigail feel dreadful to think of her father being a thief.

The sergeant was still thinking aloud, 'I wonder whether these pieces of jewellery were what Bibby was really after? He must have seen some of the items that came into the shop, but he might not have known when they went out again in your father's pockets or briefcase. He certainly flung the contents of the safe around carelessly during his rapid search.'

'Do you think he'll come back to Ollerthwaite?'

Hector stared into the distance for a moment or two then shook his head. 'Probably not. I should think he'll have stolen enough to start a new life somewhere, even without finding the more valuable pieces like these.'

Abigail shook her head sadly. It was all so embarrassing. Thank goodness she was no longer facing it alone.

Rufus's arm went round her shoulders as if sensing how distressed she was feeling. She felt quite sure he wouldn't let her down.

15

Edward Ollerton and his architect were watching the men working on the foundations of his new home and enjoying a cool but sunny day.

'I'm missing Rufus already,' Lewis Brody said. 'That man has a very efficient way of tackling jobs. He often thinks of new ways to do them and gets those working on them to do it differently without upsetting them.'

'I've noticed that too. I wonder how long it will take him to bury his mother and organise new living arrangements for himself and his sister.'

'It's a pity he hasn't got a wife to look after Nina and do the household chores.'

Edward smiled. 'Wives are not just servants, you know. They're there to love and be loved by, which is far more important to me.'

Lewis envied him. He'd never met a woman who inspired him with such love and many of the marriages he'd seen appeared to be more for convenience than for affection. On the other hand, since coming to Ollindale he'd seen a few marriages which were clearly for love. Edward's was a prime example of this. He face lit up at the mere sight of Lillian. It must be wonderful to feel like that about someone.

Before long one of the men returned from driving the cart into town and hurried across to his employer before he started unloading it. 'I saw Rufus in town and he asked me to give you his apologies but it'll be a few days before he can come back to work. He's helping Miss Dawson out, you see. It makes a lot of trouble when a man is murdered.'

Edward thanked him, but when they were alone again he exchanged puzzled glances with Lewis. 'Why on earth has Rufus got involved in the murder investigations?'

'Who can tell? Perhaps he knows the Dawson family. In the meantime, I'd like to put a couple of men on the job of making the entrance to the old cellars secure so that we can connect the two spaces below ground to the building above and then temporarily block off the parts we shan't be using.'

'I've been wondering how that would be done.'

His friend grinned. 'It's not a job I've heard of before and I'd have welcomed Rufus's input, given his mining experience. I'm having to work out how to do it as I go, so I'm proceeding slowly and carefully. Well, we don't want any people getting trapped down there if a ceiling caves in, do we?'

'Definitely not. I'm really pleased with our progress generally, though,' Edward said. 'The men from the village are very willing workers.'

'They've been short of work for a good while in the valley. Your new home is giving some of them a chance to earn a better living than they've had for a long time.'

'I wonder what they'll do for jobs once the house is finished?'

'It'll be a year or two before that happens, I'm afraid,' Lewis said. 'It's going to be a big house and when it comes to the interior, we'll have to bring a lot of building materials in from Preston or Lancaster, plus some skilled workers to do jobs like windows and the fancier parts of plastering. I'll go and check out the nearest suppliers of what'll be needed for that later on. We'd have nowhere to store them if we did bring them here now.'

'If the skilled workers come from outside the valley, we'll need to find them accommodation and there's a shortage of that here because they don't get a lot of visitors.'

'That's another thing to think about.'

'Perhaps I'd better look round for somewhere to house them. We'd like the big house to be finished before the Queen's Jubilee. Lillian has already started conferring with Walter about what we could do to make life better for other people in the valley.'

'Talk of the devil. Look who's just turned up,' Lewis said with a smile as Walter rode across to join them on his new tricycle.

Edward chuckled as they watched. 'Good thing we made a level path from the agent's house to the building site, eh? You must be setting a fashion with your tricycle, Lewis. Did you know Walter was buying one?'

'Yes. But not that it had arrived already. He asked me where I got mine.' He nudged his companion and grinned. 'If I've ever seen an old man looking like an excited schoolboy, it's now.'

'I just hope I'm as active and busy when I'm his age.'

Lewis's smile faded a little. 'I hope I take after my mother's side of the family and actually get to be that old. My father's family aren't noted for living to a ripe old age.' He moved forward to greet Walter. 'So your new toy has arrived, has it?'

He got off it. 'Yes. The chap you recommended was very efficient and he had one ready to go. I must say this is a lot easier to ride than a two-wheeled bicycle, plus having space for far bigger baskets, front and back.' He beamed down at his tricycle and patted it as if it were a live creature. 'Oh! I nearly forgot. There's a letter for you, Edward.' He pulled it out of his jacket pocket. 'I was just setting off to come here when the postman delivered my mail. When he said he had a letter for you, I offered to bring it and save him cycling up the hill.'

He turned to study the busy workers. 'They're making excellent progress, aren't they? Even without Rufus.'

Edward was studying the envelope. 'Excuse me a moment, but this looks like Rufus's handwriting so I'll just see what he wants. I wonder why he's writing and not coming to see me?'

Edward opened the letter and read it quickly, then stared across at his companions with surprise written all over his face even before he spoke. 'Good heavens! Rufus is getting married.'

All three of them stared, then Walter asked, 'Who to? I didn't know he was even courting.'

'I certainly haven't seen any signs of it. Anyway, he's marrying Abigail Dawson, the murdered man's daughter. He says they can help one another and he really likes her. He apologises but he won't be able to work here for a week or more, as they need to sort out her father's affairs. He'll understand if I want to hire someone else – which I definitely don't.'

'There's an investigation going on into Dawson's affairs,' Walter said. 'I think Rufus worked for Dawson earlier this year, doing some repairs on that house just after they moved in. He must have met Miss Dawson then.'

Edward looked at the letter again. 'He doesn't go into any details.'

'Perhaps he thought it was hopeless to ask to court her. The father wouldn't have let her marry him or anyone else,' Walter said. 'Everyone knew that Dawson kept her almost a prisoner. Her job was to look after him and from what I heard tell, only that. I doubt she'd have dared defy him. Even the people who worked in his shop were terrified of him. Well, well! Fancy our Rufus marrying her.'

'She's a bit above him socially, isn't she?' Edward commented.

'Yes. But he's a fine figure of a man. I've seen women stare at him in the street as he walks by.'

'And he's a clever chap, too,' Edward added. 'Very clever indeed.'

The three men stood there thoughtfully for a few moments taking this in. Then Walter said, 'On another subject, there's something I think you ought to know about, Edward lad. You remember Bryn, the chap who lives out at the old mill?'

'Yes. I've met him at your house.'

'Well, he's seen a man sneaking around furtively on the moors, and more than once. He didn't recognise him but he's wondering what anyone is doing out there. It's not farming land and there aren't any paths across that area.'

'How does that concern me?'

'It wouldn't except another fellow I know has also seen someone lurking a few times on the rocky patch at the upper end of your property, Edward. He thought it might be Terry Catlow, though he wasn't certain because the man was distinctly scrawny and Catlow used to be a burly fellow. Catlow attacked you a while ago and perhaps he's about to do so again. You'll need to take extra care.'

Edward stilled. 'Oh, hell! I've had a feeling of being watched lately, but I hoped I was imagining things. Could Catlow still be hanging around, do you think? One or two people warned me when I first came to live here that he'd hated my father and had boasted that he was going to wipe out the Ollerton family. I thought he'd got over that. He must be mad. I've never done anything to hurt him.'

'You're an Ollerton and I doubt he'll let the matter drop. It's who you are, not what you've done. We should tell our good sergeant about this new development and you'd better hire someone to keep watch on your house at night. Yes, and to keep watch on the new building as well.'

'Surely he's given up by now.'

'I doubt it. He's a stubborn creature when he gets an idea fixed in his mind. There's not just you to worry about now. There's Lillian too. She had enough trouble in her life with her first husband.'

'Hiring a watchman is a bit extreme, don't you think, Walter?'

'Not with that nasty Catlow chap on the prowl. The good people from that family usually move out of the valley to get away from their nasty relatives and unfortunately for us, the bad ones mainly stay. Terry is one of the worst Catlows there's been in my lifetime, that's for sure. And he's one of the most cunning too. He's never been caught stealing anything of value, so athough everyone knows he's a villain, there's not much they can do about it because the poorer people he preys on are too afraid of him to report him to the law.'

He paused to shake his head sadly. 'Well, we only had Cliff Nolan as our police officer before, didn't we? He was pretty useless when he was younger and by the time he retired he couldn't have flattened a flea – all he wanted was a peaceful life.'

Edward stared at him in dismay. 'Catlow is that bad?'

'Unfortunately, yes. If you'd lived here longer you'd have seen how he's got worse over the past few years. Even his wife won't have anything to do with him nowadays, though she won't tell anyone why. His eldest son was sent away to work for his uncle, who was one of the better Catlows, and by all accounts young Jezzy has mended his ways. He seems to have learned enough to know he'll gain more in life by honest methods like his uncle than by committing minor crimes like his father.'

Walter waited a minute or two, then said again, 'Hire a watchman to keep an eye on your current home and on your new building for the time being, lad. You can easily afford it and someone will be glad of the money.'

Edward sighed. 'I suppose you're right. Can you recommend anyone?'

'I can recommend half a dozen decent chaps who'd jump at the chance to earn some extra money. I'll ask around to find out who's most in need and send him to see you.'

'Thank you, Walter.'

Edward wouldn't have bothered if it just been himself, but he had a wife to care for now and a building he was longing to see finished.

The man they were talking about was watching Edward and the rest of the group from one of the shallow crevices in the rocks that jutted out here and there. Further up the hill there were caves and he'd now made his home in them, but these rocks were good places from which to spy on people without being noticed.

He'd spent the last few weeks watching Edward Ollerton and hadn't been able to catch the sod on his own. If he wasn't billing and cooing with that new wife of his, he was walking around gesticulating and pointing with that architect chap, or talking to the men working on his new house.

Catlow still intended to kill Ollerton, but he wasn't going to do it in a way that would send him to dangle from the gallows for the crime.

Casting a final dirty look in Edward's direction, the watcher made his way slowly and stiffly back up to the higher part of the moors. He'd tried living in the shepherd's shelter, which was closer to town, but it didn't have a door and there were gaps in the stones it was built from which he'd tried in vain to fill with earth. Worst of all, there was nowhere to hide the food and other things he had to steal because his damned wife would no longer feed him. So he had to make a longer journey each night to get back to what he thought of now as his cave.

He'd sell his soul for a pint of beer. He hadn't had a drink for weeks and water didn't ease that particular longing. He'd have welcomed regular cups of nice hot tea, too, but didn't often dare light a fire in case the smoke gave away his hiding place.

Damn his wife! She should be supporting him, at the very least bringing supplies out to the cave and letting him sneak back home for a day or two every now and then for a rest. Instead, she'd sent a message by one of his younger sons – he thought it was Ned or was it Nick? – to say she'd hit him over the head and knock him out, then hand him over to the new policeman if he came anywhere near her or the house. And she never threatened what she wasn't prepared to carry out.

She'd brought his oldest son back home again from staying with his uncle in Manchester, and Jezzy was helping her to make changes to the house. The lad hadn't got into trouble once since his return. What had his uncle changed him into? A right old softie, that's what.

She was running the old Catlow family home, which didn't really belong to her, as a lodging house these days and only taking in respectable people. Folk said she was making good money from it because Ollerthwaite was short of places for visitors to hire a bed for the night. She wasn't even sharing the money from that with him.

It was a good thing he had one or two friends still willing to help him. But they weren't in favour of attacking Ollerton, either, and last time he'd spoken to one of them the sod had warned him not to carry out his threats because of the new jobs Ollerton was bringing to the valley.

Terry had pretended to change his mind because of that but he hadn't really. He'd told his friend he was going to help out with a business in Blackpool and would be moving there permanently before winter really set in. Which was a lie. He wasn't going anywhere until he'd wiped out the Ollertons.

Whatever it took!

He spat on the ground in front of him to seal that promise, as he always did. It brought you luck, spitting on a promise did, or so his grandma had always told him.

16

Still talking, the sergeant walked towards the kitchen because they were all using what they called the back door to come and go. 'I think that's all we can do for today, Miss Dawson, Mr Shorrocks. I know you two have various other jobs to do in town, so unless anything important happens I probably won't see you till tomorrow.'

He stopped in the doorway to address his final words to Rufus. 'Keep a careful watch on Miss Dawson and don't let anyone into the house who has no business here. I won't send messages. I'll come and see you myself if I find anything else that needs your attention. The police station is only a short walk away from here.'

The two men shook hands and Abigail felt annoyed that men never included women in these gestures, just left them standing nearby. She'd love to protest about that, had read about some modern-minded women doing that. Ah, why worry about details? There were lots of things she'd have loved to do in the past few years and not dared because of her father. There was too much else to do now to worry about principles, some of it of crucial importance, like booking a wedding and finding something prettier than her father's choice of dowdy clothes to wear at it.

She still couldn't quite believe she was about to get married. She'd been wishing she had a husband and family for so long, had even imagined what names she'd call her children. And now it was happening.

Once they'd seen the sergeant out, she gave Margie instructions while Rufus went to fetch one of his many acquaintances to keep watch over the maid and Nina while he took Abigail out to book their wedding.

Nina was sitting in the kitchen eating one of the scones she'd helped Margie make. She listened to Abigail and Margie discussing which foods were running low, or used up, while she licked every last crumb off her fingers. It was lovely to always have food available if you were hungry, which she mostly was, and Abigail had told her to ask for food any time she wanted more. Her brother's fiancée must be very rich to say things like that.

'Couldn't I come with you?' she whispered to Rufus when he came back with another man she recognised as one of his friends.

'Sorry, love. Not this time. Abigail and I have too much to do. Steve will stay here with you, just to keep an eye on the place. I don't need to tell you not to let anyone else into the house, do I? Well, except for the sergeant. He's welcome any time.'

'No, I won't let any strangers in.' She shivered at the mere thought of that.

Abigail could see that the girl was still anxious and had a sudden idea for distracting her. 'Could you and Margie choose a bedroom for you to use after your brother and I get married, do you think, Nina? You can move the furniture around to suit you and generally make it ready to move into.'

Nina brightened immediately. 'Ooh, it'll be fun doing that.'

'Just take furniture from any of the unoccupied bedrooms if you need more drawers or want to change anything else.' She looked across at Margie, who gave her a little nod as if to say that she'd keep an eye on the child. It was nice to be able to communicate openly with the maid. Her father had always forbidden idle chatter with anyone.

Rufus gave his sister another quick hug and said quietly, 'It won't be like this for ever, Nina love, then you can go back to school.'

'I wish I could go back there now. I was getting ready to take the exam for the grammar school but how can I win a scholarship if I miss a lot of the work?'

Abigail saw Rufus hesitating and stepped in without hesitation. 'You'll be able to go to the grammar school anyway, Nina, because we can easily afford to pay the fees for you. You won't need to win a scholarship for that. You'll just have to prove that you're a good scholar and are able to keep up with your school work.'

'I'm sure your teacher will vouch for that,' Rufus put in.

Nina brightened at once. 'Really?'

'Really and truly.'

She twirled round several times.

Abigail watched her rather enviously. She could never remember doing anything like that in her whole life. She'd always had to be quiet and careful.

As they set off, Rufus said, 'Thank you for that offer. She's a really good scholar and deserves a chance to stay on at school.'

'You only have to chat to her to realise how intelligent she is. I wanted to go to grammar school, but my father wouldn't hear of it. He didn't even let me sit the exam. I had to leave school as soon as it was allowed and work for him.'

'He stopped you doing a lot of things, didn't he? I hope I'll be able to help you enjoy a more active and interesting life from now on.'

'I'm sure you will, Rufus.'

They smiled at one another. 'Now, we have a few things we need to take care of. Where would you like to go first?'

She hesitated. 'To book our wedding? Or perhaps we should see the lawyer first? Which do you think?'

'Let's get the lawyer's visit over and done with. I've seen Granville Osgood's nameplate on the wall outside a house in town but I've never met him.' He hadn't heard any good about the fellow though.

'I only met him once, after my mother died. She left me a few pieces of silverware from her side of the family, but my father said to deposit them with Mr Osgood, who'd keep them in his safe for us. There was a lovely gold bracelet, too. She said it came from an aunt but she never wore it, and I never went anywhere it would be suitable, so I left that with him too.'

'All right. Lawyer first it is. We can go to the town hall after that and book our wedding.'

'I'll enjoy that much more than Mr Osgood. He has a mean face with squinchy little eyes.'

'I love that word of yours.'

'What word?'

'Squinchy. I hadn't heard it used till I met you. You used it when I first worked at your house.'

'It's a nice word.'

'I agree. I use it too now and Nina loves it as well. Now, we're here so we'd better be more serious for a while.'

The lawyer's rooms seemed quite small and were only sparsely furnished. He obviously wasn't highly successful, Rufus thought. A young chap was sitting at a desk in the reception area, leaning back and staring at the ceiling but he jerked his chair back down on all four legs when they entered.

He looked at Rufus, totally ignoring the woman, as some people did when business was concerned, so Rufus said, 'My fiancée needs to see Mr Osgood about her inheritance.'

'And her name is?'

'Why don't you ask her yourself? She's not deaf and she's standing right in front of you.'

The young man blinked in shock and looked at Abigail so warily she nearly laughed. She waited for him to ask again, wasn't going to make this easy for him.

'Um – could I have your name, please, miss?'

'Miss Abigail Dawson.'

His mouth dropped open and he gaped at her, so must have heard about her father. Once again, she was glad of the years of practice at keeping her face expressionless.

'I'll see if Mr Osgood is free.'

He came back almost immediately. 'Mr Osgood will see you now, miss, but he says he'd prefer to see you on your own.'

'And I'd prefer my fiancé to accompany me.'

He hesitated.

'In fact, I insist on it.'

'Oh. Well, this way, then, miss.'

Mr Osgood was sitting at a desk and stood up as she went in, glancing sharply at Rufus then at Abigail. 'My late client specified that you were to see me on your own when you inherited. He didn't want anyone else poking their nose into his affairs.'

She drew herself up and said slowly and firmly, 'I think it's more appropriate for my fiancé to be with me.'

'Oh. You're engaged, are you? Hmm. I suppose it's all right then.' He indicated two chairs. 'Please take a seat.'

Rufus waited for her to sit then pulled the other chair closer to hers before sitting down.

'You have your father's will with you, I presume, Miss Dawson? Just to prove that this is all happening as he planned.'

'Yes.' She took the envelope out of her shopping bag and showed it to him.

'Good. There are three more pages to add to the will. And your father said to tell you not to mention these matters to the po— to anyone,' he amended hastily with a quick glance at Rufus.

Had he been going to say 'police'? she wondered but nodded as if agreeing, which she wasn't at all sure she did. She was growing increasingly unhappy with what she was finding out about her father. There seemed to be something bad revealed at every step.

'These papers list two bank accounts which will be transferred to you now that your father is dead, Miss Dawson. And there is a list of the properties he owned. We had the honour of collecting the rents for him and hope to continue helping you with them.' He pushed another large envelope across the desk to her. It was firmly sealed and signed by her father on the back. She'd recognise his signature anywhere.

The lawyer relaxed a little. 'Mr Dawson arranged for all this to happen, though I don't think he expected to die quite so soon. Shame, isn't it? Such a clever chap, your father. Have the police caught the murderer yet?'

'No.'

She took the sealed envelope from him and was about to open it when he put his hand down on it to stop her. He said hastily, 'He wanted you to read these when you were on your own. I was just to give them to you.'

The lawyer took a small parcel out of his desk and pushed that across to her as well. 'This provides identification to the bank that you're his heir. You're to take it with you on your first visit there after you've read the papers.'

The parcel wasn't sealed so she peeped inside and saw an old-fashioned document seal, one she'd never seen before even though it had her father's initials on the bottom. People didn't use seals like this on their envelopes these days. She waited for the lawyer to speak but he turned and took a small briefcase from the top of a bookcase next to his desk. 'Your father, er, thought you should take them away in this so that people won't know what you're carrying.'

Had her father gone mad? He'd always wanted to keep what he was doing secret, but this was ridiculous. What could people tell from an envelope or the outside of a parcel, for heaven's sake?

'That's all I was asked to do, Miss Dawson. I have no idea of how much money is currently in the bank accounts. I'll just repeat that if you're wise you won't mention this to *anyone*. And the same applies to you, sir. You should keep all this to yourself as well.'

He stood up and walked round to his office door, holding it open for them to leave. 'I'll say goodbye to you now, Miss Dawson, but hope to see you soon to arrange about the rents.' He nodded farewell then stepped back and closed the door behind them.

She looked sideways at Rufus, not sure whether to ask what he thought.

He put one finger to his lips then led the way past the young man in the outer office, not saying anything until they were outside the building. Were those papers an indication of more money for her in the bank? He felt uncomfortable about the thought of that because he had so little money compared to her. They needed to discuss it properly, but privately.

'Let's leave the visit to the bank about those accounts till we've had time to read the papers he's given us and think about them. There's clearly something unusual about all this.'

'I agree.'

'Anyway, it's more important to arrange our wedding and buy some food.'

But she had to say it, because she couldn't help worrying that this might be something illegal that made him back away from marrying her. 'I don't feel comfortable about the money,

Rufus, given what else we've found out about my father's activities. What if it's from him dealing in stolen goods? Should we tell the sergeant about it before we do anything else with it, do you think?'

'We should certainly consider whether this might be the proceeds of crime and act accordingly.'

'I don't like the thought of being involved in that sort of thing.'

He was pleased to hear her say that. It showed that whatever her father had done, her morals were good. He offered her his arm and they started walking along the street. 'At least booking our wedding will be a pleasant task.'

'You still think so? I wouldn't blame you for breaking off our engagement, given what we've just found out.'

He smiled at her. 'Do I really need to keep repeating myself? I shall do so if I have to, Abigail, but I'd rather this was the last time you worry about that. I shan't change my mind about us getting married. It makes absolute sense for both of us and for Nina because we neither of us have family to help us out of our difficult situations. I shall look after you in any way I can and try to make you happy. Trust me on that. And I hope you'll help me do the same with my sister, who has had a difficult life so far.'

She felt tears well in her eyes and blinked rapidly. 'Thank you. I shan't query it again, Rufus. And it'll be my pleasure to help you care for Nina. She's a very lovable child.'

'Good. That's settled once and for all, then.'

She didn't know why but he was right. This time it had definitely sunk in that he truly intended to marry her, whatever unpleasant legacy her father had left behind. She was also starting to realise how very much she wanted him to become her husband. Far more than she'd expected to.

On the way to the town hall, he stopped at the bank.

'I thought we weren't going there till we'd read those papers the lawyer gave us?' she said.

He flushed slightly. 'I've realised that I shall need to draw out some money from my own savings to pay for the wedding and, well, anything else that crops up.'

'I have more than enough money for that in my purse now.'

'It'll be my task and my pleasure to pay for our wedding, though I don't know how my money will last for our other expenses. But our wedding is, well, special. If I need to borrow money from you for other purposes, I'll repay you eventually.'

'If we're married, there won't be any need for you to repay anything.'

'I'm *not* marrying you for your money.'

'I never for a single moment thought you were.'

She could see him relax a little at that and he gave a tiny nod. 'I believe you. Now, perhaps you'll sit on one of the customer seats and wait until I've drawn out some of my money?'

She sat down, watching him and wondering whether he'd take money from her for their other expenses. She'd just have to make sure he did, because her house would cost far more to run than his former home had, she was sure, and there were Margie's wages to pay as well. She'd still need the maid's help in such a big house and knew Margie was already enjoying living in more comfort.

After they left the bank they walked the short distance to the small town hall and booked their wedding for the earliest possible date the law allowed, which was just over a week from then.

'That'll be three pounds for the special licence, sir.'

Rufus pulled a small wallet out and counted out the money. Abigail hated to see him paying this when she had so much more money, but didn't say anything.

'And what time of day do you want to book the wedding for, sir?'

They smiled at one another and she took it upon herself to confess to the clerk that they hadn't even considered that.

'Well, by law it has to take place between nine and three.'

'Really? I didn't know that. What time is best, do you think?' she asked.

On the clerk's advice they settled on midday, which he said a lot of people found a very convenient time to get married as they could go and eat a wedding celebration meal straight afterwards.

She hadn't even thought about doing that, had no one she cared about to invite to a celebration anyway. Except the man she was about to marry and his sister! She realised the clerk was speaking again, so tried to concentrate on what he was saying.

'I should perhaps also remind you that you'll need two witnesses to the wedding, sir, miss.'

'Oh. Right.'

'Or two of our clerks can do that for you if needed. Only, most people like to bring friends with them.'

'We'll be doing that,' Rufus said. 'But thanks for reminding us.'

As they left the town hall to go to the grocery shop, she looked at him and felt herself flushing as she blurted out, 'I don't have anyone close enough to ask to be a witness, Rufus.'

'Let's get our shopping done and discuss who to ask at home. I can easily find a couple of people if you like.'

'I'd be grateful. It would look dreadful to have two town hall employees doing it. Word of it would be bound to get around.'

He offered her his arm and she took it as they walked along, comforted by holding it.

They went into Prebble's, the large grocer's shop on one corner of Railway Road, which her father had said was the best one. Here Abigail took the initiative, asking to speak to the owner.

She explained that now her father was dead, she and her husband-to-be would like to transfer the account to their name, so she wished to pay off and close the old account.

The owner said quietly, 'I'm sorry about your father and I'm happy to see that you'll have help in making changes to your life, Miss Dawson. It won't take me long to make out your bill for the old account. There's only one week or so owing because your father was always very prompt in paying at the end of the month.'

'I can place our new order while we're waiting to pay.'

'Thank you. I wish all my clients were as organised and helpful. In the meantime, my wife will attend to your needs.'

He beckoned a middle-aged woman across and she took his place on the other side of the counter.

'I have a list of the items we need at once and a much longer list of what we shall need delivering. Can I leave that with you?' Abigail asked.

'Of course, Miss Dawson. But we can deliver all the things you need within the hour, so do you want to add the other things to that list rather than carry them home?'

Abigail glanced at Rufus, who nodded, so she said, 'Yes. Please deliver them all at once.'

The bill from her father's account was more than she'd expected because she knew exactly what had been delivered to the house in the last order.

When she asked about this, Mr Prebble explained, 'Your father always had a few things delivered to his shop as well as those going to his home. It was mostly tea and biscuits.'

She still checked every item on the bill before paying it, but they were the sorts of cakes and biscuits her father had liked best. She wasn't surprised at seeing the extra items. Her father had always eaten a lot of sweet things and it was no wonder he'd become so stout as he grew older.

She noticed the labels on the row of big square tins with glass tops in which biscuits were stored until weighed out for customers and that made her feel sad. The ones stored in the end tin had been his favourites, but she didn't think she'd ever order that sort again.

17

When they were outside she said without thinking, 'I wish I didn't have to go back to that house at all. It hasn't got any good memories for me. I didn't help to choose it, didn't even know he'd bought it or what it was like until the day before we moved in.'

'The more I hear about your father, the more surprised I am at his behaviour towards you. Perhaps we can change how you feel about the house and make some happier memories there from now on and—' He broke off as he saw a gentleman coming towards them.

'Rufus! My dear fellow, how are you?' I'm sorry to hear about your mother.'

'Her death wasn't a surprise and I'm well, thank you.' He turned to Abigail and gestured to the man. 'I don't think you've met Mr Ollerton, have you? Edward, this is Miss Dawson, who has done me the honour of agreeing to marry me. We've just been booking our wedding.'

On a sudden thought, he added, 'We were discussing who to invite to act as witnesses since neither of us have any close family to turn to.' He wondered if Edward would volunteer to do this but didn't intend to ask him outright in front of Abigail in case he didn't want to be involved with her family. But his instincts told him that the man he now considered a friend would probably volunteer to act in that capacity and he was immediately proved correct.

Edward looked from one to the other with a smile. 'I'm pleased to meet you, Miss Dawson, and delighted to hear your good news. You're marrying a fine chap and I'm sure you'll be very happy together.' He clapped Rufus on the shoulder and added, 'If you haven't had time to sort out your witnesses, I'd be happy to offer my services.'

Rufus smiled gratefully at him. 'I'd be delighted to have you as one of the two witnesses, Edward.'

'I think Lewis would love to perform the same service, unless Miss Dawson has a friend or relative who can do that for her?'

Rufus looked at Abigail. 'I think we can be utterly frank with Edward, who has been a good friend to me. Would that be all right with you?'

She nodded and took the initiative to tell Edward about herself in the most tactful way she could manage. 'Because my father and I led a very quiet private life for the past few years at his insistence, Mr Ollerton, I have no friends, close or otherwise, and no relatives that I know of, either.'

'Then it's settled,' Edward said at once.

'Why don't you come round for a cup of tea, Edward, and we can make the arrangements? Then you can check with Lewis and let me know if I need to find someone else.'

Mr Ollerton really did seem happy to do this task for them, Abigail thought in wonderment. She was more used to people avoiding speaking to her because of her father.

'What a good friend he is to you!' she whispered.

Rufus gave her a solemn look. 'You'll be able to make a few friends of your own from now on, I'm sure, because I shan't stand in your way.'

Would she really meet people who *wanted* to become her friends? She found that hard to believe because she felt as if her father was still casting a shadow over her life.

When they got back, they had cups of tea and could offer their guest one of Margie's currant buns, then Rufus arranged to meet Edward and Lewis at the town hall half an hour before the wedding the following week.

Rufus showed their visitor out and she heard them speaking quietly for a moment or two before Mr Ollerton strode away from the house.

Her fiancé came back and said gently, 'I was assuring him that I'm happy to be marrying you.'

'You don't have to report your every conversation to me.'

'I prefer to when I'm talking *about* you. Now, we really do need to look at your father's bequests.'

'I suppose so.'

He turned to Nina. 'I'm sorry, love, but there's something else we have to do before we can chat to you. It's rather important that we do it before the banks close, too.'

She looked disappointed but nodded. 'Can I stay in the kitchen with Margie? She doesn't mind me talking to her.'

Abigail looked across the kitchen at Margie, who nodded vigorously, so she took it upon herself to answer. 'Of course you can.'

'She's showing me how to cook and do other little jobs. I really like that. It's so nice and clean here.'

He turned to Abigail. 'It might be best if we go into your father's room to do this. There's plenty of desk space and we may need to sort out the papers into piles.'

'Good idea.'

When they went into the room, she stopped and looked at the big chair in front of her father's main desk. The other chair was two yards away. 'Please bring yours closer then we can read the papers together.'

He pulled a chair up to sit beside her and patted her hand. 'They're only papers. They won't bite, you know. Here, let me get them out of the envelopes for you.'

There were four sheets of paper, all written out by hand in her father's tiny black script. She picked up the top one, took a deep breath and spread it between them on the desk.

Dear Abigail,

These are lists to explain what you're inheriting. The list of addresses is for properties I own in Ollerthwaite, which pay a nice amount in rents. They're currently collected by Mr Osgood, who takes 10%. He does a good job and you'd be wise to leave them in his charge.

The bank account labelled 'Your mother's legacy' is just that. I haven't touched the money she left you and it has been accruing interest for years.

The final bank account contains what I've earned in various other ways.

I've enjoyed building up a fortune and I know you're careful with money and won't waste it. I'd suggest you use it to move away from this valley and live somewhere more salubrious once I've passed away, a seaside town perhaps.

Charles Dawson

'There are no words of affection, no wishes for the future, just lists,' she said in a scratchy voice. 'And where do you think the money in the final bank account comes from?'

He told her the truth, unpalatable as it was. 'At least in part from his illegal activities.'

She flicked one finger at that paper. 'I don't want it, then.'

'We shall need to go to the bank, whether you use his money or not. Do you want to go today or tomorrow morning?'

She looked at the clock on the mantelpiece. 'Today. Let's get it over with.'

'I agree. Have you got that seal to introduce yourself to the manager with? Though why your father arranged something as meaningless as that, I can't understand.'

'He liked to conceal his finances under layers of paperwork and was fanatical about not letting other people know too much.'

'Hmm. Well, we can do things our way from now on: openly and honestly. But first we need to put in your claim.'

Nina's lips wobbled when he told her they'd have to go out again and leave her.

Abigail felt sorry for the child. 'I'm afraid there are always a lot of things to see to when someone dies.' She remembered her own mother dying and the fuss made by her father to get everything sorted out 'properly'.

'I haven't got anything like that from my mother dying. Just the funeral to go to in two days' time,' Rufus said.

'Oh, heavens, Nina and I will need some black clothes, then.'

'Not for our mother, and nothing is planned yet for your father.'

'Are you sure?'

'Yes. I'm afraid she won't be greatly missed. It's sad to say that, isn't it?'

'Yes. But it might be better to go into mourning anyway or people will talk. I'll see what dark clothes I can find. I still have some of my mother's old clothes stored away and they might be closer to Nina's size because my mother was quite a small person.'

'In the meantime we'd better hurry.'

When they got to the bank, they gave the seal to the clerk and he took it to the bank manager, who came out in person to escort them into his office.

She exchanged puzzled glances with Rufus, wondering why Mr Baxter was fussing over them.

When they sat down, she explained that Rufus was her fiancé and the manager nodded. 'Yes. Word has already got round about that. Congratulations.' He studied Rufus and she didn't think he approved of him, in spite of the half-smile firmly pinned to his face.

She produced the three papers. 'Could you kindly tell us what's in each account? My father left these but he'd never discussed any financial details with me so I haven't any idea of the amounts.'

'The easiest one to start with is your mother's legacy. Compounding interest has added to it considerably.'

The amount surprised her and when she shot a startled glance at Rufus she could see that it had upset him too. She could guess why. By his standards she was rich and people would no doubt be nasty about why he was marrying her so hastily. But she knew he hadn't come after her money, which was what really mattered. He'd reached out to another human being for help with Nina, as she had reached out to him for help with her father's affairs.

'And the account for the houses my father owned?' she prompted when the bank manager didn't continue straight away.

That too contained what seemed to her to be a large amount of money.

'There was a lot more money but he sold one of his smaller houses and drew a large amount out of this bank account to buy the house you're currently living in. And he had to deal with more repairs than he'd expected, as well as adding the modern bathroom.'

'I see. And the third account?'

'The money comes from his business dealings. He was in the habit of paying a large amount of cash into it every quarter.'

The amount made her heart sink. She didn't dare look at Rufus, but couldn't help reaching out for his hand. To her relief he took hold of hers and it felt comforting.

She closed her eyes and drew in a shaky breath, then forced herself to open them and speak to the bank manager, who was trying to look as if he wasn't listening to what they were saying, but of course he was.

'Can you please change the names on these accounts to Mr and Mrs Shorrocks as from the end of next week? We're getting married then.'

'Of course.'

'We'll be in touch with you after the wedding to sign any papers necessary and discuss what we intend to do with the money,' Rufus said quietly.

'But I'll draw some out now,' Abigail said, as she knew Rufus would need it.

When they were outside, she said, 'I don't want to talk about it till Nina is in bed. Then we must . . . discuss what to do with it all.'

'I agree.' He offered her his arm and when she took it, she clung to him so tightly he stared down at her and said gently, 'It's really upset you, hasn't it?'

'Yes. Well, not so much my mother's legacy, which hasn't been touched so truly belongs to me, but the two so-called business accounts. I hope that with us both to sort things out, we shall manage to do it . . . fairly and honestly.'

'I still haven't changed my mind about marrying you.'

'Nor have I.' But her voice refused to come out as anything but a shaky half-whisper.

Rufus was watching her more carefully than she realised and his heart went out to her. She'd had so many shocks today.

So he gave her another hug. He suspected she'd had very few of them, if any, in her life. And a hug was usually a welcome thing, or so he'd found.

But when she later gave him the money she'd drawn out of the bank, he hesitated.

'Please. We'll need to pay for various things and it'll look better if you do that.'

After another brief pause he nodded and put the money in his wallet. 'I won't waste a penny of this, mind.'

'You can spend it how you like. I trust you absolutely.'

This won her another of those glorious hugs.

By evening, Abigail was starting to feel more hopeful about her future and felt like playing the piano rather than chatting or reading. Music had always been a friend she could turn to in difficult times.

She hesitated as the three of them went into the living room.

'Would you mind if I played the piano for a while, Rufus?'

'Mind? Certainly not. I'd be delighted.'

'You're not just saying that?'

He looked puzzled. 'No. Why would I say it if I didn't mean it?'

'Well, my father didn't always feel in the mood for music, and I don't know you well enough to guess your moods yet.'

'I don't usually indulge in moods and I love music, so play away.'

Nina came to sit on the arm of her brother's chair. 'Rufus has a lovely voice, only our mother always said it gave her a headache to listen to him if he started singing. I like singing too.'

'So do I.' Abigail was relieved to see him smile at his sister's frankness. He didn't seem to get angry whatever she or Nina said or did, was always so calm and reasonable. How easy that was to live with!

'My sister and I would both love to hear you play and another time we'll all sing together,' he said with another of his smiles.

She went across to the piano and lifted the lid back, then took her place at the keyboard. She ran a few scales first to wake up her fingers, then played some simple tunes, feeling a bit self-conscious and not quite daring to sing in front of him yet.

When she paused, Nina clapped vigorously. 'I don't know the names of those tunes, but I liked listening to them. Didn't you, Rufus?'

'Very much.' He stared at Abigail. 'You're an excellent pianist.'

'Thank you.'

'What other hidden talents do you have? Do tell us. I've never learned to read minds.'

'Um, well, I like to embroider in cross stitch, to make up pictures myself, not follow other people's patterns. I haven't taken my embroidery out since my father died, though.'

'I shall look forward to seeing your work.'

'Did you do the one hanging on the wall in our bedroom?' Nina asked.

'Yes. Father didn't want them hanging anywhere else in the house. He was the same with the ones my mother made. She taught me to do it but we only worked on our embroidery when he was out of the house.'

'It's a lovely picture, Rufus, full of birds and butterflies and flowers. Can I show it to him when we go up to bed, please?'

Abigail looked doubtfully at Rufus, who said, 'I'd love to see it. Really I would.'

She could see Nina hesitating and asked gently, 'Did you want to say something else?'

The child nodded. 'I'd love to learn to sew. We did some at school, but my mother lost the piece I was working on so I had to sit quietly and watch the others.'

'She used it as a dish rag,' Rufus said. 'I was furious with her.'

'She got things mixed up sometimes,' Nina said. 'She grew … strange, very forgetful towards the end.'

There was silence and Rufus stared down at his hands for a few moments with a very sad expression, so Abigail turned back to the child.

'I'd be happy to teach you to sew once things have settled down. I have some spare material in my sewing cupboard and I can start you off on some simple pieces, perhaps an apron to begin with,' she offered. 'I have a sewing machine and I can show you how to use it.'

Nina looked round. 'Where do you keep it?'

'In one of the spare bedrooms. I only used it during the day because my father didn't like the sound of it. I concentrated on embroideries down here in the evenings.'

Nina clapped her hands. 'That'll be wonderful. They have a sewing machine at school, but I never got that far enough with any piece to be allowed to use it.'

When Nina went up to bed, Rufus went with her to look at the embroidery and when he came back, he said quietly, 'Thank you.'

'What for?'

'Being kind to my sister, paying her some attention.'

'That's a pleasure. She's a delightful child.'

'And your embroidery is exquisite. If you have any others that are framed we could put one or two up on the downstairs walls as well.'

'Are you sure?'

'Of course I'm sure. Stop doubting me.' He waggled one finger at her, then stamped one foot and tossed his head in a parody of an angry person, which made her chuckle.

His little sister was a pleasure she hadn't expected when Rufus agreed to marry her. And he was proving very interesting and easy to live with and chat to.

What would their life be like if they managed to sort out the mess her father had left behind him and could live like a normal family?

It'd be wonderful, compared to her previous life. Absolutely wonderful.

It was a huge improvement already, even with all the worries they still had to deal with.

18

Walter came home from a quick trip into town on business and beamed at Flora. 'I've found just the place for your clinic.'

'Really? How wonderful. Can we go and see it? Does it need much altering or renovating? They usually shove clinics for the poor into tumble-down old buildings.'

'We can go and see it this very afternoon if you like. The building is old but it's in a good state of repair and will only need a few changes made before you can get started. It used to be a small church, an offshoot of the Methodists, but the group who started it didn't flourish and no one else wanted to buy it when it was put up for sale, so I got it very cheaply.'

She smiled. 'You often step in, don't you?'

'If necessary. I don't want unused buildings falling into ruins and becoming dangerous.'

'I suppose not. And you can afford to change it into a clinic?'

'Yes. If I'm careful. It's not very big, so can only be used for a small one. I'm guessing we'll need to make at least one enclosed area to give patients privacy with the nurse or doctor. We'll also need to put in more plumbing and make a separate room for the staff to rest in. I can get that done quite quickly once you've agreed that the place is basically suitable.'

'The main thing is to get a clinic started,' she said at once. 'I don't need fancy surroundings and they'd put off some of the poorest people anyway. But what I will need is regular medical supplies and perhaps clothes for children and the pregnant women, who often struggle to find garments they can fit into as they grow bigger.'

'There are some ladies in town who will be delighted to help you get started with that side of things. I'll spread the word.'

'Good. The more folk getting involved the better. People have to face some dreadful things in their lives sometimes, especially poorer folk, and we can at least help some of them.'

A strange expression came over his face and she left him alone, but kept an eye on him. He was a wonderful man – wonderful to everyone else, but he didn't take care of himself properly. And every now and then he looked so sad it hurt her to see him, as it was doing now. She intended to start her nursing work here in the valley by looking after him.

They had a quick snack, but when Elinor joined them and Cameron came in to tell his wife that he had harnessed the pony and was ready to set off, Walter suddenly remembered his grandson saying this morning he needed the pony and trap to take Elinor shopping. He turned to Flora and whispered. 'We'll have to go tomorrow instead. I'd forgotten they would be using the pony this afternoon.'

'It doesn't matter. I've been wanting to talk to you privately about something else. We can have our little chat today and go into Ollerthwaite tomorrow.'

She watched out of the window as the pony trotted off down the hill and said idly, 'I think I'm going to have to learn to drive motor cars and if I succeed, I'll buy one to get round in when I start work.'

'No! No, you mustn't!'

She swung round to see him staring at her in utter horror.

'Surely you're not serious, Flora! Those machines are dangerous in many ways. They're highly unsuitable for a woman to drive and will break down on our hilly roads and cause problems for everyone nearby.'

She looked at him sadly. 'I've seen this happen before. Someone has only to mention motor cars for you to stiffen and start saying how terrible they are. And yet you've never tried to drive one, have you?'

'I have personal experience of the serious harm they can do to . . . to people.' His voice broke on the last words.

She got up and put one arm round his shoulders, pulling him to his feet and guiding him across to the sofa. When he merely stood next to it as if not knowing what he was doing there, she pushed him to sit down. Then she sat beside him, took his nearest hand in both hers and used it to pull him closer.

'I'm already very fond of you, Walter. We seem able to talk about anything and everything. But you need to shed the burden you're carrying or it'll weigh you right down and prevent you from having a serious, long-term relationship with anyone. You'll only get rid of your dreadful load of grief by talking about your sorrow, facing the facts and moving on.'

He tried in vain to pull away. 'I don't know what you mean.'

'Dear man, of course you do. I know about your son and grandson, but from what I've heard, that terrible accident was the fault of bad handling of a young horse and the fact that it was pulling too great a load, not the fault of the motor car.'

'I still don't want to talk about it. Some feelings are not for public display.'

'This isn't public display, Walter. This is you and me, no one else. What's more, we two are growing rapidly fond of one another, but we won't be able to do much about that till you sort out your emotions about your loss and unlock all your feelings again.'

'I can never forget my son and grandson, but that's my own private business. I certainly don't wish to let it intrude on others.'

'I agree that you will always feel sad about your lost ones, but have you let yourself grieve properly? I don't think so. You've kept your feelings bottled up inside yourself and they're sitting there like a nasty festering sore. Have you wept long and hard for those you lost?'

He closed his eyes as if in acute pain. 'That's not how men do things. You just . . . you don't understand.'

'Actually, I do. I lost my twin sister in a railway accident when we were both twenty. We were so close, sharing our lives and hopes for the future and . . . well, everything. Then suddenly, I was alone. That was so hard.'

Tears welled in her eyes and ran down her cheeks and it was those tears that were Walter's undoing, because he could feel tears rising in his own eyes and sobs pushing their way out of what felt like his very soul.

She pulled him into her arms and the soft warmth and gentle kisses on his cheeks unlocked the final door to his grief and it burst out like a flood. These tears were nothing like the furtive trickles of grief that he'd always cut short, even in the privacy of his bedroom. These tears could not be stopped; they overwhelmed him.

He didn't know how long he wept but he suddenly realised that he was cradled in Flora's arms and she was still occasionally kissing the cheek nearest to her, stroking his hair or pressing her lips to his forehead.

He'd now stopped making those desperately harsh noises, and it felt as if he'd emptied out a darkness from the very depths of his being.

When he looked at Flora, her cheeks were wet, too.

'I don't know what got into me,' he said shakily.

'You've held your grief in for over a year, my dear. It's what got *out* of you that matters today. It matters very much. You can't live your own life to the fullest with your most important feelings so tightly enclosed and suppressed.'

'Men aren't supposed to cry.' He fumbled for a handkerchief and couldn't find one.

'Whoever told the world that lie about men not crying was utterly wrong and did a lot of harm.' She pulled a handkerchief out of her sleeve, not a tiny, lace-edged lady's handkerchief but a man's useful piece, big enough to wipe her cheeks and then his too.

'You'll sleep better tonight, Walter, I promise you. You'll weep again, of course you will. But all that proves is that you're a normal human being and that you loved them dearly. They wouldn't have wanted you to hold such pain inside you, though, I'm quite sure of that. Not if your son and grandson were anything like you.'

'You are an amazing woman.' His voice was still wobbly.

'Yes, I am, aren't I? And you're an amazing man. We're well matched. I wish we'd met before now. We shall have only a few years together at best after we marry, but they'll be good ones, enriched by our love, I'm sure.'

He gaped at her. '*Marry!*'

A gurgle of laughter escaped her. 'I just proposed to you, didn't I?'

He began to smile too, for all that his eyelashes were still wet. 'So you did. And I have no hesitation in accepting. What's more, we shouldn't waste any time in doing something about it.'

By the time the others came back, they'd both calmed down and were discussing how soon they could get married and how to do it without any fuss.

Cameron and Elinor stopped dead in the doorway to stare at the way the two older people were cuddled up close and holding hands like courting youngsters.

'Come in and congratulate us. We've just got engaged,' Flora called our cheerfully. 'And we'll need the pony and trap tomorrow to go and book our wedding. You don't waste time doing something this important and wonderful at our age.'

Cameron went across to shake his grandfather's hand but this turned quickly into a enthusiastic hug, while the traditional words of congratulation offered by Elinor to Flora met the same fate.

The following day Walter and Flora drove into Ollerthwaite and he shocked the clerk at the town hall rigid by booking their wedding for a month's time. After that they strolled up to the lake and stood holding hands and staring across the water.

'It's sparkling like diamonds today, with the gentle little breeze,' she said dreamily.

'I'd like to buy you a diamond ring to celebrate our promises to one another. That combination makes a perfect day for us!'

'I don't normally wear fancy rings.'

'But then you've never been married before. We can buy an unfussy ring.'

'Very well. But only if you also wear a gold wedding ring.'

'Men don't usually do that.'

'Some do. And it'd mean a lot to me.'

'Then I'll do it and hang what people say or think. With a wife like you I shall be very happy to show the world that I'm a married man.'

Silence fell, then a few moments later he said suddenly, 'I'm still finding it astounding that this has happened.'

'So am I. Proposing was the last thing I expected to do yesterday. Or at any time.'

'I loved that you asked me. I'm usually the one who nudges people into doing things. You're a very modern woman, my dear.' He gave her a look every bit as loving as that of a younger man. 'Let's sit down on that bench and continue to enjoy the view across the water. I don't feel like rushing around today. I want to be quietly happy with you.'

They held hands again and sat in silence. After a while he gestured towards the far end of the lake. 'I'd expected to have the path round this finished years ago but the top end still needs quite a lot of attention. Older people and mothers with prams or small children have to stop and turn back.'

'Why? I haven't been up to that end yet.'

'Because the ground is so rough, and there are some quite big shrubs that need removing and a few lumps of rock. Our volunteer working parties were making a good solid path, stretch by stretch, one that would be safe for everyone till the Russian flu struck. And after more than one outbreak, people were more concerned with staying healthy and keeping away from crowds than creating a new path round the lake.'

'You can't blame them. I lost a good friend to that first wave of Russian flu.'

She lifted his hand and plonked one of her stray kisses on it. 'Perhaps it's time to nudge the locals and get them to work again.'

He rolled his eyes heavenwards. 'How? I've nudged and hinted and they're always going to do it, but later.'

'We'll find a way.'

He smiled. 'We?'

'If you don't mind. I think parks are good for people's health. Open spaces get them out and about and help them forget their troubles for a while. They give children somewhere to play and older people can sit on the benches and chat to one another. Is there an area for children planned as part of it?'

'Well, no. I just thought of creating a path to let folk walk right round the lake.'

'We'll talk to a few people about a children's playground and spread the word about that. If we make one at the top end of the lake, they'll be attracted to it and walk further.'

'The trouble is, I think people are more concerned about their own safety after the recent murder. There's never been one here before that I remember.'

'We'll see.' She smiled. 'Lots to do, as well as you to love, Walter Crossley. Life is wonderful. Come on. I've got sturdy shoes on. Let's see if we can walk right round the lake, however rough the ground at the top is. We should manage as long as we take it slowly. It's a lovely fine day and that nice man at the livery stables said he'd look after your pony for you.'

'I'll only do it if I can continue to hold your hand.'

'Oh, very well. You are such a bully, Walter Crossley.'

19

Once Nina was in bed and presumably sound asleep Rufus said, 'We need to talk about your various bequests, Abigail, and then I think we should discuss them with the sergeant. He seems a very capable man and I'd trust his opinion.'

'Yes. That's a good idea.'

'You're certain of what you want to do?'

'Sort of.'

'What does that mean?'

'I'm happy to keep any bequest of money or equivalent that was earned honestly, like my mother's money, but I don't want to keep the results of theft.'

'I feel the same. Let's discuss it with the sergeant tomorrow. And then the day after is my mother's funeral.'

'I'm attending it with you.'

'I'd been hoping you would. It's the simplest and cheapest "proper" funeral I could get. I'm doing it more for Nina's sake than my own because I lost patience with my mother years ago. She's always been lazy and uncaring about others.'

Abigail nodded. 'I think it's important to give Nina something positive to remember, though. Unfortunately I don't yet know when I'll be allowed to bury my father, and I think it'll have to be a quiet affair, anyway.'

'They won't be able to leave that much longer.'

'Well, I'm not giving him a fancy send-off for another reason: he doesn't deserve it. Now, I need to sort out some dark clothes for Nina and myself. I can make alterations quite quickly if I do it roughly.'

'So that's two things we have to do tomorrow: speak to the sergeant about the bequests and sort out some clothes for you and Nina. You surely can't fit making alterations in as well as everything else. Or are you a miracle worker? If so, why don't you go and dance on the moon while you're at it?'

'You sometimes make me feel as if I could do that.'

Which remark led to another of those silences while they gave each other warm smiles.

Abigail pulled herself together first. 'Your sister needs a whole new set of clothes, Rufus, not just something for the funeral. Most of hers are too small for her and she feels embarrassed about being seen in them. Would you mind if I dealt with that as well?'

'Don't you have enough to do? If she's managed this long, she can manage for a week or two longer, surely?'

'I have some difficult and unpleasant things to do. Going shopping for materials and partly made-up garments for your sister will be sheer pleasure.' A yawn took her by surprise and when it ended, she stood up. 'I really do need to get some sleep now.'

'So do I.' He came across to give her another hug and walked with her to her bedroom door.

'I'll go and check all the doors in the building to make sure they're locked, and have a word with Steve.'

She watched him walk across the landing and down the stairs, then went into her bedroom. It felt different tonight with a child sleeping peacefully in the bed they'd brought in – better somehow. Nina was fast asleep and Abigail smiled at her a couple of times as she undressed. She carried the feel of that last hug by Rufus with her to bed as well.

How strange! The past day or two had been both the worst and the best in her whole life.

Her last thought was of Rufus and she fell asleep with a smile on her face.

In the morning Rufus thanked Steve for keeping watch and asked if he would call in at the police station on his way home and tell the sergeant that they had news for him.

'Happy to.'

'And can you come and keep watch tonight as well? Just to be sure everything is all right. I'll pay you the usual.'

'Even happier to do that. Jobs have been a bit scarce lately.'

As a result of his message the sergeant turned up at the house thirty minutes later and Rufus showed him in.

'I'll just go and fetch Abigail. She's altering a skirt for Nina to wear at my mother's funeral tomorrow.'

'Eventful times for you in several ways, aren't they?'

'Yes. And for Abigail.' He went out and came back a couple of minutes later with his fiancée.

When they were all sitting, he asked her, 'Do you want me to explain what we discovered to the sergeant or do you want to do it yourself?'

'I'd be happier if you'd do that. It still upsets me. I'll just ask Margie to make us a pot of tea. I'm sure the sergeant won't say no.'

He nodded. 'It'd be nice.'

She came back, sat down and gestured to Rufus to start explaining.

When he'd finished, the sergeant studied the pieces of paper with the information about legacies and sat frowning down at them for a while. Eventually he looked up and shook his head. 'I have to commend you on your honesty, Miss Dawson. I don't actually know how we stand legally on this. If the police take you to law about it, you and your money, even your mother's legacy, could be tied up in the courts for a long time.'

'I need some money to live on, but I don't want to use my father's money if it's the proceeds of crime. 'I just . . . I can't bear the idea of that.'

'I can understand your feelings but we have no solid proof of how your father got that money, nothing to tie it to actual crimes. He was very cunning.'

'He can't have made that much money just from the shop, he just can't.'

Both men nodded at her comment.

Silence reigned for a few moments then Margie brought in a trolley she'd found with a pot of tea, cups and saucers and a plate of biscuits on it.

After they'd finished the refreshments, Rufus began, 'How about—' Then he stopped suddenly.

The sergeant flapped one hand at him. 'Go on. How about what?'

Rufus aimed his words mainly at Abigail. 'How about you donate the money we think might have come from crime to charity? It would be unusual but it'd show good intent, wouldn't it? We can't return it to the original owners of the pieces he sold because we have no idea who they are. He seems to have dealt mainly in things from outside the valley.

'That would ensure it was put to good use,' the sergeant said slowly. 'Though I'm not sure of the legality of it all.'

There was silence as they all three considered the idea.

Hector tapped the pieces of paper. 'I'll have to consult my inspector about these and I don't know what he'll say about them. This inspector is new to me, so I don't know him well enough yet to guess. It'll probably take a few days to get any sort of answer from him.'

'The money we're uncertain about can sit in the bank for as long as necessary, but I'm going to assume I can use my mother's legacy as I please,' Abigail said. 'There are wages to pay and food to buy. And I know from the bank manager that the money in that account has never been touched since it was first deposited there.'

The sergeant nodded, hesitated, then said, 'I shan't even think about that legacy till I've discussed the general situation with my inspector, so you should just go ahead and use the money. I'd guess it'll be yours legally, especially if the bank manager can confirm that your father never deposited any money into the account.'

They nodded, then Rufus asked, 'Do you think Bibby will ever be caught? It seems wrong for him to get away with murder.'

'Ah. I got some news about that late last night. Not good news as far as I'm concerned, unfortunately. I received a telegram from a fellow policeman I've known for many years. He's an inspector now. I sent the information to a few people in the parts of the country near here, asking them to put the word out in case anyone saw Bibby and the woman. It was waiting for my friend when he got back from a meeting in London.'

After another short pause, he added, 'Sometimes the smallest thing can point in the right direction. He'd noticed a couple getting on the train to London and had been amused by her dyed frizzy hair and the fact that the two of them were carrying large, heavy bags as well as suitcases.'

There was silence before he added, 'I doubt anyone will see where Bibby goes from London, though. It's easy to get lost in a big city. He could be overseas now for all we know.'

'So he's getting away with it.'

'Probably. We'd love to catch every thief and solve every crime, but sadly we can't manage it. Um, out of curiosity, which charity would you give the money to?'

'I'd put it in Walter Crossley's hands and ask that it be used to help the poorer folk of this valley,' Abigail said without hesitation. 'That thought came to me in the middle of the night. He wants to open a clinic for poor women and children, for one thing.'

'Sounds a good idea.'

'Does the sighting of Bibby in London mean we don't need to keep guard on this house any longer?' Rufus asked.

'I think you need to be careful for a while but yes, I think our villain has got away with it and I doubt he'll come back to attack you. I don't know of any other threat to your safety. Do you?'

'No. I don't go round making enemies and we don't usually have attackers stalking people here in the valley.'

The sergeant grimaced. 'Actually, we do seem to have one lurking around at the moment. There's a chap who has been threatening another of your friends, Edward Ollerton. It seems someone called Terry Catlow has been spotted a few times following him or lurking nearby. Do you know anything about this Catlow fellow?'

Rufus shook his head. 'Not much. I've never had anything to do with him and I've worked away from home for years. But it's generally known that he's not to be trusted and that his wife has thrown him out of their home for good. Oh, and that the eldest son of theirs has come back from temporary employment with his uncle and is surprising people by working hard and not trying to bully anyone. He's called Jezzy.'

Abigail smiled slightly as she added some information, 'Mrs Catlow is known to be a woman who can be very fierce with anyone who upsets her. I've seen her at the market a few times. She has a very loud voice.'

'I'll remember that.'

Rufus frowned. 'I heard one chap say that Terry Catlow has been looking increasingly strange since she threw him out. He said he'd as soon poke an angry tiger as push Catlow too far when he gets a certain look on his face.'

'Did he now.'

'The important thing is that Abigail and I can get married next week.'

'Yes. I wish you well. You'll be in good company. Have you heard that Walter Crossley is getting married too?'

His companions both gaped at him, then Rufus asked, 'Walter Crossley? But he's about seventy, isn't he? Who is he marrying?'

'That nurse who's come to live in the valley recently, the older woman who's been helping the new lady doctor. I've been told about it by several people.'

'She's a lucky woman,' Rufus said. 'Walter is an admirable man, doing so much to help other people. He'll use Abigail's charity money to good purpose, I'm sure.'

The following morning at 10 o'clock, the funeral of Mrs Shorrocks took place. It was a brief affair, officiated at by the minister from the small Methodist chapel and only four people attended. One of them was Mrs Lucas from next door to Rufus's old home, the rest being him, his fiancée and his younger sister.

Nina was wearing a black skirt and a plain white blouse. The skirt had been tacked in big, hurried stitches at the waist to make it fit reasonably well, and shortened as well. She had a black shawl over her shoulders to hide the improvised seam at the back of the blouse and a straw hat with a black ribbon round it that Abigail had lent her.

Rufus saw Nina stroke the skirt a few times when she thought no one was watching. It was of a lovely soft woollen material and he guessed it had belonged to Abigail.

His fiancée was wearing all black garments but when he commented she said they were rather old-fashioned in style, having been used a decade ago at her mother's funeral. Her hair looked more reddish than brown against the dark colours. He loved the way it always shone and seemed to change colour in the sunlight.

He endured the funeral, held Nina as she cried and was relieved when it ended.

'How about some refreshments?' he asked.

When they all nodded, he led the way across to a small café next to the cemetery and ordered tea and a selection of small cakes from the waitress, then turned to his mother's neighbour as they waited. 'Thank you for all you've done for my family, Mrs Lucas. And for making the long walk to attend the funeral today.'

'Neighbours should help one another, but I didn't walk. There's a new service taking people up and down the hill from the railway station for only tuppence a head.'

'I hadn't heard of that. Who's doing it?'

'A man from Eastby End who's got a pony and who's put bench seats into a covered cart. It's a bit rough and ready, but it's a lot easier than walking, and you'll be dry when it's raining. He told me he doesn't know yet what times he'll be going up and down the hill from the station in Ollerthwaite. He's just trying it to find out if it makes money and he said he'd keep doing it if it did. I hope it does. It'll be a godsend if he keeps on providing the service.'

They didn't stay long in the café but it had seemed the right thing to do and Mrs Lucas had clearly enjoyed the refreshments. Rufus thanked her again for all her help before she left to go to the shops and then, she hoped, ride up the hill on the new cart.

He suggested they walk home straight away and get on with their day.

He'd done the right thing by his mother, but it was really for Nina that he'd arranged the funeral.

When they got to the town centre, Abigail said, 'Can you stop a minute, Rufus? If the sergeant is right and there isn't likely to be a problem now that Bibby has left the valley, Nina and I could do some shopping.'

'I'll come with you.'

She chuckled. 'Do you really want to hang about outside shops selling women's clothing, underwear and shoes?'

'Well, no.'

'Then leave us to it. We'll be a couple of hours at least, I should think.'

He looked down at his sister's excited face. 'I'd be grateful if you could buy her whatever clothes she needs. Let me give you some money.'

She took a quick step backwards. 'No. This is a gift from me to my future sister-in-law.' She added in a lower voice, 'Please let me do it, Rufus.'

'Very well. And thank you.'

It was the first time Abigail had had someone to go shopping with since her mother's death a decade ago and the first time Nina had ever in her life had new clothes. It would have been hard to say which of them enjoyed the outing more, and since Abigail had noticed how tight the girl's shoes were, they visited the one and only shoe shop in town first and she wore her new shoes to go shopping.

As they came out of the shop, Nina kept staring down at her feet as she walked in obvious delight, because the new shoes fitted properly and wouldn't cause blisters or cramp her toes. She spent as much time staring down at them as looking where she was going and tripped several times, so Abigail took hold of her hand.

She hadn't brought enough money with her so they also called in at the bank for her to withdraw some more.

When they went back to their house, Nina threw her arms round Abigail and twirled them both round. 'Thank you. Thank you so much.'

'My pleasure.' She looked across the kitchen and saw Rufus leaning against the door frame watching them with one of his gentle smiles.

'If those are your new shoes, they look very smart,' he said.

Which made his sister beam down at her feet again.

'Some of your new clothes have already been delivered,' he said. 'Why don't you try one or two on to show them to me?'

Nina rushed up to her bedroom with the parcels and bobbed up and down the stairs no less than five times to show him her new clothes before hunger took over and she joined them for a snack, wearing her new house slippers and only glancing down at them now and then.

Later in the afternoon, however, the worries started again because the sergeant called round to say that the following day his inspector was catching an early train to Ollerthwaite to see them. This visit had surprised him, he admitted.

So they were to do nothing with any of the money until he'd checked everything, which would include calling on the local bank to view the three accounts and decide what to do about them.

'Oh dear! I took some money out of my mother's legacy today!' Abigail said anxiously. 'Nina needed some new clothes.'

'Just today or ever before?'

'Just today.'

'That will probably not matter since we can check what you spent it on if necessary.'

After he'd gone Rufus looked across at her. 'You may be in trouble for spending that money on my sister's clothes. Let me pay you back.'

'You don't need to. I wanted to help her.'

She wondered whether to tell him about the banknotes and coins she'd found among her father's things and the other money she'd been sneaking away for years in a hiding place in her old bedroom, then in a similar cache in her new bedroom. She could have come home before shopping to take some of that money but she hadn't wanted to reveal it to anyone yet.

No. Best not to say anything, she decided. At least, not yet. She had such a burning need to know there was money to fall back on if necessary. It made her feel safer, but she wondered if she'd ever feel truly safe again.

She wished she'd had a normal father and family life. But what was normal? It certainly wasn't a perfect life because even a capable man like Rufus had had trouble with his mother.

20

Edward joined Lewis in the cottage he was living in, which was also being used as an office for matters to do with the new building. They spent some time studying and discussing the plans and rough sketches.

'The main thing that needs doing at the moment is clearing and re-establishing the passage connecting the cellars of the old and new house, and making sure it's safe for future use,' Lewis said. 'That will involve some messy work removing the fallen earth currently blocking access. I don't want to put the roof on the main house till all the underground work is finished. I don't think we're likely to get a slip but I'm not risking it.'

'Absolutely. Even more importantly we don't want our workers affected by further collapses down there,' Edward said. 'We aren't even sure what caused those areas to collapse in the first place.'

'I'm hoping our excavations will show what went wrong.'

'And it's not just the building workers. We need to make sure that any servants we employ will be safe once the house is up and running. They're the ones who'll be going down to the cellars to access the stored food and an occasional bottle of wine.'

Lewis nodded. 'I'd like to make sure the wooden props and planks that are being taken to the site are good and strong.'

'So if we go slowly, we should be all right, surely?'

'You never know with underground work.' He hesitated. 'I know what to do in theory, Edward, but I've never done anything even remotely like this in practice. I can't ask Rufus to supervise this job at the moment so perhaps we should find someone else to take over careful supervision of the underground rehabilitation, someone with experience in mines maybe.'

'You're right. I can't see Rufus being free to give our project his full attention for a while. He's getting married on Tuesday, after all. And I don't want to spoil that for him.' Edward smiled. 'I've had recent experience of how wonderful it is to marry the woman you love myself and I'd not spoil that for anyone else. And though he says it's a marriage of convenience, he looks at her fondly, if you ask me. And she him.'

After another hesitation Lewis said in a sharper tone of voice, 'And there's our other problem: we need to make sure the cellars are not easily accessible from outside, both while we're working on them and when everything is finished because of that madman who is trying to kill you simply because you're an Ollerton.'

Edward scowled. 'Do you think he is really so dangerous?'

'Yes, I do. You make light of it but I don't. Your safety has to be our primary consideration until he's caught and locked away.'

'I'm being careful, aren't I, not going for walks on the moors on my own, even though you can see for miles whether there's anyone else around. I find it infuriating not to be able to go up there because I love it on the tops. I've been waiting years to get back here and enjoy going there. As for being careful, I've hired a nightwatchman to keep an eye on my current home and the building works each night. What more can I do?'

'It's also what *we* can do, working together. I intend to secure the underground workings at all times. And I want you to promise me you won't go down there or anywhere else on the site alone, never, ever.'

He saw the stubborn look settle on Edward's face and sighed even before his friend said, 'I'll do my best but I intend to be involved in every stage of building my new family home. *Every – single – step.*'

'But not on your own for the time being . . . please humour me on this. Building sites can be dangerous even without our madman.'

Edward patted his friend's shoulder. 'I'm touched by the way you care about my safety. Really I am. Now, let's get back to the specifics of what we should do next. How about I ask Rufus if he can recommend someone to come and help us sort out the underground parts? It seems obvious that he'll be too involved with his new wife and her rather neglected home to work for us in the near future, perhaps never again even. She's got money even if he hasn't and he's talking about converting the house into a small hotel.'

'That might be a good idea. There isn't one in the valley. He'd make a good host, he's so calm and amiable.'

'I agree. And both Lillian and I like the look of his fiancée.'

'She seems nice but rather reserved. I only wish I could meet someone I care about as much you two care about one another, but I never have.'

'It's not too late for that to happen, Lewis.'

He shrugged. 'We'll see. Abigail's house will need a lot of work doing on it to make it more attractive if they're going to turn it into a hotel. Rufus has the necessary skills to do most of that.'

'He seems able to turn his hand to anything. All right. It's agreed that we ask Rufus about getting someone else in to help with the underground work. Surely after all those years working in mining he'll know someone with the right practical skills?'

'Let's go and ask him now. I could do with stretching my legs. I'm sure he'll be able to spare us half an hour. He might even be glad to get away from the wedding fuss for a while.'

As they set off, Edward said, 'By the way, Lillian has reminded me that we'll need to buy wedding presents for the happy couple. She also wants me to find out whether she can attend the ceremony. Apart from the fact that she'd like to be there, she says it'll look better if they have women attending as well as men. She also wants to know whether they're having a wedding breakfast afterwards. Stupid, isn't it to call a wedding meal a breakfast whatever time of day it's at? Are they having one?'

'I don't think so. Women are good at the social details, aren't they?'

'My Lillian is. I don't think Abigail has had much chance of learning them, the way her father kept her more or less locked up for all those years. I'm under strict instructions from Lillian to put on a meal at our house if the pair have got nothing planned. I'm also to ask the baker in town whether they've ordered a wedding cake and if not, order one and a few other suitable refreshments from him.'

'That'll put a smile on the baker's face.'

'Well, you've nothing else to do with your time, have you?' he joked.

They both laughed and continued striding down the hill towards Railway Road.

When they got there Lewis didn't waste any time in asking how to find someone to oversee the work of connecting the two sets of cellars.

Rufus stared at him for a few seconds as if he'd spoken in a foreign language. His mind was still lingering on the memory of Abigail and Nina laughing over something this morning, both looking carefree and happy. It did his heart good to see them getting on so well.

Then his mind switched back inevitably to worrying about this inspector chap, who would be with Sergeant McGill at this very moment and would no doubt come here to see Abigail soon.

He realised his visitors were looking at him as if waiting for an answer, so he tried to pull himself together and think clearly how to help them.

'There's a chap called Dan Makersby who might be able to help you. He'd be as glad as I was to get out of the dangerous mine we were both working in under a particularly stupid foreman. I know he'd do a good job for you.'

He had a quick think about what might be needed to attract Dan to the valley. 'The trouble is, you'd have to offer him somewhere to live and a permanent job afterwards to get him to move here. He's worth it. He and I were good friends, even though I'm a few years older than him. We've been keeping in touch, writing to one another every few weeks since I left to come and look after my mother. In his latest letter he said his wife has just found out that she's expecting their first child. And that makes accommodation even more important in any move.'

'He sounds possible. Not sure about the accommodation. I might see Walter about that.'

'They're living with her mother at the moment, can't find a decent place to rent. That puts a roof over their heads, but it's going to be very difficult once the baby arrives because another daughter has recently come back to live at home as well, and it's not a big house. Dan is even thinking of heading down south to see if he can find somewhere offering a house to rent as well as a job that isn't as dangerous.'

'What skills exactly does he have?'

'He's rather like me, has been working in mining for a few years but enjoys doing anything with his hands.'

He fumbled in his inside jacket pocket. 'I think – yes, I did shove his letter in my pocket. It has his address on it and I don't care if you read it.'

'I'd trust your recommendation, Rufus. If he's anything like you he'll be a useful fellow to have around permanently while we're building. More than that I can't promise.'

He turned to Edward. 'This problem of accommodation is going to keep cropping up, you know: where to lodge the more skilled people who'll need to come here to work on the finer details of your building. It'll probably put some people off coming to work here.'

'Walter might have a house he could rent to you for this chap at least, though he's just had a couple of his places rented out. If you can get him to stop smiling at Flora, he might be able to help.'

Lewis chuckled. 'They do seem happy to be with each other, don't they?'

'At their age? He's seventy, isn't he? A bit old to marry again.'

'Yes. But he's still a lively chap. Our trouble is, we'll be needing more than one place to house a skilled worker as we get further along with the building.'

Rufus sighed. 'And yet Abigail and I have too many rooms in our house. If we do turn it into a small hotel we'll have to put in a lot more plumbing because we'll need more lavatories and bathrooms, which will mean digging up the backyard. The house was badly designed in the first place and is woefully old-fashioned now, but it's a good, solid structure at least.'

He'd love to do something about that and bring the whole house up to scratch but before he could make even a small start, there was the question of Abigail's inheritance to sort out as a matter of urgency. Would the house still belong to her or would the law take it off her because of her father's unsavoury activities?

He caught sight of the clock. 'I'm sorry, lads, but we have the police inspector supervising this area coming to see us this afternoon, so I'm afraid I need to get ready for that now.'

'Is there some problem?' Edward asked at once. 'If so, you know we'll help in any way we can.'

'Thanks, but there's nothing you can do at the moment. I'll bear your offer in mind if I need help or even a character reference.'

Rufus saw his friends out then went back to join Abigail, who was looking very nervous indeed.

'You're sure he can't arrest me for anything?' she asked yet again.

'Of course not. *You* haven't done anything illegal,' he reminded her gently.

'I keep telling myself that but I can't seem to believe it. He might accuse me of knowing all along that my father was breaking the law. That inspector is coming all the way here to see us in person the very day after he heard from our sergeant about my inheritance. Why the haste?'

'Who knows?'

She wished she could stay as calm as Rufus seemed able to.

Someone knocked on the front door just then so he said, 'That can only be them. No one round here uses the front door. You go into the living room. I'll let them in and bring them to you.'

He opened the front door and as he'd expected, the sergeant was standing outside, accompanied by a tall man with greying hair and a very shrewd gaze, who could only be Inspector Molson.

'Do come in. It's quite a chilly day, isn't it?'

When they were all standing in the hall, the sergeant introduced them properly and Rufus found himself being given a firm handshake as well as a continuing scrutiny.

'My fiancée is waiting in the living room. This way, Inspector.' He led the way, introduced the stranger to Abigail and then suggested they all sit down.

'Let's not waste any time on chat, however polite. I'd like to see as much of the valley as I can while I'm here, as well as looking into this case,' the inspector said. 'Do you have the information the lawyer gave you about the accounts, Miss Dawson?'

'Here you are.' She passed the papers over and they waited for the inspector to study them.

He did so for a short time then turned to Abigail again. 'I gather you had no idea about these three accounts?'

'I knew about my mother's legacy but my father said he'd manage that for me so I didn't know how much interest had accrued. He wasn't the sort of man a young woman dares argue with, so I hadn't had anything to do with it since my mother died ten years ago until I saw it yesterday.'

'And the house rents?'

'That account was a complete surprise to me. I didn't even know my father owned so many houses. He was rather a secretive man and only told me about financial matters if he felt it absolutely necessary. I learned not to ask.'

'And the third bank account?'

'I'm not at all sure about that. It wasn't a surprise that he had an account for the shop but the amount in it was far more than I'd have expected. Some of it will no doubt have come from legitimate profits on his sales of pledged goods whose loans hadn't been redeemed, though not all of it. And I don't know how to find out any more details.'

'Hmm. I gather your father has an office at home. Can I see it, please?'

She was surprised but didn't quibble. 'Yes, of course. It's at the other end of the house. This way.' When she stood up, all three men did the same, then followed her along the corridor, which made her feel strange.

They'd kept the end room locked and Rufus still had the key in his pocket, so he moved forward to unlock it. He stood back to let her lead the way in, which only added to her nervousness.

'No one except my father came in here till after he died,' she said. 'I certainly didn't.'

'Not even to clean?'

'No. He did any cleaning he considered necessary himself. You can see by the skirting boards that he wasn't thorough.'

'Hmm. An unusually secretive man,' the inspector commented.

They'd left the piles of papers on the second desk and she took the inspector across to them, explaining what was on each pile, then stepping back to stand next to Rufus.

Once again everyone kept silent and let the inspector look through them.

When he'd done that, he said, 'Thank you, Miss Dawson. I wonder if you'd come with me to the bank now and give the manager permission for me to check your accounts? It'll save fussing around with court orders and such. Unless you object to me doing it?'

She felt proud of how calmly she replied when she felt so on edge. 'I have nothing to hide, so I'll come with you and tell him that.'

She was glad that she could walk to the bank with her arm tucked in Rufus's. Just being with him made her feel better, and braver.

She kept reminding herself that she hadn't done anything wrong. And it was true. But that still didn't stop her feeling apprehensive.

The bank manager looked faintly surprised when told who the man was and his expression changed from a smiling welcome to one betraying nothing of his feelings.

When she gave her permission for the inspector to go through the accounts she'd inherited, the manager looked at her sharply, but didn't comment. He found seats in a small waiting room for Abigail and Rufus before taking the two police officers away to his own office.

It seemed a long time before they returned.

'Shall we go back to your house?' the inspector asked. 'I think you'll feel more comfortable if we do our talking there. And I'll feel better about no one being able to overhear what we're saying.'

That last remark worried her. What was going to happen that might make her or anyone else feel uncomfortable?

When she looked sideways at Rufus as they walked along he winked at her but didn't try to chat. Did that mean he thought things were going well? She didn't have the faintest idea.

Once they were seated in the living room the inspector again waved away an offer of refreshments and took charge. 'I'm grateful for your cooperation today, Miss Dawson, and it's quite clear to me that you at least have done nothing wrong.'

Relief flooded through her as she waited for him to continue.

'However, I think your father had been involved in quite a lot of – shall we say dubious transactions. But I would prefer to sort this out informally. I see no value in dragging it through the courts, which would cost a great deal of public money and upset blameless people like you needlessly, as well as warning those connected to these actions that we're getting close to stopping their activities. In any case, though your father is undoubtedly guilty, he's dead and can't be held to account.'

He paused for a moment to let that sink in, then went on, 'So I repeat, let's solve this problem informally. Actually, I like your idea of donating the money you're not certain about to a worthwhile charity. Are you still of the same mind?'

She nodded. 'Yes. I dislike the idea of benefitting from theft.'

'Walter Crossley could manage the money,' Rufus put in. 'He does a lot of good work in the valley.'

'I know of Mr Crossley and he is held in very high esteem by a lot of people in this county, not just here in the valley, so if you gave him . . .' Another pause and then he said, 'Let us say approximately two-thirds of the money from the account in question, then I think the moral side of this matter would be satisfied.'

She let out a shaky breath and he smiled at her. 'Let me repeat: it's clear to me that you have done nothing wrong, Miss Dawson. We don't usually seek this sort of informal solution, but there are circumstances which warrant it this time. We have a continuing struggle against crime, as you will appreciate, and some of it appears to be connected to this case so we need to keep your side of things quiet.'

'I'm sure we can trust Mr Crossley to send an honest accounting of how he uses the money directly to the inspector. Even in my short time here I have heard nothing but good of that gentleman,' the sergeant said quietly.

The three men looked at Abigail as if expecting some comment but she was at a loss about what to say and was grateful when Rufus once again took over.

'My fiancée has been very worried about this whole situation, Inspector, so perhaps I can speak for her and myself now. Both of us very much appreciate your tactful solution, because we do wish to continue living in the valley.'

'Yes. It's kind of you,' she managed, starting to get angry at herself for being so stupidly feeble.

'We'll leave it at that, then. If you have no more questions...?' The inspector raised one eyebrow at her.

She shook her head.

'Then I'll leave the management of this matter in the capable hands of Sergeant McGill and Mr Crossley, and take my leave of you. While I'm here I shall have a quick look round the valley, which I've never visited before. I can already see that the sergeant needs his constable and perhaps a second one eventually, given the distances involved here and the lack of public transport.'

'I'll show them out,' Rufus said.

Both men nodded a farewell to her and followed him out.

When Rufus came back he sat down beside her and put one arm round her shoulders. 'We've been lucky to have that man in charge of this area, I think. Quiet solutions often work best, I've found. Less confident men might have wanted to make an example of this situation to show the world how clever they were.'

'Mmm.' She let herself nestle against his solid warmth. 'I'm sorry for being so weak that you had to take over, Rufus.'

'You've had a series of shocks in the past week and your whole life has been turned upside down. I think you've been very brave about how you've coped with them.'

'Really?'

He laughed softly. 'Yes, really. And before you ask, I'm still happy to be engaged to you.'

She had to smile. 'I wasn't going to ask that again. I believed you last time.'

'Good.'

They sat there quietly for a while then he said, 'We'll go and see Walter Crossley tomorrow, shall we? I think you've coped with enough today. Let's see if Nina would like to join us in a quick walk to the lake.'

Nina was not only delighted to do that but cheered them both up by her exuberance.

'You're doing her good,' he said softly.

'She's doing me good too,' Abigail replied.

21

Terry Catlow had made himself a hiding place in a clump of bushes that overlooked the new building. He could even wriggle across closer to it on his belly without being seen and then watch what was going on.

Just looking down at the busy scene made him feel angry and ready to do anything, anything at all, to stop another Ollerton settling in the valley.

He forgot things sometimes, blaming his poor memory on the poor conditions in which he was living, but he never forgot the need to get rid of *that family*.

After the men working on the walls had finished for the day and headed down towards the town of Ollerthwaite, he walked quietly along the edge of the moors to take a better look at what they'd done that day. He nearly jumped out of his skin as someone yelled at him.

'What the hell are you doing here?'

Terry jerked round, ready to run away, but realised he knew the person and relaxed a little. 'Just taking a look round, Bill lad.'

'Well, don't do that again. I know you and I'm not having you stealing any of the tools or mucking around with what we're doing here. An' just to get it clear, all the others who'll be keeping watch agree with me about it.'

That floored him. He'd believed he still had some allies in the valley. 'You surely don't want to see the Ollertons playing King of the Castle here again? I thought your father had a grudge against that family.'

'He's dead now an' I'm not him. Anyway, this Ollerton is a good man, treats us well, pays on time an' even asks our opinion sometimes. I'm telling you now, his plans are going to be *good* for the valley, not bad. Life goes on an' we have to move with it.'

'Don't be stupid. He's fooling you. Wants to have you slaving away for a pittance for the rest of your life.'

'Fat lot you know about it. He's not fooling me about the money. He pays a decent living wage an' I've earned more each week since he came back to the valley than I had done each month before. My wife's proper set up about it. I've not seen her smile like she does when I hand over my wages each week, not for a long time. So you can take yourself off an' don't come back! You Catlows always did spoil things for the rest of us.'

Terry scowled at him. 'Can't a chap have a look round, even?'

'*You* can't look round here. That's why there are guards being set. Me an' the lads have talked about it an' we've decided we don't want you hanging about any more. Why don't you go an' live somewhere else an' get yourself a proper job instead of stealing things from people who've worked hard for them? If you think people don't know who's behind some of these little thefts, you're not thinking straight.'

'The valley's my home. I don't want to leave it.'

'Well, your wife is telling everyone that she's never having you back to live with her, so you've not got a home here any longer.'

Terry said nothing. He'd deal with his wife later, take her by surprise, teach her a sharp lesson. A lot of women were getting uppity these days, by hell they were. They needed putting in their place. 'Modern women' they called themselves. Lazy bitches he called them. Their job was looking after their husbands and children, and doing what they were told, not lazing around half the day gossiping.

'Get off with you!' Bill yelled suddenly, waving a clenched fist close to his face.

'But—'

'I'll thump you if you don't leave. I mean it.'

He was too big to argue with so Terry turned and slipped away through the bushes, making plenty of noise as if he was leaving. But he stopped about a hundred yards away and an hour or so later he came quietly back again. He was going to set a fire here one night and mess up that fancy brickwork for them, not to mention damaging the wooden beams they were just starting to put across the top storey.

Someone grabbed him by the collar and though he struggled, Bill was a lot stronger than he was and he couldn't shake him off.

'I told you to stay away, Catlow.'

'Ow, don't do that! I'm hungry, Bill. I were just looking for something to eat.'

'We're not stupid enough to leave food lying around here. And this is to remind you not to come back.'

The punch Bill had threatened landed on Terry's jaw and sent him sprawling backwards on the ground. He scrabbled frantically and rolled sideways in case Bill tried to kick him.

'That's just a taste. I'll thump you really hard if I see you round here again, tonight or any other night.'

Terry left, rubbing his jaw. He didn't dare go back again tonight but he would do another time. Surely the other chaps keeping watch wouldn't defend it as fiercely as Bill had?

He circled round and headed towards Eastby End, taking care to move quietly. He knew this part of the valley like the back of his hand and made use of his knowledge to wander about unseen at times.

When he stood outside what had previously been his home, he muttered to himself angrily. The lights were on but the curtains were closed. It looked so cosy and warm. And he was having to live in a damned cave!

Well, madam wife, he thought. Just you wait. I'll show you what's what. He felt in his pocket, fingering the key to the kitchen door. Smiling, he went to find a sack in the shed. Then he stayed in there, sheltered from the wind, till everyone had gone to bed and all the lights had been out for a while.

He turned the key quietly in the lock and slipped silently into the house. There he began to fill his sack with food, shoving aside anything he didn't fancy and taking mainly his favourites, including a big lump of cheese. He took care to lock the back door behind him again.

It felt to be a longer walk than usual back to the cave and the sack seemed to get heavier by the minute. He had to stop and rest part way. By the time he got there, he could only be bothered to eat a slice of bread hacked off the half loaf and with it, a bit of ham cut off the chunk he'd stolen. Then he stuffed the food back in the sack and covered it with rocks to stop animals getting at it.

He'd be all right for food for a few days now, he thought happily as he lay down and wrapped himself in his blanket.

But he wasn't all right in other ways. It was getting colder now and that kept him awake. He should have taken the hearth rug as well, only he'd not have been able to carry it. He'd get it next time. Winter was late starting this year but the nights were beginning to get chilly. How the hell was he going to face the whole winter here? He needed more bedding and a warm fire, and even then the cave would be full of draughts. Only, if he lit a fire, someone would see the smoke and investigate.

Winter or not, he wasn't going away till he'd got rid of Edward Ollerton once and for all. He swore every day that he'd do that, spitting on his promise. Only he'd have to take care that no one saw him do it because he didn't intend to wind up in jail or dangling at the end of a hangman's rope.

Maybe if he stole more blankets he'd be all right at night.

When Nora Catlow got up the following morning and saw the mess in her kitchen, she screeched at the top of her voice. Jezzy came running downstairs, thinking his mother was being attacked, and he too was shocked at what he saw.

'Who did this?' He went to try the handle of the back door and looked at her in shock. 'It's still locked.'

'That'll be because it was your father who did it. He can't even steal things tidily, that one. He must have grabbed what he wanted and left everything else in a mess. Look at the waste.'

'I'll clear it up for you, Mam.'

She looked at him and said slowly and loudly. 'I'd rather do that myself, son, and retrieve what I can, but thank you anyway. What I want you to do for me is grow up into a decent person not a thief. Remember this mess and think of your father living in a cave. It's the sort of thing you might end up doing if you follow his example and live by thieving and cheating folk.'

He went across and risked putting one arm round her bony shoulders. 'I'm not going to be like that, Ma. I'd rather be like my uncle.'

She pulled him closer and hugged him back. 'Eh, look how much taller you are than me these days. You're a good-looking lad, too. *He* were good-looking when he were younger. Fair dazzled me, he did. Please don't be like him.'

'I promise you I won't, Ma. I know now how stupid his way of life is. When you sent me to live with my uncle and I saw how well off he was, I was jealous. Lucky sod, I thought. But it's not luck, is it? It's hard work mostly that does it.'

She nodded and dabbed away a happy tear.

'I saw how well the family ate every single day, and I ate well too once I was living there. At first I couldn't believe it. Then I worked for my uncle and saw him make more money in a month in honest ways than I'd ever seen my father bring home from his thieving and trickery in a year.'

He shook his head slowly at the memory of how surprised he had been. 'After a while, I knew I didn't want to live like my father, and that will never change. Eh, not only did everyone eat well but my uncle's family had happy evenings together most of the time because no one was mad at anyone for doing something bad. I'd never seen anything like it.'

She dabbed at her eyes again. 'I can't tell you how happy it makes me feel to hear you say that, son.'

'But you're not sure it'll last, are you? Well, it will and I'll make you proud of me one day, Ma. See if I don't. The other kids aren't going to bed hungry, or to school hungry either, like I used to.'

'I'm proud of you now, Jezzy. It's not every lad of your age who can see his life that clearly and change how he does things. Actually I'm not just proud, I'm *very proud indeed* of you.' She plonked a kiss on his cheek, a rare occurrence for her.

'Don't clear up the mess,' she added. 'I'll just tidy up a space near the sink. I'm going to make a list of what's missing and report this theft to that new sergeant. I'll show him what the place looked like when I got up. Terry's not getting away with this. He'd steal the last crust from a baby, that one would.'

They worked together to clear up a small space for her to work in and then he set places at the far end of the big kitchen table from the pantry, where nothing had been dumped.

'Shall I let Barney Grieves know you need a new lock putting on the back door, Ma?'

'Yes, please. I'm not giving Terry the chance to do this again. I should have thought of it sooner.'

Since it wasn't yet time for his brothers and sisters to get up, they sat down together for a good hearty breakfast because her husband hadn't taken everything. She'd been hungry so often in her life she always kept a few bits and pieces hidden 'in case'. She chewed slowly then asked suddenly, 'Where do you think your father's hiding?'

'In one of the caves up on Beckshall Edge. He showed them to me once. There's nowhere else near enough to the town.'

'There's that shepherd's shelter on the moors.'

'Too near the track an' it might keep most of the rain off but it won't keep the wind out, will it? It only has three walls and one side is completely open.'

'You're right. He's going to be freezing cold even though he'll be dry in the caves come winter. He might find enough wood to light a fire, but someone will see the smoke and go after him. He's done too much thieving and a lot of folk have lost things to him over the years, especially recently. That new sergeant has given them hope of sorting that out.'

He frowned at her. 'Why did you take against him so fiercely after all these years, Ma?'

'He started thumping me just before he left even though I told him when we married that I'd never, ever put up with that. So I told him to get out of the house. Life's so much calmer now. I used to be worried all the time that he'd get caught, and we didn't always have enough to eat, did we? He isn't even a clever thief, or maybe he's just lazy.'

'Serve him right if he gets caught and put in prison.'

'He's always boasted that they won't catch him and lock him away, that he's too clever for them. Ha!' She gestured towards the mess her husband had left. 'He got away with it when Cliff Nolan was the policeman here because Cliff was old and too lazy to do his job properly. This new fellow isn't like that.'

Jezzy nodded agreement. 'He reminds me of my uncle a bit, the new one does. Got a good sharp brain, you can tell from his eyes somehow.'

'So have you got a good brain when you bother to use it.'

He grinned. 'It's getting used every day now, Ma.'

'Good.' As she pushed her chair back and stood up, the other children came down to join them one by one. She waited till they were all there and told them what had caused the mess, then ordered them to sit close together at the end of the table if they wanted a treat for breakfast.

She made them boiled eggs and 'soldiers', their favourite breakfast. Thank goodness Terry hadn't taken her eggs and had missed the new loaf on the top shelf, where she kept it to stop the kids pinching slices between meals.

There was silence for a while as they dipped their strips of toast into the boiled egg yolks. As she looked round she felt tears well in her eyes. If only she didn't have to worry about Terry, she could have a really good life from now on, what with her occasional lodgers, a cleaning job or two, and Jezzy bringing regular money in.

They were good kids, given half a chance, as Jezzy had proved.

You shouldn't wish for someone to be dead, and she didn't, not exactly. But she did wish she need never see her husband again.

Then she realised the kids would be late for school if she didn't chivvy them along, so she did that and told them she'd be asking the teacher how they were doing regularly from now on. She wanted them to be far better educated than she was, wanted so much more for them in life.

She'd changed as she'd grown older, changed for the better, she now felt. Grown up a lot, she admitted to herself. Better late than never growing up and realising what a waste of time her husband was. Well, not a complete waste. He'd given her some good kids.

She watched Jezzy and smiled. She'd saved him from growing up like his father by sending him to live with his uncle. Now she was going to save the others, every blessed one of the little devils. The next generation of Catlows was going to be very different from their father's one.

22

The Tuesday of the wedding dawned clear and sunny, if rather chilly. After a leisurely breakfast Abigail said shyly, 'I'm going to have a nice hot bath now, if no one needs to use the bathroom, then I'll change into my wedding clothes.'

Rufus nodded. He'd had a bath late last night, using the same bathwater as Nina, bless her. He was taking it easy this morning because he too wanted to look his best for the wedding ceremony. It might only be a simple town hall marriage but he wanted everything to feel as special as possible for Abigail.

His sister had put her new clothes on straight after breakfast and was moving round carefully to keep them clean. He'd seen her go into the hall a couple of times to sneak peeps into the mirror there.

He sat in his shirtsleeves enjoying a final cup of tea while Margie cleaned the living room next door, humming to herself. He still couldn't believe he had a live-in maid but it was a big house and not easy for one woman to keep clean.

When someone knocked on the kitchen door he shouted, 'I'll answer that, Margie.'

He opened it to see a lad holding out a cardboard box containing a bouquet of flowers tied with pale blue ribbons which had long dangling ends, and there were two buttonholes made from roses and sprigs of fern in the box as well, ready to pin on their coats. Who could have sent those?

'Compliments of Mr Crossley.'

'Thank you.'

As the lad turned and walked away, Rufus nudged the door shut with the back of one foot and walked across to set the box on the kitchen table. He stared down at the flowers then lifted one of the buttonholes out to sniff it. These must have been made from some of the last flowering roses of the year. He loved their delicate perfume.

Nina came into the kitchen. 'Who was that? Oh! Flowers.' She went across to stare at the contents of the box. 'Aren't they lovely?'

'Yes. It's going to be a beautiful wedding. And you look pretty in that dress.'

She smiled and smoothed down her skirt with one hand. 'I've never had anything half as nice.'

He stared at the flowers again. He hadn't invited Walter to the wedding and wished now that he had. He'd been trying not to attract too much attention because of the murder. Perhaps he'd been trying to keep things too quiet. He didn't want people to think he was ashamed of his wife-to-be, because he wasn't, far from it. She wasn't like her father any more than he was like his mother.

Before he could do anything else, he heard a vehicle draw up outside this end of the house, so went to the window to see who it was.

The fancy cart that was hired out sometimes by one of the farmers for posher valley wedding parties was standing in the street near their gate. What was it doing here? He hadn't booked it.

It too was decorated with ribbons and as he looked, Edward let down the extra step and got out of the back followed by Lewis, both raising a hand to wave at him. They were followed rather more slowly by Walter Crossley. All three men were wearing similar buttonholes to the ones delivered by the lad.

As Rufus watched, they helped four women out of the cart and then they all came across towards him.

'The ladies are taking charge here now,' Walter announced. 'We men are under strict orders to escort you to the town hall on foot, Rufus lad, and they'll come there in the cart bringing your bride and sister to join you in time for the ceremony.'

Edward's wife Lillian flapped one hand at Rufus. 'Go and put your coat on and take one of those buttonholes. Leave the other for your sister. Then get off to the town hall. We ladies will join you there in time for the wedding.'

She, Maude, Elinor and Flora went into the house, leaving the driver sitting on the bench at the front of the cart grinning broadly. The three men were standing waiting at the gate, so Rufus hurriedly got his coat and waistcoat, and picked up a buttonhole, trying to pin it on quickly.

'Here. Let me do that.' Elinor stopped him at the door, knotted the tie hanging round his neck to make it lie neatly and pinned the little flower arrangement to his lapel. Then she stood back and studied his appearance. 'You look very smart. Now, get off with you.' She turned back into the house and shut the door on him before he'd even started moving.

'Come on, then!' Walter called. 'A nice brisk walk will do you good. Oh, and Riley sends his regards and would have joined us but he'd booked a job for today so can't let them down. He wishes you well.'

Flora looked across the kitchen at the little girl. 'You must be Nina. I'm Flora. How pretty you look. Is that a new dress?'

She nodded vigorously and spun round in a circle to show it off, holding out her skirt.

'That's lovely. Now, we've come to help Abigail get ready. I brought her a hat to borrow that's just right for a bride. How do you like it?'

Nina came across to stand closer to her and study the hat. 'It's beautiful.'

Next to them Lillian shook out a rather elegant coat that she'd been carrying over one arm. 'We thought this would look good on the bride. It goes well with the hat. It's the tradition for a bride to wear something borrowed, you know. And I see that the flowers arrived safely, so she'll have her bridal bouquet too.'

Nina smiled shyly. 'She's just finishing getting ready.'

'Good. You're the bridesmaid, aren't you? So this buttonhole is for you. Shall I help you pin it to your lapel?'

She looked surprised. 'It's not that sort of wedding. They aren't having bridesmaids or fuss. Isn't the buttonhole for Abigail?'

'No. They weren't having a bridesmaid when this wedding was first planned, but we've changed the arrangements and they are now, which is you. The bride will have this bouquet to hold so you get the flowers to wear, just like the rest of us.'

That made Nina beam at the ladies again.

Flora held the bouquet out to the child. 'Just smell that. There's something wonderful about late roses and their fragrance.'

'It smells lovely.' She let the ladies pin the flower to her coat then went into the hall to stare solemnly at herself in the mirror again.

The ladies exchanged smiles and nudges as they watched her, but she didn't notice that, was too intent on peering at herself in the mirror, twisting from side to side.

Shortly afterwards footsteps came down the stairs and Abigail joined them, wearing her best clothes and holding a hat in her hand.

'I think I left my hatpins down here when I took my hat off yesterday, Nina, and—' She broke off as it sank in that several ladies were standing in the kitchen as well as Nina and all of them were smiling at her.

Elinor moved forward and twitched the hat Abigail was holding out of her hand. She put it on the sideboard, gesturing to Flora, who was holding out the much more elaborate wide-brimmed hat that was trimmed with tulle and delicate artificial roses.

'This one will be much more suitable for a wedding, don't you think?' Flora asked.

'It'll go nicely with the coat I'm lending you as well,' Lillian added. 'But first let Maude do your hair at the back in a more flattering style. She's really good with hair.'

'But I—'

'Shh.' Maude pushed the bride down on a chair and set to work on her hair, pulling out the pins holding the low bun in place before Abigail could protest and letting the shining mass tumble over the bride's shoulders. She deftly coiled the hair into a more flattering style, higher up her head, inserting hairpins in strategic places to hold it firm. After that she carefully set the other hat in place, threaded in a hatpin and stepped back.

'There you are. That's more like it. Take a look at yourself in the mirror. You should always do your hair like that.'

Abigail went into the hall to stare at herself, smiling at what she saw.

'You look lovely,' Nina told her from the doorway.

'Just as a bride should look,' Flora said.

Margie, who had been peeping in from the scullery doorway smiled and nodded across at Abigail. 'You look really pretty, miss. And this is the last time I'll be calling you miss.'

'Your maid is in on the secret and Margie and a friend will be keeping an eye on the house for the rest of the afternoon,' Elinor said.

'That's why she was so insistent I save my bath till just before we got ready to leave for the town hall. Thank you, Margie.' She glanced at the clock. 'We'd better leave now, hadn't we? I don't want to be late.'

'We won't be late. We have the special wedding cart outside waiting to drive us ladies to the town hall in style. The men will be waiting for us there by now.'

'Thank you,' Abigail said as they all walked outside. 'This is so kind of you.' She blinked her eyes furiously, shook out her handkerchief and blew her nose quickly, then took a deep breath and got up on the wedding cart.

It seemed part of the magic of the day that a woman passing by stopped to call out best wishes and the remaining clouds slid away, leaving the sun to shine more brightly on them all.

She'd never had such a pretty outfit to wear nor friends to help her, either. Once she and Rufus had sorted out the money situation she was going to buy some nicer clothes, if she could afford it. And she'd definitely do her hair this way from now on.

Well, she would if Rufus liked it. Her father had always told her to 'dress modestly' and not 'flaunt' herself. But she didn't want to dress like a dowdy old woman now, she wanted to make the most of her appearance so that her husband would be proud of her.

As she sat in the wedding cart, she felt Nina slip one hand into hers. The child let out such a happy sounding sigh that Abigail smiled down at her, whispering, 'You look very pretty in those new clothes.'

The other women beamed at her from the bench on the opposite side of the cart, so she smiled back at them as well.

She had never expected to feel like a real bride, but she did now. And she thought that, for once, she really did look quite pretty.

As their party waited in the outer room at the registry office for the previous marriage ceremony to conclude in the inner room, Edward glanced at a noticeboard to one side of the door.

The list of coming marriages was pinned up for the public to see, as was required by law, and to his surprise he saw Walter and Flora's names there. He tried to hide his reaction, but Walter saw where he was looking and grinned.

'Congratulations, Walter,' he whispered.

'You and Elinor have started a new fashion,' Walter whispered back. 'But we're not doing it in as much of a hurry as you two. Flora wants a new dress made and a fancy cake, and you name it. And I want a big party afterwards, to which you are all invited.'

Then the previous couple came out of the inner room, smiling rather bashfully as so many people stared at them.

Once they'd left, the registrar called, 'Shorrocks and Dawson,' and their group filed into the inner room.

Rufus caught hold of Abigail's hand and kept hold of it as they led the way in and stood at the front where the registrar was pointing.

While everyone else was seated and making themselves comfortable, three women dressed in everyday clothes and wearing headscarves filed in and took seats in the back row. He knew that by law there had to be an open ceremony where anyone who wanted to attend was allowed in as well as the wedding party, but he wished these strangers hadn't come because he didn't think Abigail would like being stared at.

Then she leaned towards him and said in a soft voice, 'Isn't it nice that people want to watch marriages take place? It makes me feel even more special today.'

So these minor worries slipped away. It hadn't upset her. Indeed, she seemed almost luminous with happiness at the moment. Rufus hadn't realised quite how pretty she could look.

Then the registrar whispered to them to pay attention and the brief wedding ceremony began.

Rufus repeated the words the registrar intoned slowly, looking at his bride as he made these important promises. He was hoping she realised that he really was happy to do this.

She must have done because for once her shyness seemed to have vanished and she smiled warmly back at him when their eyes met.

After they had been pronounced man and wife, he kissed her on the lips, not the cheek, and nice soft lips they were, too. Then he offered her his arm and they led the way out. The three old ladies in the back row called out good wishes for the couple's future happiness as they passed.

When the wedding party made their way outside to the front of the building they found that the sun was still shining brightly.

'Even the weather is doing its best for us today, Mrs Shorrocks,' Rufus said, holding his wife's hand.

'This is the best day of my whole life,' she answered quietly, then added, 'Mr Shorrocks.'

'So far. We'll do better for you than this before we're through if I have my way.'

'What a lovely thing to say.'

Then Nina was tugging at their hands and keeping hold of Abigail's. 'You really are my sister now. Isn't that lovely?'

'Very lovely indeed, Miss Shorrocks.'

'I agree, Mrs Shorrocks.' When the child giggled at that and repeated the new name, everyone smiled.

A photographer appeared from the side of the building and stopped at the front, accompanied by a lad carrying a stand for the camera. 'Sorry I'm late!' he called out. Then he started chivvying them into place, first the bride and groom, then various small groups, and taking photographs.

The only people surprised by his appearance were the bride and groom.

Who had ordered this? Rufus was annoyed at himself for not thinking of photographs. Of course they'd want to remember this special day.

Fortunately Edward came out of the town hall bringing the completed documentation from the marriage ceremony, which he'd offered to collect, in time to be included in the photos.

When the photographer said thank you and started packing up his things, the wedding cart moved forward to collect them and everyone squeezed into it, with Nina sitting on her brother's knee.

To the newly-weds' surprise it took them up the hill towards Walter's farm not back to their own home.

'We can't let a wedding go without a party,' Walter told them. 'Come in, all of you.'

What looked like an absolute feast was laid out on the kitchen table, covered by a couple of clean tablecloths which Lillian and Maude quickly pulled off.

Walter came in to join them and they heard the sound of the cart driving away.

'One of the lads will drive you three home in our cart later,' he said. 'Now, let's enjoy this lovely meal that Elinor and Maude have prepared for us. Then we'll drink the health of the bride and groom in cider.'

When the newly-weds and Nina at last got back to their own home, Margie was nowhere to be seen, but the two single beds had been moved from Abigail's bedroom and a double bed had been moved into the room and made up with one corner of a sheet turned back temptingly.

Abigail walked Nina to her new bedroom and offered to help her get out of her clothes but the girl smiled and said, 'I can do it myself, thank you.'

There was a large new doll sitting on the bed waiting for her. It was a splendid creature and though she'd considered herself too old for dolls when she turned ten, she couldn't help picking it up and cradling it in her arms. Then she sat it on one rear corner of the desk that she'd chosen to have in her new bedroom and looked round in great satisfaction.

It felt absolutely wonderful to have a well-furnished bedroom all to herself for the first time in her life.

Leaving Nina to see to her own needs, Abigail walked back along the upper corridor to her bedroom, feeling rather nervous now. She'd heard or read all sorts of tales about wedding nights, but surely Rufus wouldn't be rough with her? And surely it wouldn't be too painful?

She hesitated in the doorway, then took a deep breath and stepped inside.

He was waiting for her and came across to take her in his arms gently, as if to prove that she was right and he wasn't going to hurt her.

'We don't have to rush anything, Abigail. We can wait to consummate our marriage until you're more used to me, if you'd rather.'

'I'd rather get it over with.'

He looked astonished. 'Get it over with? What on earth have people been telling you to make you think it'll be an unpleasant experience?'

She could feel herself blushing and didn't know what to say.

He pulled her gently back into his arms and kissed her cheek. 'Abigail, making love is usually a very pleasant experience. Shall I show you?'

For two of the years he'd been away from Ollerthwaite, he'd had a happy association with a very generous lady whose husband had died and she'd shown him how to make a woman happy in bed.

Thank you, Reba! he thought.

Abigail watched him step back a little. He didn't do anything else after asking her permission to take her to bed, simply waited for her to reply. For some reason that made her feel better, so she nodded and only then did he blow out the oil lamp and take her into his arms again.

After that the world faded and with it her worries. There were just the two of them and the wonderful kisses made her feel he did care about her.

By the time she realised that he'd undressed her, she was lost in these new sensations, lost in the pleasure of being held close and cherished in such delightful ways.

Afterwards he didn't move away, but pulled her gently into his arms and lay there quietly, cuddling her close.

'Was that very bad, Mrs Shorrocks?' he teased as he reached down to pull the covers up over them properly.

'Dreadful. But I was brave.'

'So you'll put up with it again?'

'I'll be happy to.' And feeling very daring she drew his head closer and took the initiative, kissing him on the lips.

'We both need practice at doing it together.' He returned her kiss, then let out a soft laugh. 'But I think you need sleep more than anything else at the moment and so do I.'

'Mmm.' She nestled against him.

He sighed happily. Some women didn't enjoy making love, he'd been told. But his new wife had been surprisingly responsive. Perhaps that was because it was love he was offering her, not merely a physical encounter. He blinked in shock at that thought and lay staring into the darkness as it sank in that it really was love. It hadn't taken him long to start to care about her. She was so gentle and yet brave, and she'd been kind to his sister as well.

How did she feel about him? She must have had to guard her real feelings for many years, poor lass. He hoped she wouldn't try to guard them from him.

23

Dan Makersby turned up unannounced in Ollerthwaite on the Friday of the same week. He asked directions to Rufus Shorrocks' address from the porter at the station and found his way there easily, surprised at how big a house it was.

When Rufus opened the door, he gaped to see his friend standing there with a battered suitcase in his hand. 'Dan! I can't believe you're here already.'

'I got a letter from your Mr Ollerton, saying you'd suggested me for a job with him. It arrived the day after I'd been fired by that sod of a foreman, so couldn't have been better timed. I was going to go and look for work in the Midlands but his letter, which was nice and polite, decided me to come here first and see what was on offer. If I don't fancy the job, or the employer, I'll have to carry on southwards and see what I can find elsewhere. My wife will be safe with her mother.'

'Well, I'm glad you've chosen to visit us first. And what am I doing keeping you standing on the doorstep? Come in, lad! Cup of tea and a sandwich?'

Dan put the suitcase down and grinned at his old friend. 'Do I look hungry?'

'Yes. And I heard your stomach rumbling.'

'I've been economising a bit on food lately, I must admit.'

'I've had to do that a time or two.' Mainly because he'd never let himself dip into his savings. 'But we've plenty of food to spare so you're welcome to a meal or two. Let's get you a jam buttie to put you on.' He didn't wait for an answer but quickly cut a thick slice of bread and slathered it with butter then jam.

In between mouthfuls and sighs of pleasure, Dan said, 'It's nice to see you again but to be honest, the most important thing of all to me is the possibility of a job. What sort of job is it? How much does it pay?'

'Didn't Edward give you any hints as to what he wanted or was offering in wages?'

'Just that he wanted someone with expertise in underground work and that he'd pay my expenses to come and talk to him about it.'

'Then let me tell you about Edward and what he's doing here, as well as the sort of job it is. Oh, and to set your mind at ease, we can offer you a bed for as many nights as you need so you've plenty of time to check out what's going on in the valley. You'll have to excuse everything being in a mess in this house, though. We got married on Tuesday, you see, and I've only just moved in. The house needs a lot of sorting out because half of it has been unused for years.'

Dan gaped at him. 'I never expected to hear that you'd got wed. You've held out against marriage for years. What changed your mind and who did you marry?'

Rufus glanced towards the door, not wanting to explain while Abigail was within earshot in case she misconstrued what he said. He was moving along very slowly and carefully with her, and guessed it would take time for her to learn to completely trust him. Or anyone.

'I'll explain in more detail another time, but I'm very happy about my new wife and situation. This is Abigail's house and it needs a lot of renovation, not to mention modernising, so I've started work on it.'

'I'll help out where I can while I'm here.'

'Thanks but getting you a job is the most important thing, so let me tell you about the situation.' He explained briefly

about Edward's return to Ollindale and the big new house
that was being built. As he was finishing his summary, Abigail
came in and he introduced her to his friend.

'You'll stay with us, won't you, Mr Makersby?' she offered
at once.

Rufus grinned and winked at his friend.

'Please call me Dan. And yes, I'd be grateful for a bed, if it's
not too much trouble.'

She looked at him, seeming to sense the anxiety about a job
that was behind his polite responses, then turned to her husband. 'Why don't you take Dan to meet Edward and Lewis
straight away? There are still a couple of hours of daylight left
for him to see the building work.'

Rufus smiled at her. 'Great minds! I was about to suggest
that. Come on, Dan. Leave your case in the corner. We can
walk up to the Ollerton estate from here.'

'I'll get a bedroom ready,' she called after them.

'Thanks, love.'

'Your new wife has a lovely smile,' Dan said as they set off
up the hill. 'You can tell a lot about people from their smiles.'

'Yes. She's had a difficult life. No shortage of money but a
big shortage of kindness and affection.'

'I can tell you're fond of her.'

'Yes. Very. And she's good with my little sister too. Not so
little these days. Nina's up to my shoulder and growing fast.'

As they walked out of the town and up the hill Dan breathed
in deeply. 'Lovely fresh air here.'

'I think so too. No big mill chimneys pouring out filthy
smoke.'

At the crossroads, he stopped and pointed to the left. 'We
go that way and this is where the Ollerton estate starts. The
first house is the former lodge. The architect is currently living there because he's also supervising the building work.
The roof you can see further along belongs to what used to

be the agent's house, and that's where Edward and his wife are living for the time being – they've only been married for a few months, by the way, so no children yet.'

'Nice outlook they must have, right down the valley.'

'Yes. And as you can see, up the slope from the lodge is the start of the building work. The new house will one day have an even better view. They're getting on well with the walls but they need to sort out the cellars before they can put on the roof beams and close up the building, which is why they need someone with experience of underground work.'

He explained briefly about the two sets of cellars and by that time they'd reached the agent's house. When he looked beyond it he saw Edward and Lewis standing near the ruins deep in discussion, pointing here and there, then looking down at a big piece of paper to study what appeared to be plans.

'There they are! Edward's the taller one. Let's go and join them.'

As they walked across, the two men noticed them and stopped chatting to smile.

'What brings you up here at this time of day, Rufus?' Edward asked.

'This is my friend Dan. He got your letter and set off straight away. He's interested in the job you wrote about.'

Dan shook hands and said, 'Just so that everything is clear from the start, I got sacked two days ago for refusing to do a job at the mine in a highly dangerous passage that needed much better reinforcing put in. I'd also told the other chaps working there how dangerous it would be to go down there, which upset the foreman even more. I'll not even consider taking any job where the work isn't done carefully. I've seen several good men killed or maimed in mines over the years, you see.'

He was obviously still upset by the recent incident, Rufus thought, or he'd not have blurted it out like that.

Edward gave him a sympathetic look. 'I'm glad you told us why you left. I feel the same way about the people who work for me. I want them to stay as safe as possible and I want to end up with a sturdy building to house my family and their servants for many years to come – and that includes the cellars there being safe too.'

He frowned and added, 'There have been a couple of cave-ins underground here in the past and I don't want that to happen again, so I need to find out why it happened and perhaps do some work to prevent another occurrence.'

Lewis joined in. 'It's too late today to do anything but we could show you round first thing tomorrow. There are two lots of cellars to look at, the ones belonging to the newer house which got burned, and those that belonged to the old house which was demolished decades ago. After that we can discuss what will need doing to reconnect the cellars in a safe way.'

'I'd be happy to look into that, Mr Brody. It sounds to be an interesting problem.'

'Yes, but I'd rather not have a problem at all and we're hoping you'll be able to help us find a long-term solution.'

They chatted for a little while longer then Edward said suddenly, 'Dan, you're looking utterly exhausted and here we are nattering on at you. How about you go back with Rufus and rest? We'll see you tomorrow morning and take you underground.'

'Thank you, sir. I shall look forward to that.'

As he and Rufus walked back down the hill, Dan said, 'Well, that's a good start. A potential employer who speaks politely and who actually noticed how tired I was. I like the looks of those two. Unless they're the best actors and liars in the county, they're a decent pair of gentlemen.'

'They're decent, believe me. They've never lied to me and actually, I consider them my friends now. We're on first-name terms, at their suggestion.'

'That's unusual, though in a good way.' A yawn suddenly overtook Dan and he slowed down for a moment, giving in to it and wriggling his shoulders about. 'Eh, Mr Ollerton's right. I'm exhausted. I hardly slept at all last night for worrying and it's been a long day.'

'Well, we'll give you a proper meal then you can go straight to bed if you like.'

Before they went into the house, Dan thrust his right hand out and said in a gruff voice, 'Thanks, lad.'

'My pleasure.'

The two men stayed clasping one another's hands for a few more seconds before going in to join Abigail.

She greeted them with a smile. 'There's a stew simmering on the stove so I can serve a meal straight away. Our maid usually eats with us but Margie has already had hers and gone to bed. She said she was tired, but I think she was being tactful and leaving us alone.'

Dan ate heartily but went straight up to bed afterwards.

'Your friend seems nice,' Abigail said when they were alone.

'He's a good bloke and clever with it.'

'Like you, then, Rufus.'

He smiled and gave her a quick hug. 'I wouldn't mind going to bed early, either.'

She blushed but didn't seem upset at the prospect.

The following morning Dan woke early and got up as soon as it started to get light. Since his host wasn't up yet, Margie made him a quick breakfast and he was up at the building site by eight o'clock. The bosses weren't there yet so he had a good look round on his own and then chatted to the various workmen as they started to arrive, explaining that he'd come about a job.

They all looked calm and friendly to him, and were sorting out tools and materials for their current tasks without anyone ordering them around or hassling them, another sign of good employers, he felt.

He turned as he heard a door bang shut in the distance and saw Lewis walk rapidly up the slope towards the new building. He stopped on the way to answer a question from one man and then gesticulated to an older man to show how he wanted something done.

By that time, Edward had come out of the agent's house and walked across. 'Good morning, everyone. Looks like being a fine day. Glad to see you, Dan. I think everyone knows what they're doing today and Charlie can keep an eye on them.'

The older man nodded and turned to speak to a lad standing next to him.

Edward swung round to speak to Dan. 'I thought Lewis and I could start by showing you the two cellars. This way.'

As they walked up the slope, he said, 'Once we've been round them, we can discuss what might be done to make things safer and how best to do it.'

Lewis put in, 'You were honest with us yesterday and I'm going to be honest with you today about my own experience, Dan. I'm well aware that though I know about working underground in theory, in practice I've never taken charge of any projects remotely like this one. So I'll understand what you say but probably not have a good idea of the details of what it will entail.'

Dan was surprised at this frankness but it made him feel happier to have his own expertise recognised before they even started, no doubt thanks to his friend Rufus. 'Lead on, sir. I'm looking forward to seeing what's left down below.'

They were soon standing above the cellar, which had once been under the earliest old house and was now surrounded by the workings of what would be the new house. 'When the original house was demolished the stones were re-used on the second house. Since the fire destroyed that, some of the stones have been taken away and have no doubt been used here and there on other buildings in the valley. We've sited the new building above the first cellar in the expectation that it'll save us the job of digging out new ones but the house is also there to take advantage of the best views.'

He turned to Lewis. 'Shall I go down and leave you standing guard at the top?'

His friend shook his head. 'I'll do it this time.' He turned to Dan and explained, 'I don't like going underground but I can tolerate it when necessary. However, we always leave someone at the top next to the entrance in case there's a problem. I'll go down first. Oh, and call me Lewis. I don't stand on my dignity with a friend of Rufus.'

'And I'm Edward.'

The two of them saying that surprised and pleased Dan, especially after the brusque way he'd been ordered around in his last job as if he were an idiotic child.

When he joined Lewis below, Dan stood for a moment at the foot of the ladder, holding up his lantern and looking round the underground space, which was larger than he'd expected with stone pillars here and there to prop up the roof, and rows of shelves on parts of the walls. It must have been created two or three hundred years ago, when they did all their own preserving and there were no tins and jars of food available in the shops or elsewhere.

He looked across and saw that Lewis was now standing holding up his lantern at the entrance to a passage that led off the far side of the space, waiting patiently for him.

When he went across Dan saw that the passage had been completely blocked part of the way along, by a cave-in, and he looked up hastily to check the ceiling. No, that looked perfectly sound. So what had made the far end collapse and block that part of the passage? Something about the way it looked made him think this had happened quite a long time ago.

Just before they got to the sloping pile of rubble, Lewis led the way into a side cellar and showed him that this too had had a cave-in, presumably at the same time as the one in the passage.

'We don't know what caused this whole area to collapse,' Lewis said.

'Could you wait in the big cellar and give me a few minutes to give it a quick check. All right if I use that shovel I saw in the big cellar to poke about a bit?'

'Fine as long as you don't poke too hard and bring it down on us.' Lewis moved away, not trying to hide his uneasiness.

Dan thought that if it had collapsed so long ago and been unstable it would have crumbled further by now, but it hadn't. He checked the main passage and side chamber carefully just to be as sure as you could with a quick inspection, then went back to join Lewis, frowning.

'I think the cave-ins were caused deliberately, Mr B— I mean, Lewis. Apart from where the falls were, the walls and ceiling nearby seem sturdy and stable to me. However, I'd not try to clear it without propping up the open part of the passage very carefully indeed and the area of roof nearby in the side room as well, just to be sure. We don't know how much they damaged the walls and ceiling to get the rest to cave in like that.'

'We did wonder if it had been done on purpose. Some strange things have happened round here in the past two or three decades. What we'd like to know now is whether you think you can make the cellar safe to use from now on?'

'Yes. Given good props, mind. I won't try to work with rubbish pieces of wood like they gave us at my last job. And I'll need a couple of strong chaps to help me.'

Lewis seemed surprised. 'Have you had to do that sort of thing before?'

'Aye. More than once. Rufus has too. Some folk economise too much on quality of materials and then it's not as safe down below as it could be. There's no such thing as perfectly safe, of course.' He let that sink in then added, 'I'll just have another little look round, if you don't mind.'

After he'd poked at the walls of the main cellar and muttered to himself, he came back across and said, 'Could you show me the other cellar now, please? I'd like to see the other side of this cave-in.'

They climbed the ladder and Dan heard Lewis let out a huge breath of relief at being in the open air again.

When he glanced sideways he saw how carefully Edward was watching his friend. These were people who cared about others. That, and what Rufus had said, reassured him that it would be all right to work here.

24

Lewis led the way up the slope and showed Dan the two entrances to the upper set of cellars. The second entrance, presumably added later, had been hidden at the side of the flat piece of land.

As they walked along, Edward said in a low voice, 'Are you sure you're all right to go down again, Lewis?'

Dan tried to pretend he couldn't hear what they were saying, even though he had excellent hearing.

'Yes, I'm all right,' Lewis said. 'It doesn't feel as bad when I have someone with me who clearly has considerable expertise. I trust Dan like I trusted Rufus. You should see the careful way he checks everything. And when he explains, he's so clear and succinct it becomes obvious, even to someone not used to that sort of analysis, what's needed. And then you're even more certain he knows what he's doing.'

'I'm glad to hear that.'

Lewis turned to include Dan as well. 'We'll go into the hidden older cellar first, I think.'

'You're sure you want to do this?' Dan asked him directly.

'Yes. I find it unpleasant, as you must have noticed, but I feel safe with you.'

That compliment pleased Dan, but for all Lewis's brave words, when they went down the ladder he noticed the other man take a deep breath, as if bracing himself. And when Lewis insisted on leading the way and being the first to crawl into the very low passage at the side, Dan wasn't sure whether to consider that an act of bravery or stupidity, given his inexperience underground.

He'd seen miners who felt a similar discomfort when underground carry on going down day after day and pretend they were fine with it. You did what you had to in order to feed your family. He didn't think this man needed to worry about that, though.

The low passage, which they crawled along on hands and knees, led them into a huge, high-ceilinged cellar. When he looked round Dan saw that it had been built out from what looked like a natural rocky cave. It was a strange formation, unlike any he'd seen before, but then nature did unexpected things at times.

The next space led off the main area and was, he thought, a fully excavated normal cellar. He was surprised when Lewis showed him some furniture had been carefully covered and wrapped, then stored there a long time ago.

'We have no way of working out how many decades it's been here, but several for sure,' Lewis said. 'Good thing the place isn't damp, eh, however well it's wrapped?'

They went back up to the surface and then down into the nearby main cellars, which had previously been directly under the house that had been burned down, so he guessed the cellar made from the cave had been a secret or hidden place originally, perhaps a place to store valuables. If you were lucky enough to have some.

He smiled at that thought. This remote valley didn't look to him like a part of the country where people got rich. He'd never even heard of the place till his friend Rufus moved here.

The second set of cellars were straightforward, nothing special about them that he could see, though he wondered whether there was a faint odour of burning.

Lewis confirmed that. 'The house fire was deliberate, set by the people who bought the house from Edward's family due to his ancestor's gambling debts and then didn't like living here. They got a large payout from their house insurance, but had trouble selling the estate afterwards without a building on it.'

He gave a grim smile. 'It served them right that they had to let it go very cheaply in the end. Edward was the only one to offer to buy it and that was several years after the fire, so he at least benefitted from their wicked act by getting his family estate back more cheaply.'

They went out of the main space of this set of cellars into a sort of hallway but he couldn't open the door, only move it two or three inches.

'This leads into the remains of the house,' Lewis told him. 'We managed to check it from the other side by hanging a piece of cloth over the top of the door so you could tell where it was. Someone has put huge rocks on the other side of the door. We guessed they did it before the fire because though there is some charring to one of the top corners of the door, it's still intact.'

'Eh, to think of them doing all that! They must have been real villains.'

'Yes. Planning to steal things and take them away later, I'd guess, only they never got back here to profit from their thieving.'

He smiled at Dan. 'I'm going to recommend employing you because it stands out a mile that you know what you're doing underground, so I'd better tell you that we have a present day villain hiding nearby who'd be happy to burn down the new building we're erecting and who's tried a couple of times already to kill Edward. If that makes you think again about taking the job, better that we find out now.'

Dan gaped at him. 'Why would anyone want to kill Edward? He seems a decent chap to me.'

'This man, whose name is Terry Catlow, is a layabout – no, worse than that. He's an out and out villain who bears a grudge against the Ollerton family because of something one of them did many years ago to a member of his family. We don't even know the actual details.'

'And he's still holding a grudge? He must be mad.'

'Yes. That's what I reckon. He seems to be losing his wits, as some people do when they get older. If he ever had any wits in the first place. He's always lived by thieving and cheating, and has tried to teach his children to do the same. His wife recently threw him out of the family home, which says something.'

He waited a few moments then prompted, 'So, are you still interested in the job?'

'Yes, I am. But it's better that you told me about this chap, so that I can watch out for him.'

He held out his hand and the two men shook. 'I'm glad to hear that. I think we'll work well together.'

When they rejoined Edward, Lewis said simply, 'I've already offered Dan the job. From the way he talks, he's very much like Rufus with a range of skills. That'll be useful in other ways too as the house goes up.'

Dan was amazed at this praise, even more amazed when Edward nodded to his friend then turned to ask, 'Will you come and work for us, then, Dan?'

He didn't hesitate. 'I'd like to very much, sir, but there's just one thing I need to sort out. I have a pregnant wife and we'll need somewhere to live. There are still several months to go before the baby is due. Are there any houses for rent round here?'

'A friend of mine has a cottage that's empty. It's weatherproof but old-fashioned and it needs work doing on it. I can show it to you if you like. It's on the far side of the lake on the outskirts of the town, so you'd have a bit further to come to work each day. Might be worth your while to get a second-hand bicycle. We've a chap in town who sells them.'

Dan grinned. 'I've got one already.'

'If the cottage suits, I'll pay the rent for the first three months as long as you'll make any small repairs necessary.'

'And my wage? You haven't said what you're paying.'

'Haven't I? Sorry.'

The sum Edward named made Dan feel even happier, because it was half as much again as he'd been earning recently. 'Thank you. That's very acceptable. I'll give you good value for your money, I promise. Could I see the cottage now, do you think? I don't want my Polly to live in conditions that are too primitive and she'll be eager to hear what it's like.'

'It's not bad enough to call "primitive", but we can go and look at it straight away, if you like. I can call in at Walter's farm on our way and get the key from him.'

As they walked down the slope past the men working on the partly finished walls, Edward stopped for a moment to smile at what would one day be his home. 'I can't wait to have it finished and move in.'

'It'll be a few months yet, at best,' Lewis warned him. 'Perhaps even a year.'

'I know. But one day it'll happen.'

They stopped at the far side of the crossroads and Edward went round to the back of the big farmhouse nearby. He returned brandishing a key and they set off again, this time continuing along the track instead of turning right and going down the hill.

Lewis looked sideways at his friend. 'By the way, I've told Dan here about Catlow.'

'I suppose you had to, but I can look after myself now I know about him.'

'Not if you're taken by surprise. Lillian's told me how he threw a stone and knocked you out once and if she hadn't turned up, he'd have killed you then.'

Dan said nothing. This was clearly an ongoing disagreement between the two men, not because they were at odds, but because they were good friends and cared about one another.

After a few hundred yards they had to go round the top end of the lake, which meant walking across rough ground on an ill-defined path, which twisted this way and that to avoid shrubs of various types and sizes.

'This is the part that hasn't been cleared yet,' Edward said. 'It will be, I'm sure, because Walter is absolutely determined to finish the walk round the lake before Her Majesty's Diamond Jubilee. He'd have done it for the Golden Jubilee, but the Russian flu stopped work and then kept returning so that people were wary of getting together to do unnecessary or voluntary jobs.'

Dan nodded. 'I remember that. I was just a young chap then.'

When they reached a shabby cottage with the remains of an overgrown garden at the front, Edward unlocked the door and led the way inside. As he had said, the roof seemed to be water-proof, because there were no stains on ceilings or in corners, but the main problem was that the cottage was old-fashioned. It had an outdoor lavatory and a rather stained slopstone in the scullery instead of a modern white sink, not to mention dingy walls throughout the whole house that were in need of whitewashing.

They went outside and walked round the back looking up at the roof.

'The roof definitely looks weatherproof to me,' Dan said, 'which is the main thing. I'm sure I'll be able to make the interior lighter and more comfortable. But it'd be better if we could get connected to gas and there was a bathroom.' He sighed and muttered, 'Still, beggars can't be choosers. It'd be a start.'

'Walter usually sees to putting in proper bathrooms and modernising the cottages he owns once he has a tenant, so I can't see why he'd treat yours differently. He says it's no use doing that when it's empty, as some were for years during the period when more people left the valley than came here to work. In the meantime, I'll have a load of wood delivered for the kitchen range.'

'Thank you.'

'If there's anything you need to do maintenance work on, the materials will either be provided or you'll be recompensed for what it costs you. But check with me before you make any big changes and I'll discuss them with Walter. I'll ask him about getting a bathroom, too.

Dan smiled at his words. 'That'd be grand.' Even old-fashioned as it was, the cottage was better than the single bedroom he and Polly were presently sharing in her mother's house, with their bits and pieces of furniture stored in a friend's garden shed.

After they'd looked round the cottage, Edward stopped at the gate and gestured towards a large structure on the far side of the small field that bordered the cottage. 'I hadn't really noticed that barn before. Is it my imagination, or does it look unused?'

'It does. In fact it looks as if it hasn't been used for a year or two. There's not even a well-defined track leading to those big double doors. This is certainly not a thriving farm,' Lewis said thoughtfully.

Dan wasn't interested in the farm but in how quickly he could move here and start work. 'I'll go home tomorrow and pack up our things. Polly will be relieved. She's desperate to settle somewhere well before she has the baby. We'll be able to send the furniture and boxes here by rail. We, er, don't have a lot because we had to move out of our old house a few weeks ago.'

He looked expectantly towards his new employer, waiting for him to lead the way, but Edward didn't move on and still had a thoughtful expression as he stared across the field.

'I must ask Walter about that barn,' he said slowly. 'It might be just the thing.'

For what? Dan wondered but didn't ask, being more interested in considering the practicalities of making the move to a place of his own again.

They said goodbye to Dan at Crossways Farm and stood watching him stride down the hill towards the town.

'He'll be good at that job,' Lewis said. 'He seems to me to have a real feel for the underground spaces and he looks strong, too. Which never hurts in such jobs.'

Walter came out of the farm to join them. 'Did he take the cottage?'

Edward nodded. 'Yes. I'll pay the rent at first and he'll make some minor repairs to the house, if that's all right with you.'

'It's particularly all right because that's my last unoccupied cottage, which is a nice change from twenty years ago, when there were quite a few of them and the valley seemed to be dying. I bought most of them for practically nothing. I'd better arrange to have a bathroom put in, as I've done with the other cottages. It was no use doing that till I had tenants. Tell your man he can move in whenever he wants, but it'll be chaos for a while with the plumbing changes.'

'He's eager to get here, so I think he'll put up with the conditions.'

Walter beamed at him. 'At this rate we'll have to build some more houses in the valley. Now, wouldn't that be good, more people coming here to live and perhaps new jobs or businesses created?'

'It'd be excellent. Um, there's something else I want to ask you about, Walter. I noticed a barn in the next field, quite a big one, but there's no sign of activity at the nearby farm and the barn looks neglected. Does it belong to them?'

He looked sad. 'Yes, and you're right. It isn't being used at the moment. Hale Farm has belonged to the Halliwell family for several generations but the last owner, Geoff Halliwell, died suddenly a couple of years ago and they only had the one daughter so there's no son to take over. His widow is still living there, though she's withdrawn into herself since losing her husband. Her daughter moved back in with her a few months ago because her husband died too. He was only thirty and had a seizure out of the blue and that was it. This has been a desperately sad year for them both and I sincerely hope nothing else bad happens. Only time will help them recover.'

He sighed, then continued as if feeling a need to finish the story. 'The two women can't farm it on their own because Rhona has never done outdoor work and isn't physically strong enough to do half the tasks. And poor Gwenda is expecting. She's got a few months to go yet, I think. Eh, her husband didn't even know about the baby when he dropped dead. Rhona sold the stock and the two women are just ticking along quietly, waiting for the birth and then I should think they may have to sell the farm. Sad, isn't it?'

'Very sad. Maybe I can help them out a bit financially by renting the barn. What's it like inside, do you know?'

'I know the outside looks a bit of a mess but it's actually quite well built and waterproof. There's nothing inside it at present and there isn't likely to be. Rhona got offers for the farm machinery so she sold that as well. I don't know what'll happen to the place if she doesn't sell it. It's not a working farm any longer, that's for sure. What they do will depend on whether Gwenda's baby is a boy to give them an heir who can farm it, in which case they may try to keep it.'

He frowned thoughtfully. 'Though I suppose she might remarry. She's a nice-looking woman, healthy and sturdy. If she had a husband who knew about farming they could build things up again gradually, since they'll own the farm outright.'

'Sad story. I wonder . . .' Edward's voice trailed away and he didn't say what he was wondering about.

As the two men walked back to the building site, he seemed lost in thought so Lewis didn't interrupt that by chatting.

When Dan got back, he found Rufus repairing a cupboard door in the scullery and told him he'd got the job with Edward and would be moving to the valley within a few days. The two friends then spent the afternoon going round the little town so that Dan could describe it to his wife, and later walking up the path that led from the town to Jubilee Lake.

'Walter's going to try to nudge the townsfolk into clearing the ground at the top end and making a path there to finish it off properly,' Rufus said. 'He's determined to give people a good walk all the way round so that old people and small children can use it for pleasure. I think Flora, whom he's going to marry at the end of next week, agrees with him on that. She's a nurse and a firm believer in outdoor leisure activities for good health.' He grinned. 'Actually, she's a firm believer in all sorts of things, including better health care for women and children and heaven help anyone who tries to stop her achieving them.'

'That sounds a good quality to me.'

'She's going to try to get a Queen's Nurse based here in the valley to help with looking after the health of poorer folk.'

'For a quiet valley, there's a lot going on underneath the surface. I don't mind helping make a path at the top end once I've sorted out our house. Polly likes to go for walks but at the moment she gets tired more easily.'

'I'll take you up on your offer of helping with the path when we can. It'll please Walter, I'm sure. He wants to make a big push to finish it off before we get ready for the Diamond Jubilee celebrations – if the Queen lives that long. It feels as if she's been the queen for ever, doesn't it?'

'Aye, it does. Someone told me she's been our longest reigning monarch. I don't know whether that's right or not.'

'I think it's true. It'd feel strange to have a king now and what sort of king will her son make anyway? He sounds a real playboy type from what you read in the papers.'

A short time later he said, 'Oh, I nearly forgot. There's one other thing Abigail said to ask you about. She'd be happy for you and Polly come and stay with us while Walter is having better plumbing put into your house.'

'That'd be a big help. Eh, you and your wife are helping us in so many ways. I'm really grateful.'

They walked on for a bit and Dan breathed in deeply. 'I shall be glad to come and live here for another reason. I love this clean air and my Polly has always had trouble with her breathing when it's foggy or the mills are blowing out more smoke than usual, and that's got worse now she's expecting. I can guarantee she'll love the fresh air here as much as I do.' He sighed happily. 'I'll take the earliest train back in the morning, if you don't mind. I want to set her mind at rest about me getting the job and I can't afford to waste my money on a telegram.'

'How long do you think you'll take to pack up and move in?'

'Only two or three days if I have my way. I was going to send the luggage and furniture in advance then set up the cottage before going back for her but your offer of a bed for a few nights will be a big help. I hope we won't be making a lot of trouble for you.'

'Not at all. We've plenty of space as you might have noticed.'

'I have. It could be a lovely house with some care put into it.'

'I've only just moved in but I'm looking forward to making a few changes and improvements.'

As they got back Dan paused to look along the street then smiled at his friend. 'Eh, I really like it here. It hasn't been easy living with Polly's mother, who likes to boss people round and has old-fashioned views of what women who're expecting should do. I'm sure Polly will feel a lot better living here as much as I will.'

25

Edward sat by the fire that evening chatting to his wife and telling her about Dan Makersby.

'He sounds a good find,' she commented.

'Yes, but it's made me realise that lack of accommodation will stop other skilled men coming here and that'll probably slow down the work on our house. I've been wondering if we can do something about that and provide them with decent temporary accommodation at least.'

'What could we do? You can't build new houses over-night.'

'I know. But Rufus has a big house, most of which is standing empty. Perhaps he'd like to rent out some rooms and find someone to cook and clean for the men staying there. Some accommodation will only be needed for a few weeks, if that.'

As she thought about the suggestion, he was tempted to kiss away the delightful little crease that deep thinking always brought to the centre of her forehead. But he didn't because he wanted to hear what she said. She often had useful ideas to contribute to their discussions and the way they were sorting out the agent's house now they lived there together.

'I don't think their house would be suitable for that. Nor would it fit in well with their lives at this stage. They're newly-weds, Edward. They won't want to live at such close quarters with a series of strangers. I definitely wouldn't want to do that, either, I must admit.'

Another pause for thought, then she added, 'And besides, let alone she hasn't been brought up to be a servant, she has a – well, what would you call it? An educated air.'

It was his turn to frown. 'No. I suppose you're right. So I wonder if . . . Hmm.'

'Tell me. Two heads are better than one.'

'My other idea was about the big old barn in the next field to the cottage we visited today. That barn isn't being used at all. The farmer died and Walter says there's just his widow and her recently widowed daughter living there now. I did wonder if it'd be worth fitting out that barn for the skilled tradesmen we need to come here temporarily.'

'Depends what it's like inside. It's worth asking, isn't it?'

'Yes. I'll call in and see Mrs Halliwell tomorrow. You're right. It is definitely worth asking about the barn.'

When someone knocked on the door just as Rufus and Abigail were finishing their breakfast the next day, Margie answered it and didn't hesitate to show Edward and Lewis straight in to them.

Rufus pushed his chair back and stood up. 'You're out and about early.'

'We wanted to catch you before you start your day's work. I hope you don't mind.'

'Come and sit down. There's more tea left in the pot, if you'd like a cup.'

They both nodded and he gestured to Abigail, who was queen of the teapot, they always joked, to pour them cups. 'Go on. How can I help you?'

Edward explained about his discussion the previous evening with his wife and his idea of using the barn for temporary accommodation.

'I think it's a good idea,' Rufus said at once.

'We wondered if you could spare the time to look at it with us now and see if you think it could be made into temporary housing without too much cost or trouble. I'll pay you for a morning's advisory work.'

Rufus looked at him thoughtfully. 'Even if the interior is in good condition, it'll depend on whether the town's water supply runs nearby. Yes, and the gas pipes. You'd definitely need to put in a bathroom and hot water geysers, and gas lighting would be better than oil lamps. Skilled people won't want to live too roughly, especially after a day's work leaves them sweaty and dirty. They'd need hot water to be easily available for a good wash at the very least.'

'Yes. There would be a lot of details like that to sort out, wouldn't there?' Lewis said thoughtfully.

'Keep tossing ideas at us,' Edward added. 'You're better than us at that, Rufus. Do you think your friend Dan would be up to managing work on the barn for us as well as the underground jobs? He seems like a capable chap.'

'Oh, yes. He can turn his hand to nearly anything. And Riley Callan might let you jump the queue of customers and put another bathroom in for you quickly, Edward, because it'd bring more people into the valley. Some of the tradesmen may even settle here.'

Lewis laughed. 'Riley's getting to be as bad as Walter about attracting people to move here. He's got a young chap working with him now and learning the trade because his services as a plumber are increasingly in demand. Once people see what it's like to have a proper bathroom with running hot and cold water they want one too.'

They looked at one another thoughtfully, then Edward said, 'So can you spare us the time to check the place out?'

'Yes. It won't take more than a morning to have a look round the barn and do a preliminary check of the amenities.'

'Good. We came by bicycle. You've got one, haven't you? It'll be much quicker to ride than walk and it doesn't look like rain. We'll wait for you outside.'

When they were alone, Rufus put his arms round his wife. 'I shall miss you.'

She smiled. 'You won't miss me that much in one morning apart. You love getting out on that bicycle. I'm wondering whether to get myself one, too. Lots of women are riding them now. I think that's one of the reasons they're making skirts shorter these days. What do you think?'

'I think it's an excellent idea.'

She frowned down at her own clothes, which were not only old-fashioned and reached almost to the ground, but dowdy. They always had been dowdy, even when newly made. At one stage her father had forbidden her to have leg of mutton sleeves, though they'd been in vogue for several years, and she'd have loved to look smarter.

'Stop worrying about clothes. I'd find you appealing if you were dressed in a sack.'

'Shhh! Margie will hear.'

He grinned. He enjoyed making her blush. 'We'll get a bicycle for both you and Nina. You don't mind if I go with Edward and Lewis this morning? Apart from anything else, I'll be earning a little money.'

She hesitated. 'Are you doing this because you're worried about money?'

'I don't have a lot saved, so I am a bit concerned. A bicycle for Nina may have to wait a bit. But I'm also interested in what they're thinking of doing.'

She took a deep breath and said what she was thinking, 'Look, I have quite a lot of money from my father, you know that. You should regard it as joint money now that we're married, like I do. We really don't have to worry about money.'

He stiffened. 'I didn't marry you to live off your money, Abigail.'

'I know. But it's there in the bank doing nothing and you're putting in a lot of work on the house. There's more than enough to pay for what we're thinking of doing to it as well as buying bicycles. I must say, I really like the idea of turning this place into a hotel and meeting new people regularly. Only, well, I don't know enough about the details of how to run one. I've only read about them, never actually stayed in one.'

That surprised him. 'Never? Not even on holiday.'

'No. We never went away on holidays. Father didn't like them.'

An idea struck him and it felt so right he shared it with her straight away. 'We could go away for a day or two, stay in a hotel somewhere and watch how they run it, even ask the owners' advice if they seem friendly.'

'Go away!' She stared at him, wide-eyed and rather shocked. 'I've never left the valley.'

It was his turn to be surprised. 'Not even to go shopping for the day in a bigger town?'

'No. My father said he didn't like staying in hotels nor would he leave our home unoccupied, even when we lived in a much smaller house. He said I could get anything I needed here in the valley.'

'I wouldn't leave this house unoccupied for several days, either, at the moment. I'd get one of my friends to live here temporarily and Margie would be here too, of course. Though she's a bit old to defend the place.' It surprised him how quickly he'd grown used to having a maid.

Abigail looked thoughtful again. 'I bet Nina would love to have an adventure like that, too. She's never been anywhere either, has she?'

'No. I'm the one who went away to work in the mines. And you're right about Nina loving it. I'm sure she would, and I'd love to give both of you a treat like that. Your father kept you a prisoner in more ways than one, didn't he? Mentally and physically.'

She nodded then dared to ask, 'Do you think there will be enough people coming to the valley, the sort of decent people who would want to stay in a proper hotel, I mean, not just casual workers needing cheap lodgings?'

'There will be if Walter Crossley has any say in the matter. That man has saved this valley and town from fading away just about on his own. Without him I reckon it'd have turned into a sleepy village by now. He deserves a medal.'

'He's a really nice man. And he looks at Flora so lovingly. It makes me feel happy to see that.'

He suddenly caught sight of the clock. 'Eh, look at me nattering on and keeping Edward and Lewis waiting outside. Take your time thinking about a little holiday. We could do it after Walter's wedding. I'll probably be out all morning today.'

'Am I being a coward needing to think about things so carefully, Rufus?'

He stopped again to smile at her. 'No, of course not. You're simply acting like a normal human being about not rushing into uncharted territory.'

'You are so kind and understanding,' she said wonderingly. 'I'm still not used to that.'

Just then Nina came into the kitchen.

'Tell my sister about our coming adventure.' Then he was gone.

She peeped out of the window to watch the three men ride away on their bicycles up the street. She didn't notice much about two of them.

Then she turned back to tell an excited Nina about their possible holiday.

Edward led the way round the lower end of the lake, cycling past the run-down cottage where Dan would be living, and on to what had once been a farm, judging by the lines of fences. But it was now land that was untended, with gaps here and there in fences and hedges, and no animals or crops to be seen except for a few hens pecking about in a run near the house door and a kitchen garden containing the last of the year's crops.

The latter wasn't as bare as it would normally be at this time of year because of the mildness of the winter so far, but they were nearing the end of the Indian summer, as a lot of folk were calling it. There wouldn't necessarily be snow before Christmas but there would probably be a few frosts.

When the three men cycled into the farmyard an old dog heaved itself up to let out a few rusty barks and a woman came to the door.

'Can I help you?'

'Are you the owner?'

'Yes. I'm Mrs Halliwell.' She sagged against the door frame, looking lethargic and more interested in getting rid of them than anything else.

Edward introduced himself and his friends.

'I know who *you* are, Mr Ollerton, but I don't do refreshments or have eggs for sale.' She started to step back.

'That's not why we're here. It's your barn I'm interested in.'

A young woman came to stand behind her. 'I'm Mrs Lockyer. I live here with my mother. Just a minute.' She tugged her mother away from the door. 'You go and sit down, Mum. I'll deal with this.'

As she turned back it became obvious that she was well into a pregnancy, which made Edward feel sad. How these two women must have suffered in the past year, each losing a husband unexpectedly.

Mrs Halliwell shuffled back inside the house, moving like a weary old woman. Her daughter faced them, arms folded across her swollen belly. Her eyes were slightly reddened as if she'd been weeping earlier but she looked to be in good health physically.

She gave Edward a long, cool stare. 'Now, Mr Ollerton, may I ask what you want with our barn?'

'I'm looking for somewhere to lodge the skilled tradesmen who'll be coming and going to build and fit out my new house.'

She looked at him in puzzlement. 'What does that have to do with us? We don't run a lodging house.'

'You own a large barn which isn't being used. I wondered if it'd be suitable for me to use to house the various skilled men for the next year or two.'

'There's nothing inside the barn. How can they stay there?'

'I'd furnish it with bunk beds – well, I would if there's a water supply available. That's the most crucial element.'

She stared at him. 'Oh. Well, there is one. The water pipes pass quite close to the barn on their way to the farmhouse, so Dad had a connection put into the barn. How much rent were you thinking of paying?'

He named a sum, saw interest flare in her eyes and added, 'Per year. I think I'd need it for about two years.'

'What would you do with it then?'

'Whatever you liked. Either clear out the furnishings completely or leave them for you to use in the same way.'

'What about cooking for the men and such?'

'I'd put in a stove and sink, and a simple bathroom. The men would have to pay someone to shop and cook their meals.'

She stared at him, frowning, saying nothing for a moment or two, then straightening her shoulders in a decisive way. 'I'd better show you the barn, then, hadn't I?'

'Thank you. Will your mother be all right about you doing this, do you think? About renting the barn to me if it's suitable for what I need, I mean? She's the owner now, isn't she?'

'I'm sure she will be fine with that. We're agreed that we need to earn money whenever we can. I might even persuade Mum to do some of the cooking for the men. She used to enjoy cooking – before Dad died, that is. She's hardly done any since he passed away, sadly.'

'Perhaps she's been lacking something to keep her busy.'

'Yes, probably. We both have, actually. It was a worse shock my Ronny dying. You don't expect that to happen to a man his age.' For a moment her voice wobbled and she took a deep breath or two before continuing. 'People using our barn might be good for her and me both. Just let me get my shawl.'

Edward admired her attitude and her stoic coping with such a major double loss as her father and husband.

They walked across to the barn and she started to pull open the door, which didn't seem to be locked.

Rufus quickly took it out of her hand and dragged it open, kicking aside some gravel that must have been washed there by the rain and was getting in the way of it moving freely.

Lewis took out a small notebook and scribbled in it, muttering, 'Entry needs paving.'

It felt warmer in the barn which provided a big, light space with windows to one side, an upper area previously used for storing hay and a couple of rooms roughly separated from the rest of the space by a variety of pieces of wood forming uneven walls. Each room had a small window on the outside walls and an inside window overlooking the interior of the barn. In one of them there was a desk covered in dust, an old kitchen chair and a chest of drawers to one side.

Mrs Lockyer stopped outside the room with the desk, not attempting to go inside it. 'Father used to do his farm business here. There's nothing in the desk these days, though. Mum took all the papers out and stored them in the house.'

'Very wise.'

There were fireplaces in the two side walls of the barn, one in each. 'Dad lit fires in the worst of winter to take the chill off.'

'And the water supply?'

'Over here. There's a rough slopstone and a cold tap. If Dad needed hot water, he used to boil it in an old kettle on one of the fires. Take as long as you like to look round. I'll wait for you in the office.'

Rufus paced out the floor, counting his steps and noting them down to gain a rough idea of the barn's size. 'Plenty of space and you could use those two rooms as places of a better quality, charging the men a bit more to use them.'

After she'd left them to explore, Gwenda hesitated then went inside the room that had been used as an office. It still felt strange not to see her father sitting here. She sat on the rather dusty chair to wait, leaving them the privacy to discuss the situation.

'It's better than I'd hoped,' Edward said. 'Or it could be.'

Rufus nodded. 'It certainly looks promising. You'd need to get gas brought in and proper plumbing fitted. A gas cooker would be a lot safer to cook on as well. Gas lighting too, of course.'

They went over to the former office again and Rufus asked Mrs Lockyer about gas, but she only thought she remembered that the pipes went somewhere nearby, wasn't sure.

'Dad never bothered with it, though Mum would have liked to have it to cook on and for lighting the farmhouse but she couldn't persuade him to pay for changes that big. He got tired a lot towards the end so she stopped pestering him. We didn't realise he was ill and fading rapidly, any more than we knew my husband had a weak heart.'

She took a few deep breaths then frowned at him. 'If you get gas connected out here, it'd make sense for us to have it brought to the house as well. Be cheaper for both of us if we do it at the same time and share the costs. It'd make it easier for us to run the house. We're so old-fashioned there. I had gas at the home I shared with my Ronny.' She sighed and stared into space for a moment, then turned back to him and waited for him to speak.

'We'll consult you when I find out about exactly where the gas pipes are and how much it'd cost.' He turned to Lewis and Rufus. 'Have you seen enough?'

They both spoke at once. 'Yes.'

When the other two went back outside, Edward said, 'If we can get gas brought in, I'd very much like to hire your barn, Mrs Lockyer.'

'Good. I'll give you a week to find out and decide, then if you're not interested, I might ask around to see if anyone else would like to hire it. We shall need money to live off and for baby things, and it'd be better not to break into our savings.'

She nodded and walked briskly across to the farmhouse, shutting the door without looking back as they started walking away.

'She's a brave woman, that one,' Edward said. He turned to Rufus. 'Could you come back to the house with us and discuss the practicalities?'

'Of course.'

They cycled the rest of the way in silence.

26

Terry Catlow watched the three men pedal across to the Halliwell farm on their bicycles. He moved gradually from one hiding place to another to get a better line of sight.

He wondered if those things were hard to ride. He'd ignored them when he lived in town, but it'd save all the damned walking he was doing these days if he had one. Only he didn't really fancy balancing on two narrow wheels, so once again he dismissed the idea. You could fall off and break your leg easy as anything from one of those contraptions. And if he did that out in the middle of nowhere, he'd be in serious trouble.

Why were those three sods visiting those two widow women, though? He didn't want Ollerton and his pals messing around near there, because he needed to be able to get to that house one night soon. He would be wanting more food and was sure they'd have plenty at a farm.

He continued to watch, only able to pick out a slightly blurry picture of what was going on in this dull light because his eyes were giving him trouble. He let out a low growl of anger as he blinked and still couldn't get his vision to clear completely. If it wasn't one thing, it was another as you grew older.

He had to get all this sorted out quickly and get rid of the last of the Ollertons, though he needed to do it in a way that no one could blame him for. That was what was stopping him acting straight away. Killing someone if you crept up on them would be easy but doing that and no one even suspecting it was you who'd done it would be much more difficult.

Especially as folk knew how he felt about Ollerton and that he'd attacked him before.

After that man was dead the valley would become quiet again, with no one building ruddy great houses, or teaching your wife to forget her promise to 'love, honour and obey', especially that last bit. The bitch needed a good thrashing and one day soon he'd give her what for. Only, teaching her a lesson was second on his list. It came well after getting rid of Ollerton.

After that the third thing would be dealing with his son. Jezzy had been a promising lad till he went to stay with his uncle. Now, he'd got himself a bloody job and was off every morning to work on that house. Of all the betrayals, working on the Ollerton house was the most shocking. He'd teach the little sod to do as he was told, the first rule of which was never, ever to help or deal with a member of that family.

He didn't want his lad working for wages, either. Slavery, that was, bloody thought they owned you, employers did. He wanted better than that for his son.

Terry watched the three men till they disappeared from view, still wondering what they'd been doing at the farm. He'd find out eventually, he always did. He was good at eavesdropping.

He hoped his next attack would be successful. He'd got it all pictured in his mind. He'd kill the sod, then walk away across the moors and go on walking till he came to a village or town. Then he'd stay away for a few weeks. He'd have to get a job labouring unfortunately. But not for long.

When he came back he'd act surprised at Ollerton being killed. As long as no one saw him do the actual killing or walk away from where it happened, they'd not be able to claim it was him who'd done it.

He'd have to make a hidey-hole nearer the building site, find a place from which he could watch Ollerton then choose his moment when the sod was there on his own. The easiest way would be to shoot him. Do it quickly and get straight away from the valley. He knew where there was a gun and it shouldn't be too hard to pinch it, then put it back where he'd found it the same day.

The owner of the gun was dead now and his widow hadn't made any attempt to get rid of the thing. He'd peeped through the window at their farm and seen it hanging on the wall, in the same place as always with a packet of ammunition sitting on a shelf nearby. And it looked dusty as if no one ever even took it down.

It was as if fate was helping him. The gun was crying out to be stolen while they were out, used and then put back.

But he'd have to get rid of that dog of theirs before he could do it. The creature might be old but it still had plenty of teeth left and had bitten him the other week when the two women were out at market and he was scouting round.

He could still outrun an old dog and now spent a happy hour working out how to kill it and hide the body before he went inside to borrow the gun. He wasn't used to guns but how hard could it be to point the thing at someone and pull the trigger? He could fire it more than once if he didn't hit the sod the first time.

He had no trouble getting to sleep that night because he'd pinched another blanket that had been airing on a clothes line in someone's backyard. But it was still damned cold when you woke up in the mornings.

He'd have to risk a fire soon or he'd freeze to death. He had the firewood drying out in a corner of the cave so that it wouldn't give off smoke when used. He could just light a small fire to brew a pot of tea on and warm himself up a bit at the same time. He had the makings for the tea all ready to go.

He sighed as he got himself a meagre breakfast with the last of the food he'd pinched. It always seemed to get eaten up more quickly than he'd expected. How the hell did women know what to buy to keep their families fed every single day? It baffled him.

Maybe he could break into that little corner shop in Eastby End. He could get a bigger load from the storeroom there than from the cupboards in people's houses.

The shop was run by another damned widow. The town was littered with the bitches. They wore out their husbands then carried on living for years. Well, Nora wasn't going to outlive him. By hell she wasn't.

After he got his home back, he'd work her to death, one way or the other. And that son of his had better be careful what he did, too. If Jezzy was so keen to work, he could do it for his father.

27

The next big event in Ollerthwaite was Walter Crossley's wedding, which they'd managed to fit in before Christmas and before Elinor's baby was due, too, since these events were likely to happen around the same time. She had, thank goodness, started feeling well again once she was over the sickness of the early days.

Walter told everyone that he didn't want a lot of fuss made and refused to let them put on a big party for him. All he would agree to was inviting his family and a few close friends to celebrate with him at the farm after a simple church wedding.

He'd have been happy to have an even shorter civil ceremony at the town hall but Flora wanted to be married in church and he wanted to make her happy.

She was in agreement with him about not having a big, fussy wedding, thank goodness. She was still a bit bemused at times to think she'd fallen in love at her age, not only so quickly but so deeply. When they were alone together, it felt as if the two of them had known each other for many years.

He felt as bemused as she did by all this. He'd never expected to remarry and as for falling in love so quickly, he hadn't even done that the first time round, fond as he'd been of his first wife. Folk talked about falling head over heels in love, and that exactly described how he'd felt this time.

It was a great relief when the wedding day arrived. It'd soon be over and he could get back to his normal life, but with one important and wonderful addition – Flora in his bed.

He woke at dawn, put on a dressing gown and went down to make himself a cup of tea and say hello to the world. He found the fire burning brightly, the kettle still hot and the teapot full of brown liquid. He was about to pour himself a cup when he heard a sound behind him and turned to see his grandson's wife come into the room.

He smiled at her. 'No sign of Flora waking up?'

Elinor stood for a moment with her head on one side, studying him as if she'd never seen him before.

'She's been awake for ages and I made her a cup of tea, but she won't be coming down for breakfast. It's bad luck for the groom to see the bride before the actual ceremony, so you're to have your breakfast quickly, get ready early, and then Cam can drive you down to Rufus's house. He's expecting you and you can easily walk to the church from there.'

'Superstitious rubbish,' he muttered.

'It may be but Flora has never been married before and she deserves all the little frills and fun activities that go with it.'

She paused and stood staring at him, arms akimbo. 'Well? Are you going to do as you're told about this or do I have to drag you screaming all the way down the hill?'

He smiled at the thought of a highly pregnant woman dragging him anywhere. 'I suppose fear of your violence will force me to do as I'm told.'

She laughed and came across to give him a kiss.

He kissed her back on both cheeks. He might be her husband's grandfather, not hers by blood, but he felt as close to her as any relative could, so acted accordingly. Apart from the fact that he liked her a lot, she'd made his lad happy and that was extremely important to him.

His breakfast was served quickly and then Walter was chivvied out of the house by Elinor and the woman who normally came to do their washing, but who would be keeping an eye on the farm while everyone was in town getting Walter and Flora 'married off' as they kept calling it, a phrase he detested.

After the ceremony they would all come back and eat the food that was now sitting covered by clean cloths on the shelves of the pantry. He'd been threatened with severe torture if he so much as lifted a corner of those cloths and disturbed the contents, so hadn't touched them. He guessed they wanted to surprise him with some lovely food and he'd enjoy that.

When he got to Rufus's house, Walter found that his host too had been given instructions. He and Abigail were to walk to the church with him when the time came. Which meant they must have been added to the guest list. Still they were a lovely couple so one more pair like them wouldn't matter, but he hoped his family hadn't added too many guests. He really didn't want a big party.

'Nervous?' Abigail asked when the time came for them to set off for the church.

By then Walter was feeling a bit grumpy, rather than nervous, already fed up of all the fuss people were making. He'd rather have strolled down the hill to church hand in hand with his wife to be. But he didn't say that because they meant well and anyway, it was too late to change anything now.

Rufus grinned at him as they left the house. 'You'll not stop them fussing over you for the rest of the day, Walter, so you might as well give in and enjoy your wedding.'

That seemed a strange thing to say to the bridegroom but then everything felt strange today. Walter shrugged and continued to stroll towards the church beside the two of them.

He was a bit surprised that they didn't meet many people he knew as they walked along. Strange that, because he'd half expected to be waylaid and congratulated several times.

When they got there, Abigail said, 'Let me look at you.' She raised one hand to smooth down his hair then kissed his cheek.

She was coming out of her shell since her marriage and it was good to see.

Rufus consulted his watch again. 'It's stuffy in that old church. Let's wait out here for a few minutes longer and enjoy the fresh air.'

'All right.' Walter had given up trying to have any say in what they did today, so if his escort wanted them to stay outside he'd do it, even though it was rather chilly if you asked him.

After a while Rufus took his watch out of his waistcoat pocket yet again and flicked the top open. 'About time we went in.'

Why did he keep checking the time? Walter wondered.

When he entered the church he found out why and stopped dead in shock, because the place was full, absolutely full of people. Every pew was crammed with them and some were standing up at the back, grinning at him.

As he scanned the crowd he saw just about everyone he'd ever known, not only his own family but people from the town.

Cam was waiting for them inside the entrance. How had he got here without Walter seeing him go in?

'Come on. You and I have to stand at the front.'

Walter took a deep breath, gave in to the rueful smile that was dying to settle on his face at all these machinations and walked slowly down the aisle. As he stood next to his grandson at the far end, he muttered, 'You sneaky devil!'

'Worth it to see your face. Anyway, people care about you. They want to see you get married and then wish you well. How could we deny them that pleasure?'

There was the sound of a cart outside, a bigger one than his own, and he caught glimpses of some people fussing round at the entrance to the church, but he couldn't see Flora.

'Got the ring?' he asked Cam, suddenly afraid of something going wrong.

'Of course I have.'

Then Edward stepped into the church and stood at the end of the aisle, holding out one arm. When Flora joined him and linked her arm in his, Walter's anxieties vanished. She was here.

She wasn't wearing a white gown but a pale blue one made of some material that gleamed. It skimmed her body and ended just above her ankles. She had a hat with flowers on it and looked absolutely lovely, years younger than her age. And yet Walter could tell that she was a little nervous.

He beamed across the church and her face lit up when she saw him, then he turned obediently in response to Cam's tugs on his sleeve to find himself facing the minister.

He never afterwards remembered the ceremony clearly because he was looking at his bride, thinking mainly of her. He slipped the ring on her finger when told and obeyed the instruction to 'kiss the bride' with great enthusiasm.

After that, he and his wife followed the minister into the vestry to enter their names into the church records, then they came out to face the crowd of people still inside the church. He was astonished to see others lining the path outside and, oh hell, they were holding packets of confetti which they scattered lavishly over Walter and Flora as they moved forward.

He got some in his mouth and stopped to spit it out, then couldn't resist putting his arms round Flora and kissing her again, confetti and all.

Which made everyone nearby cheer and shout.

All of a sudden he was enjoying the fuss and he could see that Flora was too. Why had he not agreed to it sooner?

Then came another big surprise. They didn't go home but were told by Cam to walk across to the church hall. There they found everything ready. Two big tables at the sides were loaded with plates of food. A lot more scrubbed wooden tables than usual were set out in the body of the hall for people to sit at and eat.

He was kissed by all the women and his hand was shaken by all the men as he and his bride made their much-interrupted way across the room.

Then everyone nearby stood back and gestured to the food. He and Flora filled their plates first and were then escorted to the only smaller table set with a white cloth, where they were joined by their family.

The wedding meal seemed to go on for a long time and he wasn't really hungry. What he wanted now was to be alone with his wife.

He leaned sideways to mutter to her, 'How soon can we escape?'

'There are the speeches to be given yet.'

'Oh, hell! I'd forgotten that.'

She gave him one of her mischievous smiles. 'Be brave, my lad.'

So he listened and laughed or blushed – he hadn't known he could blush like that, but the things they said would make a stone blush!

And then, at long last it was over. They were escorted out to the big wedding cart and allowed to make the journey back to the farm on their own.

As it set off, he looked sideways at her. 'I love you, Flora Crossley.'

'I love you too, Walter Crossley. You're my very favourite husband.'

So he pulled her across to sit closer to him and managed to give her another quick kiss in the process. After that they sat quietly, each with one arm round the other and their other hands tightly clasped on their laps.

When they arrived, they tried to shake off all the remaining confetti before going inside but of course they couldn't manage to get rid of it all.

'I wish there were just you and me now,' he whispered as they opened the front door.

'So do I.' She looked down the hill. 'But the others are in sight already.'

'Give me another quick kiss before they arrive.

Eventually, however, they got their wish and were the only two people in what had been his bedroom with hearts and bodies sharing a wonderful wedding night.

And if the loving didn't last for as long as a younger couple might have managed, it was nonetheless very sweet.

28

When Dan and Polly Makersby arrived in Ollerthwaite, they brought some boxes with them on the train, but even so it was only a smallish pile of luggage, considering there was a whole cottage to furnish and all their minor possessions to move.

'Is that everything?' Edward asked when he met them at the station driving Walter's cart.

'The rest will be arriving by road. It was cheaper,' Dan said frankly.

'Well, you can't get into the house to live yet, so maybe that's a good thing. Riley says it'll be too full of dust and mess, though that will only be for two or three days longer. And before you ask, there have not just been the plumbing changes inside but bringing the gas into the house.'

He turned to Polly. 'The bathroom is half finished, as I'm sure you'll be glad to hear. Luckily there was a small room at the side of the kitchen which could be turned into a bathroom.'

'That sounds fine,' Dan said.

Polly merely smiled and nodded, seeming a bit shy. She didn't look at all well to Edward, so he offered to take them straight to Rufus's house, where they were to stay for a few days. They'd be helping Margie to keep an eye on the place while Rufus and Abigail were away on their little holiday.

'Could we have a quick glance round the cottage first, do you think?' Dan asked. 'Then Polly and I can start working out in our heads where things will go.'

'Of course.'

'Was it you who arranged to get the bathroom put in?' Dan asked. 'If so, we're grateful.'

'No. It was always Walter's plan. He hasn't put bathrooms into any of the houses he owns till there were tenants wanting to move in. The gas company has connected the pipes to your cottage, a nearby barn and a farmhouse at the same time and there will be gas water heaters installed in your bathroom and kitchen.'

'That's really good news, isn't it, Polly?'

'Yes, it is.' She smiled at them. 'Very good news.' But her voice sounded weak and tired.

'Rufus and Abigail asked me to tell you they don't mind how long you need to stay with them. They have a large house with several rooms not being used.'

'That's so kind of them and we're extremely grateful,' Dan said and Polly nodded again.

They had a quick tour of the cottage but as Riley's message had said, it was full of dust and clutter at the moment and Polly had to be helped to move around safely. Still, they now knew the layout of the rooms in their future home.

By the time they got to Rufus's house, Polly was chalk white and moving even more slowly. In fact she looked as if she might faint at any minute and Edward could see that Dan was watching her anxiously.

After they'd been introduced to their hosts, she apologised in a breathless sounding voice, and asked if they'd mind her taking a short nap.

'Of course not,' Abigail said. 'I'll show you to your bedroom then you can make yourself at home there.'

'I get so tired,' Polly explained as she walked slowly and wearily up the stairs with her. 'I've been like this ever since I've been expecting.'

Abigail had to wait for her at the top. 'Well, you won't be in our way because we're leaving tomorrow and as far as I'm concerned you can sleep as much as you want, even when we're at home. Our maid Margie will still be doing most of the housework, so you don't need to worry about that, either.'

There were tears in Polly's eyes. 'You're so kind. I'm sorry to be such a nuisance.'

'You're not a nuisance at all. It's a poor lookout if we can't help one another.'

When she had closed the bedroom door on her guest, however, Abigail stood still for a moment or two at the top of the stairs feeling rather worried. Polly didn't look merely tired; she looked downright ill.

She decided not to comment on that to Dan but ran lightly down the stairs and rejoined the others. She'd worry to her husband about their guest when they were on their own.

Was there something really wrong with Polly or was she just having a really bad start to her pregnancy?

The next day Rufus, his wife and his sister set off early in the morning for their brief holiday, the first time two of them had ever gone away for a holiday or even left the valley. They were heading for Blackpool, where Rufus felt sure some hotels would be open, even in the winter.

Nina was nearly wild with excitement, couldn't sit still on the various trains they had to change to, was up and down looking out of windows at the scenery on one side of the train then the other.

Abigail was quieter, looking a trifle nervous. 'What shall we do if we can't find a nice hotel that's open?'

'I'm sure we'll find one in such a big resort, whatever time of year it is. Trust me on that.'

He was more concerned about the prices. This holiday was costing a lot by his standards and Abigail had insisted he accept money from her to pay for it.

Since it was mainly for her benefit that they were going he shouldn't feel bad about it, but he did. He'd pay her back with hard work on the house improvements once they returned to Ollerthwaite, but he wished he could have afforded to treat her.

The journey took a few hours, what with two changes of train, and even Nina was tired enough to have calmed down by the time they got there. It was mid-afternoon by then and they found a smiling cab driver waiting for custom at the station.

When he asked where they wanted to go, Rufus had to confess that they didn't know and would welcome his advice about a hotel. He listened to what sort of place they wanted to stay in and took them to The Grand Sea Vista right on the seafront.

'They stay open but they don't get a lot of custom at this time of year, so they'll be really happy to see you, sir,' he said. 'And you'll find it extremely comfortable.'

He was right. They were treated like royalty by the manager and shown up to two big bedrooms on either side of a private sitting room, for which the winter price wasn't as high as Rufus had feared it might be.

'Would you be wanting an evening meal, sir?' he asked.

'Yes, please.'

The manager beamed at that.

The food was good and was brought up to their sitting room on a trolley because the dining room wasn't open that evening, though the lounge was available if they wished to sit there and have a drink later on.

They were all ravenous by now and tried every single dish, Nina making little murmuring noises of pleasure.

The beds were as comfortable as they looked and Nina fell asleep in her own bedroom almost immediately after the meal. She was tired out by excitement as much as by the journey, Rufus thought fondly.

The two adults stayed up longer, going down to the lounge where they daringly ordered a beer for Rufus and a glass of shandy for Abigail. They chatted to the waiter since they were the only customers that night and he seemed happy to fuss over them.

When they got back to their room, they went straight to bed. Abigail fell asleep in the middle of a sentence even before Rufus got in beside her, and he wasn't far behind in surrendering to sleep.

In the morning they were told that the dining room was open so they had breakfast downstairs at a table by the window overlooking the seafront. Once again they were the only customers.

Afterwards Rufus managed to speak to the manager and ask his help about them learning what would be needed to run their own hotel in a small country town, a smaller hotel than this one, of course, but hopefully with the same high standards.

'The hotel is very quiet at this time of year,' the manager said, clearly as susceptible to flattery as the next person, 'so I have time to show you what goes on behind the public spaces here, if you like?'

'That would be marvellous.'

Nina opted to sit by the window in the lounge, reading a ladies' magazine and watching the sea while they did that.

Afterwards the manager sat with them in the lounge to discuss exactly what they were hoping to do and made some very helpful suggestions.

Once he'd gone back to work they went out for a short stroll and Nina bought a postcard to show her friends where they'd been. But there was an icy wind, so they didn't linger on the seafront but went back to the hotel where there were plenty of newspapers and magazines to read.

In the afternoon the same cab driver came to pick them up, as arranged, and drove them along the promenade all the way to Fleetwood and back, stopping for a while now and then to point something out, and stopping for longer at a café in Cleveleys so that they could all get a nice warm drink.

Nina looked at the beach longingly but the driver said it was too cold for a stroll on it and besides, the tide was coming in.

He was very good at explaining what was what in the area, and suggested taking them to Lytham St Annes the following day, which was on the coast in the other direction.

The day after that was their last one and they walked into the town centre to explore and look in the shop windows, another treat which Abigail and Nina had never enjoyed in a big town before.

In the evening, they invited the manager to join them and Rufus offered to buy him a drink. But he smilingly declined this, so they could only thank him.

'You've been enormously helpful,' Rufus told him. 'And if I hear of anyone going to Blackpool from where we live, you can be sure I'll recommend this hotel.'

'Thank you, sir. I'll do the same. What are you going to call your hotel?' he asked. 'You didn't say.'

They looked at each other in surprise, because they'd not even considered this.

Then Abigail said slowly, 'How about The Jubilee Hotel, Rufus? It would fit in with our local lake.'

The manager said, 'Aha! You have a lake there, do you? Is it pretty?'

'We think so.'

'How about walking? Are there any good country walks nearby?'

'Plenty of them. You can walk for miles across the moors, or the "tops" as we often call them,' Abigail said. 'My father used to take me up there sometimes on sunny Sundays.' Though it had only been to the nearer parts of the moors and she'd longed to go further.

'Then when you open your hotel, you should check all the walks nearby and advertise walking holidays,' the manager said. 'Get some maps and leaflets printed if there aren't any available already. It'll be worth the expense as it will likely pay dividends in bringing customers to your valley. If you do that and send some leaflets to me, I'll put them out for our guests.'

Rufus and Abigail exchanged happy glances. Another good idea.

Then a staff member beckoned to the manager from the door of the dining room and he excused himself.

Nina had been standing across by the window looking out on to the promenade and now came across to join them. 'I'm sorry we're going home tomorrow.'

Abigail's comment was more predictable, Rufus thought.

'I'm not sorry to leave. But I've enjoyed this visit and I'd like to come here again in the warmer weather so that we can walk about more and go down on the beach. The sand looks so clean and smooth.'

She turned to her husband. 'Thank you for bringing us, Rufus. This was a wonderful idea. And we were lucky to have a helpful manager here, weren't we? I have a head stuffed full of information and ideas about running a hotel now.'

Ollerthwaite looked dull and ordinary when they got back, but only Nina commented on that.

'I can understand better now why Walter wants the path round the lake finishing at the top end,' Abigail said as she and Rufus chatted over a cup of cocoa before going to bed. 'The town does need some features to attract people.'

'He has a lot of good ideas. I must tell Walter about the suggestion of printing brochures about the area for visitors, and finding out about nearby walks that might be suitable for strangers.'

After a brief pause for thought, he added, 'Walter will be interested in that, I'm sure. This town owes him so much and I bet he hasn't finished improving people's lives yet.'

29

Two days after they got back Abigail decided on a step she'd been longing to make.

'I think I'll go out this morning and order some clothes to be made by the dressmaker in town,' she said over breakfast, trying to sound casual. 'Not dark clothes this time, but something prettier and in a more modern style, perhaps.'

She held her breath in case Rufus thought that extravagant and looked at him anxiously, relaxing when she saw him give her an understanding smile.

'What an excellent idea, Abigail!'

'You don't mind, then?'

'Of course not. I think Nina needs a few more clothes as well before we send her back to school, don't you? She looks to me to have grown even in the short time since she's started eating properly. Could you see to that too, please? I'll pay whatever it costs.'

'No, you won't. She's my sister now, too.'

'Thank you – for the clothes and the loving care of her.'

After a brief hesitation, he added, 'I confess I don't like to see a woman as pretty as you dressed in clothes as dull as that lot. What was your father thinking of to insist on you wearing such garments when he could afford better? Perhaps you could give them all to some poor person in need after you've replenished your wardrobe?'

'Really? Oh, I'd love to get rid of them.'

Nina had been listening with a happy look on her face. 'Does that mean I can come shopping with you?'

'Yes, it does.'

Abigail gave her husband another slightly anxious glance but he said firmly, 'I'm not coming shopping with you for clothes, so don't ask. You two are on your own for that.'

'Good!' said Nina. 'Men don't know about clothes.'

'And you do?' he teased.

Her smile faded a little. 'I used to look at people in the street and envy them.'

'Soon they'll be looking at you and envying you,' Abigail said firmly.

A blissful sigh greeted this remark.

When she went into town to consult Miss Parten, the dress-maker the better-off ladies used, Abigail took her favourite dress with her to be altered, because it was the only one she wanted to keep. Then she told Miss Parten the absolute truth: that she had a wardrobe full of old-fashioned clothes, thanks to her late father, and now wanted to replace them with some modern garments.

'And the styles?'

'Fashionable but not too young or silly for a woman my age,' she said, feeling nervous that she might make bad choices. 'I'd welcome your advice on that, actually. I'm going to buy a bicycle so will need clothes I can use when I ride it. My present clothes are all too long. Anyway, I'm giving them away.'

'A lot of the ladies are shortening their skirts,' Miss Parten said. 'But first you'll need to buy some fabric for me to make your new clothes. I have some pattern books and can send for lengths of anything you fancy, but I also keep a few lengths here for ladies in a hurry to get some new clothes – which I think you are.'

She got out some folded lengths of winter cloth and Abigail chose two of them, delighted at the rich colours. She then chose two more lengths from the pattern books. She also wanted prettier underclothing and some blouses, but would get them elsewhere.

Miss Parten was looking a lot happier than when they'd come in. It felt so good to help this kind woman earn more money.

'I shall look forward to making these for you, Mrs Shorrocks. And I can have this skirt and jacket altered by midday tomorrow. I'll have one of the lengths cut out, too, and tacked together to try on for size if I bring in a friend who sometimes helps out when I'm busy. To be frank, she'll be as delighted as I am about the additional work.'

She hesitated, then added, 'Do you know what you're going to do with your old clothes?'

'No, not yet. Do you have a suggestion?'

'My church takes clothes and other goods for people in need. They'd be happy to receive such warm clothing, especially in winter.'

'That would be very helpful! Can you take them for me once I've got my new things?'

'I'd be happy to. Thank you.'

'Now, as I said earlier, my sister needs some new clothes too.'

'I have another friend who makes clothes for children. She has some clever ways of making clothes that can be made bigger with very little effort later on. Children can grow out of things so quickly.'

When she and a very excited Nina got home, Abigail found Rufus working on the kitchen cupboards and couldn't wait to tell him about what she and his sister had chosen.

Then she asked hesitantly, 'When you can spare the time, could we go out and look for a bicycle for me? And a smaller one for Nina? I think it'd be a good use for my father's money.'

His face lit up. 'That's even more wonderful news. We can all go for rides together. Let's go out after lunch to get the bicycles. It'll make a nice walk across town and Peter will be as delighted with your custom as Miss Parten was.'

'I'm not . . . spending too much, am I? I don't want to upset you.'

'Not at all. And I'm coming to terms with you having that money. You really need to change your life and start enjoying it, and for that you need to spend money. And remember, every time you spend money locally, you help someone else in the valley to make a living.'

'That's a wonderful thought. I saw how happy Miss Parten was with my order.'

'There's something else you and I need to do now that the wedding fuss is over, and that's discuss the money that has to be used for charity with Walter. We haven't told him yet.'

Her smile faded and Rufus said, 'He'll be delighted with it because he'll be able to help a lot of people.'

'I suppose so.'

Nina interrupted them, looking reproachful. 'I'll go up and wash my hands quickly, shall I? I'm very hungry indeed now and Margie's been waiting to serve the food.'

That lightened the mood again and they both laughed.

'Yes, you do that,' he said. 'You're turning into a stomach on wheels lately.'

She stuck out her tongue at him, so he pretended to chase her and she ran out shrieking with laughter.

Abigail waited till his sister had run up the stairs then gave in to temptation, put her arms round her husband's neck and kissed his cheek which turned into a lingering kiss on the lips for them both.

'I really like being married to you, Rufus,' she murmured.

'I like being with you, too.'

'Truly?'

'I wouldn't say so otherwise.'

So they kissed one another again.

As if fate wanted to help get the charity money spent, Rufus met Walter and Flora in town the following morning when he was out buying some more screws and nails. He hesitated then went across to them, explaining that he and Abigail had something important to tell Walter, so invited them both back for a cup of tea and a slice of one of Margie's delicious cakes.

He and Abigail had been planning to go out to see if they could buy bicycles after he got back, but that would have to wait.

When they got to the house, he took their visitors' coats and hats, and as he was hanging them up, managed to whisper to his wife that he'd brought their guests back for her to tell them about her father's money.

Abigail's happy expression faded, but she knew this had to be done, so she took a deep breath then led the way into the sitting room. After they were seated, she said, 'I have something important to tell you, Mr Crossley. To ask you, really.'

'Should I leave you on your own?' Flora asked. 'You look so nervous perhaps you'd rather tell him privately?'

She shook her head. 'I don't mind you being with us. Actually, you'll probably be involved in what will be happening afterwards.'

She took a deep breath and explained about her father's money then sat quietly, waiting for their response, even perhaps a scornful glance or two.

It didn't happen. Instead Flora stood up and came across to sit closer to her and take hold of her hand. 'That was very brave of you, Abigail, and it'll be wonderful to have the money to help poorer people with. So your sad story will have a happy ending.' She then looked at her husband as if inviting him to speak.

'I'll be very happy to use this money to help people. Flora and I will discuss what to do with it and talk to you about that. Um, do you have any idea of roughly how much it is?'

When she told him the approximate amount, he looked shocked rigid. 'That much?'

Abigail could only nod, then remembered something else. 'Oh, and the authorities want you to discuss what you're doing with Sergeant McGill and report on progress, so that he can let his inspector know as things happen.'

'I'll have a little chat with him before we start.'

'Can we go to the bank when it's convenient and transfer the money to you?' she asked. 'I'll feel better when I've passed it on to use for good.'

'We can do that this very day,' he said at once. 'I don't guarantee to use it straight away because with that much money I'll need to think about it extremely carefully and perhaps use it in a series of schemes. I promise you, though, that I'll make sure it's well used. Flora's help will be invaluable.'

He saw that she was still looking upset and said gently, 'It's not your fault that your father earned money that way, Abigail, so please don't feel guilty.'

She sagged against the back of the sofa in utter relief. They were such kind people and hadn't given her any looks of disgust when they found out about her father, had never shown scorn of any sort.

When they'd finished the refreshments the four of them walked into town and Rufus and Flora waited outside the bank while Abigail and Walter dealt with the transfer of money. He was well known there so the bank manager took them into a side room to do this in privacy.

It helped afterwards that Rufus walked home with her and she could cling to his arm.

'I don't like to see you so upset,' he said in a low voice.

'I can't help it. My father had a lot to answer for.'

'Well, with a bit of luck, this moral use of the money will cancel out some of what he did.'

That comment made her feel so much better.

The following day they went to see Peter about bicycles for her and Nina. She and Rufus smiled at one another as the child once again grew very excited. She had such a bright, happy smile.

Peter already had a bicycle that was suitable for Nina, and said he'd give them some money back and exchange it for a bigger one when she grew taller and needed an adult bicycle. But the seat of this one was adjustable so it should last her a year or two.

'Can I ride it home?' Nina begged.

Her brother shook his head. 'No. You're not learning to ride on busy streets. We'll go and try it out later on the path at the town end of the lake. There's a little park you can ride round a few times till you're steady.'

'Aww.'

'No.'

Peter smiled regretfully at Abigail. 'I haven't got anything suitable for you at the moment, Mrs Shorrocks, but I can get you one within a day or two, as long as you don't mind a second-hand bicycle. You'll want one with a basket at the front for your shopping, won't you, like the other ladies?'

'Yes. And I don't mind it being second hand.'

The three of them walked home together, with Nina pushing her bicycle and Rufus promising to give her a lesson and some practice at riding it before the day was through.

Abigail was worried about Polly Makersby because their guest was looking only slightly better for her recent restful days. She took Dan aside and asked him straight out whether his wife needed to see a doctor.

He closed his eyes for a moment or two, looking anguished, then said, 'We did see a doctor. He told us there was nothing anyone could do except let her rest as much as possible and hope for the best.'

'What did he mean by that?'

'That the baby would be born safely and that she would recover afterwards. But later he took me aside separately and said if she recovered – *if!* – she shouldn't have any more children.' He stared down at his feet. 'She insisted on knowing what he said to me and says she'll do her best to prove him wrong. She's a wonderful woman and she's much more important to me than the child.'

He shook his head and gulped audibly before adding, 'I think she finds it easier not to talk about it, by the way, and she says she has felt better for the way you've cosseted her.'

'We have a good woman doctor in the valley. Perhaps it might not hurt to consult her as well. And I'll speak to Walter's wife Flora and see if she has any suggestions for you. She's a very experienced nurse.'

When Rufus asked why Abigail was looking so worried, she explained. He was silent for a while then said gently, 'I don't think there's anything you can do, love. We all know that childbirth is a dangerous thing for women to face. Sometimes people just, well, fade away or die whatever you do for them, and not just in childbirth. If anything goes wrong, I hope the child will survive to comfort him.'

'You sound as if you don't think she will survive.'

'I've seen it in the mines. When people get a certain look on their faces you know they're in very poor health. Only it's usually older people that happens with, not young ones like Polly. And yet because she's young, she may surprise us all.'

In one way it was a relief when Dan and Polly left to move into the cottage. Abigail and Margie cooked them some food to help during the first day or two, as the two of them would no doubt be busy sorting out their new home.

There was nothing else they could think of to do.

'I'll take them some food every few days,' Abigail said.

They were both silent for a few seconds then she changed the subject to something more cheerful. 'I'll have a bicycle by then, surely? I'm *dying* to get one. I'll be able to get around so much more easily.'

The thought of the bicycle cheered her up considerably. Her life was now so interesting with so many different things to do. She'd hardly read any books since her marriage.

30

Jezzy Catlow was horrified and angry when his father way-laid him on his way home from work and dragged him to the side of the road. As he struggled in vain to get away, Terry said, 'Be still. I'm not going to thump you. I just want a word with you.'

'Well, I don't want a word with you.' The trouble was, for all his father was looking scrawnier and had that undernourished look on his face you sometimes saw on hungry children, he was still taller and stronger than his son. So Jezzy stood still, trying to droop as if giving in. In reality, he was waiting for an opportunity to get away.

'You have to stop working for that Ollerton chap.'

'What? Why should I do that? Mam needs my wages to buy food for everyone. And anyway I like working for him. And not just for him but also for Mr Lewis.'

'*Like?* How dare you like an Ollerton or his stuck-up friends! He's fooling you and if you don't stop working for him, I'll make sure you damned well regret it.'

'Well, I won't stop. I'm learning how to lay bricks. It's a good trade, bricklaying is, and Gavin's going to take me on as an apprentice so I can become a proper bricklayer myself one day.'

Terry backhanded the boy before he could stop himself, he was so angry at this. That sent Jezzy sprawling on the ground, but it also gave the lad the opportunity to roll sideways, jump to his feet and run off, which he did before his father could stop him.

He pelted along as fast as he could towards the village of Upperfold, looking over his shoulder from time to time to make sure he wasn't being pursued. When he bumped into someone while doing this, he cried out in shock and fear as two hands settled on his shoulders and forced him to stop. He was about to try to run off again when he realised it was Mr Ollerton. 'Sorry, sir. I thought you were someone else.'

'Who were you running from?'

Jezzy froze. He didn't want to say it had been his father, because he was ashamed to have a father like that, but on the other hand he didn't want his kind employer to walk into a trap and get attacked. 'My father.'

Mr Ollerton pointed to his cheek. 'There's a bruise starting. Why did he thump you?'

'Because I won't do as he wants.'

'I can guess what that is: he told you to stop working for me. Do you want to do that?'

'No, I don't, sir. He has some stupid ideas, downright wicked some of them are, my uncle says. Let alone my mother and the kids need the money I earn to buy food, I like laying bricks. And I like working with the other young fellows who're learning trades. I've never had friends like them before.'

Mr Ollerton smiled at him. 'I'm glad to hear that. I've been getting good reports about your work.'

'You have?' He couldn't help smiling at that.

'Yes. But Jezzy, be careful how you go in future.'

He could only nod. His father was cunning. Maybe he could walk home with someone from now on, or take a longer way round. His father couldn't catch him when he ran, but he couldn't run all the way home, could he?

'I'll let you get along now. I'm sure you're as hungry for your tea as I am.' He turned and started walking off again towards his home.

Jezzy realised suddenly that his employer was heading towards where his father was lurking and rushed after him. 'Please come back, sir.'

Edward stared at him. 'Why?'

'It's, er, not safe.'

'Is your father lying in wait for me?'

He could only nod, he was so ashamed.

'It must be hard for you having a father like him, in many ways.'

He nodded again. He hadn't realised till he went to live with his uncle that other fathers treated their children differently, could be kind and helpful towards them, teach them useful things about life, large and small, not push them around and pinch their food from them.

One of the chaps working on the house came along the road just then and Edward called out, 'Have you a minute?'

'Yes, sir.'

'I'm told Terry Catlow is lurking again, waiting for me. Could you walk home with me, do you think? I'll make it worth your while. I doubt he'll attack two of us and I'm not afraid to fight if I have to.'

'I don't need money to do that, sir. I'd rather you stayed safe. We all would.'

'Thank you. I really appreciate that. But I insist on paying you for your trouble.'

As they nodded to Jezzy and walked away together, the lad set off walking quickly, this time taking a roundabout way home. Just in case.

His mother looked up as he flung the door open so hard it banged back against the wall. 'Watch what you're doing.' Then she saw his expression. 'What's the matter, Jez?'

He told her about his father lurking nearby and grabbing him. 'I don't want Mr Ollerton to get hurt, either. He's a good man. Everyone who's working on the house likes him. He's even bought a big urn and teapot so that we can make hot drinks with our snacks and midday meals.'

'I think – no, I'm sure your father has started losing his wits in the past year or two, like one of his old uncles did.' She looked sad. 'I've got my life sorted out at the same time as he's started losing his.' She gave her son a sudden hug. 'Don't ever take after him, love, and above all, don't do what he tells you about where to work and . . . and such.'

'Would he really *kill* Mr Ollerton?'

'Yes, he would. I told you, he's lost his way, got so that he can only think about the one stupid thing. I like Mr Ollerton too and I don't want to be married to a murderer.'

She was very quiet that evening, which wasn't like her, doing a lot of sighing and staring into space.

Jezzy was quiet too. It felt as if the day's events had battered his whole body physically as well as his mind. He wished he didn't have a father like that, wished his uncle or someone like him had been his father instead.

He felt tired when he went to bed but couldn't get to sleep for ages, not until he'd decided to keep a more careful eye out for his father and if necessary stop him trying to hurt Mr Ollerton or stealing from people. When it came down to it, his father should work for his daily bread like everyone else did.

Jezzy was proud of giving his mum most of his wages every week, very proud indeed.

Sergeant McGill watched from a distance as a man stopped a lad in the street and dragged him to one side. He didn't like to see people ill-treating the young and asked a passer-by who the man was. The woman scowled and said it was Terry Catlow and the lad was his eldest son. Poor thing having a father like that.

'I've heard about Terry Catlow. Is the lad a chip off the old block?'

'No, he's nothing like his father. Well, not these days he isn't. He was a naughty youngster then went to live with his uncle and came back a year or so later a different person. He's a nice, lively lad these days. He's labouring for a bricklayer who's working on Mr Ollerton's big house, and he's doing well, from what I've heard. Anything else you need to know?'

'No, thank you. That's very useful information.'

'You're welcome, Sergeant. And can I just say that I hope you like living here in Ollindale. We're all glad to see you. We needed a breath of fresh air, someone who'll help maintain law and order, and above all stop the thieving that's been going on more often lately. A lot of it's by that chap you were asking about, Catlow.'

'I'll do my best to put things right. Again, thank you for your help.'

'You're welcome.'

As she carried on walking briskly down the street, he moved to one side, standing where he wouldn't be as noticeable and continued to watch. It looked as if Catlow was telling the lad off for some misdemeanour. Well, it would have been something like that with a normal father and son. But Hector had heard enough about Catlow to know that he wasn't a good father, didn't even bother with his kids most of the time. So what was he furiously angry about?

Was he really intending to murder an important member of the community, one who'd brought jobs to people struggling to make a living in the valley? Not if Hector could help it. He intended to maintain law and order in what was now *his* valley.

He was too far away to catch Catlow this time, but he'd know him at a glance from now on. Apparently, the man had already stolen food from several places recently, quite a lot of it from the sound of things, even from his own wife, and he mustn't be allowed to get away with that.

The trouble was, Catlow seemed to be rather skilled at creeping around without being seen and Hector didn't know the valley all that well yet. And to add to the difficulties of stopping him, not many people seemed willing to confront the man. They'd been letting him get away with stealing for years from what Hector could make out.

Well, that was going to change. Oh, yes.

Had Catlow been so violent in the past that some of the weaker people were terrified of him? It looked like it. The previous policeman didn't seem to have done anything about catching him, either. Well, Cliff Nolan had looked worn out and far older than his actual age to Hector. And he'd had little to say about how he'd been involved in valley affairs when they had a chat and he handed over the various keys belonging to the small police station.

That was a pity because usually when someone was retiring and handing over control, the one leaving would tell you who to watch out for and who could be helpful, even if only un-officially, which could be very useful.

Since information wasn't offered, Hector had asked him straight out about this, but Cliff had just shrugged and said the valley was fairly peaceful these days because a few villains had either left town or been killed recently.

When Hector mentioned Terry Catlow and asked where he was to be found now, Cliff said he was living rough on the moors.

'Where exactly?'

'I'm afraid I don't know.'

'Doesn't he have any family round here?'

'Sort of. But Mrs Catlow won't have her husband back liv-ing with her, not at any price she won't. No, you just keep him out of the town and he'll die out there of pneumonia or frostbite once winter really sets in, and good riddance to bad rubbish.'

'I'd rather find out where on the moors he hides out and go after him now so that he can't hurt Mr Ollerton. Someone must know where he is, surely.'

'Well, I can't tell you anything. I didn't grow up round here and I've never been one to go wandering over the tops. In some parts there are sudden drops and cliffs, all sorts of dangers. I reckon you have to be born here to know your way around out there.'

Clearly Cliff didn't intend to get involved before he moved away from Ollerthwaite to live with his eldest daughter in Yorkshire. Hector thanked him for his help and saw him to the door of the police station.

When he went back inside he set to, clearing out all the cupboards and drawers, and they certainly needed it. Half the history of the valley's misdemeanours was in them. That sort of stuff could be useful. He set a whole pile of letters and papers aside to read when he had more time.

31

Dan settled Polly in at the cottage as best he could and after some thought he decided to get a young lass to live with them and help around the house. He'd been intending to do that as she got closer to her time and afterwards for a while too, just to make sure she recovered properly. He would be able to afford that on his higher wages.

He intended to take his wife to see the woman doctor here as soon as he could, too. She'd be able to tell them about finding a reliable and skilled midwife, surely, and she might be able to help Polly in other ways.

All this with a new job to get used to, a job he thoroughly enjoyed. Mr Ollerton had praised him several times already for suggestions that helped the work go more smoothly.

To his surprise, Walter Crossley came across to speak to him at the building site the second week he was there, just after they'd moved into the cottage. By now he was well aware what an important man this was.

'My wife is going to call in and see your wife today. I hope you don't mind. We heard that she's not well and that you'd hired young Sadie Foxton to help her with the housework and such.'

'Sadie's doing most of the heavy work at the moment. She's a very capable lass, thank goodness.'

'Aye. All her family are. The thing is, my Flora is a nurse with many years of experience. She's worried about what she's heard and wants to see if she can do anything to help your wife. Is that all right with you?'

'More than all right. I'd welcome any help at all, especially from someone who knows what she's doing.'

'You wouldn't object to my Flora driving your wife over to see Dr Coxton, then? Our lady doctor has a good reputation for helping women who're expecting, especially those who're not having an easy time of it.'

'As I said, I appreciate any help I can get. I've been trying to persuade Polly to see this doctor, but she keeps refusing, so I hope your wife can get her to change her mind. To be honest, I'm at my wits' end as to what to do for the best, Mr Crossley.'

Walter patted his shoulder. 'Sometimes there's nothing you can do. And sometimes other people can do more than you can, however hard you try. My Flora will find out if she can get your wife to accept help and we'll see what the good doctor says as well. They're both skilled, caring women.'

'I'm truly grateful.'

Walter felt upset for the young man as he walked away. Dan Makersby was clearly having a hard time. As was his poor wife. Some women had a really bad start to their pregnancies, as if their bodies were rebelling against what was happening to them. Most of them got over it after a while, but if this woman didn't perhaps his Flora could help. She was one of the most capable women he'd ever met. And the best wife a man could have.

When a small cart pulled up outside the cottage, Polly was asleep on the sofa, so Sadie answered the door.

'Is Mrs Makersby in?'

The lass glanced quickly over her shoulder and spoke in a low voice, 'She's having a nap at the moment, Mrs Crossley.'

'How is she?'

Sadie looked at her as if afraid to say anything.

Flora lowered her voice to barely more than a whisper. 'I've heard she's not well, so I came to take her to the doctor. Can you get on with the housework while I'm gone?'

'Oh yes. I'm doing most of it already.' She held the door open, glanced over her shoulder and said in a louder voice, 'Do come in Mrs Crossley. I'm sure Mrs Makersby will be happy to see you.'

Flora followed her inside and hoped she hadn't shown her shock at how pale and weak the poor woman was looking, even worse than she'd expected. And this was before the baby was even showing. 'Don't get up, my dear. I can find my own way to a chair.'

She didn't waste time chatting but said straight out, 'I heard you weren't well, so I've come to take you to see our lady doctor. You'll like Dr Coxton and she's got a lot of experience at dealing with women who're expecting. I have our cart outside so I can drive you there straight away. I'm a nurse myself, by the way.'

Polly studied her then sighed and looked sad. 'I doubt this doctor will be able to do much for me, Mrs Crossley. I've been sickly all along and my mam was the same.'

'Well, it won't hurt to go and chat to the doctor, will it? After all, people usually call her in when someone is actually birthing the baby, so she'll need to see you before then.'

Polly shrugged and sagged back as if giving in to a stronger will than her own. 'I suppose you're right. So long as you can bring me back as well as take me there. I'm having trouble walking very far at the moment.'

'Of course I'll bring you back.' Flora turned round and called, 'Sadie, can you fetch your mistress's coat and hat, and a nice warm scarf, please? Oh, and a blanket to wrap round her.'

Dr Coxton was expecting Polly. She'd been told how ill the newcomer was by several people, and when Flora Crossley asked her to see the woman after her usual surgery had finished, she had said she'd stay late and check everything she could to see if they could help.

The doctor sucked in her breath sharply when she saw the poor woman, who looked as if she ought to be in bed. Sometimes it was the only solution, and it could help.

Her patient had to be helped down from the cart by their gardener and Flora, and then she leaned heavily on the older woman as she walked slowly across to the house.

Maria Coxton forced a slight smile as Polly was brought in to see her.

'This is Polly Makersby, Doctor.'

'Thank you for bringing her, Mrs Crossley. So nice to meet you, Polly. I like to see all my mothers-to-be before they get near the birth.'

She then proceeded to check every single thing she could think of, but the only reassuring finding was that the baby seemed to have a strong heartbeat, and the mother's wasn't as bad as she'd expected.

Mrs Makersby gave her a long, thoughtful stare after she'd finished the examination and surprised her by asking, 'Do you think you can manage to save the baby? Will it be strong enough to live?'

She didn't try to pretend. 'It has a strong heartbeat, my dear, which is a good sign. And your own heart isn't showing any signs of weakness.'

'I'm glad to hear that. And, Doctor, I know I don't have long to live. I haven't told my husband that I know and I'd appreciate it if you didn't either.'

'You're already feeling sure about that? I don't agree. Not if you can get a lot of rest, anyway. It's the main thing that can help you through this stage of the pregnancy.'

'Are you sure it could help?'

'One is rarely sure about anything at this stage. Your husband will ask me what I think and what he should do and I shall tell him you need rest.'

'He's already hired a girl to help in the house.'

'Good for him. And I can give you a tonic that may help too,' Dr Coxton offered. 'It's worth trying. Will you take it?'

'You're sure it'll help the baby?'

'It usually does. And can help you too.'

'Then I'll take it. Just tell me how often and how much.'

Flora, who was sitting behind them near the door, didn't say anything. But she'd keep an eye on Polly from now on. That was a nurse's job more than a doctor's.

When they went outside again, she managed to get Polly up on the cart without any other help, then drove her home.

They didn't chat but once Polly murmured, 'It's nice to get out and see a bit of the town.'

'We'll see if we can get you out occasionally.'

'You're very kind.'

'I like to help mothers produce fine healthy children.'

After she got back to the farm, Flora went to find Walter and sat holding his hand.

'Is Polly Makersby too bad to save?'

'I never like to give up on someone, especially a young woman.'

After a while she became her usual brisk self and sent him off to find Dan at the building site. He was to tell the young husband that Dan should try to stay cheerful and concentrate on helping his wife get through the first few months.

After that the days continued to tick slowly past and Polly found she could hardly lift a finger without someone telling her to sit down and leave that for others.

The doctor's tonic seemed to be helping her cope a little better too and the women from the village popped in to chat sometimes, which was nice. This was such a lovely friendly place to live.

32

A few weeks later, Edward Ollerton was standing just outside his kitchen door for a breath of fresh evening air.
He'd given up his solitary walks around the valley and still had
men posted around the estate, but he'd never considered he
could be in danger so close to the house.

Suddenly there was the faint sound of gravel moving
nearby. A subliminal sense of danger made him swing round
so that the knife stabbed into his arm instead of his body.
He yelled at the top of his voice and kicked out, managing
to strike Terry Catlow hard enough to send him staggering
backwards.

His assailant wasted precious seconds scrabbling around for
the knife he'd dropped, so that by the time he jerked to his
feet, Edward had managed to get into the house again and was
starting to shut the door.

Terry stuck his foot in the gap and stopped the door closing
fully then grabbed hold of it with one hand and tried to shove
it back open, but found it hard to do that against Edward's
greater weight and strength.

By this time Lillian had come running to her husband's aid.
She took one look at the scene and grabbed the frying pan in
which she'd cooked their tea, ignoring the fatty fragments that
splashed around as she used it to batter the would-be intruder's hand that was clasping the door.

She hit out with all the force she could muster and when
Terry yelped in pain and let go of the door, she managed to

jab the pan sideways through the gap kept open by his foot, this time hitting him lower down in a very vulnerable spot.

He yelled again in agony and curled up to protect himself involuntarily, allowing Edward to close the door completely. Lillian at once slid the bolt into place.

Edward slumped against the wall with a groan, clutching his bloody upper arm. 'Well done, darling.'

From outside Terry yelled, 'I'll get you next time, Ollerton. I know this valley better than you do.'

They heard the sound of his running footsteps, growing fainter as he escaped into the dusk.

'Dear heaven, that man has gone completely mad,' Lillian gasped.

Before she could help her husband further into the kitchen, they heard footsteps running towards the house from a slightly different direction and a voice calling, 'Are you all right, Mr Ollerton?'

Lillian peered out of the kitchen window and recognised the man coming towards them. 'It's Patrick. He must have been on his way here to keep watch tonight.'

Edward joined her, leaning heavily on a cupboard. 'Catlow's a cunning devil. He must have watched and seen the times the men keeping guard change over. Hell fire, is nowhere safe from that scoundrel?'

'There's blood all over your arm. Let's get you sitting down before you fall down.'

Patrick came up to the house and stopped near the window. 'Are you all right, Mr Ollerton?'

'He's hurt. Catlow just stabbed him,' she shouted.

'He only managed to hit me in the arm but thanks to my wife's quick thinking, we drove him off.'

'Keep the back door locked, sir, and I'll check the garden, then send someone for the sergeant.'

'Keep your eyes open for Catlow.'

'I will. Just let him dare come near me. I've got my weighted walking stick to wallop him with.'

'I think he's run away now, damn him.'

Lillian had now seen Edward's arm properly. 'There's a lot of blood. How bad is the arm? Stop trying to hide it from me.'

'Go and check that every single window is closed before you do anything about my wound,' he said. 'I'm a bit dizzy, that's all.'

She picked up a clean tea towel and pushed him down on a chair. 'Here. Use this to staunch the blood while I check the windows.'

He held it to his arm, glad he was now sitting down because he was feeling faint and finding it hard to think clearly.

She was back a short time later. 'It's all locked up. Now, let me see that arm properly.'

He let her help him take his jacket and shirt off and check the wound properly, then said, 'You're shivering, darling. Come and sit on one of the armchairs near the warmth of the kitchen range.'

He couldn't help groaning as he turned and bumped the arm on something.

'I think it'll need stitching. We'll have to send for the doctor.'

She knew he was feeling weak when he didn't argue, so she called to Patrick and he came running.

'I've sent a lad for the sergeant, Mrs Ollerton.'

'Can you send someone for the doctor as well. My husband has a deep stab wound on his arm that needs attention.'

'I'll find someone straight away but I'm not leaving you on your own in case that sod is still waiting nearby.'

When she went back to her husband, she muttered, 'We're buying a loud bell so that we can ring it for help if he attacks you again. I wish we had neighbours close by.'

'Mmm.' He leaned back, eyes closed.

She kept a careful eye on him but didn't speak or mess with the wound.

It seemed a long time till Dr Coxton arrived, brought by her usual driver. She left him outside keeping an eye on the pony, and dealt with the wound, cleaning it carefully, then stitching the big cut together.

He couldn't help moaning at the more painful moments.

'Sorry, but it's quite deep. You're lucky not to have been stabbed in the chest, Mr Ollerton. That must have been a very sharp knife.'

'Mmm.'

'You'll need to stay at home for a day or two and not move that arm around more than you have to. Keep it in the sling until I've taken out the stitches. You've lost quite a bit of blood, so you'll feel very tired. Drink plenty of fluids and eat some good red meat.'

'I'll make sure he takes care, Doctor,' Lillian said firmly.

Edward stifled a sigh but nodded. He still felt shocked that such a thing could happen to him right on his own doorstep. He'd be a lot more careful in future, even near his own home, but he couldn't spend his whole life watching out for Catlow. They had to find some way of dealing with him. But how?

Closing his eyes, he leaned back in his armchair while the doctor told Lillian what to do and said she'd call round some-time tomorrow afternoon to check the cut.

When his wife came back from the door she echoed his own thoughts. 'Something will have to be done about Catlow or you'll never be safe. And what's taking the sergeant so long?'

He grabbed her hand with his good arm. 'He'll be here soon, I'm sure. Thank you for your help, love. I feel so stupid for standing out there alone.'

'Well, done is done. But you'll not be standing there alone again. Sit quietly and I'll make us a mug of cocoa.'

She hoped she'd hidden the tears that welled in her eyes now the danger was past. What would she do without him? He wasn't just a husband, he was her dearest friend.

Sergeant McGill arrived shortly afterwards and questioned Edward about what exactly had happened. He left him and went away looking grim and determined and asked Patrick, who was still keeping watch nearby, whether he knew someone who would help him search for Catlow.

'He'll be long gone, that one,' Patrick said.

Nonetheless, Hector went to find Patrick's friend and they scoured the town for any signs of Catlow. But no one had seen him and when Hector looked beyond the town at the big, dark expanse of the moors, he knew it'd be no use going out there to search.

What he really needed was to find some men who knew the moors well to help him.

He'd send a message to Walter Crossley first thing in the morning, he decided. If anyone knew the people as well as the area, it was him.

The following day, Lillian told Edward firmly that she'd sit on him if he so much as tried to poke his nose out of the house.

'Well, will you ask Lewis to come and see me here then. We really do need to discuss the house. I'm not too badly hurt to talk, for heaven's sake.'

'I will after you've had something to eat and a little rest.'

So it was over an hour later before Lewis arrived.

When the two men were settled together with a pot of tea, Edward said, 'I think this might be a good time for you to finish sorting out the cellars. I had trouble sleeping last night so thought about the whole situation and what I really need.'

Lewis shook his head. 'Are you sure you were thinking clearly. I gather it's a deep wound, so no wonder you couldn't sleep.'

Edward shrugged. 'The two of us together should be able to sort it all out.' He gave a wry smile. 'In one way, the injury has done me good, given me some thinking time. Have you thought any more about what we discussed last time we met?'

'Yes. And since you don't need most of the cellars and you do want to get the house finished so that you can live there, I think you were right. We should work out a way to close off the cellars you won't be using and deal with them later. We've perhaps been over-ambitious about what we can achieve. The main thing is to get your home finished and let you move into it.'

Edward smiled and nodded. 'I have a great desire to be living in the house by the time of the Queen's Diamond Jubilee. What do you think?'

'I think that if we change our plans and postpone finishing a few jobs, we should be able to do it. Does Lillian agree with you?'

'Yes. We rarely disagree about anything.'

Lewis didn't say anything else for a few moments. He was used now to the fond smile Edward sometimes got when talking or even just thinking about his wife.

'So you'll prepare some variations on our plans?'

'Yes.' Lewis stood up. 'And I think that's enough talking for the moment. That's a nasty wound and you're looking a bit pale. You'll need time to recover properly.'

'I'm hoping someone will help me work out how to capture Catlow and lock him away for a long time. I don't want to spend my life needing bodyguards or peering over my shoulder when I go out. It still rankles that he caught me right next to my own home.'

He sat for a while after Lewis had left. He was doing the right thing, he was sure. What's more, Walter had told him the time had come for someone to catch Catlow and lock him away. And when Walter Crossley decided something needed doing as a matter of urgency, it usually got done.

He hadn't taken Catlow's threats to kill him as seriously as he should have done, Edward admitted to himself. They were nearly in the twentieth century, for heaven's sake, not in the Middle Ages. Why did that man think he had the right to behave like this? Or had he lost the ability to think clearly? Who knew all that went on inside another person's mind?

He hoped the new policeman would be better than the retired one and able to help them sort this out.

There had to be a way to make the valley safer.

33

When word got round about Catlow's attack on Edward Ollerton, a lot of people in Ollerthwaite were extremely angry. Not only did they like the injured man, he'd brought much-needed jobs to the valley and would continue to do so.

And no one had any respect for Catlow, who was following the same path as the other villains in his family and getting worse as he grew older and lazier. He'd brought nothing but trouble to Ollindale in recent years.

'We can't put up with any more of this,' Walter said to his wife. 'Catlow is making life a misery for a lot of people, what with his stealing and violence towards those who cross him.'

She stared at him in surprise. 'I don't think I've ever seen you quite so angry.'

'I've not often felt like this. I'm absolutely furious. It's gone on for long enough and if no one else will do something about it, I shall.'

'I think our new sergeant would be happy to do something but he doesn't know the valley very well, does he? Why don't you offer him your services and find a few others to help you both?'

'Good idea. We have to *do* something. And soon.'

'Promise me you'll be careful.'

'Of course I will. I've got far more reason to be careful these days.' He smiled at her.

She smiled back and it was a minute or two before she carried on speaking. 'And if I can help in any way, Walter love, you only have to ask.'

'Thanks. I'll start by putting word out that we need to do something, then I'll call a meeting of certain friends of mine, a couple of people I know I can trust completely.'

Before he'd even sent notes to his friends, Hector turned up at the farm to ask his advice and the two men had a long discussion. Then Hector went back to the police station and Walter decided to discuss the situation with a wider group of men.

He was determined to stop Catlow's depredations permanently and before he succeeded in killing Edward. The man could be put in prison for what he'd done already because folk had seen him attack Edward, but first they had to catch him and as he'd proved in the past, that was very hard indeed. Few people knew the valley and moors around it as well at Catlow.

The following day he sent out further messages to some of the stronger young and middle-aged men, inviting them to a meeting at his farm, as agreed in his conversation with Hector. He included the new police sergeant and his young constable and sent them the details.

Walter liked Hector McGill and thought the man had made a good start here. He seemed intelligent and honest. The young constable had only just started work here, so no one knew him yet. He was tall and looked strong but was more of a lad than a man still. Luckily young Neil had the sense to watch what his sergeant did and listen carefully to everyone he came into contact with. He'd quickly become known for not wasting words.

Among the people at the meeting was Jezzy Catlow. Walter hadn't been sure whether to invite the lad to take part in this attempt to capture his father. However, when he'd discussed this dilemma with a couple of men whose opinions he valued, including Gavin, the bricklayer Jezzy was working for, they'd assured him that the lad loathed his father and was both angry and embarrassed about his ongoing thieving.

'Terry Catlow has upset nearly everyone in the valley now,' Gavin said grimly. 'Even his own wife will have nothing to do with him these days. She's a changed woman from when she was younger, my wife says, and my lass is a good judge of character. She's getting quite friendly with Nora Catlow nowadays.'

'I'm glad to hear that.'

'And what's more, that lad is a hard worker. I couldn't ask for a better apprentice.'

So Walter had asked Jezzy whether he wanted to join in the attempt to catch his father and suggested the lad discuss this with his mother first.

Jezzy arrived for the meeting early with a message from his mother that she wished Mr Crossley well in what he was doing and would be glad to be rid of her husband, and if she could help in any way to let her know.

'So you'll join us, then, Jezzy?'

'Yes, sir.'

The lad then stood quietly to one side of the room, leaning against the wall. He seemed to be noting everything that happened, Walter thought, and had bright, intelligent eyes. After a while he was flanked by two other young men from good valley families who seemed to be on good terms with him. That spoke well for him.

The other people stared at Jezzy at first not even trying to hide their surprise at his presence, then as the meeting started, they mostly forgot he was there as their anger at the situation took over.

Walter had got his womenfolk to provide refreshments and bottles of ale or cider, which were all well received by the group, some of whom ate rather heartily for once, as he'd hoped they would. A couple of women had accompanied their husbands, he was glad to see, and they were standing with his wife to one side. He wanted as many people ranged against Catlow as possible.

After a while he called for silence. 'I asked you to come here to decide what to do about Catlow. Are you all right about us discussing your father, Jezzy?'

The lad turned red in embarrassment but said immediately in a firm, steady voice, 'I don't call him my father any more, Mr Crossley. He's never acted like a real father anyway. Me and Ma want him stopped. He's already raided our house and stolen a lot of her winter food stores.'

There was a murmur of growling disapproval at that, as it hadn't been general knowledge.

'She's worried he'll break in again, even though we've had the locks changed. She told me to say that if you catch him, you should shut him away for a long time, so that other people can get on with their lives.'

He so clearly meant what he said about not feeling as if Catlow was his father that Walter was pleased to see nearly all the remaining doubters relax visibly.

He turned to the two police officers. 'There are definitely two sorts of Catlows, you'll find. The law-abiding ones usually leave the valley, unfortunately.'

'I'll remember that,' the sergeant said.

Walter nodded and continued speaking. 'Let's get started on some practicalities then. Does anyone have any idea of where exactly he's hiding? He must have found some sort of shelter at this time of year.'

He saw Jezzy open and shut his mouth, then wait to see if anyone else spoke. When heads were shaken and people murmured that they didn't know except that it was somewhere up on the moors, the lad took a deep breath and spoke up.

'I think I know where he is, Mr Crossley.'

Everyone there swung round to stare at him.

'Good lad,' Walter said quickly. 'Tell us.'

'It's hard to tell you exactly because it's tricky to get to, but he's in the caves at Beckshall Edge.'

'We've looked there,' someone said. 'We saw signs he'd been there, but nothing to show he was still living there.'

'He is, though. There's a passage right at the back of the cave at the far left. It doesn't show very clearly so people don't often notice it. And even if they do, it doesn't look as if it's going anywhere because you have to crawl through a low tunnel to get to the hidden cave. So most people pass it by.'

'Are you sure?' It was the sergeant who asked.

'Oh, yes. He goes to the inner cave when anyone is nearby. He keeps his stores of food there all the time an' he sleeps there too sometimes.'

'I've not met the fellow yet,' the Sergeant said, 'but if there's as much proof of his thieving as some of you have said today, he's breaking the law and that needs dealing with. If you catch him, don't do anything drastic. Bring him to me and I'll arrest him.'

'We'll do that if we can,' Walter said. 'We have to go carefully though. I've seen some of the members of his family get really violent as they grow older, sergeant, an' this man is showing signs of it. He doesn't hesitate to hurt folk who're weaker than him if they won't give him what he wants. But we've had enough of it.'

He broke off as there was a murmur of approval, then nodded and continued.

Someone at the back said loudly, 'We're not letting him hurt anyone else, if we have to kill him to stop him.'

The sergeant raised one hand to show that he wanted to speak. 'Don't do that or you'll be in trouble.'

'Then you do something,' one man called out.

'I will. I'm interested in this cave. Does he really live in one? There'd not be much light or air in a back room?'

They all looked at Jezzy again.

'The ceiling in the back cave is higher once you're inside and there are a couple of openings high up in the cave roof that let in some light and air, but the ceiling is well above head height and the holes are too small to get out through.'

'How do you know all that?' the sergeant asked.

'*He* showed it to me years ago, said it was a family secret and I was the eldest so I ought to know, but he threatened to give me a good thumping if I ever told anyone. It felt horrible inside and he laughed at me when I said I wasn't going in there again. I haven't done because I don't like going into caves at all. I panicked in that hidden cave and rushed outside again. He's mocked me about that for years.'

'We won't force you to go through to the back but you can still show us what cave it's in, can't you?' someone asked. 'We have to catch your father, lad.'

'I'll show you the way whenever you like.' Jezzy hesitated, then added, 'Please will you stop calling him my father. He doesn't feel like one. An' Ma doesn't want to call him her husband, either. She says she threw him out for good when he started hitting her and she's not having him back ever again because even if he promises not to do it again, he always breaks his promises.'

'It's not right, hitting women isn't,' a man with a deep voice said. 'Eh, you've changed a lot, lad, an' I'm glad to see it. You were a bit wild yourself when you were younger.'

'I felt differently after living with my uncle, who was always *kind* to me and to his own children. He never hit me. Not once. I couldn't believe how nice it was there at first, kept waiting for something to go wrong.'

His voice wobbled on the last words, so Walter moved across and put an arm round his shoulders, giving him a hug. 'What happened at your uncle's was that you learned a better way to treat other people. And we're all very proud of you for coming today, lad. It's not everyone who can try to do the right thing by others after being taught to face the world the wrong way.'

Jezzy sniffed hard and wiped his sleeve across his eyes. 'Thank you, Mr Crossley.' He leaned his head against the kindly old man's shoulder for a moment longer, feeling the warmth of that embrace in more ways than one.

When he stepped back, he squared his shoulders and said, 'I'll take you to that cave whenever you like.'

'Thank you. I don't think we should any of us go rushing off yet, though,' Walter said.

The sergeant nodded. 'Definitely not. We need to plan this very carefully.'

'And we need to make sure no one will tell Terry Catlow that we're going after him. And that includes you, Frank Barker. You weren't invited to come here today but since you did, I'll tell you straight to keep your mouth shut. We'll know who tattled if he finds out.' He looked across towards a man at the back who was staring down at the floor now, not meeting anyone's eyes.

Someone else chimed in. 'If you say one word about this to anyone apart from those who're here today, Frank, me an' my brothers will make sure you're run out of the valley for good.'

Frank looked round with panic on his face. 'I won't say a word. I promise I won't.'

'See that you keep that promise.'

'I will. Honest I will!'

Walter nodded a thank you to the man who'd just spoken to Frank, then looked round. 'I'll need to come up with a plan. I believe in careful preparation with such a cunning sod. I'm hoping the sergeant will get together with me about working that out and then we'll try to do something.'

'Happy to.'

'And I think we want Edward Ollerton to act with us. He should be well enough to join our group soon, though he's not coming with us when we go after Terry. He lost a lot of blood when he was stabbed, and the doctor said it'd take him a while to recover fully. We're not putting him at risk again.'

'Don't take too long to make your plan, Walter,' someone called from the side of the room. 'I'd like to see Catlow captured and locked away by Christmas. We don't want that oik spoiling things for our families. We'd been planning to have a good time, for once, with a bit more money in our pockets, thanks to Mr Ollerton.'

'If it's humanly possible, I'll make sure we do that, believe me.'

When the meeting broke up, one of the lads fell into place beside Jezzy as he walked down the hill. 'You can come and play kick-around with us, if you like. We weren't sure before whether we could trust you but now we are and we're short of a player.'

Jezzy looked at him in surprise and then delight as these words sank in. If Larry Gregson and his friends had accepted him enough to invite him to join them, he'd been well and truly accepted in the valley instead of kept at a distance and treated warily.

This invitation was particularly important to someone of his age because people said that one day Larry would be an important person in the valley. He was what folk called a 'likely lad' and his family were well respected.

'Thank you, Larry. I'd like that.' He hoped he'd sounded calm because he didn't feel it, felt happy for once.

'Don't let anybody down and you'll be all right for life here,' Larry warned.

'I won't let people down. I'm not like *him*, really I'm not. An' I don't want to move away from the valley. I found that out when I was living with my uncle. Eh, I was so homesick those first weeks. Nothing but streets and smoky factory chimneys. I really missed the moors. And the lake.'

Larry glanced sideways to where a glint of water could be seen occasionally between the houses. 'That lake is going to be a good place to go for walks once it's finished.'

'Yes, it is. And thank you again for the invitation to play kick-around with you.'

He clapped Jezzy on the back. 'I wouldn't have asked you if I hadn't thought you'd fit in.'

Jezzy had gone to the meeting feeling apprehensive, but now he felt hopeful and far happier. He couldn't wait to tell his mother how well things were working out, in spite of his horrible father. How lucky it was that he'd been sent to stay with his uncle.

Something else occurred to him. From now on he should help his mother make sure his brothers and sisters behaved themselves. None of the younger ones seemed to have inherited that nasty nature that cropped up sometimes in his family. He'd been watching them carefully since he got back. Very carefully indeed.

If they could just get rid of his father, life could be really good for them all.

34

One of the men Dan was working with surprised him by asking if it would be all right for his wife to go and visit Polly. 'My missus knows how hard it can be when you're expecting and not well, because she was sick as a dog a lot of the time herself, poor lass.'

'I'd be grateful. Polly hasn't got the strength or energy even to go to the shops. The neighbour at the farm does that for her, or young Sadie sometimes. But I know my wife would appreciate a bit of company.'

'Good. My lass said she'd be willing to help out now and then in ways that would have meant a lot to her when she was expecting, so she's going to bake a meat and potato pie that'll last you both a couple of days, as well as one for us.' The man licked his lips at the mere thought of that. 'She makes the best pies, the very best.'

'Eh, that's kind of her. We'd be so grateful.' He knew Polly got lonely but she never complained.

'She doesn't like to think of a sick woman struggling on her own. It's a pity you don't have family here.'

Dan nodded, looking worried. 'I know. But we're managing better than I'd expected because folk round here have been so friendly and helpful. I'm hoping to settle here permanently.'

The next day the woman took the pie round and Dan went home to a hearty meal, for once. He could also tell that his wife had enjoyed the company because she looked a bit brighter.

Two days later at work a chap called Bertie said suddenly as they were sitting eating their midday sandwiches, 'My wife thinks you're looking strained an' no wonder, Dan lad. She suggested it might do you good to get in an occasional walk at the weekends. It gets dark too soon to do one after work at this time of year.'

'I'd love a walk but I don't like to leave Polly for long.'

'Even an hour in the fresh air can help. That's what I do when I need to think. My wife says she'll come and sit with yours for a while. If you ask me, the best thing of all would be for you to go for a stroll near the lake. There's something soothing about the sight of water.'

Dan couldn't remember the last time he'd been able to stride out and relax in the fresh air at the weekend, knowing his wife would be all right without him. 'You're right. A walk would be something to look forward to and it'd do me good, I'm sure. I'd thought that sort of thing would have to wait months, till after the baby's born and settled down. Are you sure your wife wouldn't mind visiting mine?'

Bertie grinned. 'You don't know her. If she sees something she thinks is needed she finds a way to do it. She said to tell you she'll come over on Sunday afternoon if it's fine and sit with your wife while you and I go out for a walk. You've not been right round the lake since you came here, have you?'

'No, I haven't.'

'We can do that, if you like. Your house isn't far away from it. You get some nice views on a walk there as long as you don't mind the rough ground at the part furthest away from the town. We call it the "top end", though of course it's on the same level as the rest or the water would all drain away.'

He laughed heartily at his own mild joke, so Dan forced a smile too. Then it turned into a real smile at the thought of enjoying a long walk without feeling guilty or worried.

At the weekend, they were lucky enough to have a sunny Sunday, so Bertie's wife took over and shooed them out of the house.

The two men strode round Jubilee Lake at a cracking pace, not even talking most of the time. It was only when they got to the far end that Dan found out how rough the ground was there, with well-established shrubs and rocks scattered around like a giant's playthings.

'Why didn't they finish making a path at this part when they did the rest?' he asked.

'Because of the Russian flu. It hit the valley hard just before the Golden Jubilee, and then came back again every year or two. Walter's tried a few times since then to get the work finished but something's always cropped up to stop people getting down to it. And he's nearly ten years older than he was then, so he's a bit old to do the hard digging himself.' He grinned. 'Even if he tried, I don't think that nice new wife of his would let him overdo things. Eh, I'd not go against her wishes, nice as she is with people.'

Dan studied the area at the top end of the lake. 'If we got some of the chaps that are working on the big house to bring their shovels up here, we could sort this out in a day or two. A couple of weekends' work would probably do most of the clearing needed.'

His companion looked startled then stared round thoughtfully. 'You're right. People have always said it'd be weeks of work and take a lot of men.'

'Well, those of us working on the house are experienced at digging and sorting patches of land out, aren't we? If anyone could do it more quickly, we could.' Dan tugged at a small bush and with a bit of effort shook it loose from the ground.

'See. It wouldn't take that much effort if we all joined in. I soon found out how much Walter Crossley does for this valley, so how about we do something for him? I can only be in on it if the women will take it in turn to sit with Polly.'

'My wife will soon get them organised to do that.'

'She's a treasure, as well as a good cook, then. That pie was delicious. Mind you, I'd have to get my share of the work on the lake done before the baby arrives. Polly will need my help even more after that.'

After another careful look round at what was needed, Bertie said, 'You're on, lad. I'm sure my wife and her friends will look after yours and I'll speak to the other lads about helping with the digging. Let's just hope the mild winter continues. It doesn't usually snow till February or even March.'

He grinned as something occurred to him. 'How about we spread the word not to say anything about it to Walter? We could just do it then take him for a walk and give him a nice surprise.'

'Excellent idea!'

The following weekend was rainy and cold, so the men had to wait a fortnight to make a start on the lake path. Dan told Polly about it and she too was very much in favour of them finishing it.

'You won't mind me leaving you?'

'I've not been on my own all day at weekends since you got friendly with Bertie. Not even once! Eh, it makes a difference. A couple of people that I'd not met before have popped in to introduce themselves and say hello as well. They said Bertie's wife told them about me being on my own. Sadie's a good little worker in the house but it's been lovely to have a natter with other women nearer my own age and I can still make a good cup of tea for a visitor.'

Polly had been looking quite a bit better lately, what with the doctor's tonic and some pleasant company, so he was starting to feel more hopeful about her coping with having the baby.

Surely there was a chance of that? But he still reminded himself that could only happen as long as things went all right at the birth. He didn't dare tempt providence by being too optimistic. Polly hadn't talked about plans for the future and that worried him. Did she think she was going to die? Surely not?

Women were more vulnerable when expecting than at other times, even the healthy ones, and sometimes bad things happened inside their bellies and they died.

It didn't only happen to the weakest women either, from what he'd heard or seen since his own wife was expecting.

The second weekend was fine and the group of men who'd volunteered to work on the path met near the top end of the lake, bringing digging tools and taking it in turns to push a wheelbarrow which also had tools in it.

They'd taken Walter's wife into their confidence about this and she'd agreed to keep him away from the lake for a couple of weeks.

When they got near the top end Bertie took charge, as he often did, and they set to work. They made rapid progress, chatting happily and not needing telling what to do once the path had been marked out.

'Does Walter Crossley really not have any idea that we're doing this?' one of them asked idly when they were taking a break.

'His wife said he didn't know. It'd be nice if we could keep it a surprise, don't you reckon?'

'I agree. And we should do it well. The rest of the path has been really carefully done, made to last.'

'I'll make sure of that.' Bertie's voice was very determined. 'It's the old saying: if a job's worth doing—'

'It's worth doing well,' they all chorused, then laughed.

'I've been thinking,' another man said when they took their next break. 'We could get some of the bits and pieces of the wood that's lying around the building site, the ones that are too short to use on the roof or window frames, and patch together a couple of benches for folk to sit on up here. They don't have to be posh ones, just without splinters and sturdy enough for the older folk or women with little kids to rest on for a while.'

'That's another good idea. Well done. I'll check with Mr Brody that it's all right to take the wood from that pile of offcuts. Now, back to work, lads. We can fit in another hour or so then we'll have to start for home before it gets dark.'

35

The men Walter had brought together, and their families too, had been keeping their eyes open for Terry Catlow for a while. Or trying to. It wasn't easy. They caught sight of him here and there, but usually only in the distance, and no one could find a way of working out where he might turn up next.

They kept a careful watch on Edward Ollerton, taking it in turns for one of them to join the man he was paying to guard his house overnight. They were determined to prevent Catlow hurting him again.

And there was usually someone, females as well as males, hovering nearby when he went out and about in town or to the building site. He knew what they were doing, but the stabbing had shaken him and he didn't protest. Indeed, he told one chap he felt honoured by the way they cared.

Even the young constable was brought into it and strolled past the former agent's house as many times as he could each day, especially when he was patrolling the upper part of the valley near the building works.

In fact, a lot of people were determined to prevent anything like that stabbing from ever happening again.

There were a few people who didn't care about Edward particularly, but they did care about their own families, especially their children, and didn't want them to be ostracised so kept their own views quiet.

Catlow had brought it on himself, most thought. It'd been bad enough when he'd committed minor crimes occasionally but it felt as if he'd crossed an invisible line when he started trying to murder Edward Ollerton and they were *not* having it.

Besides, who would Catlow attack next if they let him get away with a murder? He'd be a very big danger to other folk then.

Some of them were keeping an eye on Walter's safety, too, and he knew it and felt grateful. He had always considered himself tougher than the next chap, and maybe when he was younger, he would have been easily able to defend himself. But he wasn't as strong physically now, however good he was for his age.

After a couple of weeks of futile watching for Catlow, he gathered the same group together again to discuss the situation. 'I don't think we're going to catch him this way. I've been trying to keep track of where he goes and when he's likely to come into town and it seems to be random, no pattern to it at all. Some days no one sees him, either in the valley or on the moors. Other days he's spotted two or three times, and in different places.'

He let that sink in then said firmly, 'I think we're going to have to set a trap. Well, we are if we can find something that'll attract him.'

He looked across at Jezzy, who was now an accepted member of the group. 'You probably know him better than any of us do, lad. Do you have any suggestions about what we could use as bait?'

'I might have a bit of an idea, Mr Crossley, but I was going to come and see you after this meeting to find out what you thought of it before I said anything to the others. I don't want to waste people's time.' He looked round rather nervously, knowing some were still not fully sure of his loyalty.

Walter's voice was gentle. 'If your idea isn't right, we'll tell you, but we'll still think better of you for trying to think of a way to catch him, because it shows you're on the side of right, not wrong. So you might as well tell us all about it now then we'll discuss it and tell you if it's got any merit.'

'Well then, sir, there are two things *that man* goes after these days,' Jezzy said slowly. 'One is Mr Ollerton and the other is food. He must be running low on food again by now because it's a while since he pinched anything noticeable, other than when he knocked old Mrs Velden down and stole her loaf a couple of days ago.'

There was a rumble of anger at that act, because the old lady had hurt her knee quite badly when she fell and was now limping. Jezzy waited till the men had settled down again before he continued.

'What if we let it be known that there has been a big delivery of food to someone in the village?'

He waited, heart thumping with anxiety, but no one ridiculed his idea so he continued, 'I doubt he'd go right into the town centre, even for a lot of food, but he's been seen several times in Upperfold village and Eastby End. If he heard that someone there had bought a load of food in for the winter maybe he'd go after it.'

That brought several comments.

'You're right. He doesn't go into the town centre.'

'But who knows where he goes in the middle of the night, eh?'

'He's always gone out wandering after dark, that one, even when he was a lad,' an old man said.

One woman waved her hand to get their attention. 'He hangs around the outskirts of the village regularly, even in daylight. I've caught glimpses of him from my garden when I was pegging out my washing. The back of my house looks out on to the moors, so someone might see him coming if they kept watch from my son's bedroom. I'd not mind someone coming into my house to do that.' She smiled. 'I might even give them the odd cup of tea.'

After listening to a chorus of 'Good for you, missus!' and similar phrases, Walter took charge again. 'We'll remember that kind offer. And Jezzy lad, I think it's a good idea to tempt him with food. But how do we do that in a credible way?'

A man spoke up loudly. 'Maybe we can pretend someone got lucky and won a hamper of food? A cousin of mine won one once.'

Walter thought about this for a moment then shook his head. 'I don't think he'd be fooled by that.'

Another woman said, 'There aren't any competitions going on at the moment. My church held a raffle only last month.'

There was silence then Jezzy took a deep breath and spoke again. 'How about we ask Mrs Crossley to announce that she'll be collecting food items to make up Christmas boxes for the poorest families? *He* might believe that and it might tempt him to try to get hold of the food before she hands it out.'

He glanced round at their faces and couldn't see anyone looking scornful so asked, 'Would your wife do that, do you think, Mr Crossley?'

'She'd be happy to, I'm sure, but I'm not having her put in danger. Someone will always have to go with her while she's collecting the food.'

'She wouldn't need to collect it herself. People could bring it to that old church hall she's going to use as a clinic,' a woman called out. 'She's there part of the time anyway. We could make sure there's always another woman or two with her in the day-time, so she'll be safe enough. And that won't look as strange as if she had a man hanging around there with her.'

'Good idea!'

Another man chimed in. 'Once the food starts piling up, we'd have to keep a couple of men hidden nearby during the night as well. I don't think anyone should try to tackle him on their own. He fights dirty and he's already stabbed Mr Ollerton so he's probably carrying a knife all the time now.'

'Hmm. We'd need to get hold of some food supplies and store them where people can see them.'

After a few moments of thoughtful silence, Walter said, 'Let's do it for real, then, collect food supplies for needy people to be given out to them at Christmas? There are a few folk who struggle to put enough food on the table through no fault of their own. Doing that to help them would give us a good result from a bad situation, even if we don't catch Catlow.'

There was another chorus of approval for that.

'But leave it to your wife to be the one doing this publicly, Walter,' one man said. 'If you were thought to be running it, that might make him stay away because he's always been wary of upsetting you.'

'I suppose so.'

By the time the meeting broke up, the basic plan had been worked out, even to the extent of having a day fixed for when genuine Christmas parcels would be handed out.

Bertie Garson was voted unanimously to be put in charge of telling people about it because he was well known to be efficient at little jobs like that and he'd get the word out quickly.

Flora hadn't become a member of this group, since she had her own charitable work, but when she got home she listened to Walter's explanation about the trap they wanted to set for Terry Catlow with great interest.

'I'm happy to be involved and I hope it does work out, because it's a good cause anyway,' she said fervently. 'That horrible man is now a danger to this whole valley and to steal food from poor people because you're too lazy to work for your own keep is a horrible thing to do. How he's got away with it for all these years, I can't think. Why did no one stop him?'

'People on their own are afraid of him. And he only used to take small things here and there, making sure he was never actually seen doing it. We knew it was him but couldn't easily prove it – and was it worth bothering for a loaf or a few eggs?'

'Well, I'm not afraid of him, thank you very much. His behaviour since I've been living here has been beyond shameful. Catlow needs locking away in prison and never letting out again.'

'I agree. And I'm glad you approve of what this will be leading to.'

'I'd always approve of giving food to those in need, Walter love. I can't bear to see hungry children with their pinched little faces.'

'I know, love. I've seen you buy them penny butties at the baker's.'

She blushed slightly and shrugged. 'One slice of buttered bread doesn't break my bank.'

He changed the subject. 'How's Polly Makersby coming on? Have you seen her lately?'

Flora's smile faded a little. 'She continues to be weak, but she does seem a little better. It's hard to tell whether this is only likely to be a pause in her downhill journey or whether the improvement will last.'

He looked shocked at that. 'You think she might die?'

'Who knows?'

'Is there nothing else we can do?'

'I'm afraid not. Sadly, the doctors don't know how to help with some ailments. I worry about her husband, too. He loves her dearly. I wonder if he'll be left with a child to raise? I hope not. But I'll keep my eyes open for someone who's expecting a baby around the same time and who looks fit and well, just in case.'

'There's Gwenda Lockyer, Halliwell as was. She was widowed before her husband even knew she was expecting. What's more, she lives just across from Dan and Polly at the family farm with her widowed mother.'

'Yes, of course. How could I have forgotten her? I'm still learning who's who in the valley. On a happier note, we should make a start on collecting food for Christmas parcels. Tell Bertie to hurry up and begin spreading the news.'

'There's something else you should know. Be very careful not to talk about our real plans anywhere in public, not even in a whisper. That rat has found out about other things without anyone seeming to have betrayed the information. Some of us wondered whether he could have overheard people talking. He's very cunning about finding hiding places, you see, and he knows every inch of the valley and the moors.'

'I'll make sure all my friends know not to chat about it in public, then.' She winked at him. 'Except the things we want him to hear about, of course.'

Walter couldn't resist pulling her to him and giving her another hug. 'And no going anywhere outside the house after dark on your own till this is sorted out, my bonny lass. If you have to visit a sick person in the evening I'm coming with you. I don't want that man attacking you as he did Edward.'

She looked even angrier. 'If someone's really ill, I absolutely have to go and see if I can help them, Walter. Ooh, I'd like to throw that man over the nearest cliff.'

'You'd have to join a queue of people wanting to do that. This time he's stirred up more anger than he ever did before. I wonder if he realises how strong the feeling is against him?'

'I doubt he'd care.'

'No, and he's definitely not thinking clearly these days, only seems to care about hurting Edward.'

Word got out and spread rapidly that Flora Crossley, helped by some of her women friends, would be getting together a collection of food so that they could give the poorest families parcels for Christmas.

Terry found out about it when he was hiding near the centre of Upperfold village. It always amused him how much he could get to know this way.

It seemed people were being asked to give what food they could, not just tins or packets, but also promises of baked goods nearer to Christmas.

He sneered mentally about that as he walked back to the cave that night. What a stupid thing to do. If they couldn't find food, let those fools starve.

He trudged on, scowling because he was utterly fed up of the long walk back to his uncomfortable temporary home. He was too old for this. Going up the hilly parts of the moors made him breathless after a day's scrounging, he was so tired, and though he picked up the occasional old newspaper to read, he got very bored on the days he stayed in the cave.

If his bitch of a wife had done her duty she'd be looking after him still and he'd not need to do this, because she was younger than him. But no, she had to steal the comfortable house he'd inherited from his family and teach his children to disobey him.

'One day I'll make you regret that, Nora Catlow, see if I don't,' he muttered, as he often did when he thought about her. It was a good job he knew which caves were safe and which liable to subside after the winter storms had sent temporary streams flooding down any crack they could find.

One day people came to look in the cave that led to the hidden place and he watched them from a crevice in the upper level of rocks, alternately sneering and laughing at their efforts. Good thing he'd had time to hide the remaining food supplies and blankets. He felt like king of the castle sometimes when he watched people search for him.

During the days that followed, he overheard other conversations in town about the food parcels and it gradually sank in that people were serious about this Christmas collection and would be donating a lot of food. Best of all to him, they were going to store all the food in the small hall that had once been a tiny chapel in Eastby End.

The town council hired out the hall for occasional functions and gatherings, but it had been loaned free of charge for a few weeks to those making this charitable effort to help poorer folk. There would be people there during the daytime, but to Catlow's delight there wouldn't be anyone there during the night. They were just planning to lock all the doors very carefully then.

That gave him an idea. If the contributions were stored there with no one guarding them at night, he might be able to get hold of a nice big supply of food, one that would last him for several weeks. He could continue to pinch the odd fresh items now and then, as he often did, but wouldn't have to trudge into town as often on days when the weather was bad.

He kept an eye on their efforts and decided to wait for enough food to come in to make it more worth his while to break into the hall. Every time he passed he smiled to see through the windows how the piles were growing higher. The idiots hadn't even thought to cover them up so that no one would see them and be tempted to pinch them.

Actually, he was rather surprised at how much people were contributing to the poor. He wouldn't have given them a box of matches. They should look after themselves, as he was doing.

When he next peeped through the windows of the hall one morning in the pale grey light of early dawn, he grinned. There was plenty piled on the table, ready for him to stuff into some sacks and carry away.

That made him think how best to do it as he walked slowly back to the cave. If he stole a handcart at the last minute, he could find a hiding place for some of the food near the outer part of Eastby. He'd be able to pinch half a dozen sacks full or more, hide them here and there, then take them gradually back to his cave. He'd push the handcart over the edge of a steep slope once he'd finished using it.

He didn't dare take the handcart right back to his cave because someone might follow its tracks and find the outer cave he was using and then keep watch on it. He could take a load part way and leave it then go back for another load. He'd have to get rid of the cart then so it'd take three or four journeys to carry all his hidden stores from some other hiding place in town to his cave on foot.

It wasn't likely anyone would find the stuff he had to leave for a day or two on the moors because there weren't many people walking for pleasure at this time of year.

Now, where could he hide the stuff he left in town? Hmm. There was that garden shed he used occasionally in Eastby End to hide in during the winter. Its owner was getting old and didn't use it much these days. To passers-by it looked abandoned. He didn't even put a padlock on the door because he didn't want to show that it was in use, did he?

He knew the shed was still waterproof, though, because he'd risked sleeping there two or three times recently when he was simply too weary to trudge all the way back to that damned cave in the pouring rain.

Or was he being too optimistic about hiding the food? Should he risk leaving it so close to where people lived? Oh, why not? What had he to lose, after all? It didn't even belong to him yet. And he could always pinch some more.

He snickered, thinking how it'd annoy that Crossley woman and her arrogant sod of a husband to lose it.

36

One of Walter's friends came to see him, looking thought-ful. 'I'm fairly sure that sod is on the point of stealing the food.'

No need to explain who he was talking about.

'What makes you think that?'

'A friend of mine has seen him near the hall a couple of times now, Walter lad. And I've seen him near that old shed on Roy Torring's plot of land.'

'Hmm. You're sure he didn't see you?'

'Certain. Catlow seems to have been looking round for something else as well and we had a bit of luck because Tom was nearby when he found it. We reckon he's planning to steal Griff Potter's rubbishy old handcart. Griff just leaves it tipped up against the wall in his backyard and bolts his gate. Tom saw Catlow climb up and stand on the handle of the gate to look into the yard. Then he checked the gate to see how it was locked. Griff's a fool. He's only using a bolt that anyone can lean down and pull back. Not even a padlock.'

'That is promising. I wonder when exactly Catlow is intend-ing to go after the food.'

'Who knows? Soon, I should think, but there's no way of working that out, I'm afraid.'

'We'd better keep a continuous watch on the food every night from now on.'

The sergeant joined in. 'If we do catch him in the act, tell everyone to be very careful and not try to capture him on their own. He stabbed Edward Ollerton, remember, and we don't want him killing anyone.'

'You're right to remind us. No trying to capture him single-handed, lads.' Walter turned back to the sergeant. 'We don't want you risking your life, either. We value what you're doing in our valley.'

'Thank you, but I won't be on my own. I've got my constable to help me now, most of the time anyway.'

The following day someone stole a pile of old sacks from the back of the small grocery store. It seemed obvious they were for Catlow to put the food in, so the theft must be imminent and he must be intending to steal a larger quantity than they'd thought. They decided they'd better set more men to keep watch every night from now on.

But the next day was not just rainy; it was stormy, with lots of thunder and lightning during the afternoon. There was hardly anyone to be seen on the streets and they knew Terry had never been seen out on days like that, so Walter didn't call out all the men he could have done to keep watch. And those he did nominate grimaced at the thought of a cold, wet spell of duty.

That night the young constable strode along on his last town patrol of the day, looking forward to getting in out of the chilly rain. When he heard something, he stopped, because the other streets had all been empty and quiet. He followed the sound to the back alley that led to the church hall, making sure he wasn't seen. There was a man pushing a handcart along it.

He followed and saw the fellow fiddle with the locked front door and get it open, with several glances over his shoulders.

Ha! Neil thought. Good thing they'd put a big padlock on the back door so Catlow had to go in the front way. The sergeant was a clever man.

Catlow went inside and Neil peeped carefully through a small side window and saw him begin loading the goods from the table into a sack.

The constable wondered what to do. They'd been wrong about that fellow not coming out during a storm. But the sergeant had warned him very sternly not to try to tackle him on his own.

He edged across into a useful patch of shadow and waited. The handcart was four-wheeled but not very big and only held a few sacks, so it didn't take long to load it. He wasn't going to disobey his sergeant but he decided to follow Catlow and find out where he went before he reported what was going on. They didn't want to lose sight of him, after all.

The man surprised him by not taking the track that led to the moors. Instead he made his way slowly through the streets to the outskirts of Eastby End and on to the patch of rough ground with a shed at the far end. It looked abandoned.

Thank goodness it had stopped raining and the cloud cover was only intermittent. The storm had passed more quickly than anyone had expected. There was an almost full moon tonight, too. Neil hid behind a fence at one side and saw Catlow open the shed door and start carrying the sacks inside one by one.

He seized the moment to go and wake his sergeant who didn't live far away, moving quietly at first, then running the last part of the way.

Hector cursed when he heard about Catlow doing this tonight and sent his constable off to wake John Forster, the burly landlord of the small pub nearby.

He made his way back to the church hall where there was a lot of food still left on the tables. Since their thief had apparently been unloading food into the shed, it was his guess that Catlow would return for at least one more load.

He went round to the side of the hall and stood waiting in the shadows. A few minutes passed and there was no sign of Catlow which worried him. Had he guessed wrongly? Wasn't the fellow coming back for more?

Then there was the faint sound of wheels in the distance and he smiled slightly. He had been right. He hoped the constable and John would join him soon, though. Even with his years of experience Hector didn't fancy trying to capture a man carrying a knife, especially one who had already proved that he wasn't afraid to use it.

Catlow appeared pushing the handcart. Oh hell, he was coming round to this side of the building. Hector looked round and managed to squeeze behind some big bins of rubbish. From there he watched the other man leave the cart near the door and go inside.

Hector risked coming out from behind the bins and peering through the side window again.

There was enough moonlight now that the sky was clearer to see that Catlow was cramming things into another sack. He didn't seem to be picking and choosing what to take, just tossing one item after another into the grubby sack and when that was full he started on another. Perhaps he didn't care what he ate and anyway it would be hard to sort things out with so little light to see by.

As Catlow picked up the first full sack, Hector quickly went back to crouch behind the nearest bin, where he had to put his feet in a damned puddle.

He could see the smile on the sod's face as he came out and dumped another sack on the cart then went back inside again. It wasn't long before he reappeared with more food. This time he closed the hall door behind him then set off along the street, moving slowly, clearly trying to make as little noise as possible. Once he stopped to clap one hand to his chest as if it was hurting then set off again, but more slowly.

Hector continued to follow him, trying to keep quiet and taking great care not to get too close. He was just wishing that the others were with him when someone did appear beside him and he nearly jumped out of his skin. But it was Neil, thank goodness, and behind him John Forster.

Hector put one finger to his lips and stopped to whisper what had happened, then sent John back to rouse a couple more men because although Hector felt he and Neil could probably handle Catlow, there would be the cart and sacks of food to bring back as well. He didn't want to waste food that would be much appreciated by people struggling to feed their families.

He led the way again, keeping back out of sight because he didn't want to start a fight here where some well-meaning person might rush out of their house trying to help and get in the way or even be injured. He'd seen that happen before now.

Catlow stopped at the old shed and dumped two of the sacks inside, leaving only two on the handcart. Just as Hector was wondering whether to try to capture him now, a man he didn't recognise hurried along the street, stopping in shock at the sight of them.

Hector managed to stop him calling out and since Catlow didn't look out of the shed, he assumed he hadn't heard anything. The man was apparently going for the doctor because his young child was ill, so he sent him on the way with instructions to move quietly.

That encounter made Hector decide to let Catlow get right out of town before tackling him. The door of the shed opened and they just had time to hide before Catlow came out and shut the door behind him.

He picked up the handles of the cart and moved off, turning onto a narrow track that clearly wasn't much used. Hector wasn't sure about where that led. He hoped it'd go out of Eastby End and up to the moors.

As he moved along he tried to work out where would be the best place to grab Catlow without warning him of their approach. He didn't want to give him a chance to abandon the cart and run off across the moors, because he knew them better than Hector did.

Unfortunately John hadn't returned with reinforcements, so there were still only the two of them, both strangers to the area. He decided to let Catlow go a little further before pouncing.

He was surprised at how far Catlow was going. They must be getting on for halfway to the cave if you cut straight across the moors, because he could see the higher ground and outcrops of rock in the distance.

What was the fellow intending to do with the handcart? Take it to the cave and use it again? Surely not?

After a while this part of the track started going more steeply uphill and Catlow looked to be struggling with the cart. He was moving along the edge of a small but steep drop now, one of several that made up the start of the higher area called Beckshall Edge.

Hector didn't know this part of the countryside very well and it seemed a bad place for an ambush with the drop on one side, so he still held back.

Catlow was now walking more slowly as if looking for something, then he stopped moving and let go of the cart to glance over the edge of the cliff. Just as Hector was considering pouncing, Catlow shook his head as if something was wrong and picked up the handles of the cart again.

Hector sighed. If he'd been living here longer he'd have known the outer parts of the district better and been able to plan his next move more surely. He was now wishing he'd tried to catch the fellow at the edge of the town rather than in a dangerous place like this.

When he heard faint footsteps behind him he turned to see two more men coming to join him and his constable. Thank goodness.

Then one of them tripped and fell, crying out involuntarily. Catlow must have heard the noise because he swung round and stared into the semi-darkness before setting off running, still pushing the cart.

Hector started running too but to his delight Neil overtook him. He hadn't realised how fleet of foot his young deputy was.

Neil had nearly caught up with Catlow when the man suddenly turned, swinging the cart round and shoving it so that it rolled back towards his pursuer. Then he took off across the moors.

As the cart ran into Neil, he had no way to avoid it and it knocked him sideways. The narrow strip of land at the outer edge of the path was made of slippery rock and his foot slid across it and tumbled him towards the very edge of the small cliff where he scrabbled desperately for a secure foothold.

Unfortunately the cart was now lying on its side and one of the sacks had spilled its contents between him and the cart, making it difficult for him to find something solid to hold on to.

Hector reached his constable just in time to help him avoid going right over the edge. He grabbed one of Neil's arms but it took all his strength to hold on to him because the young man was no lightweight. And the rock was damned slippery after so much rain. When someone flung himself down next to him and grabbed Neil's other shoulder and arm, he groaned in relief.

Together the two of them were strong enough to heave the young constable back to safety, then another person joined them to help complete the job. All four of them lay among the debris from the sack panting for a few seconds.

It was John who pulled himself to his feet first and stared across the moors. 'No sign of the bastard, Sergeant. How the hell has he managed to vanish when he's crossing open land?'

'There are sometimes gaps that run along the tops like big cracks,' Ted said. 'He could be crawling along one of those or simply be hidden by the heather and waiting for us to leave before moving on.'

'Well, we know where Catlow will be heading, don't we?' Hector said grimly. 'He'll think we don't know which cave he's in or that there's a hidden inner cave. Surely we'll be able to trap him there?'

'He might not go back into the cave,' Neil said.

John shook his head. 'I bet he does. He probably has done already. There's nowhere else he could hide for long near here. It's all open moors except for the area round Beckshall Edge, so we'd soon catch sight of him if he tried to run away in another direction. No, I reckon he'll be prepared to lie low for a while in that inner cave his son told us about.'

'Let's press on and see if we can find him and it then,' Hector said.

The four men left the cart and its spilled contents and moved as quickly as they could across the tops till they came to the highest part of Beckshall Edge, where the biggest outcrops of rock were. At no point did they see any sign of Catlow.

'I reckon he must have got back to the cave more quickly than we expected,' Roy said.

'Desperation can make people run faster.' Hector sighed. He'd hate to lose track of their villain.

When they reached the entrance to the end cave, which they'd been told was the one used by Catlow, he asked the two civilians to wait near the entrance while he and Neil went inside. If their man had a different hiding place or there was a second hidden exit from the cave, and he came out again unexpectedly, they were to do their best to grab him and yell for help as loudly as they could. However, if Catlow flourished a knife at them, they were to stay back.

The two policemen then moved into the outer cave as quietly as they could, pausing for a moment just inside the entrance till their eyes grew more accustomed to the dimness after the moonlight outside. They'd not see him easily in here.

Then Hector saw a box of candles on the ground behind a rock and smiled as he grabbed it, together with the box of matches next to it. He didn't hesitate to light a candle then use it to light a second one and hand that to Neil. He set the box down, hidden in another spot in case Catlow was counting on it.

He nudged his constable and pointed to the right, whispering, 'One of us check along each side.' He moved along the left-hand side of the cave, which was where Jezzy had said the entrance to the inner cave was located. If there was any risk to be taken, he'd do it himself.

Moving forward slowly and methodically, the two men shone their candles alternately across the cave walls and then the central space. It was narrow enough and only about five or six yards long, with the roof sloping down to the ground at the far end.

If anyone had been there, they'd have seen him, but there was definitely no sign of Catlow.

So Hector pointed to a place for Neil to station himself near the entrance and began to search for the half-hidden opening that led to the inner cave. It wasn't obvious even when you knew it was there, but he found it suddenly, lower down than he'd expected and half-hidden behind a deep fold in the rock. The tunnel had a narrow entrance and was just above ground level, only big enough for him to get into if he crouched or crawled.

He didn't go straight in, trying to work out how he was going to come out at the other end without being thumped or stabbed into oblivion. The best he could manage was to set his candle down here so the tunnel would be in near darkness. Surely Catlow would have some sort of light at the other end?

He strained his eyes, sheltering them between open hands, and yes, there definitely was a faint light there. That told him that they'd found Catlow, so he took off his scarf and tied it round the end of his truncheon. If he waved that out of the other end of the tunnel, he hoped it would be enough to distract Catlow briefly so that he could move into the inner cave safely.

He beckoned to Neil and tried to give him some guidance as to how to act, speaking in a low whisper. 'If he manages to hit me, he might get out, so you'll have to stop him. He'll do anything he can to get away, so watch out for his knife. Stand to one side of the tunnel so that he can't see you and get your truncheon out. Hit him before he realises you're there if you can.'

The young chap nodded and unhooked his truncheon from his belt.

Hector took a deep breath and began to edge along the tunnel, bent almost double and only able to move forward slowly through the near darkness in an awkward crab-like manner. It was only about three yards and he stopped just before he got to the end to listen.

There was no sound at all but just as he was about to risk moving on he heard a slight noise to the right as if someone was walking on loose bits of rock, followed by another silence.

Aha! he thought. Gotcha!

He tried to wriggle into a better position to get out of the end of the tunnel quickly, then held his truncheon out of it at arm's length, shaking it so that the scarf dangling from it waved about.

Catlow grabbed the scarf and tugged, but Hector held on tightly, pulled it back a little then suddenly let go. The other man let out a yell of surprise as that caused him to stumble backwards.

Hector managed to get part way out of the low passage, hoping to get into a position from which he could defend himself before Catlow stood up. But the man was too quick for him, grabbing a rock as he got to his feet and raising it as if about to hurl it at his opponent because he was too far away to hit him with it.

The sergeant put up one arm to defend himself, only the rock didn't come whizzing across at him as he'd expected. He was surprised to see it drop suddenly to the ground. Catlow let out a choking sound then crumpled slowly down to lie still on the rocky floor.

Was he faking a collapse?

Hector edged forward, still prepared for this to be a ruse as a prelude to another attack by Catlow. Only, nothing else happened. He stared down at his adversary, still ready to defend himself but there was no sign of movement.

Keeping an eye on the body on the ground he reached out slowly to pick up the lighted candle, which had been placed on a rocky protuberance in the wall near the tunnel. As he bent again, holding the candle closer to Catlow's body, he saw enough to realise that this man wasn't likely to attack him again. In fact, he wasn't likely to attack anyone ever again.

You couldn't mistake that look and Hector had seen it in the course of his work many times. Catlow had just dropped dead. Must have had a seizure or some such thing.

Shuddering in relief, Hector stood motionless, his pulse still pounding but starting to slow down. He stared at the man they'd been chasing. Catlow looked older than his years, as if he'd shrivelled up, and he smelled bad, presumably from lack of washing facilities for himself and his clothes.

Hector held up the candle and looked round the small inner cave. There were a few personal possessions scattered around plus some food. How on earth had the fellow managed to live in such poor conditions for so long?

A voice called from the tunnel. 'Sergeant?'

'I'm all right, Neil.'

'Isn't he there?'

'He is but he's not going to hurt me or anyone else. He's just dropped dead.'

'*What?*'

'Go outside and tell the others then come back and help me get his body out.'

He looked round and called, 'Actually, I don't like the feeling in this cave. It smells foul. I'm going to come outside with you to get some fresh air before we do anything else.'

Then he felt the ground quiver slightly beneath his feet and that terrified him. He couldn't get out of there quickly enough. He scrabbled his way along the tunnel on hands and knees, yelling, 'Run outside quickly!'

He only just refrained from sobbing as he pushed Neil to move faster and they erupted out of the cave.

'Get away from here!' he yelled and followed as the other two men ran further away from the entrance.

The fresh air was wonderful but he'd heard a faint rumbling sound and there it was again. The ground was shaking beneath his feet once more as he led the others even further away.

As they stopped to look behind them, the sound turned into a deep growl that grew louder and louder and the ground shook so violently beneath their feet that they called out in fear, desperately trying to stay upright.

Hector watched the rocks round the cave entrance shifting very slowly. In the gleam of the moonlight he saw the rocky entrance change shape, moving slowly but inexorably, giving off a cloud of dust.

The ground shook a few more times, but the quivers of movement grew gradually weaker.

The moonlight was bright enough to show them a tumble of rocks where the entrance to the cave had been.

Hector felt sick. If he'd stayed inside that cave even a couple of minutes longer, he'd have been killed. He had to take several deep breaths before he could manage to speak at all, then he tried again but couldn't seem to find the right words to explain what he'd seen and left behind.

The other three men stared at him in shock, then looked towards the cave.

'Take your time, lad,' John said. 'You two just had a very narrow escape.'

Hector nodded and took some more breaths of the wonderful fresh air. 'It was – terrifying,' he managed.

'Yes. You must be the luckiest chaps in Lancashire tonight,' John said.

He nodded, swallowing hard, still finding it hard to string words together.

'We can't dig our way back into that cave without proper tools and even if we do—' John broke off and stared at the sergeant, then finished what he had been saying. 'Even if we do try, we'll be risking our lives because the rocks might shift again at any moment.'

'Catlow must have been killed,' Ted said.

Hector stared at the tumble of rocks fanning out towards them. He took a deep breath and managed to speak. 'He dropped dead before it happened. I know what death looks like. I'm not prepared to risk my life or yours trying to get inside. If the authorities want his dead body dug out, they'll have to find someone who is prepared to run the risk. I certainly won't.'

He shuddered violently and didn't care who saw him do that. 'I don't intend to ever go into a cave again.'

'My parents used to warn me never to go near these caves,' Roy said. 'They said the ground sometimes slipped. It put the fear of God into me and I never even tried.'

'Do we need to leave someone here to keep watch?' John asked. 'And what about that cart of food?'

'No need to keep watch. Catlow was definitely dead. I'd stake my life on that. And now he's been buried, as far as I'm concerned. As for the cart, it won't run away. Someone can come for it tomorrow.'

'Then let's get back home. I don't know about you, but I'm exhausted.'

'I am too. But it'll be a long time before I get any sleep. I need to find a magistrate and report this at once.'

In the end the magistrate took a solemn deposition from Sergeant McGill, then commended him for his devotion to duty and his lucky escape.

He would need to check with his superiors what they wanted doing about the body so Hector said it again, 'You won't get me back in that cave or any of the other caves nearby, not for anything.'

'I doubt they'll want to risk anyone's life trying to retrieve a dead body. There are enough witnesses to declare Terence Catlow well and truly dead.'

37

What had happened on the moors was a nine-day wonder in Ollerthwaite and Upperfold, and a source of much debate on what, if anything, ought to be done about it.

Some people even took the long walk across the tops to look at the jumble of rocks and marvel at the sergeant and constable's narrow escape.

Others simply said good riddance to Catlow and got on with their lives.

The man's death had a more lasting effect on a few people.

His wife was very quiet for a day or two but refused to waste her money on buying mourning clothes. She didn't even consider holding a gathering of the sort that usually followed even the meanest funeral, and she gave short shrift to people who tried to persuade her to do it.

'I've better things to do with my money than pour it down your throats, thank you very much.'

Jezzy Catlow was rather quiet. He didn't care about his father being dead, well, not much, though it was a horrible way to die, but he wasn't sure how the family would cope with life from now on.

When his mother gathered him and his siblings together, he was greatly relieved to hear what she was planning to do.

'Now that your father's definitely not coming back, I'm going to open a proper boarding house and I'll need your help with this. First of all we're going to make the attics more suitable for you six to sleep in. There are some dividing walls up

there already and a plank floor that just needs a bit of smooth-
ing with some sandpaper. And we can have any other walls
that are necessary put in. The bedrooms you're in now will
then be available for paying guests. Your new rooms will be a
lot smaller because of the slope of the roof, but you'll have one
space each at least.'

They all gaped at her when she added, 'And I'm putting
in modern bathrooms, too, one up there for the family and
another on the first floor for the guests. It's hard work staying
clean if you have to lug buckets of hot water around before
you can have a bath. And I can charge guests extra for a bath
to help pay for the alterations.'

The smallest two children cheered at that and she smiled
at them fondly before continuing. 'I'm improving the kitchen
too, putting in a gas cooker and a hot water geyser.'

Jezzy stared at his mother because there was something
more important to him than being able to have a bath more
easily. 'Can I keep working at the big house with Gavin, Ma?'

'Of course you can, son. If you continue to be a hard worker,
you can go through an apprenticeship and be set for life as a
proper bricklayer.'

'Won't you need me to help you in the boarding house?'

'No. Why should I? You've got three sisters and two brothers. Everyone can lend a hand, even little Bertha. Your father
never helped me. In fact, he more often hindered me and
wouldn't let me make your brothers toe the line. Well, they'll
do as they're told from now on, I promise you.'

She gave them such a fierce look that they gaped and didn't
even try to answer back let alone claim, as they'd heard their
father do, that men didn't do housework.

'It'll be good to know that *he* won't come back and ruin all
I've done. Though of course, you'll continue to do the odd
chore for me in the evenings, Jezzy. You *are* the eldest and the
biggest.'

There was a new and more confident tone to her voice, so he simply nodded and said, 'Yes, of course, Ma.'

She looked at the others. 'You can stay on as a maid at Mrs Hodgett's, Sally, but you'll still hand most of your wages to me. If this place is successful you can stop work there later on and start here – and I'll pay you a wage.'

Sally didn't look best pleased at this series of orders. At fourteen she considered herself grown up, but their mother always treated them as children.

It was Linda's turn next.

'I'll take you out of school half-time when you turn eleven next month, Linda, and you can help me in the house.'

His sister beamed and his mother added warningly, 'I'm not doing that so you can play out, Miss Cheeky-Face, but so you can help with the housework and shopping, and learn how to run this place. We all have to learn honest ways of supporting ourselves from now on.'

She waited for that to sink in then went on, 'I also intend to make sure you girls don't go out with lads till you're eighteen. If I catch any of you making eyes at a lad, you'll be in serious trouble. *Very – serious – indeed.* And when you get old enough to walk out with lads, you'll only be allowed to see honest chaps who can keep you in reasonable comfort and live decently. We don't want any of you marrying someone like your father.'

Linda was the only one who dared to ask, 'Why did you marry him if he was so bad?'

'Because I was stupid back then and my mother only wanted to get rid of me so she pushed me into it. Anyway, he wasn't as bad in those days. He got worse and worse as he grew older. I didn't know how lazy he was, though, right from the start. Think how you'd feel if you married a bad provider and had to do all the jobs around a house while your husband spent half the money he earned at the pub and didn't lift a finger at home, only sat and smoked.'

That seemed to make even cheeky Linda think harder about life.

Nora stared round at her children thoughtfully, the sort of stare that made them say, 'Yes, Ma!' to whatever she wanted these days. 'The rest of you had better work hard at school. Since the law says you have to go there, you might as well learn as much as you can. I wish I had more book learning, I do indeed.'

Martin looked at her speculatively. 'I enjoy schoolwork, Ma. It's really interesting to learn things. And I like reading books.'

She looked surprised. 'You'd *want* to stay at school after you turn twelve?'

'The master says I'm good enough at bookwork to stay on. Only I thought Pa would stop me going there so I didn't dare say anything.'

'He would definitely have stopped you. But if you pass the exam, I'll pay for you to go to the grammar school for as long as you work hard there.'

'You'd have to buy a uniform as well as the books I'd need,' he warned.

'I know that. By then, if you all work hard and help me, this place should be bringing in decent money.' She smiled. 'I'll bring in Mrs Fowler straight away to do the cleaning regularly. She'll be pleased to earn more and I hate scrubbing floors.'

'Will you have enough money to get all this started? We'd need to buy beds and other stuff if we were taking in lodgers,' Jezzy said. 'I can still give you most of my wages, but I only get apprentices' rates and I heard you tell Dad you were short of money just before you chucked him out.'

'That was to fool him, so that he wouldn't pinch my money. I have enough saved to set the place up *and* to manage for a few weeks until we get it running. After that the lodgers will be paying to stay here. There's a shortage of decent lodging houses in the valley so I'm not going to do it too cheaply. And

I'm going to give them good value for their money, so they'll want to stay on here.'

She didn't tell them but one of the reasons she'd been saving had been to leave the valley once her children were old enough to manage without her. She hadn't intended to spend her declining years being bullied by Terry. Now, she could stay and make a better life for them all here, where she knew people, which she'd much prefer.

When the other children had gone to bed, it was still too early for Jezzy, so she said, 'Why don't you sit and chat to me for a while, son?'

He took the other armchair and when she didn't speak he asked, 'Shall you miss him at all, Ma?'

'No. I'd not mind marrying again if I could find a decent chap who'd make a proper husband, but I'd not have one like him who didn't have a steady job or who tried to thump me. It's lonely being a widow and you kids will all grow up and leave home one day, so I'd like to have someone to turn to then.' She pulled a face. 'But it's not likely I'd meet anyone who's decent and free to marry.'

'You still look nice when you dress up, so you might meet someone.'

She rolled her eyes. 'We'll see.'

He could see that she was pleased by that compliment, though. 'We've changed in the past year or two, haven't we, you and me, I mean.'

'Yes. Took me a long time to grow up. I'm ashamed of what I put up with when I look back.'

'I'm ashamed of what I was like till I went to live with my uncle.'

'Well, we'll both do a lot better from now on, eh?'

'Yes we will, Ma. And if you want to find yourself a husband, I'll look around for one as well.'

She flapped one hand at him, laughing. 'Get away with you!'

But he meant it. He'd seen how happy his uncle and aunt were together, and he'd like to see his mother that happy too.

Later, when he stood up to go to bed, she got up and suddenly gave him a big hug. Then she pushed him away, looking embarrassed, because she didn't often hug anyone. 'You've turned into a good lad, Jezzy. See you carry on like this because I'd like to keep being proud of you.'

'You're proud of me? Really?'

'Yes, I am. You've turned out all right.'

She hesitated again, then added, 'And whatever people say, I'm *not* going into mourning. I gave up on Terry long before I chucked him out. I'm glad he's gone for good, glad I haven't got a grave to remind me of him and need tending.'

As he turned to leave, she added, 'He left a few clothes behind when I threw him out. If any of them fit you, I'll wash them and you can have them. Have a look through them tomorrow.'

'All right. And, Ma – I'll do my best to keep on making you proud of me.'

'I just told you. I *am* proud of you already. Just don't change back into what you used to be like. Eh, you were a bad lad for a while. I thought you were turning into another Terry. But I warn you now, don't try to boss me around as you grow older. No man's ever going to treat me like that again.'

He chuckled. 'I wouldn't dare.'

She smiled. 'Good. Now, get yourself off to bed, son. We're going to be very busy here in the next few weeks.'

'I'll help all I can after work and at weekends.'

Which won him another quick, half-embarrassed hug.

Edward Ollerton was also greatly affected by what had happened. It took him a while to feel safe again when he left the house because even though he knew Catlow was dead, he still felt vulnerable and couldn't stop himself from jerking round to check whenever some sound surprised him.

Lillian seemed to understand and so did his friend Lewis, but he felt a fool at times.

Some places affected him more than others and it was a while before he could face going down into the cellars to see how the changes looked as the men gradually walled off the parts they were not going to use for years, if ever.

He sat chatting one day with Lewis who was not only a good friend but a good architect, he believed, and was managing the work needed to create the new house well too.

'I'm feeling fairly sure that with the changes we're making to our original plans, I'll get your house finished in time for the Queen's Diamond Jubilee,' Lewis said. 'I can't actually promise you that but I can promise you it's likely. Well, unless something major and unexpected goes wrong, it'll probably get done on time.'

'Will it still take that long?'

'I'm afraid so. We'll soon be having to bring in skilled workers from outside the valley, as I'd warned you. The barn we hired is nearly finished now, and we've built enough bunk beds for our needs, so at least we'll have somewhere reasonably comfortable to house them. That'll make a big difference. But it takes longer to find such people than if we had locals capable of doing that sort of skilled work, so it slows down finishing the job.'

Edward nodded. 'Is it my imagination or do you think Dan's wife is looking a bit better? One of the women took her out for a ride in their cart last week.'

'I saw them and I was wondering that.'

'If I can do anything to help them or they need money, let me know, Lewis.'

'It's not money but help and companionship, I think. I really admire the way folk here step in to help when there's a major problem for someone.'

'I like the people here too.'

'You know about the lake, don't you?'

'Yes. Is Walter still unaware of what the men are doing?'

'I gather so, mainly due to his wife keeping him extra busy at weekends on preparations for her clinic and for the Christmas handouts to the poorer folk. Dan has invited us to join them for the grand opening of the new top end path next weekend. Mrs Crossley is going to invite her husband to go for a walk with her and the people who've done the work on it will be waiting for him at the top end. At least they will if the mild spell continues.'

He chuckled. 'It won't be all that grand but it'll be safe and comfortable to walk on, and that will please Walter.'

38

A few days later Rufus met Walter at the market and since his friend didn't look to be in a hurry, asked if he could speak to him privately about something.

'Yes, of course. Is there a problem?'

'No. It's just that I had an idea about the valley and lake, and I wanted to share it with you and see what you thought. Why don't you come and have a cup of tea with me and I'll tell you about it.'

'I'll be happy to listen to your idea.' He smiled. 'And I'm always ready for a cup of tea at this time of day.'

'Thank you.' Rufus took him home and since Abigail was out he made them a pot of tea. He would have taken Walter to sit in the living room, only his visitor insisted he preferred to sit at the kitchen table, if that was all right.

When they were seated, Rufus began to explain. 'When Abigail and I were in Blackpool, we spoke to the manager of our hotel about our idea of running our house as a hotel – a smaller one than theirs, of course. He showed us round behind the scenes and also made a few suggestions about how we might be able to attract visitors to the valley in general. Some of them would inevitably stay at our hotel once we get it finished and open.' He stopped and looked at Walter as if wondering how that was going down.

'Carry on.'

'Well, we hope to open our hotel in the spring, as you know, and the manager thought we might be able to attract hikers and walkers in particular to the area during the better weather, with it being so close to a lake and the moors. It'd not only give us custom but bring money into the valley's shops too.'

'Which would be an excellent thing, I agree. What exactly did he think you could do?'

'He suggested we should have some investigations made into where the interesting walks across the moors are located. You're on the town council and I wondered what you thought of the town putting up signposts round the area indicating short or long walks. He also suggested having brochures printed and distributed to various places, travel agents and railways here in the north for a start, and to hiking clubs too if we could find some. That'd all help bring people here.'

Walter held up one hand to stop him going on. 'Hold on a minute. Let me take that in.'

So Rufus waited patiently until Walter looked up again and said, 'It might be a good idea, but we're still going to be short of accommodation.'

'There will be our hotel by then with six bedrooms. And Mrs Catlow is apparently going to open a better class lodging house now she's free to organise it without interruptions. Hikers often want cheaper accommodation apparently, because lots of ordinary working people who enjoy hiking as a hobby can't afford fancy hotels. So she could have a room or maybe a couple of rooms with bunks, as well as normal guest rooms.'

He waited until Walter nodded to continue. 'Then there's the barn where Lewis and Edward will be housing skilled workers from outside the valley. It'll be free to be used in a different way after his house is finished.'

'True, true. And there may be a few people in the town with a bedroom or two to spare as well.' He stopped to stare at his companion and smile.

'Why are you smiling at me?' Rufus asked.

'You sound to care about the valley like someone born here.'

'Do I really? Well, I like living here very much indeed, and it's unspoiled countryside nearby and really pretty. I think the people of the area could use that to bring outsiders here and therefore create a few jobs. I admire what you've done already, Walter, but I just – well, I want to do more. It's such a lovely place to live in.'

'You've put forward some interesting ideas, lad. I'd like to think about them and discuss them with other councillors, then talk to you again. You must have been thinking about it for a while.'

'Yes. Ever since I married Abigail and discovered wider horizons had become achievable for me because of her money and the house. Lack of money can close people's lives in so tightly, make them give up trying.'

'You're right about that.'

'And my wife feels the same. Indeed, she's helped pull together the ideas I've been telling you about. She's got a really sharp brain. She'd have been with us today only she's visiting an old lady she's met who turns out to be a distant relative of her mother's and who hasn't been well.'

'That's kind of her. You've got an excellent brain, too, Rufus. That stands out a mile. You're doing Abigail good in many ways. She's like a flower coming into blossom since her father died and she married you. It's lovely to see.'

The way Rufus smiled betrayed how fond he was of his wife. 'She is coming out of her shell, isn't she? And it's thanks to her that I can afford to do a few more things with my life, so we're doing one another good.'

'The other women speak well of Abigail, too, now that they're getting to know her,' Walter said.

'I'm happy to hear that. I think I'm very lucky to have met her.'

'And she's lucky to have met you. That's how marriages should be. But to get back to your ideas, which I think might well translate nicely into ways of attracting people to the area, I'd better warn you: we have one or two chaps on the town council who want to keep life here quiet. They've got enough money to live on comfortably and they don't think about others, above all don't like change. The poorer people who're short of work and therefore money, can't take advantage of the wider opportunities life can offer if they're always worrying about where the next meal is coming from.'

'I don't know much about our councillors. I went to work in other towns because I could earn more money but not everyone is free to do that. I'm now looking forward to getting our hotel up and running, not just for the money but because I like meeting people. And if anyone tries to stop me I'll find a way round it.'

'By all accounts you and your wife are using her father's money for good purposes. I've heard that you've helped one or two people already. We've got the money you gave me safely set aside for the mother and baby clinic and whatever else is needed to help people stay healthy.'

'I'm sure you'll use it wisely, Walter.'

'So will you.'

'Sometimes it doesn't take much to give someone an opportunity. So . . . you'll think about these other ideas, Walter?'

'Yes. But I'm not rushing into anything. Before we can do that, I have to get people to finish off the lake path. If we can't even get that done, we'll never be able to cater for tourists.'

Rufus opened his mouth then closed it again. He felt guilty about keeping the secret of the work on the lake from Walter, though. 'Well, have a think about it. I have a lot to do yet to finish our hotel. Just give me a week or two then perhaps we can discuss the possibilities further – if you're interested, that is.'

Walter beamed at him. 'I'm very interested and glad you raised the matter.' He smiled and added a confidence. 'When I first started trying to improve our town, I was rather doubtful that I'd get much done because a lot of people seemed to have given up hope. But lately, well, things are getting better all the time and it's not just me who's pushing it along.'

'I can see that.'

'It's wonderful, that's what it is, Rufus lad. And after we get our lake walk done, which I'm going to nag people about next, we'll study your ideas and see if we can take another step forward as a town.'

When he was alone again, Rufus smiled. Walter definitely didn't know about the work on the lake path. Or if he did, he was a better actor than anyone had ever realised.

The work had gone well and a surprise revelation to Walter and the rest of the town was being planned for ten days' time. The main thing they were worried about was the weather. They needed this coming weekend to be fine so they could finish the path off, and then they were hoping for more fine weather the weekend after that so they could spring their surprise on Walter and hold a celebration picnic.

Mrs Crossley knew because they needed her help. She'd already promised to get her husband to walk round the lake with her on the morning of the grand opening without telling him why she wanted to do that.

The first weekend was fine and they managed to do nearly all the work necessary to finish the path, and the wooden benches were being constructed in Riley Callan's new workshop.

Then on the Tuesday after that it rained and people good at forecasting the weather were anxiously consulted. It rained even more heavily on Wednesday. Most thought it would clear by the weekend though one or two were rather pessimistic.

It was still raining on the Friday morning but light showers only and people all over the town kept peering out of their windows.

It stopped raining completely around noon and the sun peeped out briefly during the afternoon.

There was a lot of toing and froing on the Friday afternoon to get the final details finished. The two benches that had been made from offcuts of wood were to be taken to the lake on a cart as soon as it was light the following morning, covered up by tarpaulins so that even if Walter was out and about, he'd not know what they were.

As the light faded on the Friday, Dan looked round the area at the top end of the lake and everyone waited for him to speak. 'That's the best we can manage, lads. It's ready to show off. Well done!'

He sent a youngster with a written note to Flora. If Walter was there he was to pretend it was from a friend of hers. It confirmed that everything was ready and asked her to please bring her husband to the top of the lake for about eleven o'clock the following morning.

The lad came back saying he'd given her the note while Mr Crossley was over in his office in the backyard and she'd read it quickly then whispered to him to tell everyone that she was all set to take her husband for this very special walk.

39

As Flora served breakfast on the Saturday she said, 'Look at the weather, Walter. It's going to be a beautiful day. Let's go for a walk round the lake.'

'I was going to do some more work on my accounts. I didn't manage to finish them last night.'

Elinor was with them and in on the conspiracy. 'Save those for a rainy day, Pops. You should take advantage of days like this before the worst of winter sets in. I might even drag Cameron out for a while.'

He glanced out of the window. 'It does look as if it'll stay sunny even if it is a bit chilly. This has been a real Indian summer, hasn't it? Hmm. You've tempted me, love. I should get on with my work but—'

Flora winked at the younger woman. 'I have a couple of jobs to do. How about you put in an hour's work and we set off at about half past ten, Walter? We can work up a good appetite for our dinner by going right round the lake.'

'All right. You've persuaded me.'

He was ready on time and held out his hand to her. 'Let's pretend we're courting youngsters and hold hands openly.'

'We usually do.'

He beamed at her. 'Yes, and don't ever try to stop doing it.'

'I promise I won't.' She stood on tiptoe to kiss his cheek then led the way out, hoping she hadn't given away how excited she was. She was so looking forward to seeing how happy the progress on the lake path would make him.

Most of the younger men and women who'd been involved in finishing off the path round the lake and preparing a celebratory picnic tried to find hiding places behind some bushes. They were all rugged up with winter coats and scarves because though it was sunny, it wasn't warm.

Some of them moved a bit further down the path on the other side from where Walter and his wife would arrive. A slight rise in the path would hide them there.

The main conspirators stood in a group, chatting quietly as they waited for Flora and Walter to appear.

'Mrs Crossley told me yesterday that he still has no idea that we've finished the path,' one said.

'I'm dying to see his face when he comes over that rise and realises what we've done.'

'I'm dying to start on the food,' a rather plump young man said.

His wife waggled one finger at him in a mock threat. 'Don't you dare touch a single crumb till our special guests have been served.'

He rolled his eyes. 'I wouldn't.'

Someone pulled out a watch. 'It's nearly eleven o'clock. Where are they?'

Then the young chap keeping watch came running over the rise to join them. 'They just came into sight. They'll be here in a minute or two.'

Walter was looking at Flora and didn't at first notice the changes to the path or even the group of people waiting for him, so she nudged him.

'Look down at the path ahead, darling.'

He planted another kiss on her cheek then did as she'd told him and gasped, stopping dead in shock. 'The path's been finished!'

The whole group started cheering, and Walter looked around in astonishment before turning to his wife. 'You knew about this, didn't you?'

She gave him a smug look. 'Of course I did. Someone had to keep you away from here while the final improvements were being made.'

More people erupted from behind some bushes and others rushed from the other side to join the group, but no one trod on the path.

Dan Makersby stepped forward. 'You have to be the first one to walk along this stretch of path now that it's officially open, Mr Crossley.'

'That's . . . wonderful.' Walter's voice sounded husky and he was fighting to keep calm. As he stared at the path he also stared into the past. Ten years ago he and some friends had started work on this, intending to finish it for the Queen's Golden Jubilee. Then the Russian flu had hit the world and it had to be postponed.

He'd promised himself it'd be ready well before the Diamond Jubilee, but hadn't managed to stir up enough interest. He'd begun to lose hope.

And now – now it had happened. He didn't even try to hide his tears of joy, couldn't move for a few moments and his wife had to nudge him with her elbow to get him to reply to Dan.

'I shall be honoured to christen the path. I can't believe my hopes have been fulfilled sneakily like this. I'm utterly delighted, though. The valley folk will be so grateful for this. You'll see.'

He swallowed hard and held out his arm to his wife then they moved slowly forward together. He hoped they would always move forward together.

The conspirators formed lines by the sides of the first part of the path. Amongst the crowd he spotted Lillian and

Edward, his arm still in a sling; Maude and Riley beaming at him; Rufus and Abigail, arm in arm. As he stepped onto the neat path, he tried to say something meaningful that people would remember, but his voice came out rather wobbly.

'I can't believe this is happening! It's been so long. You're all wonderful, absolutely wonderful, doing this for our town.'

They couldn't hold back their excitement and interrupted one another.

'It was Dan's idea.'

'We wanted to surprise you.'

'The path is completely level and smooth now.'

'You have to try out the benches too.'

Walter hadn't noticed those and now stopped to stare at the nearest bench.

Flora took it upon herself to tug him off the path and sit down with him on the first bench as the people milled around, beaming at one another and treading on the path now that he'd christened it.

'How does it feel?' she murmured.

He kept hold of her hand and stroked the smooth wood of the bench with the other hand. 'This will be perfect for older people and women with small children. They've done really well, haven't they?'

'Very well indeed.'

One of the young women beckoned to them and once again, Flora had to tug him to move on. The two of them continued slowly along to the second bench and tried that one out too.

'You did well, choosing places with good views,' he called out.

There wasn't a face without a proud smile. 'That was Dan's idea,' someone said.

At the other end of the new path he found an impromptu table made of planks and on it were a couple of cakes and plates of scones and buns.

Walter recognised one of the cakes and turned to look accusingly at his wife. 'You said you were taking that cake to an old friend yesterday.'

'Well, I didn't exactly lie to you. The person who looked after it overnight was old and has become a dear friend since I moved here.'

He managed to pull himself together to address the now bigger group of well-wishers before he ate anything. 'What a wonderful surprise you've all given me! I can't believe I didn't know what was going on.'

Someone pushed Dan forward. 'This was Dan's idea.'

Walter stepped towards him and shook his hand, then shook any number of other hands that were held out to him one after the other.

His voice was still suspiciously husky with emotion as he said, 'Thank you. I can't thank you enough. The whole valley will be grateful to you. Thank you so much.'

Someone pushed a young woman forward to join them. 'Enid organised the food.'

'Cut the cakes, Enid.'

She picked up the big knife and Walter stood there, smiling and still fighting tears as the pretty young woman cut the cake into small slices.

He felt happiness surging through him. He'd been wanting to finish the walk round the lake for so long, had just about given up hope. And now here it was.

Flora took his hand again. 'Aren't they clever?'

'They're wonderful.'

'If you sit down on the bench, Mr Crossley, Mrs Crossley, I'll bring you some cake.'

So he sat there like a lord while he and Flora were waited on.

Gradually the fuss died down and as people stopped staring at him and began chatting to one another, he was able to turn to his wife and say, 'Isn't this a wonderful day for our valley?'

'Yes. I knew it would be.'

Then something occurred to him. 'What about Dan's wife?'

'A couple of women are sitting with her so that he can be here today, and they got together a roster to do the same thing while he was working on the path. There are some kind young people living here.'

He looked down at the bench he was sitting on. Cheap off-cuts of wood, but lovingly polished and he couldn't have been happier sitting on a throne.

'We shall have to get some more benches made come the spring,' he said to Flora. 'We're going to need them all along the path when the visitors come to our valley.'

'You're sure they'll come?'

'I'll do my best to get the news out to the world about how beautiful our moors and the walks across them are.'

After another few quiet moments watching the happy group of people round them he murmured, 'These enterprising youngsters make me feel hopeful about the future of our town, they do indeed. And we've been offered another wonderful idea for our future by Rufus, attracting visitors.'

She tucked her arm in his and they fell silent again, smiling peacefully at their world, the people around them and the views down the valley.

Dan came across to join them shortly afterwards. 'I need to get back to Polly now. She'll be dying to hear how things went.'

'How is she?' Walter asked gently.

'A little better than she was. We'll both be glad when the baby arrives. Maybe then she'll start to get truly better.'

They sat quietly for a few more minutes watching him walk away.

'I'll pray for that,' Flora said.

'So will I. At least there seems to be a chance of her recovering now.'

Walter looked down the hill for a while then said, 'In spring we should plant some pretty flowering shrubs here and there. And some rhododendrons. I think their flowers are so beautiful.'

'Good idea.'

He patted her hand, which he was still holding. 'I think it'll be all right for us to leave now.'

As they walked round the rest of the lake then back up towards the farm he said, 'You and I have a lot to look forward to next year on a personal level.'

'Yes, indeed. I shall try to set up my clinic properly and help as many people as I can.'

'I shall help with that and see what we can do with Rufus's ideas to attract people to the valley.'

'And the year after that will be Her Majesty's Diamond Jubilee,' she added quietly. 'Don't tell me you aren't already planning some big celebrations for our town.'

'Guilty as charged. It's an important thing, a Diamond Jubilee. And she's been our queen for a long time. That is something to celebrate.'

She stopped to reach up and pull his head towards hers, then kissed him. 'Until then, I shall celebrate every day I spend with you.'

They stood there for a few moments hand in hand, staring across the lake, then began to stroll slowly on.

He stopped just before they went into the house. 'I love you so much, Flora. Even the Queen's Diamond Jubilee comes a long way behind that for me.'

She squeezed his hand. 'I feel the same. Who'd have thought I'd find the love of my life when I came to Ollindale?'

And they stepped over the threshold of the farmhouse together.

CONTACT ANNA

Anna is always delighted to hear from readers and can be contacted via the Internet.

Anna has her own web page, with details of her books, some behind-the-scenes information that is available nowhere else and the first chapters of her books to try out, as well as a picture gallery.

Anna can be contacted by email at
anna@annajacobs.com

You can also find Anna on Facebook at
www.facebook.com/AnnaJacobsBooks

If you'd like to receive an email newsletter about Anna and her books every month or two, you are cordially invited to join her announcements list. Just email her and ask to be added to the list, or follow the link from her web page.

www.annajacobs.com

The best books live on in your head long after they are finished. As you read, you are turning the pages faster and faster to find out what happens next, only to feel bereft when you reach the end.

If that is how you feel now, you might like to join us at www.hodder.co.uk, or follow us on Twitter @hodderbooks, and be part of our community of people who love the very best of books and reading.

Whether you want to find out more about this book, or a particular author, watch trailers and interviews, have the chance to win early limited editions, or simply browse our expert readers' selection of the very best books, we think you'll find what you're looking for.

And if you don't, that's the place to tell us what's missing.

We love what we do, and we'd love you to be part of it.

www.hodder.co.uk